Copyright © 2019 Robel

All rights reser

The characters and events portrayed in this book are fictitious. Any similarity to real persons, living or dead, is coincidental and not intended by the author.

No part of this book may be reproduced, or stored in a retrieval system, or transmitted in any form or by any means, electronic, mechanical, photocopying, recording, or otherwise, without express written permission of the publisher.

ISBN-13: 978-1089991830
ISBN-10: 1089991835

Cover design by: Art Painter
Library of Congress Control Number: 2018675309
Printed in the United States of America

To my family, thank you for supporting me and the hobby I chose to pursue. I couldn't have written anything resembling a good novel if it wasn't for the constant support of my mother, as well as the proofreading done by my father. One more special person I need to put into this category is my wonderful girlfriend. Thank you for putting up with my constant typing and obsession with history.
There were many others who helped, especially a few people from the Goodreads forums. Bob and Ralph, you both provided excellent feedback I am lucky to have received; thank you.

CONTENTS

Copyright
Dedication
Characters/Maps
Prologue - 425 CE
Chapter I   1
Chapter II   25
Chapter III   50
Chapter IV   68
Chapter V   99
Chapter VI   124
Chapter VII   151
Chapter VIII   177
Chapter IX   190
Chapter X   221
Chapter XI   244
Chapter XII   263
Chapter XIII   272
Chapter XIV   284
Chapter XV   297
Chapter XVI   304
Chapter XVII   313

Chapter XVIII	323
Chapter XIX	331
Chapter XX	341
Chapter XXI	361
Chapter XXII	376
Chapter XXIII	394
Chapter XXIV	413
Chapter XXV	436
Chapter XXVI	461
Epilogue	478

CHARACTERS/MAPS

Abhartach---Great Chief of the Gaels

Amiram --------------------------------------Lead Rower of the Fortuna

Lord Ambrosius Aurelianus---Lord of Powys and brother to King Uther

Prince Ambrosius Aurelianus----Prince of Powys, Arthur to his friends

Aosten--King Ceneus' guard captain

Bastakas----------------------------------Second in command to Titus

Bishop Germanus-------------------Christian bishop from Rome, leader of Christians in Britannia

Braxus--Jorrit's second in command

Bors the Elder-----------------------Friend of Hall, former Roman auxiliary

Bors the Younger--------------------Friend of Drysten, son of Bors the Elder

Catulla--Slave, lover of Gaius

King Ceneus--King of Ebrauc

Citrio Bardas---------------------------------Soldier fighting for Titus

Colgrin------------------------Husband to Inka, brother in law to Jorrit, leader of army containing Saxons, Frisians, Jutes, Angles, and Danes

Cynwrig----------------------------------Childhood friend of Drysten

Dagonet---Scout of Ebrauc

Diocles----------------------------------Former Roman deserter, friend of Drysten

Drysten---Son of Hall

Ebissa---------------------------------Saxon, once followed Colgrin

Prince Eidion--------------------Eldest son of King Ceneus, ardent follower of Bishop Germanus

Fortuna------------------------Deceased mother of Drysten, wife of Hall

Gaius---Son of Titus

Gawain---Scout of Ebrauc

Prince Gwrast---------------------------Second son of King Ceneus

Hall----------------------------Commander of the Fortuna and its men, father of Drysten

Heledd------------------------Wife of King Ceneus, mother to all his children

Inka---Wife of Colgrin

Isolde---Lover of Drysten

Jorrit---Frisian boatbuilder

Maebh----------Isolde's dog

Maewyn----------Deacon serving Bishop Germanus, Christian name is Patrick

Magnus----------Healer of the Fortuna's men

Marhaus----------Slaver, son of Servius

Marivonna----------Wife of Titus

Matthew----------Former Priest, officer of Powys, rebaptized as Galahad by Bishop Germanus

Maurianus----------Most hated member of the Fortuna's crew

Prince Mor----------Youngest son of King Ceneus

Oana----------Titus' daughter

Octha----------Saxon, once served Colgrin

Servius----------Former Roman naval officer. Slaver in Frisia

Titus Octavius Britannicus----------Roman Centurion turned mercenary

Vonig----------Second in command to Eidion

Princess Ystradwel----------Daughter of King Ceneus

Historical Name-------------**Present Name**

1) Burdigala-------------------------------Bordeaux, France

2) Servius' Island-----------------------Hooge Platen, Netherlands

3) Rodanum------------------------------Aardenburg, Netherlands

4) Londinium----------------------------London, U.K.

5) Jorrit's Village-----------------------Leeuwarden, Netherlands

6) Petuaria-------------------------------Brough, U.K.

7) Eboracum-----------------------------York, U.K.

8) Din Guayrdi-------------------------Bamburgh Castle, U.K.

9) Ostia Antica------------------------Ostia, Italy

O.G.-Oceanus Germanicus-----------North Sea

O.B.-Oceanus Britannicus------------English Channel

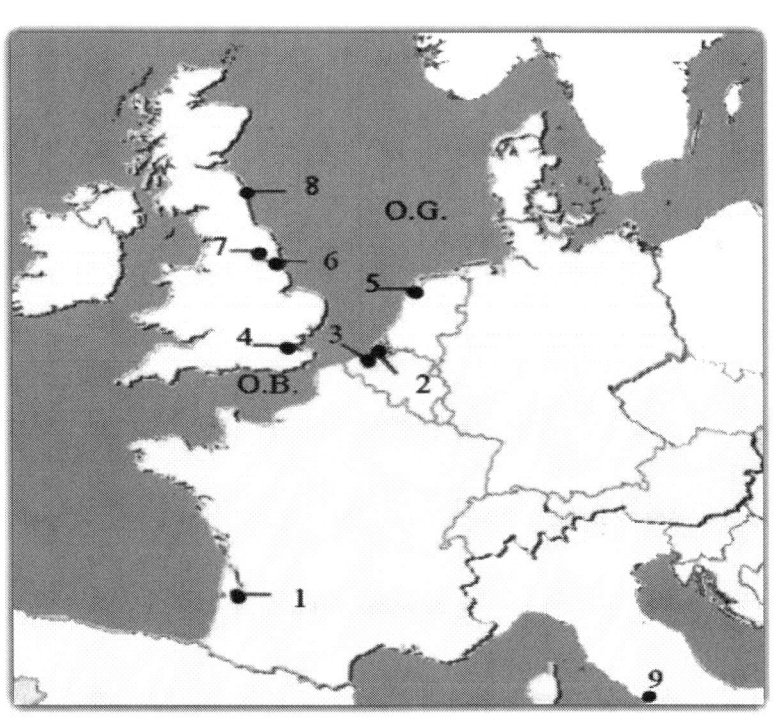

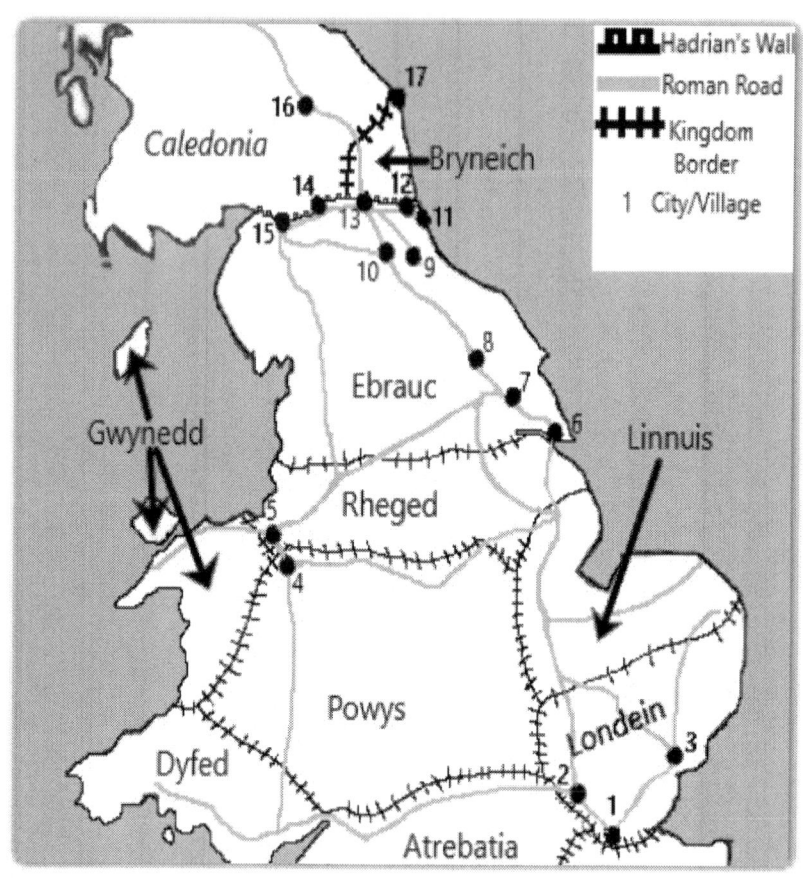

Historical Name--------------------Present Name
1) Londinium--London

2) Verulamium--St. Albans

3) Camulodunum--Colchester

4) Viroconium--Wroxeter

5) Deva--Chester

6) Petuaria----------Brough

7) Eboracum----------York

8) Isurium----------Aldborough

9) Concangis----------Durham

10) Longovicium----------Lanchester

11) Arbeia----------South Shields

12) Segedunum----------Wallsend

13) Corstopitum----------Corbridge

14) Magnis----------Greenhead

15) Luguvalium----------Carlile

16) Trimontium----------Newstead

17) Din Guayrdi----------Bamburgh Castle

PROLOGUE - 425 CE

Bishop Germanus spent the better part of the ride South bellowing insults into the ears of the king. "Their lives are meaningless," the bishop screamed. "You care more for the lives of the nonbelievers! The *heathens* of all people!"

King Ceneus rode on, attempting to pay no heed to the rabid cleric freshly arrived from Londinium, and Armorica before that. It had been two days since the portly man with the wrinkled brow disembarked, and ever since that moment, the king knew his legitimacy was being questioned.

"You hear me, Ceneus?" the bishop growled as he prodded him with a finger. The king was even more perturbed by the fact he was only able to perform the motion by leaning far off his horse. It seemed the man put more effort into his insults than his duties as a man of the cloth. "You cannot ignore the will of God, and where *I* go, God follows."

"My name is *King* Ceneus ap Coel. That is how I have always been addressed as king of Ebrauc, and you would do well to remember our Lord and savior has no place for pride," the king responded as he glanced to the bishop's deacon, Maewyn. For some odd reason, he was the lone representative of the bishop's which Ceneus could find tolerable.

Germanus began to cackle at the defiance, producing a sinking sensation in Ceneus' gut. "I could have a Christian army raised and ashore within a year. You believe I wouldn't? *Test* me. The pope and I have great plans for this accursed series of islands, and it remains to be seen if you have a place in those designs."

The thousand legions of Rome at my back, Ceneus recalled Germanus saying. *There haven't been a thousand legions in Rome since... God knows when.*

Maewyn gave the king a strangely commiserating glance as Ceneus dejectedly turned back to the road ahead.

It had been a slow ride South from Eboracum, taking a couple of hours until Petuaria finally came into view. Despite the sun's glare darting from the waterlogged streets and directly into Ceneus' eyes, it was a strangely welcome sight all the same. But even before he could see it, he could easily discern the stench of fish and the smoky odor of the pottery kilns from over the ridges.

Those aromas were rather familiar to him, bringing back numerous memories of Census' youth. The times he went hunting with the local chieftains before great feasts, the times he spent with those same chieftains 'daughters, and the times they prepared for wars of Rome's making.

It was as though the winds themselves were carrying such thoughts straight into his nostrils. But the nostalgia now caused his head to throb with a dull, constant aching. It could be expected, afterall. This was the place which fought against his claim to the throne the hardest. And it was because of that he now hated this area of his kingdom above all others.

Though at the moment, he did not fear these men. The rabble could be considered dangerous in the safest of times, but now he not only traveled with his own household guard but that of Bishop Germanus as well.

It was always easy to distinguish the two groups. The king's men wore Roman-made plates under their royal blue cloaks. His standard of a golden anchor on a royal blue background was prominently displayed at the front of the column, just behind the king himself. The bishop's men also wore Roman armor, but their cloaks were black as pitch, and they held no standards. The bishop's men never needed one, truth be told, as Ebrauc's people knew to stay away from any man clad in black.

"What is that horrible stench?" the bishop angrily shouted as he glanced toward the river.

The king noted Maewyn peering around before smirking toward the bishop. "I believe it is the Lord's bounty of the sea; that which fills our bellies every night."

"Gah!" the bishop exclaimed. "The Lord should attempt to make them smell a bit less like shit, if you asked me."

"That's the funny thing about our Lord and Savior, Your Excellency," the deacon resonded, ever smiling. "He rarely does anything without having good cause for it."

Finding it hard to stomach more talk of religion, the king sighed and glanced behind him toward his children. The princes Eidion, Gwrast, and Mor all accompanied him on their short journey south. But his daughter was who he noticed first. Ystradwel always stood out above all others. Bishop Germanus had noticed this as well, offering an impressive sum for a night with her, to which Ceneus adamantly declined.

It would have been one more reason his wife, Queen Heledd, would have abandoned all consideration of joining them on their journey should she had found out. "It is an affront to three-quarters of our people!" she had screamed the night of Germanus' arrival.

And maybe Heledd was right. Only a quarter of the population in Ebrauc even worshipped the Christian god. But the bishop had promised him power and sole kingship over the whole of Britannia for converting the nonbelievers. He just wished his sons all shared his aspirations.

"How have you enjoyed your stay thus far, Your Excellency?" Gwrast, the second-oldest and most diplomatic of Ceneus' sons, dutifully inquired.

The bishop gave a look of disdain toward the dark-haired man of roughly fifteen years. "I smell as though a fish shat on my garments and my pecker received a rash from one of your servant girls. How the *fuck* do you think I am doing?" he hissed back.

Prince Eidion could be heard snickering to himself. "I think I know of that servant girl."

"Then, Your Excellency, you likely have my oldest brother to thank for the rash," Mor put in, drawing a gaze of absolute contempt from Prince Eidion, along with a muffled giggle from their sister.

King Ceneus' heart was stalled by the comment. Fearing the anger of the bishop, he immediately narrowed his eyes and turned to his children. "You will remain silent, or you will hang with the traitor!" he rebuked. Though in truth, everyone but the bishop understood the likelihood of that happening was next to nothing. The king's love for his children was well-known to all.

Nevertheless, the threat referred to the purpose of their visit to Petuaria. There was a lord who dwelled there, a noble soul and faithful servant to Ebrauc, but a man who betrayed the values of the king and his faith. It was found he erected a statue of Cernunnos, the horned god of the local Britons, in an effort to bring wild game to the surrounding forests. There was a recent food shortage over the harsh winter which saw many people lose loved ones to fevers and malnourishment. This resulted in a desperate plea to the god of the forests, wildlife, and plenty. One of the numerous deities which Ceneus' father, High King Coel Hen, had once held his own feasts in honor of.

"How long until we hang the man, father?" Prince Eidion asked with impatience.

Ceneus turned and saw his boy sporting the eager expression one would only see on a dog awaiting its meal. All the king could do was sigh as he was reminded of the cruel nature of his eldest son. "We will have a trial of sorts to make certain—"

"He will hang the moment we arrive, boy," Bishop Germanus declared. "No trials for traitors, simply the rope."

The king saw a narrow smirk form across Eidion's face as he stared in admiration toward the bishop. *Who have I aligned myself with?* Ceneus wondered as he ran a hand over his brow.

The king glanced up into the overcast heavens as he remembered what led him to roughly half a decade of servitude. Prior to this moment, the kingdom of Ebrauc was ruled by King Ceneus' father, High King Coel Hen, the lord over all of Britannia. Representatives of Bishop Germanus approached Ceneus on behalf of Pope Innocent of Rome, bringing to him the idea of succeeding his father after his eventual death.

At first, Ceneus was reluctant, as it would mean usurping the throne from his widely loved elder brother, Garbonian ap Coel. But he ultimately caved to the courting of the Christian emissaries. There was an ensuing struggle, but eventually he gained the throne along with control over much of the Northern portion of Britannia. The popes may have changed twice since then, but Germanus was a constant presence in his life ever after.

"Lord King!" a voice called, snapping Ceneus from his daydreams.

The king's eyes widened as he peered around, quickly realizing they were about to enter the village. Its old, dilapidated Roman walls were drawing nearer and nearer as their horses clapped forth. A man approached from the town gate, having three guards on either side and every one of them dressed for war. One brandished the old standard of a horned snake, the symbol of Ebrauc before its current status as a Christian nation.

Ceneus glimpsed toward the bishop. Germanus' strong wrinkled brow protruded over his hooded eyes, giving the impression he was much older than his actual age of fifty-three. The smile across his face was that of a man who knew he would soon see his enemies writhing in agony at his feet.

"The fools believe they can fight the will of God," Germanus growled before a hearty scoff.

King Ceneus shook his head. "They wish a fight with me. God has nothing to do with it, Your Excellency."

"Bah!" Germanus exclaimed. "You Britons are simpletons. You have yet to comprehend your actions are bound to *His* will," Germanus explained in annoyance. "God is everywhere."

"Not your cock, apparently!" a woman's voice chirped from behind.

The king instantly recognized it as Ystradwel. He glanced behind him to see all his children but Eidion attempting to stifle their laughter as best they could. The sight warmed Ceneus' heart for the briefest of moments. His children were acting as one true family, something which hadn't happened since he forced their conversion to the new religion from the East. Instead of betraying his joy, he glanced back toward the bishop to discern whether the comment was overheard, and was relieved when it was apparent it hadn't been.

"Lord King, are we truly going to execute a man without trial?" Aosten, King Ceneus' captain of the guard inquired as he eased his horse up beside him. Maewyn too was paying close attention to the exchange, wearing a solemn expression across his worn face.

King Ceneus lowered his head, with his response feeling as though it was stuck in his throat. "It... would seem so," he whispered. He had executed men before, but this was different. The man in question, Drumond, was one of his greatest childhood friends in his early years. He knew this man well, as he was the captain of Ceneus' guard for a time and fought beside him during the war for Ebrauc's throne. The man was rewarded for his exemplary service with the large villa in Petuaria's center.

"This... *priest* does not rule here, Lord King. We can put an end to this right now. Let me..." Aosten gestured to the dagger hanging at his waist.

From the corner of his eye, the king could have sworn he saw the slightest of tilts from Germanus' head. "No, Aosten. I need this man alive for a while longer," Ceneus responded. "If word got back to the pope we killed his emissary, he would undoubtedly send men to overthrow me."

Aosten shook his head with wide eyes. "No, Lord King! The Bishop simply speaks out of his arse."

"Would you bet a kingdom on that, Aosten?" Ceneus asked through a hushed tone. In his mind, he wanted the man to say yes, but such displays of courage were rare to Ebrauc.

Aosten dropped his gaze, and the group rode on. Their horses clopped their way toward the now dozen men gathered to meet them. In the front, with his son at his side, was Drumond.

King Ceneus didn't know he could hang his head any further toward the dirt, but hang it did. The emotions flowing through him caused the hairs on the back of his neck to dance along to the fluttering of his heartbeat. He slowly raised his gaze to meet that of his supposed enemy, seeing a man who knew his end was near but wished to defy it all the same. His long, grey hair seemed matted to the side of his head, while the scar across his left cheek was deeper into the man's face than Ceneus remembered.

"Lord King!" Drumond beckoned, "it is my *honor* to welcome you home," he maniacally screamed, causing the men around him to smirk.

"Quiet this rabble, Ceneus!" Bishop Germanus commanded.

King Ceneus gradually raised his hand before motioning his guards forward, creating a shield wall between them and those who were once their comrades in arms. Prince Eidion's men, clad in black in the same manner as the bishop's, moved their way in front of the king's men. The act drew looks of contempt from the warriors in royal blue, as well as that of the king.

"They are always so eager for a bloodletting," Ceneus whispered to Aosten, who was wearing an equally disdainful expression. "Where did my boy find them?"

Aosten shrugged. "Saw one or two of them in the prisons, Lord King."

The king sighed. "Eidion!" he beckoned.

The prince's eyes lit up as he yanked his horse's reins toward his father, spurring the beast forward before impatiently halting once he was on Aosten's other side. "Yes, Lord King."

King Ceneus raised a finger to his son. "Only one needs to die," he explained through a heavy breath.

Eidion smiled and returned an eager nod. "I will see to it." He quickly dismounted and moved toward the wall of shields between him and Drumond's men, maintaining his smile with each step. "Lord Drumond!" he yelled, "I believe it is time for you to come to terms with the decisions which led you here. As you have shown me kindness—"

"Shut your mouth, you fucking twat!" Drumond interrupted. "Come fucking die." The grey-haired man with the scar across his left cheek quickly drew his sword, the same sword which had slain Ceneus' enemies everywhere from this very town to north of Hadrian's Wall.

The king knew it was his obligation to watch what unfolded, but ultimately knew what he would see. His old friend gutted by his son in front of a crowd, likely in a way which would typically be below a lord of Ebrauc's court.

"As you wish, Lord Drumond. I always felt words were meaningless in these times anyway," Prince Eidion responded with a smile. He slowly unclasped the brooch holding his black cloak and let it fall to the ground. "Vonig, pick this up," he said to his captain.

"Eidion!" King Ceneus called, briefly catching the uninterested attention of the prince. "Make it quick," he ordered. It pained him to know his oldest son would likely ignore his command.

The prince drew his blade as he and Ebrauc's traitor slowly began shuffling toward one another.

King Ceneus felt his bowels begin to stir in anticipation. *The ground is wet,* he thought, examining the muddy fighting space. *Maybe, he'll actually beat him.* He hoped this would be true, but it wasn't his son he worried for, it was Drumond. He knew one day his son would inherit all that he has, and that idea terrified him more than anything. He wanted nothing more than to turn his reign over to his second son, Gwrast, who was likely the most honorable of all his children.

Bishop Germanus began coughing as the rains slowly approached from the East. "Gah! Gut the man and be done with it, boy. I won't be dying of a fever for this."

King Ceneus could not see his son's face, but easily imagined the smile which must have sprouted from ear to ear as Drumond wildly swung, opening the contest with a miss over the prince's head. Eidion leaned back as another swipe narrowly passed in front of his chest, clearly snickering at the older man's ferocity.

Your age is showing, brother, the king thought. *He'll draw you in when he grows tired of mocking you.*

Drumond, seemingly reading his king's mind, slowly took a step back, and proceeded to wait for the prince to make a move of his own. "Come on then, you miserable shit."

Prince Eidion smirked as he stepped forward, raising his blade over his head, and catching the reflection of the sun as he did so. He brought the glittering blade down toward his enemy's head but was quickly parried away before being struck on the cheek by Drumond's off hand.

Man always hated fighting with a shield.

Eidion glanced to the traitor as he raised his blade once more, but this time, instead of bringing the edge down, he kicked the lord between his legs. Drumond forward and exposed his neck to the swift stroke of Eidion's fury.

"I'm sorry, brother," King Ceneus whispered as he watched the head dangle by a small patch of skin atop the dead man's neck. His gaze lowered to his hands as they fidgeted with a loose string sprouting from his gloves. He heard an agonizing wail from the village's entrance, instantly recognizing it as Drumond's wife.

The prince glared toward the men who had lined up to bar the way into the village. "Vonig!" he called, "they wish to commune with the old gods! Let's send them on their way!"

"I... What?" King Ceneus abruptly lifted his head to see two dozen black-clad men charging their wall of shields into the handful of dejected men who stood across from them. Drumond's band had broken their formation, with some even beginning to venture back to the village when the order for slaughter was called.

"Your Excellency!" Maewyn yelled as he gestured toward the crazed prince.

"Ha!" Bishop Germanus began with a full-bellied laugh, "send them to their ancestors, indeed!"

"Wait...," Ceneus attempted.

Aosten quickly put a hand on his king's shoulder. "We have to stop this, Lord King."

But the damage was already done.

Eidion's men quickly hacked their way through the first of the individuals to resist them, slicing into their opposition without a single notion of mercy. The first few to mount a defense made the ill-advised choice to press their backs against a wall, swinging wildly at the half-circle of men now prodding their weapons playfully toward the frantic defenders.

King Ceneus glanced back to his children and saw horror displayed across his beautiful daughter's face. The same look of disgust he now saw on the faces of Gwrast and Mor. Despite it all, he was still unable to give the order for his kingsguard to cease the killing.

"Now," Germanus began as he coughed toward the king, "to the matter of the invaders to our North. Per old Roman military documents, there is a sizable portion of silver to be had under the principia in the fortress of Segedunum. The very same fortress which your people failed to hold."

"I do not recall your men sending aid to the fortress either," Aosten hissed. His eyes were watery, as Drumond was one of Aosten's greatest friends in their youth.

"Ah," Germanus mocked. "The man in command of the forces which *lost* said fort wishes to speak."

Ceneus glanced toward Aosten and shook his head, signaling him to leave the matter to his king. "What he means, Your Excellency," turning back to the bishop, "The losses we took from the famine caused us to reinforce more vital areas with men stationed at Segedunum," he explained. "It was not as vital as—"

"You are to send men to retrieve it from the Northmen," the bishop replied with a scowl. "I have *need* of that silver."

"You wish for me to send my people to die for *wealth?*" the repulsed king demanded in a shock.

The bishop nodded. "Their sacrifices will bring us the means to build a Christian nation on Britannia's shores."

Aosten contorted his face in disgust as Germanus began to ride off. "The man we would have sent to lead the army now lacks a head, Your *Excellency.*"

Germanus shrugged. "God finds a way, as I am certain your king will as well," he responded. He spurred his horse forward, indeed smelling of fish.

The Fortuna was nearly fit to depart were it not for a few stragglers reciting farewells to their loved ones. Drysten, Hall's son, was one such man. Hall noticed him clutching his woman tightly in his arms, almost as though Drysten thought he would never return from his journey. One could hardly blame the boy. His woman's name was Isolde, and even Hall had to agree she was a rather unique beauty. The idea of leaving her was likely torturous for the young man.

Hall stood on a small hilltop overlooking the piers of Burdigala, the renowned wine country in Western Gaul. He was still rubbing the sleep from his eyes as he observed the gulls circling overhead through the brisk morning air. He always enjoyed gazing at wild birds, often seeing them swoop down for any crumbs of food among the cargo being stowed away. It was always hard not to envy their freedom.

He brought his attention back down to his vessel and fondly reminisced how he had found the quinquireme rotting away on a sandbar not far from town. It was totally abandoned by its crew, likely after a storm. Hall rushed home from hunting with his son and brought the workers from his warehouses and fields to free the wreck from its lonely end.

The ship's condition was less than favorable, yet Hall was able to refit the old warship into a trading vessel. Another great sail was applied, and the lower benches once used to seat its rowers had been removed, with the entire lowest area being turned into a cargo hold. Much of the wood not essential to the ship's stability was removed and three levels were constructed, a top deck, a middle tier for the crew, and the cargo hold.

The ship was slightly cramped in some areas but the sturdiness of the original Roman craftsmanship was taken advantage of quite well. The last addition to the vessel, and to Hall it's most important, was its name. He quickly settled upon Fortuna, after his loving wife who passed shortly before he departed from Britannia. The men seemed agreeable as well, with Fortuna herself having been named after the Roman goddess of luck.

Hall looked to his crewmen and spied his most trusted friend saying his farewell to his own son. "Bors," he called to the man, but earning the notice of both.

The elder Bors, who served under Hall in their Roman days, and his son of the same name. Bors the Younger he was called, as the resemblance between himself and his father was uncanny. The two men turned to face Hall, with Bors the Elder playfully swatting his son's head in the opposite direction before strolling to his commander.

"Lord?" Bors asked as he sauntered over.

That title always felt strange to Hall, especially when it was his oldest friend addressing him as such. Regardless, it was what most people called him. Hall was not a lord by birth, but always provided steadfast leadership for the people of Burdigala. This title was not established by any authority, it was simply well earned.

Hall turned from Bors to the ship, looking it over one last time before he departed on his own journey to Britannia. "Keep my boy from making any stupid decisions. I may not be there to guide him, but I need him to conduct himself the same way he would if I were present."

Bors chuckled and turned his gaze toward Drysten. "The boy is hardly a *boy* any longer, Lord. He's grown much and has a knack for making a bargain." He nudged Hall with an elbow. "Not unlike his father."

"That wasn't what I meant," Hall explained with a slight shake of the head. "Ever since his first taste of war, he's understood he's a rare talent with a blade in his hand. I don't want him to get himself into any trouble now that he knows he has something he can put on display." His voice dawdled off as he watched a pair of seagulls grapple over a scrap of bread thrown to the ground. "Just push him in the right direction. It's hard to trust his judgment at times. He relies on sense he does not yet possess."

Bors looked up toward the sky. "I wouldn't worry about your boy, Hall. He's got a better head on his shoulders than we give him credit for. Besides, how can the boy go astray when gods themselves whisper into his ear."

Hall looked to his feet, feeling a twinge run down his spine at the thought of such deities tugging at the soul of his son.

Drysten had long been known to hear their voices. Sometimes it happened during the most dismal of times, and sometimes in the brightest moments when the people were at peace. Occasionally, he even saw beings off in the distance; faceless wretches surrounded by ravens.

Hall's wife had believed it to be a sign that the gods favored him over all others, but Hall was not so sure. In his Roman days, he saw much of the same from men who suffered from similar beliefs. Most were discarded from society and viewed as having a damaged soul. They would slowly become distraught and unpredictable, changed by anger and resentment. Drysten had never had a traumatic experience to bring about the voices; he simply heard them since childhood. They would produce fits in his earliest years, but he learned to weather those storms with the help of his mother. It made no true difference to Hall. He loved his son just the same.

"Brother, the boy will be fine under my watch," Bors assured him, placing a hand on Hall's shoulder.

Hall glanced to his friend and gave a slight nod before the two men observed Drysten marching toward them. He wore linen breeches with a white tunic over his chest. To improve his appearance as a tradesman, Hall instructed his son to embroider the sleeves in blue to show his higher standing. Many people in the empire did not indulge themselves in such intricacies, meaning Hall knew the ways for his boy to stand out when trying to sell their goods.

"I presume we'll be seeing you in Britannia, father," Drysten announced with a smile.

Hall guessed his happy demeanor was a slight ruse, as this was the first time he was journeying to the mainland unsupervised.

Hall smiled back, seeing Fortuna's eyes in the face of the sole child she was able to give him. "That you will, boy."

He was pleased with his son, peculiar as he could be. He'd grown into a fine man who would take over the freighting trade. That was what Hall hoped for, as the sea travel demanded by the occupation was growing stale to him. He was now hoping for other adventures on land, and a stable income with them.

But these new desires did not come about on their own. The men of the Fortuna were recently met with a messenger from Britannia. The stranger explained the king of Ebrauc wished for Hall to become a lord of his court and lead his armies.

This king's name was Ceneus, and Hall guessed if the man were anything like his father, the great Coel Hen, he would be a worthy individual to serve. Coel Hen was the last man to bear the title of High King of Britannia during the waning years of Roman rule. When he passed away, his first-born descendant was initially chosen to rule in his absence. For reasons Hall never discovered, the various kingdoms determined Ceneus was not the proper man to head a unified Britannia. This pushed the island into its current state, with over a dozen territories under the rule of chieftains or former Roman aristocrats.

After Hall and his son shared a brief hug, Drysten gently gave his father's shoulder a quick pat before turning to make his way to the ship.

Hall and Bors were about to resume their conversation until the two men were alerted to a stout sea captain nearby. The heavyset man was screeching obscenities to some women as they walked away from their spouses now boarding with Drysten.

"Have a go at a real man, love?" the fat pig of a man shouted.

Bors scoffed at the man, having remembered explaining his previous night to Hall when they first arrived to the docks that morning.

As usual, Bors was in the local tavern only a few hours earlier when the swine of a man first docked near Hall's ship. The captain strolled away from the dockmaster before handling his docking fee and tried to gain admittance to the city. He created a bit of an uproar when reminded of the payment he owed, and eventually attracted the notice of the

Fortuna's crew. When the Fortuna's head oarsman, Amiram, noticed what was occurring, he took a handful of men from the ship to help de-escalate the situation. Once the irrepressible captain noticed a group of men walking in his direction, he commanded his own crew to obstruct them. A struggle ensued, which thankfully saw no deaths. When it was over, the only injuries to speak of were a handful of swollen lumps on the faces of the instigator's crew. The large-bellied man's name was Servius Antius Crassus, and he was commonly recognized to be a Frisian slave trader.

Hall let out a deep sigh as he was reminded of the man Bors gestured to. "I heard about what happened last night. Why is he even here?"

"No idea. I just pray he doesn't decide to maintain a grudge, seeing as how we knocked his people around last night," Bors replied with an amused snort. "Saw the whole thing from the tavern. Amiram sure fights like a savage."

Hall smirked as he pictured the sight. "No weapons?"

Bors shook his head. "Servius' people had a few, though they apparently had no idea how to use them compared to our boys. I watched Amiram disarm one man, turn to another, and swing the blade so hard at him it knocked his shield clear off his arm! The *look* on the fucker's face!" Bors began to cackle to himself as he watched Servius glare at the Fortuna.

"Amiram...," Hall said proudly. "I remember when he still had a tongue, couldn't shut him up."

Bors smirked. "Then he had his tongue taken and we suddenly missed his humor."

"Still retained some of it," Hall replied with a smile.

The two men stood near the Fortuna, peering over the crew as they boarded under the dawn sky. Every man was noticeably droopy eyed following their final nights with their families. Most of the men had spent much of that evening drinking and whoring, or if they had families, they were doing much of the same activities with their wives. Hall never cared for wine, cider, or ale, but acknowledged if the men needed to soothe their nerves before a journey, then finding the bottom of a cup was the best way.

Servius was still staring intently over the Fortuna as well, agitating Hall into wanting to know what the bloated swine of a captain was imagining. It was clear he had ill intentions, but considering his crew was outnumbered by experienced veterans of war and sailors seasoned by years of rowing, the odds of him outright assaulting anyone were laughably small. The one characteristic Hall understood about the man was he was certainly no fool. If he genuinely wished some sort of reprisal, he would plan to strike at a moment of strength, something most likely learned when he sailed for the Roman navy.

"How does a prominent Roman turn to the slave trade?" Hall wondered aloud. It was something he grew curious of once he learned of the slaver's prominence in the region. Servius was rumored to have multiple ships under his command until roughly a decade before Hall encountered him. He had the typical assortment of riches from his service, namely gold and multiple villas in Gaul

Bors shook his head. "No clue. You would think such a profession is beneath his talents. From what I gathered, he did well under the Roman flag."

The two men shared a strong distaste for slavery. So long ago, in their days struggling against the Gaels in Western Britannia, they saw firsthand how slaves were treated in the places the Romans held no influence. To some extent, there were laws in Rome intended to protect them. This was not always the case in the Empire, but ever since the foundation of Christianity, much had changed. Old gods were now beginning to be thrown aside in favor of the one from Judea, apparently the one true god according to his clerics and priests.

How could anyone know that? Hall had wondered. He once tried to wrap his head around this idea, but quickly decided it was much too grand for him to comprehend.

Of course, there were still people who idolized the old gods such as Jupiter and Mars, but most were now turning away from them. Many of their still-loyal followers now occupied the territories the empire had abandoned, though Christianity was still making its way West and trapping them between the Christians and the sea. It was the beliefs of these Christians which altered the Roman views of slavery, and the importance of a life in general.

In the uncivilized areas, a person's slave could be shown the whip for any reason they chose. Servius was rumored to take great pleasure in the regular abuse of his slaves. It was well known he would brand them with the symbol "FVG," meaning fugitive in the Roman dialect. If a slave with this brand was caught anywhere in the empire, they could easily be executed for abandoning their master. This particular brand was normally applied to those who tried to run from their duties, while Servius used it as one of his many deterrents against runaways from the start. Though his actions would have consequences in the Empire, he was free to do as he pleased outside of its influence.

Hall vividly remembered when he first saw the man. It was eleven years ago, and Burdigala had been attacked by one of the many nearby tribes of barbarians, an incident more routine than Hall liked to admit. The enemy was driven back once Romans were able to rally a defense, much as Hall himself would do five years later. Houses and walls needed to be rebuilt, requiring additional manpower that had been unavailable. A large portion of the men who would typically be the ones counted on to restore the city were lying dead within its walls, creating an uneasy feeling of the city becoming nothing more than a grand mausoleum.

When word of the city's condition quickly got out, Servius showed up like a moth to a flame a few short days later. The first time Hall saw him, he set up his own slave market near his ship and paraded two dozen haggard looking men around for the surrounding people to bid on.

The men were all bought up and put to work, but the locals started noticing the strange behaviors they exhibited as they were given their new tasks. They rarely interacted with each other, something Hall could not understand considering they shared the same hardships and backgrounds. It was assumed people in the same plight could find ways to tolerate each other, but these men were different. Hall could not understand why they were so mentally handicapped, so he ordered his men to free anyone bought by Servius after the work was completed. At first, the slaves were reluctant to be freed of their bondage, almost as though they considered it a cruel trick or jest on the part of their new masters.

But slowly, over the course of the next few weeks, they began to open up to the people of Burdigala. Then the rumors came of how Servius had strange rooms in his Frisian villa; dark places underground where people would be brought in the dead of night but never leave.

Later, when Hall first claimed the Fortuna, Servius attempted to convince everyone it belonged to him and he had been forced to abandon it in a storm. Since then, he showed himself to be a nuisance every time he journeyed to Burdigala. The man displayed an almost impressive capacity for greed and enjoyed flaunting his wealth in front of everyone he came across. He wore golden rings on most of his fingers and wrapped himself with the most delicate fabrics available to this part of the world. His very appearance made the Fortuna's people uneasy, and Hall knew that type of man would forever hold a grudge against them for the previous night's actions.

"So long as he leaves soon, I suppose it doesn't matter where he docks for the night," Hall decided as he rubbed his drowsy eyes.

Bors grumbled to himself, obviously just as annoyed by the man's presence. "Should just kill him. Most likely deserves it for one reason or another."

Had Hall understood what the man was about to do, he would have agreed.

The snow was beginning to vanish, signaling the conclusion of another harsh winter and ushering in the Spring. This was usually the happiest time of the year in Jorrit's village. His home was located in the Frisian islands located in the northwest region of the continent. The evening before, Jorrit was summoned into the chieftain's hall to drink and feast. But when everyone withdrew for the night, the reason for his summons was finally revealed. He would have a small, yet vital purpose in their ambitions during the approaching raiding season.

The Saxons had come to an understanding with several Pictish tribes of Northern Britannia, as well as a tribe of strange Gaels on the islands directly to its West. The plan entailed those two groups luring away the Britons governing over the Northern kingdom of Ebrauc, freeing those lands so the Saxons and their allies could move up through a river passing directly into their capital city of Eboracum. They would then overwhelm the city and use it as a foothold in the area as they routed out nearby kingdoms. After the slaughter had ended, the Saxons, Picts, and Gaels would divide their newly conquered lands amongst themselves. For all their ferocity in battle, the one thing the Saxons were lacking was ships. Ships and men enough to crew them across the sea.

The leader of the Saxons, Colgrin, came to Jorrit's chief because he understood he could use his brother-in-law's talents to fix this issue. Colgrin and Jorrit were brother-in-laws by way of a pair of twin sisters, Inka and Maiki. Jorrit married Maiki first some years prior, with Colgrin seeing an opportunity to marry into what he considered a prominent family shortly thereafter. It was rumored the man only wanted the marriage for just such aspirations, but it was not known for certain until his arrival in Jorrit's village.

Jorrit dawdled his way through his neglected village built atop a series of terps. A terp was a man-made hill created to be more easily defensible from attackers. In Frisia, these structures were used more to endure violent storms from the sea than protection during war. But before long, Jorrit found his way to the entrance of the chieftain's hall, slowly entering to be greeted with the scents of cooked meat and spilled ale.

Colgrin heard Jorrit's footsteps as he entered and turned from the fire. "It's been too long, brother," he stated as he grinned and slapped his hands on Jorrit's shoulders, though Jorrit perceived any happiness the man displayed was likely a ruse.

"It has, Colgrin. How is Inka?" Jorrit answered.

The Saxon shrugged. "Well enough. Though I came to propose a job of you, not converse of our wives."

Jorrit watched as the burly man with long, braided hair the shade of fresh blood stepped closer to him. His breath stank of roasted pig, while Jorrit was able to discern dried ale on the hairs near the corners of his mouth. He stared Jorrit in the eye and began to grin, making Jorrit feel uneasy.

"How insensitive of me! I had forgotten your most recent loss." Colgrin laughed as he uttered the words, but Jorrit failed to see the humor in them.

"I... yes, she passed giving birth to your nephew, Lanzo," Jorrit responded. Colgrin walked up and settled a hand on Jorrit's shoulder. The tone of the man as he referred to Jorrit's late wife infuriated the Frisian, but he was intelligent enough to recognize what would befall him should he react as he desired.

"We will simply find you a younger one!" Colgrin remarked as he casually swung his hand through the air. "A *Briton*, perhaps?"

Jorrit felt a pang of guilt at the notion of marrying anyone other than Maiki, especially after she had surrendered her life so their son could have his own. Yet here was Colgrin, making it seem like that sacrifice was small or petty.

Jorrit moved away from the man, doing his best to disguise his aversion toward the newcomer as he marched toward his chieftain, partly asleep in his crudely assembled throne. Jorrit remembered the man's father ruling over their people when he was a small boy. Their people thrived through both trade and raiding, but such was the life under a great leader. The man who followed him fell drastically short of his father. The current chieftain's name was Dieuwer, and he most likely understood the only way he would have wealth flowing through his village was by siding with Colgrin against the Britons.

"Lord," Jorrit dutifully greeted. "I trust you are feeling well," he inquired, referring to the fact the chieftain was known to have contracted some illness from a whore in another village. Nobody understood the ailment well enough to cure it, so once the disease corrupted his mind, he was humbled into being an even more incompetent and blubbering fool than he already was.

Chieftain Dieuwer perked his head up, apparently startled by being addressed. "I... I am quite well. What was your name again? It has been so long since we have spoken last."

Jorrit hung his head. It was offensive to be sworn to such a vulnerable fool. "My name is Jorrit, Lord. We were friends growing up."

"Ah!" Dieuwer said as he perked up, "I remember you now! Your father serves me well!"

"He did, Lord. Sadly, last winter he was taken from us by a fever," Jorrit responded.

The chieftain reduced his gaze, visibly disheartened by the knowledge. Though in reality, he had spoken at the funeral for Jorrit's father. "I am sorry for your loss, as well as for the loss to our people."

Jorrit thoughtfully nodded, the only thanks he wished to give the man. It was apparent he had no memory of the fact Jorrit's father had once been favored to rule over the village. But now under Dieuwer's leadership, it was hardly worth ruling at all. Most of the people who used to reside there were now further East due to the growing water levels sweeping away their land. Chieftain Dieuwer made no attempts to organize their relocation, so the people simply abandoned him. Were it not for the fact every one of Jorrit's ancestors was cremated into urns buried nearby, he too would have abandoned the man to die a lonely death.

"To business, brother," Colgrin said in an attempt to regain Jorrit's attention. "This plan of mine will require a man of... *flexible* talents."

"Then what specifically is this little errand of yours, Colgrin?" Jorrit replied through a rather caustic tone. He did not wish to anger the man, but saw it fit to show his frustration at the man's tone toward his deceased wife.

Colgrin shifted away from Jorrit as he began to pace, either from excitement or frustration, Jorrit could not tell. He slowly turned back as he neared the fire in the center of the room, with the flames illuminating his stern brow and narrowed eyes. He appeared to loom a little larger in the flames, and the sinister grin he produced across his scarred face made Jorrit feel uneasy. "I am sending out a few different ships with the intention of being captured by the Britons."

Jorrit raised an eyebrow at the thought of voluntarily being captured. "You're asking me to do *what* exactly?"

Colgrin's smirk slightly widened. "I need a man I can trust. A man with more authority than just being the leader of a raiding craft plying the coast of Britannia. You, Jorrit, are going to have to be that man."

Jorrit scoffed. "I have no desire to be a captive."

"But what would you say to being a king?" the Saxon retorted.

Jorrit was suddenly intrigued at the prospect of being a strong lord ruling over scores of men. Men conquered and battered into submission. "And you would make me a king in these new lands you wish to conquer?"

"There is more than enough land for the both of us, brother! Additionally, you speak the tongue of the Britons and those vile Romans well enough to truly be an asset to our cause," Colgrin responded with wide eyes and a cheerful tone. "Think of the power we could own." Colgrin's eyes began to glitter with happiness as he crept back and suddenly grasped Jorrit's shoulders.

Jorrit returned Colgrin's enthusiasm with a fake smile of his own. "I suppose becoming a king would have its own... advantages. Watching my son grow up as a prince and handing everything down to him when he comes of age would certainly be something."

"Ah, yes," Colgrin began, "think of little Lanzo, Jorrit. Think of your family's legacy!"

Jorrit glanced away from Colgrin's sly smirk as he contemplated whether to hear the man further. He genuinely could not tell if he could trust him or not, but at the moment, he could not believe in his own chieftain either.

"Let us talk," Jorrit eventually answered.

CHAPTER I

Hall chartered passage over the Oceanus to Britannia shortly after his son set sail in The Fortuna. Being a prominent man in Burdigala proved useful, as he only needed an afternoon at the docks to find a suitable ship. It carried pottery from the very village Hall needed to travel to, and routinely made the voyage from Petuaria to Burdigala in the early days of spring. The crew was cheerful enough, with them urging Hall to play games of dice below deck. Though intrigued at first, Hall politely declined, as he was quite familiar with the luckless side of gambling from his days in the service of Rome. The sun gleamed overhead each day of their brief voyage, with sporadic rain as they sailed along the coastline of Britannia. So long as no harsh winds were accompanying them, Hall speculated the vessel would make it to Ebrauc with no difficulty through the channel. The plan after they traversed the Oceanus was to let Hall disembark in the Parisi tribal settlement of Petuaria, where he was slated to appear before the king of Ebrauc.

He was adorned in a set of polished lorica segmentata, the Roman style of armor which was once widely used in the empire's past. The lorica segmentata was a series of iron plates secured together by hide straps, strong against stopping arrows or even glancing blows of a sword or spear. This was once the typical battledress worn by Roman legionnaires, but Hall simply wore it because he preferred the look. For warmth as well as added extravagance, Hall wore a bearskin atop a dark green linen cloak fashioned for him by his son's woman, Isolde, a few years before. With the bearskin, he not only looked like a warlord, but a wealthy one at that.

At his waist, he displayed his old spatha, the short sword which served him well throughout his time as a Roman auxiliary. But what Hall made sure to make noticeable was a dagger awarded to him by the king's father, High King Coel Hen, following the war with the Gaels. The Romans won the conflict, but during one such engagement Coel was wounded by a Pictish arrow, and Hall had personally commanded a group of men to shield him while he was recovered from the battlefield. At the time, the current king was merely a prince, second in line to the throne of Britannia. He was present when Coel Hen gifted Hall with the dagger as well as a pouch of gold pieces which were used to acquire Hall's first home in Eboracum.

Two individuals were guarding Hall on his voyage. Two good men and proven fighters. Both men originally desired to journey to Ostia, but were commanded by Hall to accompany him to Ebrauc. The truth of it was both men simply weren't essential additions to Drysten's journey into what was deemed safe territory. Thus, they were left behind when the Fortuna sailed East, and both joined Hall about a month later when they departed for Britannia.

One's name was Cyrus, a man born in Rome of about thirty years, and rumored to be the descendent of wealthy Romans who were killed by the barbarians from Hispania many years ago. The other's name was Elias, a Greek who Hall served with in Britannia during the time he saved Coel Hen. Both men were currently strapping their leather armor onto their shoulders and chests as they drew closer to their destination.

"Looks like a touch of rain once we arrive, Lord," Cyrus announced as he peered into the sky. "I *hate* the fucking rain."

"Well, rain wouldn't be the most unfortunate thing to run into here," Hall replied as he spun his ring around his finger. It bore the insignia of the legion he served with, which he routinely ran his thumb over when he was thinking.

Cyrus glanced toward his lord with a disconcerted look. "Anticipating trouble?"

"Doubtful, but this crew was telling me the king we are about to face is... odd," Hall responded. He gave a casual glance behind him, meeting the gaze of the ship's captain and received a reassuring nod.

Cyrus chuckled. "I wager most kings are."

The three men stood under dreary skies as they waited for the ship to dock. The gulls were hovering overhead, eyeballing the pier for any small crumbs worth swooping down for. There was a pungent odor of salt and fish as they drew closer, something the three men had grown familiar with in their many years navigating the nearby waters. Before long, the boat made it to port and the three men stepped off, with Hall tossing a small pouch to the captain to cover the docking fees. The payment for Hall's passage was already taken care of, but Hall simply wished to display his appreciation for the crewmen's joyful demeanor.

"Much appreciated, Lord Hall," the bright-eyed captain responded.

Hall grinned and gently bowed his head. "It was a pleasure to sail with you and your men. Safe travels, friend." Hall patted the captain's shoulder and turned to step alongside Elias, who was patiently awaiting him on the pier.

"Doesn't look like much," Elias remarked as he gazed into a row of small huts erected near Roman ruins.

"It's not a Roman town, Elias," Hall informed him. "It used to be a fort many years ago, even before our grandfathers were born. These souls are from the local tribe that migrated in and made it their own when the fort was abandoned. The same thing that happened much more recently to the rest of Britannia when the Romans finally left."

"Explains the thatch roofs on top of the stone buildings," Cyrus noted. "Unusual sight when I recall what these structures are intended to look like."

"You believe the Romans will never come back?" Elias probed.

Hall tilted his head to the side as he considered his answer. "I don't think there's any motivation for them to consider coming back. This place broke entire legions as the Romans fought to hold it. On the other hand, many of these people still think themselves to be Roman, so I don't know for sure. Either way, get used to seeing thatch roofs, that much won't be changing."

This type of home wasn't unusual for the Britons. When the Romans left, they took all the people who had the knowledge for building their customary marble or concrete structures. Upon their departure, the remaining Britons turned back to building in the styles of their ancestors through the use of wood and thatch. Even the lucky few who claimed the now-vacant Roman buildings didn't understand how to maintain the structures, making necessary repairs in the older styles and creating a uniquely Roman-Briton look.

The three men marched from the dock, moving around the backside of a walled structure they presumed would be the old fort before they stumbled upon the small market square. Hall stopped off at a baker's stall and purchased a fresh loaf of bread, splitting it three ways with his two companions. They strolled along the exterior of the walled enclosure on their right, attracting suspicious gazes from the locals as they stepped.

"Not exactly a welcoming bunch," Elias remarked as he met the eyes of a grumbling old man.

Cyrus looked behind them and nudged Hall's elbow. "Lord," he whispered as he pointed toward their followers. It was a pair of black-clad men in old, worn Roman helmets, both sporting suspicious stares.

"The sooner we find our way to the king the sooner we won't need to worry about brigands," Hall muttered.

"Let's trust he's on time then," Elias wearily remarked.

The group finally found their way to a sharp turn on the wall, rounding it to discover a pair of obviously bored sentries outfitted similarly to Hall, but adorned in royal blue cloaks. They were both standing adjacent to a banner depicting a golden anchor with a small circle at its summit, resting atop a royal blue background. One of the guards noticed the trio and sauntered over. "Lord Hall?" he asked through a worn-out tone.

"That would be me," Hall announced as he stepped forward.

"I figured as much, Lord. Not too many outsiders wear armor like this anymore. The king is inside," the guard answered as he peered over Hall's shoulder. "Made friends already, have you?" he asked, snickering at the sight of the two followers. "They belong to a harmless bunch in the service of the prince. Don't let'em intimidate you."

"I didn't," Hall noted, inducing a chuckle from both Elias and Cyrus as well as a grin from the guard.

The guard turned and knocked on the entrance to what the men had assumed to be a fort, but upon the gate being opened were surprised to discover it was a well-maintained villa. The clay tiles on the roof were all intact, and much of the concrete was without fissures to betray wear in the walls or foundations. There were Roman-armed sentries posted, servants roaming about, and in the center of the courtyard stood a regal looking middle-aged man clothed in a finely crafted toga patterned with purple on its edges. He was a pleasant looking individual, with abundant golden hair and a short beard of the same hue. The man noticed Hall approaching and produced a glistening smile as he began waltzing toward him. An older priest whispered something which seemed to dim his happy demeanor, but his only response was a slight nod until he looked back to his guest.

"You look older, Hall!" the finely adorned man remarked with a chuckle.

"As do you, Lord King," Hall answered with a smile.

The pair shared a short embrace before breaking, with the king turning to direct them inside the main building of the compound. It was indeed an impressive site, having mosaics crafted into the floors and various murals on most of the walls. They made their way to a table which had been set up in the middle of the courtyard, overlooking a shallow pool in the courtyard's center.

"How was your journey?" the king inquired as he fidgeted with his toga.

"Uneventful, Lord King," Hall returned while still admiring the craftsmanship of the home. The Romans built similar structures in Burdigala, but Hall never expected any were still standing in Britannia.

"I would think uneventful is most certainly better than treacherous," the king happily stated as he leaned forward and nodded to Hall's two companions.

Two servants approached, each bearing a tray with vessels containing fine wine. A cup was placed in front of both Hall and the king before each attendant disappeared to fetch food at the king's direction. King Ceneus conversed with his guests for a brief period, mainly about Hall's trip, the Romans neglecting Britannia, and various other matters before finally addressing why Hall was asked to meet him.

"To business then, as I am certain you come bearing questions which my vague message did not offer answers to," the king announced. "First and foremost, I have few true leaders for my army. There certainly are former Roman administrators under my employ, but none who can do little more than stand in the front of a marching column. What I need is a proven leader who can think on a... *wider* scale."

Hall inched forward in his seat. "You're talking of guiding men through a war then?"

"I am, and most likely more than one war if we are being sincere with one another. My kingdom is fragile, and the peace among its numerous tribes even more so. They need a good man to stand behind," the king answered.

"And you believe me to be that man?" Hall said as he rose out of his chair to stretch his legs and admire more of the mosaics.

"Yes, yes I do. You served effectively with my father. He named you before he died. He said you would be someone to try and bring into my service if I found myself in this very situation."

Hall stood in silence as he pondered his options. He could turn the king down and forego any titles or wealth that would come from working in his service. Or he could accept the king's offer and command men through wars likely spanning into Northern Britannia. Elias and Cyrus were listening eagerly for what their commander would decide, as this choice would influence them as well. The two men glanced between Hall and the king before a decision was ultimately made.

"You will have your man, Lord King, but I would require definite assurances," Hall stated.

King Ceneus smirked. "I supposed you might."

Hall was relieved when the king took no umbrage to the firmness of his tone. But the king likely expected as much. The stories of the frivolous oaths of Britannia's lords were widely-known. When Roman rule was beginning to come into question, many lords immediately turned their backs on the occupying forces and helped to secure the Roman exit from behind the scenes.

On top of that, one could argue Hall was entitled to such a tone. He had a reputation in these lands, afterall. It was one merited from his years of dedicated military service to Britannia's people. One could understood how that reputation could allow him to project an air of authority other men could not get away with.

Though he was no longer serving the Empire, not long ago he had been a Roman auxiliary fighting beside the VI Legio Victrix, or the Victorious Sixth Legion. It was one of the more prestigious legions in Rome's history. Their renown was easily turned into employment opportunities as military administrators in the service of petty kings or tribal chieftains following the departure of Rome.

Hall knew this standing would no doubt entitle him to the desired compensation for service to Ebrauc. "I will serve, Lord King. But I do not wish to wholly be met in gold or silver. I wish to have a haven for myself and my people. I need for this home to be located away from raiders and bandits. I do not want my people to ache from raids or small wars as they have in Burdigala."

Hall's people had been weathering the constant threat of barbarian raiders during their stay in Burdigala. They knew all too well the dangers of being located so close to violent tribesmen and hostile brigands. Interestingly, a sizeable portion of his men were from the less hostile neighboring tribes of these attackers, all joining Hall for protection from the brutality of a common enemy.

A priest, who to that moment had stayed to himself, contorted his face into a rather annoyed expression before puttering over toward the king, sneering at the three newcomers as he moved. Ceneus craned his neck toward the man as something inaudible to Hall was hissed into the king's ear. Whatever the comment was had caused a slight grimace to cross Ceneus' face as slowly turned his head to meet the priest's gaze. Hall glanced toward his two companions, receiving a look of confusion from Cyrus and a shrug from Elias before turning back.

The king glared into the priest's eyes as he abruptly stood and agreed to Hall's terms before gracefully motioning to a servant nearby to serve their guests some wine. "I can grant you all you request. And as for a home, there's a villa you seem to be fond of already! It was once owned by a wealthy Roman who turned disloyal in a time of great hardship for his people. Sadly, after his punishment was administered, he and his family were killed by brutish fanatics who thought they were doing my bidding. I can think of no better tenants to dwell within its walls than yourself and your family. I seem to remember a lovely woman of yours from your days residing beneath our walls."

Hall glimpsed down toward his feet. "Lord, my wife passed in childbirth before we left this place. Her grave is outside the Northern walls of the city."

King Ceneus became red in the face. "I... Hall, I had misremembered. My apologies." The king awkwardly smoothed his brow as he searched for the right words. Hall did not wish to discuss the matter, but the king had even been present at Fortunata's funeral before Hall had ventured to the continent. "You can remain here for as long as you wish and make any modifications to the home and surrounding lands you feel are necessary. You will get horses, armor, and weaponry we kept from the Romans along with fifty men to patrol the area around the Okellou. You will be paid as well, and I will be lenient with taxation until your people have their legs under them." The Okellou was the estuary which marked the approach to the Northern kingdom by way of the sea. The very place Hall's son would soon journey through to rejoin with him.

Hall graciously took the cup of wine from the servant and casually raised it toward the king. "Then I would say we have a deal, Lord King. My people will do what we can to rebuild Petuaria into a genuine trading hub, as well as shield the coast for future travelers," he proudly declared.

The king nodded before hoisting his cup and draining it at an extraordinary pace Hall only witnessed from Bors. After finishing the wine, he wiped his mouth across the shoulder of his toga before turning to Hall one last time. "I advise you to familiarize yourself with the region, as it no doubt changed during your time away." At that, he gave the servant his vacant cup and gestured toward the corner of the courtyard where a man Hall did not notice had been patiently awaiting the end of the meeting. Beside the now approaching man was another, younger priest of a significantly more pleasant demeanor than the first. "This is Aosten. He was trained by a Roman mercenary I contracted not long ago. I wished for said mercenary to take up the duties you now hold, but he felt he would do more good protecting Londinium."

Hall glanced over and nodded in the man's direction. "A pleasure, Aosten."

Aosten returned a bow of the head and walked over to Hall and his two companions, both still quiet since the conclusion of the negotiations. "Good to have you with us, Lord. If you'll please accompany me outside, I will deliver you to some of your men."

Hall and the king said their farewells before he was led out of the villa's front gate. Upon exiting, Hall observed about a dozen men relaxing by the entrance, seemingly anticipating for them to come out.

Hall smirked, and peered toward Cyrus and Elias, "I should have requested for more."

With a perplexed look on his face, Aosten looked from Hall to the men. "I *assure* you, they are proven warriors, Lord. Most here were instructed by the man our king spoke of. Titus was his name."

"That's not what I meant," Hall replied with a smile.

"Lord, I promise—"

Hall gently raised his hand toward his guide, cutting him off. "I can see by the scars they carry they have already been tested. I solely meant if the king had all this awaiting me upon my arrival, then it is reasonable to wonder what he would have given me should I have asked for more."

Aosten directed his attention to the dozen or so men as a relieved smile crossed his face. "If you only knew the half of it, Lord."

Hall promptly inspected the men before he finally introduced himself. "My name is Hall ap Lugurix." Hall presented himself in the Briton fashion instead of that from his homeland. This was due to the fact most people in Britannia would not understand what he meant should he use a surname. The 'ap' portion simply meant 'son of' in the Brythonic language spoken throughout the islands. "I will be leading you for the foreseeable future. I would assume your families will have found space necessary to relocate to Petuaria, as that will be where we are stationed. If not, I will help in the construction of additional homes for your people."

Most of the men nodded, but to Hall's surprise there were a few of them which did not speak the tongue of the Romans. While Aosten translated for the few who could not understand, Hall knew he'd found his first hurdle in leading these men.

How can I lead men who cannot understand my commands? Hall silently wondered. Once the pleasantries were through, Aosten took Hall back inside his newly acquired villa.

"Difficult to complain about our new home thus far, Lord," Cyrus announced with a grin.

"I agree, though I would like to wait a short time before I am certain." Hall glanced around at the numerous slaves now under his employ, immediately wondering if it was within his power to free them.

"Sensible enough," Elias acknowledged. "We will need additional housing for our people. These tribesmen do not seem to have many empty buildings we could move right into. The only ones I saw were about to fall over the first time the wind kicks up."

Hall nodded. "I agree. Go out and find where they gather their timber."

Elias bowed his head and rose to leave the room as Hall glanced back to a mosaic on the wall. It depicted a battle scene of a Roman soldier fending off what Hall presumed were Picts, as a fearful woman and child cowered behind him. He wondered if this was a depiction of a real event, or simply an imagining before walking through the villa's atrium. He couldn't show it, but Hall was pleased to have a little power again.

"Lord Hall," a black-clad guard called as he approached, also catching the attention of Elias as he was about to leave.

Hall turned and gestured for him to step forward. "Speak, man."

The guard drew in a sigh before continuing. "A ship meetin' the description of yer own was spotted shortly ago."

"Very good! My son has brought the first of my people. Thank you," Hall began to turn away until the man once again stepped forward.

"Lord, there is something else," the guard said shyly.

Hall perked an eyebrow and turned back. "What has happened?" he requested, identifying the hushed, solemn tone of the guard.

"I… our scouts stated there are bodies on the deck, Lord. They must have been attacked, or perhaps suffered a sickness," the guard answered.

The news drained the life from Hall's legs as he cursed under his breath. "Take me to the scouts," he ordered. He turned to Aosten and his two companions, then gestured for them to follow before making his way back toward the dock.

Drysten knew the sound of bodies being thrown into the water would stay with him for the rest of his life.

"You will have safe passage from Ostia to Britannia," Hall had explained to him. "Hostile tribesmen will not risk a journey across the seas while the rains still fall."

How Drysten wished this held true. The voyage from Burdigala to Ostia Antica, the major port in Italia, was as peaceful as one could expect. But the journey from the Roman haven to the frontiers of Britannia proved to be another matter.

Last fucking day of the voyage and they come out of nowhere…

Drysten's wistful thoughts were making his head ache

nearly as much as the voices of the gods were. He clenched his eyes shut as he rubbed a sweaty hand over his brow.

Being a young man of twenty-five years, he had done much fighting, but never once on water. In his first trip commanding his father's men, he had been pursued by a Saxon raiding party consisting of two fully crewed ships. While the Fortuna was a sturdy vessel and well suited for sailing near coastlines, it was not as swift as the vessels built by Saxons or Frisians. Two of these foreign ships had started chasing the Fortuna at the break of dawn and never let up until they finally caught her. The ensuing fight was a massive blur running through Drysten's mind, and the unfamiliar setting was causing an antsy feeling from the still-fresh battle lust. It was his first time leading men through a real battle, but thankfully he had a competent crew at his back. All he remembered was the very beginning, with men wrapped in furs leaping onto his ship and cleaving into his crew. Then the end, when he took what little plunder there was to be had from the Saxons and watched as it was finally placed below deck.

"Lord," a man announce from behind Drysten.

Drysten easily discerned it to be Bors the elder, a long-time friend of Drysten's father. Bors settled next to Drysten on the Fortuna's stern, granting a small nod as he did so. He began fidgeting with the leather cording which held the worn Roman mail onto his chest.

Drysten glanced down to the water as bodies began bobbing behind them. "What is it, Bors?" he asked as he caressed the back of his neck.

"Our losses, Lord," Bors grumbled. He paused, giving Drysten a brief moment to survey the man's face. He had been bald for as long as Drysten could remember, and had narrow eyes which seemed to be deeper into his head than most men's. Between those eyes rested a scar which Drysten had always noticed, yet never learned its cause. His short beard began to twitch as he leaned over the side and spit into the sea before continuing. "Losses were bad, but I believe it was the right move to stop and face them."

"Maybe," Drysten replied through a weak voice. He slowly peered up to the sky, moving his attention toward a flock of crows hovering overhead. He noticed a feather weaving through the air before gracefully coming to rest in the water behind the Fortuna.

Bors looked over his shoulder before leaning toward Drysten. "Was it them?" he whispered.

"Them?" Drysten asked, though he knew who Bors meant. He always knew. This was the normal, yet always awkward way in which people asked him this question.

Bors massaged the scruff on his chin before glancing behind him. "You were bellowing the order to press on toward the village when all of a sudden you went white in the face and ordered us to fight. Why?"

Drysten slowly lowered his head as the memory rang out in his mind. He had long been plagued by voices since his younger years, with most people believing it was a gift showing the favor of these strange deities. Drysten himself couldn't say for sure. Some mornings he would wake to a deafening chorus blasting through his mind, one which nobody else could hear. This morning, he awoke to an unfamiliar voice which seemed to have an agenda of its own.

"He said to kill them all," Drysten shamefully replied. Recalling the low rumble of the voice brought an uncomfortable sensation to the back Drysten's neck.

Bors leaned back, obviously interested. "Go on."

Drysten took a deep breath. "Some days I hear one voice, some days I hear many, but I never hear one which I do not recognize. They always sound like those I have known in my life. It could be the voice of my father, my woman, or even you on occasion. But when I woke today, I heard a different one. It sounded like an old man, with a voice as coarse as sand yet as clear as the air. He ordered the fight today, and I was petrified as to what would happen should I refuse."

"Even *me...*," Bors mouthed to himself. It was obvious to Drysten the man was slightly put off by the realization a being could mimic his own voice. "It is likely... *best* not to deny the gods their wishes." Bors gently placed a hand on Drysten's shoulder. "Either way, gods or no gods, we would not have been able to outrun those fuckers."

Drysten let out a long sigh as he remembered the pain and suffering of the men he had led to their deaths. They were chased along the coast of Britannia for the better part of the day, and to everyone's annoyance, they almost reached their destination, the small town of Petuaria.

"How many did we lose?" Drysten replied.

Bors began to fidget with the clasp holding his dirt-stained cloak about his shoulders. "By my count, we lost forty-seven, most of our fighters and a few of the rowers."

"We could not have waited to fight them in the village," Drysten half-heartedly asserted. "The only one we could count on for help would have been my father, and one man would have made no difference."

Drysten was not sure if he truly believed his remark, but knew this was indeed the voice's reasoning, it was understandable. His father was sent for by the king of Ebrauc to speak of leading his men into wars should it be necessary. They were to become mercenaries, patrolling the Northern lands under the king's tenuous control. Drysten and Bors had previously discussed if they were soon to be the ones in charge of protecting Petuaria, it most likely meant there was nobody protecting it now.

"The new deity who spoke to you could have known of a vulnerable village stocked with helpless women and children. For all we know, he was speaking on their behalf," Bors softly answered. It was a tone which Drysten had rarely heard from the man. "As for your father, I suppose he could've watched," he quipped with a chuckle.

Drysten showed a fake smile as he worked to pick the

sticky blood out from underneath his fingernails. Bors noticed the uneasiness in his captain and left him to himself after lightly patting his shoulder. Drysten was about to turn and make his way below deck to check on the Fortuna's captive before he stopped, noticing a man gently drifting by in the frigid water. He leaned across the side of the ship to get a better glimpse at the Saxon and immediately realized he was one of the men who Drysten had personally killed. The man was one of the first to clamber onto the Fortuna, brandishing a broad ax from side to side in the hopes of clearing space for others to follow. He made the mistake of swinging too high toward Drysten, who slightly ducked before driving his own blade to the hilt into the man's bare abdomen. Drysten remembered the strange sound the man made, almost like a squeak mixed with a gasp. It was apparent the man was surprised by the aggressiveness of someone who was noticeably smaller than him.

Just as Drysten began to turn away, he detected that squeak once again. He slowly turned back to see the eyes of a doomed man as he drifted behind the ship. He must have been unconscious as he was flung overboard and had awoken shortly after entering the river.

Drysten held no pity for the man, as he likely raped and murdered others who were caught by the Saxon vessel. "Should have stayed home," he muttered as his prey slowly began to sink further into the water. His mouth was opening and closing as he searched for air, the fear and panic evident on his wide-eyed face. The man locked eyes with Drysten, who saw them slowly close before he calmly grabbed onto the mysterious amulet around his neck, then disappear further below the river's steady current.

"Thought that one was *certainly* dead. You damn near put your entire arm through his belly," yet another familiar voice put in. Drysten knew it to be the man known as Diocles, a Greek who was picked up in Ostia. He deserted from the Eastern Roman auxiliary soon before landing in Ostia and was now in search of a new home, one which Drysten was delighted to provide to a battle-tested warrior.

"His legs weren't moving," Drysten replied. "I suppose I was the reason he died in the end. I think I took his legs from him; my blade must have nicked his spine. If it hadn't, I doubt he would have had many issues struggling his way to shore."

"Ah," Diocles grimly replied. "Bad way to go."

The two men turned and started their way toward the middle of the ship where their own dead were being prepared for burial once they anchored. Most of the men evaded eye contact with Drysten, which led him to believe they disagreed with his decision to challenge the Saxons. It's true they had the opportunity to keep running, but Drysten had been hesitant to put the wellbeing of villagers at risk without the certainty of aid from others stationed in Petuaria. Besides, a god had spoken.

"Shroud the bodies," Drysten commanded as he gestured to the few still left uncovered. "Wrap them and place their personal effects close by."

Most of the men followed his orders, though there was a small crowd which scoffed and shook their heads, causing Bors to give them a scowl. Being on Bor's wrong side was inadvisable considering he loomed over most of the men on the ship. They each hung their heads and went about their business, all but one man. His name was Maurianus, and if it were not for the fact he saved Hall's life years before, he would have no position on the Fortuna's crew. He was universally known to be a slimy and untrustworthy individual, so his opinion really held no weight to Drysten.

"The town is coming up, Lord," someone shouted.

Drysten and Diocles wandered to the bow of the ship to see the small, dilapidated docks of the village coming into view. Drysten knew it was a small town with few inhabitants, but the state of it from afar seemed as though it really held no significance to anyone other than its occupants.

"Seen nicer areas in Anatolia," Diocles put in, noticeably curious whether he would regret his decision to join Drysten's crew.

"Before you burned them down?" Drysten asked.

Diocles snickered. "Aye, before we burned them."

"How is our captive fairing?" Drysten asked, shifting the subject.

Diocles shrugged. "I saw Bors go down to him a moment ago. Probably wants to rough him up a bit before the king's men take him."

Drysten nodded as he turned back to see the village become more visible as they drew on. It seemed it had a walled building in the center, which was surrounded by thatch-roofed homes he guessed were most likely constructed after the walled area was built. The earth seemed marshy and obviously unable to be cultivated in most areas, but the one space he assessed to be suitable to farm indeed had a humble farmstead near the coastline.

They pressed forward, sailing toward the dock just as the rain started to spill from the heavens. This was yet another reminder of the battle, as the rain seemed to trail the Saxons during their pursuit. It was almost as though the Saxons were leaving a trail of gloom and darkness in their wake as they pursued their prey, creating a feeling of dread inside the nearly two hundred souls aboard the Fortuna. Even the men with the sunniest of demeanors were quiet as they occasionally peered behind them, all feeling like a rat fleeing from an owl.

Drysten recalled how he didn't need to look over the faces of his men to understand their fear. Yet the only ones who appeared to have none were his most seasoned men. The two which stood out were the lead oarsman, Amiram, and the ever war-hungry Bors. They both had been well-trained fighters with the Roman auxiliary in their past, with Amiram deserting much in the same way Diocles had. Amiram had once fought for the Western Roman Empire and left his post in Gaul many years before the trip. He soon became employed by Hall before having his tongue cut out when he was captured by a Frisian raiding party.

Bors served with Hall during a short war against Pictish invaders on Britannia's Western coast. The invaders had attempted to take the area away from the small number of Romans still in power in the present-day kingdom of Rheged. The Roman emperor, Honorius, sent his most established general known as Stilicho to deal with the invaders. He recruited men from mainland Europa to sail to the island and provide support to the local forces. Hall's father led a tribe near Augusta Praetoria, a Roman city at the base of the mountains to Italia's Northern border. Lugurix was Hall's father, and at the time, he was much too old for fighting. Instead, he sent his son to war with a handful of others. Bors was one such man, and the two had been fighting side by side ever since.

There was only one moment when the two wondered whether to go their separate ways, that being the time Bors' wife left him for another man in a neighboring village. Bors departed for the continent from Londinium, and returned a year later with his young son and news of the village being sacked by yet more raiders. Those, he said, wore strange armor more commonly known in the eastern regions, but Bors didn't seem to believe them to be dangerous to Britannia.

Drysten knew he was lucky to have such hardened warriors aboard the Fortuna. Had he not had the veteran leadership behind him, he knew most, if not all his men would be dead and he himself would have most likely become a prisoner to the Saxons. The fact they both looked worn out from the engagement gave Drysten an uneasy feeling. He couldn't tell whether the fight itself had exhausted them, or if they too were quietly second-guessing the decision to engage their enemy.

Drysten watched as the last few corpses belonging to

his crew were wrapped and hidden in the linens scavenged below deck. He only knew a handful of the deceased individuals' names but felt the sting of losing men under his charge for the first time. All he ever wanted was to lead his father's people after Hall decided to step away, but now he wished he had never been given the opportunity. A shape slowly stood beside him on the bow of the ship.

"I should have kept us moving," Drysten said in a slow whisper. He turned to see the shape was once again Diocles, who now dropped his head as he appeared to be searching for the words to say in response.

"Maybe." Diocles scratched the hair at his chin as he ultimately found the words he searched for. "Maybe not. Had I been in the same position, I don't know whether I would have done this differently. Sometimes the outcome of any decision you make will result in death."

"I just wish it was my decision to make," Drysten replied quietly.

Diocles craned his neck toward his captain. "Come again?"

"Funny how one day can change everything," Drysten answered.

"Funny indeed," Diocles sullenly replied.

Drysten simply nodded and tugged at the sword belt at his waist. The two averted their eyes away from the dead and turned their gaze toward the village. The trip had been uneventful until the day they were supposed to arrive. Were it not for the Saxons, Drysten would have told his father he enjoyed his brief stint as captain.

The two stood gazing toward Petuaria as they dragged on, each questioning what Hall may have been able to negotiate from the king of Ebrauc. Drysten found himself remembering his last interaction with his woman, Isolde, back in their home of Burdigala. Isolde had stood next to Drysten as they looked on the men loading the Fortuna. They were outfitting the vessel for their trading voyage to Rome, where they would be ferrying various amphoras and crates loaded with goods. The amphoras were filled with fine wine, and the boxes were filled with tin mined from the hills by Hall's workers.

As the final goods were loaded onto the ship, Drysten reminisced how he had turned to her with his hand outstretched. "Once I return, you have my word we will speak of marriage," he had told her.

She had taken his hand, smiling in a way that seemed to melt his mind into mush. It had been two weeks since they had figured out they were going to have a child.

"Who says I want to marry you?" she answered. Drysten recalled the mischievous grin she wore when she liked to poke fun at him.

"If you don't, you can always marry Bors," Drysten responded, referring to his childhood friend who spent more time whoring and drinking than anyone they had ever met, not unlike his father.

"As pleasant as that thought is, I suppose I'll just wait. I've seen how he is with his women."

"I have something for you." Drysten slowly turned and handed Isolde a small, linen-wrapped object. He remembered the nerves in his stomach tense as he handed it to her.

Isolde beamed, took the gift, and slowly began to unwrap it. As Drysten observed her graceful movements, he caught the faint scent of her hair and betrayed a small smile at the thought of marrying her. She was one of the most beautiful girls he had ever met, with vibrant black hair and delicate unmarred skin, which were more than uncommon for a person living an arduous life in a port city. Even now, after a fight he had won but felt as though he lost, he could still treasure the happiness she always brought him.

Everyone always said she was a stark contrast to Drysten. He was a scarred and rugged looking man of twenty-five years. He had hair black as pitch tied up at the middle of his head, with the lower layers resting just above his shoulders.

Drysten was taller than most of the men in their town, besides maybe Bors and his son, and had filled out at a young age. He was hardened by a lifetime of working on ships and fields, giving him rough hands and deceptive strength. Hall liked to say his appearance was similar to Hall's early memories of his own father, but with the eyes of Drysten's mother.

Drysten called to mind when Isolde saw the ring with the emerald stone in the center, betraying a loving smile to him as her eyes lit up. It was a rare piece of jewelry. Fit for a noblewoman of Rome, which Drysten's mother had once been before marrying his father. That was the deal Lugurix made with Stilicho, Hall would fight for him for the hand of a Roman noblewoman. Hall once said the early days of his marriage were rather tumultuous, but Hall and Fortunata grew to love each other deeply.

"It was your mother's?" she asked.

Drysten smiled. "It's yours now. She would have wanted you to have it." They shared a brief kiss before Drysten finally made his way to the docks to speak with his father.

Isolde held Drysten's hand a little tighter as she slowly turned to him. "Your father told us to follow him to Britannia. He seems convinced we'll have a new home soon, and good money to stay there for a while. A handful of us left behind have bought passage with a merchant who frequents the isles. He said he could have us in Eboracum after his next voyage North."

Drysten remembered his happiness at the idea his woman would be joining them for their new life. "Who is this captain?" he asked.

Isolde shrugged as if it didn't matter. "I have never seen him before. He anchored near Servius last night. Scraggly looking fellow but he looked to be a capable enough sailor."

Thief! a woman in Drysten's mind shrieked, snapping him from his daydreams. He wheeled around to see the two men from Crete walking toward him, each tightly wringing the arm of the man called Maurianus. "This little *fucker* was snooping near Baak's body," the older brother explained, referencing a man who had perished fighting off the Saxons.

"What exactly was he doing, Paulus?" Drysten inquired.

Paulus tugged at Maurianus' arm as the man briefly tried to free himself from his grasp. "He unwrapped the man and started eyeing his remains, Lord."

Drysten narrowed his eyes and walked toward Maurianus. "And why were you doing that?"

"He owed me a debt from a dice game. I desired to collect before the opportunity was gone. I would not have taken more than was owed, Lord," Maurianus explained. "This is a difficult life we live. Any money owed…"

"You sought to loot his corpse!" Petras wrung Maurianus' arm and screamed into his face.

"Petras!" Drysten stepped forward and casually raised a hand, pacifying the man. Petras narrowed his eyes as he turned his gaze from Drysten to Maurianus. "I understand your logic, but you should have come to me about this. Only a fool would think to search the body of one of our fallen."

Maurianus dropped his head, though Drysten suspected the man was merely seeking to persuade those gawking nearby he felt some semblance of shame. "I… I apologize, Lord. I meant no offense."

"Liar!" Petras shouted as he struck the prisoner in the stomach with his free hand.

Diocles quickly restrained the younger Cretan before he could do additional harm to Maurianus, now wheezing for air on his knees. Diocles muttered something which looked to calm Petras, then shifted to Drysten and nodded. Petras began to visibly relax as he loosened his grip and let go of his prisoner's arm before falling back a couple steps.

Drysten glanced back to the accused and stooped down to his level, whispering as he spoke. "I know the kind of person you are. If it were up to me, I would have cast you overboard with the Saxons. Were it not for the debt my father owes you, there would have been judgment upon you long ago. Get up, and consider staying out of sight for a time."

Maurianus deliberately raised his head and met Drysten's eyes, then let out a sly smile as he began to stand. "I praise you for your understanding, *Lord*."

Drysten glared into the man's eyes as he slowly turned and began shuffling away. Most of the men grew disinterested by the lack of force used against Maurianus and returned to their duties while Drysten walked back to the bow.

"I've always hated that man," Paulus noted, "particularly when he tried to pay my sister to..." causing a groan from the men as they imagined what he meant.

The three stood at the ship's bow as the Fortuna gradually settled in at the docks of the settlement before silently turning around and stepping toward the port side to disembark. Drysten finally spotted his father, donned in his magnificent Roman legionary armor and bearskin cloak. He immediately lowered his head as he passed over the slight gap between the Fortuna and the pier, mentally preparing himself for a conversation he dreaded more than anything.

CHAPTER II

The warmth of the sun was fading away from the village as Hall observed the Fortuna creep toward the dock. His original intent was to journey out and survey the area's fortifications the morning after the arrival of his forces, but the adverse turn of affairs pushed his plans back. Aosten was with him at the pier and seemed to be staring off into nothing as he leaned against the stone of the villa's Southern wall.

Hall glanced toward Aosten, scoffing as he figured out the man was staring at a pair of whores who approached from the market. This was not strange, as most whores Hall encountered typically wandered over toward oncoming vessels, hoping to be the first thing sea-weary travelers saw when they disembarked. It was obvious they were also awaiting the arrival of the Fortuna, albeit for very different reasons than his own.

Hall nudged Aosten to catch his attention. "Tell me again what the scouts reported," he commanded.

Aosten straightened his back and peered toward the Fortuna as she approached. "Two ships were going at it with one of Roman make. Appeared to be Saxon by the look of 'em. We don't know for certain yet, though, as those ships are known to find their way into Briton hands in these times."

"The Fortuna was caught?" Hall asked, though he suspected this was not the case.

Aosten shook his head. "No, Lord. Your people turned

and offered their pursuers a fight."

"I can't accept he'd be that stupid," Hall growled as he watched his ship draw closer. As it did, he noted the dozens of shrouded corpses on the top deck. *Fucking hell, he was right here. Why didn't he just keep going?* Hall felt a twinge of guilt that his first thought was to scold his boy who may not have survived.

The Fortuna eventually slowed before lines were thrown to dock workers who quickly secured the ship to the pier. Hall pushed his way through a small crowd near the docking ramp and felt a wash of relief as he looked over those making ready to come ashore. Drysten slowly shuffled off the vessel to be followed by a Roman-looking man he did not recognize, then Paulus, Bors, and Amiram. Before walking toward his father, Drysten slowly turned and gestured for a handful of men to come forward. A small group was leading a hairy looking man with a large beard from the middle of the ship.

Hall stepped up to the weary-looking group, instantly discerning the bound man was likely a Saxon, and a prominent one at that. He bore a gold chain wrapped loosely around his neck and a bearskin cloak like Hall's own draped around his shoulders.

Hall did what he could to keep himself from showing his distraught as he glanced to Bors. "Brother—"

"I—" Drysten gently interrupted.

Hall swiftly lifted his palm toward his son. "We will speak in a *moment!*" His harsh tone seemed to alarm his son as he took a step back. Looking back at Bors, he lowered his hand and nodded his head.

Looking from Drysten to Hall, Bors told the story of how the Fortuna was chased along the coast of Britannia until Drysten made the decision to face their attackers.

"And this is the Greek my son took in at Ostia?" Hall asked while gesturing to Diocles.

"I am, Lord! I am called Diocles." The Greek glanced

down as he spoke. It was evident to everyone around how the stern expression coming from Hall was making the newcomer uncomfortable.

"Did you aid in the fight?" Hall queried.

"I did, Lord. Killed four of 'em too," Diocles answered, lifting his head with a little pride attached.

Hall gave a slight nod as he turned around to gaze over the Fortuna's hull, now scarred with the shallow marks left from the impact of the Saxon ships. "Could you... could you have made it to safety?"

Hall could see the doubt running over his son's face. Not doubt that he could escape his pursuers, but doubt in his decision to choose not to.

"I'm... unsure."

"No, you aren't." Hall took a step forward, staring intently into his son's eyes. "I want a *yes*, or a *no*." He took a moment to survey his son's face, half-lit by the light of the torches placed at either side of the wooden pier. He could see just enough to understand his son feared him in that moment, creating a slew of mixed emotions. As a father, he wanted nothing more than to tell his son he made the right decision, even if he wasn't sure of that himself. But at that moment, he was not speaking as a father. He knew his son needed to learn when *not* to fight if he was going to someday lead his men.

Drysten stood frozen. "Yes," he answered weakly, "I believe there was time."

Hall's voice rose steadily as he spoke, progressing from a whisper to a full-bellied yell. "I'm having a hard time believing... you're telling me you were being pursued by *two* ships, *both* of whom had full crews, *both* of whom were far off behind you, and you decided to stop and risk the lives of *my* men? My *fucking* men!"

The color was leaving Drysten's face as he stood frozen in front of his father. "I... yes," he choked out.

Hall glared into his son's eyes as he moved even closer

than before, now coming within inches of his son's face. "And how many did you lose?" he demanded.

"Forty-seven," Drysten responded shyly, lowering his head.

"You disappoint me, son," Hall whispered before pursing his lips and abruptly turning his gaze away from his son. He didn't bother facing Aosten as he ordered him to put the prisoner in the storage shed behind the villa's walls. As he stormed away, he was having trouble understanding why Drysten had made such a rash and foolish decision. To him, it seemed his son had more to learn than he originally thought.

"Hall!" a deep voice called out, "wait!"

Hall slowly stopped and turned around to see Bors briskly striding up to him. He felt his eyes narrow in frustration but decided to let Bors say his piece. "There are innocent people here! If he had kept going, he would have been putting their lives at risk. Innocent people could have been..." Bors looked at his friend and took a deep breath as he waited for any kind of response.

Hall took a step toward his friend and calmly looked him in the eye. "Teach him to lead men, Bors. That's what I ordered you to do. That's *all* you were supposed to do. You certainly weren't supposed to allow him to fight some fucking *Saxons* along the way. They would have moved off when they saw the king's men lining up on the docks, maybe even turned away when they saw three men outfitted in the armor of the Roman legions staring *back* at them. They could have assumed the Empire had returned. The Empire still brings fear to—"

"Brother, *those* people no longer fear the Empire. They haven't for some time now," Bors replied through a hushed tone.

After a moment, Hall broke eye contact and lowered his head. "Did he... fight well?" he wondered aloud.

Bors also appeared to calm at the change of subject, relaxing his shoulders as he slowly nodded. "Yes, Lord. In time, I do believe he will make a good leader for our people. Fought like a damned *demon*."

"Like a demon..." Hall nodded before gently scratching the whiskers on his chin. "Well, we may require leaders here soon enough." Hall recalled how the great Roman general Stilicho was famous for fighting on the front lines with his men. He knew if Drysten could do that as well as it appeared he had done on the ship, then he may indeed become a man people would follow.

"There is... something else," Bors added stiffly.

Hall had begun turning away but was struck by the strange tone of his friend. "What is it?"

Bors glanced around him before edging a little closer to Hall, softly whispering as he spoke. "They commanded him to engage the Saxons."

Hall gazed down toward his feet, knowingly betraying his annoyance. He despised the voices which tormented his son. "What did they say this time? Was he to fight a war against all the tribes of Gaul? Was he to lead raids to *their* shores with a ship mainly consisting of rowers? What did these gods have to say to *my* son?"

Bors sighed before he glanced back to Drysten, who obviously had some idea of what was being said based on the embarrassed expression covering his face. "He heard a new one. He seemed frightened of it, or at least frightened of going against it."

"Lord?" a voice timidly stammered from behind him. Hall split from his conversation with Bors as he turned to see Aosten gradually stepping up to speak with him. "When you have a moment, I believe it would be wise to speak of our trials facing these same invaders."

"Hmph," Bors answered with a snort, "we already know about these little invaders quite well."

"Everyone's little to you, Bors," Hall shot back before nodding to Aosten. "Let's meet at the villa in a few moments. We will speak more of this shortly."

"Yes, Lord." Aosten gave a short bow before beginning to turn toward Hall's new home.

"And, Aosten?" Hall said with a smile, causing the man to turn back. "No whores until after we speak." Aosten cast a wide grin as he shuffled off.

"Am I to assume we will have our hands full soon?" Bors wearily asked as he glanced around their new home. Hall noticed his friend's perplexed gaze was fixed on the king's banner, gracefully waving atop the villa's rear wall.

"It would appear so, but we will need to address this new voice my boy heard. I remember when he first heard them ringing through his mind...," Hall replied.

Bors nodded as he let out a long sigh, and the two discontinued their conversation as they began walking toward the villa, moving along the outside wall toward the gate.

"Fancy looking place," Bors remarked in surprise. He sounded somewhat suspicious, but Hall couldn't figure why.

Hall snickered. "It's mine, Bors. Don't get yourself any ideas."

"There's *surely* ample room for the both of us."

Hall smirked. "For you and your legitimate boy, perhaps. Simply not the rest of the bastards you fathered back home."

Bors scrunched his face at the comment. "I'll go find some booze then. Have fun with your new friend." He veered off and walked toward the buildings across from the gate, leaving Hall as he continued toward the entrance.

Hall took little note of his new villa's outer aesthetics upon his initial arrival. The villa itself was encircled by a stone wall of about eight feet in height, with the entrance being a metal gate facing the village. There were great stone pillars outside the villa's gate, clearly worn from years of abuse by Britannia's fickle weather. Both were masterfully crafted and supported a portion of the decorative archway with an engraving overhead. Hall stepped forward and examined the engraving of a woman holding a spear toward a group of enemies. He guessed it to be a depiction of the goddess Britannia, the goddess who represented the people and spirits of the islands he was now committed to defending. Hall was pleased with the aesthetic of his new home and walked around the outside of the wall to find it surprisingly well taken care of. It seemed someone was trying to keep it in good condition for any new tenants, an observation which further convinced him the king was expecting Hall to take up his offer.

Upon walking under the archway and through the gate, he again entered the large courtyard to inspect the other buildings in view. There was a comfortable looking residence, storage shed to his left, and two other buildings which looked to be housing for his servants alongside a kitchen to feed them.

Aosten sauntered up with two others he had yet to meet. "Lord, this is Dagonet and Gawain," he explained as he gestured to the two men trailing behind him. "They're two scouts who will report directly to you." The two men seemed no older than his son, which was moderately unexpected. Most fighting men in Britannia had at least a brief history fighting under the Romans, meaning they were normally a bit older.

Hall nodded as he surveyed the two scouts. The one known as Dagonet seemed to be using a leather strip to cover a brand from a slaver on his arm, but Hall cared little for slavery and knew it would not raise any issues for him. Gawain had a strong jaw and a stern gaze whereas Dagonet had long, scraggly hair and kinder eyes but a complex demeanor betraying an inner strength.

After giving them a quick glance, Hall spoke. "It is a pleasure to meet you both. As you likely assumed, we'll be building more homes around the villa to accommodate you and your families. For now, get some food in your bellies until we find our first order of business."

The two men responded with an apathetic "Yes, Lord"

and proceeded to walk toward the kitchen. Hall detected the lack of life in their tone but judged it best to disregard it so soon upon meeting them.

When they had gone, Aosten approached to explain their present circumstances. "Lord, we should not hesitate before we begin strengthening the area. At present, we have Saxons invading to the East, men from the North crossing Hadrian's Wall, and Gaels attacking all along the Western coast. Our armies have been overstretched. Aside from yourself, we have no genuine guidance in this portion of the kingdom. Most of the commanders we've had either died or vanished for someplace more... civilized."

"Died?" Hall curiously asked.

Aosten shrugged as if it was nothing. "Most yet live. Aside from the traitor the king spoke of earlier, the few who perished did so by provoking the locals. Like any other people, they are never an issue if they are treated with grace."

Hall took a step toward the villa's entryway as he began to realize how bad the situation had become since he departed. "So, I need to worry about those that dwell within our lands as well as those abroad. Do we have any outside help?"

Aosten hesitated for a moment. "Only a small faction from Powys. We've stationed them in Cataractonium at the moment. Their prince leads them well."

"Prince?" Hall questioned.

Aosten nodded. "His name is Ambrosius Aurelianus. He's a Roman born near Armorica and technically not a prince, but he's a very capable leader."

"How is he *technically* not a prince?" Hall inquired.

Aosten shrugged. "It's truly no issue to us. He's the son of a Roman general who returned to help fight off invaders. Wealthy men tend to garner titles of importance in these times."

Hall too understood that to be true and didn't find it

hard to agree. "And are there additional allies?"

"Some lords in Gwynedd occasionally post their scouts on our shared border to warn us if danger approaches. Other than that, everyone has been too occupied shielding themselves to lend us anything more," Aosten explained.

Hall groaned at the realization the Britons were not as united as he'd hoped. "How do we normally fight them?"

Aosten's faced garnered a confused expression. "What do you mean?"

"Which side tends to incite the attacks?" Hall clarified.

After catching a quick moment to consider, Aosten eventually answered. "Unquestionably, the invaders. Much of the time they raid small villages, never reaching very deep into our territory. They'll eliminate most of the men prior to taking the women and children as slaves. They slaughter the livestock if they can't direct them back to their own lands quickly enough, though they ordinarily can as they seldom stay long enough for us to send relief. When we do get there in time to stop them, they burn *everything* before providing us a hell of a fight."

Wondering why Aosten hesitated, Hall gave a suspicious glance before responding. "That certainly sounds familiar. I would rather not be on the defensive against those men," he remarked.

A clearly exasperated Aosten gave a heavy sigh before he finally resumed. "Agh, the sorriest piece of it all is every time we try to help one area, we end up leaving somewhere else vulnerable. Then the next village gets raided, and the whole mess starts over. When we box them in for a fight, which rarely happens, we normally trounce the fuckers..." Aosten ran a hand over his head and sighed deeply.

Hall could easily sense the frustration in Aosten's voice, most likely put there by years of arriving too late to these raids. He imagined a small war band reaching their destination in the hopes of defending their people, only to find pale bodies cut up and set ablaze or hung from trees. Hall remembered fighting the blue men from the North as well as the Gaels in the West when he was an auxiliary. Sadly, he understood that frustration all too well. The enemy he knew the least about, being the Saxons, was still widely known to be ferocious, so he knew he could not ignore one of these groups to deal with another.

"The Saxons control the East coast?" an interested Hall asked. He had assumed the raiders mainly stayed to the South, near the channel with the closest crossing from the continent. He had never considered the possibility that his son had strayed within *their* territory.

"Just bits and pieces. We keep a good handle on the old sea-forts the Empire left behind. Most of our forces are split between those and along the wall," Aosten explained.

"Is there a garrison inside the city?" Hall wondered aloud while gesturing North toward Eboracum.

Aosten nodded. "Most of our major cities have a small one, but we largely have to rely on soldiers who stayed behind when the Empire abandoned us. The king has his own guard force, as does the prince. One thing to remember, King Ceneus' guards wear royal blue and earned their position based on merit, the prince's did not. The prince's guards would be the black-clad men you may have noticed wandering about when you arrived."

Hall stood in reflection for a moment, gently rubbing his whiskered chin before he eventually turned toward Aosten. "Tell the king I need the men he gave me plus another fifty volunteers."

"We're to attack someone?" Aosten responded in surprise.

Hall shook his head. "At the moment, no. I simply desire to understand which groups can be counted on to bolster us should we require it."

"Before we arrange anything, Lord, there is one obstacle we must overcome," Aosten started. "The Northmen have taken our sea fort at the Easternmost side of Hadrian's Wall.

We would do well to correct that before we commit to anything else."

Hall nodded as he remembered his brief time at the fort Aosten was speaking of. It was called Segedunum, and at one point contained a few of the older men who served him aboard the Fortuna. Hall wondered how many of said men were still alive after their attack by the Saxons. "We'll have to take it back before someone can use it to establish a foothold by the sea. Get what men we have set to move."

"Yes, Lord," Aosten responded, before shifting away and walking out of the villa's gates. Hall stood listening to the rush of the Usa's current near the village, reminiscing about how his wife had once gifted him a radiant golden chain carrying the depiction of the sun god, Lugos, on its medallion. He remembered that day so vividly he almost thought he could hear her voice once again. It was strange to him such an unrelated deed from his wife crept up in his mind.

After a moment, he ultimately shook off the sadness and turned to find his son.

Drysten was followed by Diocles and Amiram as he explored his new home. He didn't mind the stench from the sea, or even that of the pottery kilns near his father's villa. What he found unsettling were the strange stares from the locals who seemed to refuse meeting his eyes with their own. Two children scampered off as Amiram gave them a smile, and a woman went wide-eyed and plucked up her basket of food once Drysten offered to help her.

"Friendly bunch," Drysten mentioned to Diocles.

Diocles shrugged. "Heard one mention something about a new lord replacing an old one. Could just be afraid of a little change."

Amiram gave Diocles a confused look and tilted his head in confusion.

A group of people were gathered across the road from the villa's entrance, dawdling around as if they were trying to keep busy while looking on the newcomers. The perplexing thing about them was their demeanor. Some even seemed to look on in sympathy, but Drysten could not figure why.

A figure exited the villa and spied the crowd, attempting to shoo them off before turning toward Drysten. Aosten, clearly drowsy judging by the bags under his eyes, slowly wandered over as Drysten approached.

Aosten nodded to Drysten as he rubbed his hands together. "I would suggest giving your father a moment's peace. We just spoke of the many urgent matters he now needs to worry of in his new position."

Drysten hadn't realized it, but he was holding his breath as he thought of his father. He suspected that Hall wasn't sure he could trust his son's judgement anymore. "I am in no rush to see my father at the moment."

Aosten smiled and gestured for the three men to follow him away from the villa. "One day you will be, Lord. There is always an instant when you recognize you will never get the chance to see a parent again. Cherish even the roughest of times, that would be my advice."

Drysten raised an eyebrow at the counseling. "And what should I say in that moment?" he asked, still somewhat shocked by the humanity a stranger was showing him.

"You will know, Lord. It is not something one can plan for considering you have no understanding of the circumstances yet. What I *can* assure you is if you are fortunate, you will be able to see him off well and ease his passing," Aosten explained.

"And... if I am not?" Drysten wondered. To him, his father was a stalwart bastion of strength he had never seen waver, even in the darkest of times. The idea the man would die someday seemed foreign.

Aosten shrugged. "Then you must simply do what you can with what the precious few moments you may have."

Aosten patted Drysten's arm as he moved to step in

front of the group, now leading them through the docks and market square. Drysten was now directly behind him and nodded as he passed. He was glancing around and gently rubbing the back of his head while attempting to comprehend why everything he saw was nothing like his childhood memories. He had previously visited the village with his mother so long ago, but nothing mirrored the images of his mind. Though in all fairness, the nighttime's darkness had just set in.

"Where's the remainder of the crew idling?" He asked of his guide.

Aosten motioned to a series of structures across the path from the villa. "The king is permitting them to stay in an unused barracks near the compound. It's directly across the street. Once the barracks in your father's new villa is finished being repaired, they'll settle down there."

"And our things?" Drysten found himself wondering what treasures the box taken from the Saxons contained. He hadn't had the strength to open it following their battle at sea.

"It has all been delivered to the villa, Lord," Aosten answered with a nod of reassurance.

The four men moved their way out of a cramped alleyway and into a street Drysten assumed would be teeming with people during the daytime. He was unimpressed by the size of the market square when comparing it to the one he was accustomed to in Burdigala. This one was much, much different. It had fish and freshly picked crops, but it lacked extravagant clothes, fine wine, and the natural surplus of whores working on getting men's attention. There were still a few whores walking about, as Drysten had noticed when he first disembarked, with each trying to gain the attention of the newcomers. One even confronted a pair of Christian priests before noticing Drysten and his companions. She succeeded in snatching Diocles' focus, with the man turning to give Drysten a smirk before straying off toward her.

"You don't even know where we live yet!" Drysten shouted to no effect. Before he knew it, the man was out of sight in what looked to be a tavern.

Aosten scoffed in amusement and motioned his hand for Drysten to follow. "I suppose some men can wait longer than others." He led them toward the side entrance on the eastern wall of the villa, walking beside the two Christian priests currently making an effort to redeem a pair of whores. All it really succeeded in doing was getting one to walk away without a word, and another to grant them the same suggestion.

Drysten was familiar with the aesthetic of smaller villages in the area from his early years living in Eboracum. As a young boy, he had wasted many hours wandering the countryside with his friends and invariably ended up running home later than he was supposed to. He reminisced how he used to hide in the wheat fields near the city and try to frighten his mother as she was strolling home from purchasing food inside the city. It was that image that first made him think of Isolde.

When is she going to arrive? Drysten asked himself.

Death will find you!

Drysten was alarmed by another, profoundly wicked voice, resembling that of Maurianus crying out through his mind.

You will never outrun it! The moment will soon arrive, it hissed.

Drysten pinched his eyes shut as the shock of hearing the voice achingly displayed over his face. An icy shiver rushed down his spine, almost producing a wail of agony from deep beneath his chest. He somehow managed to stymie it down into a low, almost inaudible murmur of discomfort. He took a moment before glancing to his left to see a knowing Amiram gaze at him sympathetically, along with a perplexed Diocles looking between the two from the door of the tavern.

Amiram shook his head toward Diocles before gently placing a hand on Drysten's shoulder.

Thankfully, Aosten turned around and interrupted the uncomfortable exchange, pointing in the direction of a large, walled home with the depiction of a woman carved over the archway of its main gate. "Lord? Your home's through here," he stated.

Drysten shook off the unpleasant sensations and somehow managed a nod before moving through the archway. To bring his thoughts away from the sinister voice, he glanced up to admire the craftsmanship as he passed through the torchlit entrance. As he walked into the courtyard, he noticed a group of about a dozen men relaxing around a small fire. The sun's light had gone for the evening, opening the way for the chill of darkness to creep in.

One of the men noticed Drysten and smiled wide as he stood up and proceeded to walk toward him. He was about as tall as Bors but with perhaps forty pounds less of muscle and a face which Drysten had no difficulties placing.

"Cynwrig," Drysten pronounced with a smile as he remembered all the times he spent eating with him and his siblings during his younger years.

The two men shook hands and embraced one another before Drysten turned back to Aosten. "Are these my father's men?" he questioned.

Aosten peered from Drysten to those gathered around the fire. "Most are, Lord. Though a few appeared soon after your father's coming. I assume they're looking for work." He glanced back to Drysten. "I guess that would make the newcomers yours if your father has no place for them." Aosten patted Drysten on the back before he pleasantly smiled and walked through the gate. "Tell your father I'll be dutifully honoring his arrival in that tavern we passed. The one your friend disappeared into." At that, he meandered off through the gate.

Drysten turned back to his childhood friend and

slapped him on the shoulder. "It's been a long while, Cynwrig. How's your family?" he inquired as he started toward the entrance to the main house of the villa.

His face shifted to an expression one could only describe as a deep, hopeless grief, Cynwrig slowly turned to him. Drysten was startled by the anguish in his eyes, with the dark bags of fatigue and lack of sleep more noticeable than before. "All of them are gone, my friend. The Northmen got to them at the village beside Segedunum a few days ago. I'm only alive because I was in a neighboring settlement across the river. Do you remember Arbeia? I was there peddling off the barrels of fish I caught with my father and brother. I had no idea what was happening until I turned back toward my home and saw smoke blooming up into the sky. It was not long after that I began hearing the screams of my people along with it. I grasped what was happening and immediately journeyed my way here. I was the one who brought the news to the king."

Drysten felt his mouth fall open as the two kept walking. All he could manage was a sorrowful stare.

"That was it," Cynwrig added. "The end to the line of great Sarmatian knights once in the service of Rome."

"I am... there are no words. I am sorry for your losses," Drysten managed to whisper. He had dealt with so much death the previous day that he had not considered there would be more waiting for him when he arrived in Britannia. As he began to grasp the tragedy that had befallen his friend, he remembered the voice's words which vexingly rang through his mind moments before. Cynwrig responded with a melancholy smile and accompanied Drysten through the open doors of the villa, where he too gazed upon the exquisite murals painted by a gifted Roman many years before.

The painting had a profound effect on Amiram, who stopped following the other two men and just stared in wonderment at the craftsmanship demanded to create such art. He looked on the depiction of a great battle between blue faced men and a fearless-looking Roman boldly standing in defiance of them. Blood coated the hill they fought on, with anguished faces attached to wounded men who had fallen to the lone Roman's ferocity.

Amiram turned and smirked when he recognized his companions were now waiting on him, then rejoined the group as they stepped into the central common area of the elaborate home. There was a shallow pool of water in the center, enveloped by flowers on three sides, leaving a bench on the fourth side nearest to the entryway.

"Wow... just, wow," Cynwrig exclaimed.

This was indeed an improvement upon the home Drysten had resided in during his time in Burdigala. That home was a small shack compared to the decadence and grandeur of his new dwelling.

"Could use a woman's touch, no doubt. *Everything's* better with women," a man announced from behind him. Drysten turned and saw Diocles walking through the entrance. "Bitch took my money and ran. Didn't feel like chasing after her," he explained.

The group shared a quick laugh and made their way to the center of the common area, where Diocles noticed the chest containing their plunder. "Why don't we take a look?" He chuckled toward Amiram before sauntering over and raising the lid. "Already had myself a quick peek before we reached the village. Good stuff to find in here." Drysten, Amiram, and Cynwrig all eagerly followed him to examine the chest's contents.

Drysten observed the other men, momentarily unsure if he should be one of the first to open the container. After a brief pause, he turned to the men who were present during the fight at sea and instructed them to choose one item for themselves, while the rest shall be distributed among the remainder of the crew. He then comforted Cynwrig, who was obviously feeling somewhat left out. "Your fortunes will come soon enough, brother. I'm sure of it." Then briefly placed his hand on the man's shoulder.

Amiram fancied a small ring with an engraving written on the side in a strange, curved language before he deliberately paused and plucked up a gold chain. Drysten did not immediately grasp why, as it was laborious for the man to articulate without a tongue. Puzzled, Drysten looked on as Amiram anxiously stared at it as if he wanted with every fiber of his being to say something. Diocles took a silver brooch for his cloak, one he thought was worthy of a lord as he raised it up toward a torch for a better view. Drysten's smile evaporated as he peered deeper within the chest, gently pushing away tiny trinkets to reach the one glistening object which caught his eye. As he gazed deeper, a pit swiftly formed in the center of his stomach, swelling up into his chest.

Voices began whispering messages of death into Drysten's mind. Each one reverberated louder than the last before any other sound was drowned out by their painful messages. He felt as though he had been stabbed, tortured, or struck by lightning from the impending storm which still lingered out at sea.

"Where is the prisoner?" Drysten managed to choke out.

Because there sat Isolde's ring.

The cellar was cramped and stank of rotten grain, but Jorrit understood it was a triumph to be there. He knew he was about to usher in a war, one in which triumph meant relocating his people away from the frozen dirt they currently inhabited and into the lush pastures of a crippled kingdom brought to heel. The people of these lands were unprepared and undisciplined, something which delivered joy into Jorrit's heart. From there, a hope the conflict will conclude that much sooner began to take shape inside his mind.

No more of those fucking winters, he mused as he leaned his head against the stone walls of his confinement. *Let's hope all the men here make impulsive decisions like that fool of a commander.* Jorrit let out a quick smirk as he recalled the events of the day. He immediately concluded the two ships under his command could have taken the bigger, yet slower and less outfitted Roman ship he assaulted earlier in the day. At one point, Jorrit even feared he would accidentally win the battle.

The rival commander was a young man who he speculated was mildly inexperienced in the role. While Jorrit witnessed the skill the man held in battle, his tactical blunder to turn and offer himself up to the pursuing Frisian and Saxon crews would ordinarily be one to lament. Jorrit feared his men would quickly overwhelm the Britons and force him to wait for yet another vessel to prey upon. Even though that would have meant victory and plunder for his men, he understood the greater prize would have had to wait that much longer. Fortunately, the Britons showed more resolve than he anticipated.

Though he understood he could have killed them all should his goals have been different, Jorrit was able to act the role of a beaten commander strongly enough to convince the Britons they had truly won. In exchange for discontinuing the fight, Jorrit submitted himself as a hostage, but only after ordering his men to slaughter the enemy crew should they not have accepted his offer.

His reminiscing was disrupted once more by the echoes of shouts overhead, each roaring in the old language of Rome, one which Jorrit had only encountered a handful of times in his life, but still managed to learn bits and pieces of off traders. He raised his head in an attempt to catch some familiar words between the two angered parties but ultimately failed to recognize any at all. There appeared to be a gradual intensification in the volumes of each voice, until a low thud was heard, immediately replaced by a tense stillness.

He determined what was transpiring overhead must

not have concerned him, and once more he reflected upon Colgrin's plan. Not the killing required, as Jorrit was never a real proponent for slaughter, but power. The power he would be compensated with for his pivotal role in seeing it through. How Colgrin would grant him a fertile parcel of land to call his own, and how he would erect an altar to Woden in its center. Gone were the days of cattle raising and weathering the storms and high tides his Frisian birthplace was susceptible to. Many formerly occupied areas were now underwater or close to meeting the sea, and people had been migrating away from those areas for years.

Jorrit was now intent on claiming his new home in Britannia, one where he could start his own tribe. A powerful, yet mostly peaceful tribe reliant on trade to be led by himself, then eventually his son. Everything he did was for his son, Lanzo. He was born nearly to the day two summers ago, though his mother tragically perished delivering him into the world. At the moment, he was home in Jorrit's village and under the loving charge of his aunt and Colgrin's wife, Inka.

"Too bad Colgrin does not let her be a mother to her own boys," Jorrit whispered aloud, reflecting on the twin boys of about age twelve who had never had the loving embrace of their mother. Colgrin had feared too much time with Inka would have made the two soft, and soft men cannot lead a war.

She's rather good in the role.

Lost in thought, it took Jorrit a moment to notice further shouting above him. However, now they were accompanied by footsteps advancing toward the space in the shed's floor which allowed access to the cellar. The light from a torch began to beam through the hatch as it opened, and the ladder dropped to the soggy earth below. A lone individual seemed to fall alongside it, and before Jorrit could say anything, the enemy captain was rushing toward him with a knife drawn.

It seems the pup wants another go, a startled Jorrit thought as he gradually rose from the dirt.

The man quickly advanced until he was able to reach out and tightly clutch one of Jorrit's arms as he pressed the knife to his stomach, roaring something in the Roman speech as he did so. He shouted until his voice was hoarse before moving his hand from Jorrit's arm to his throat.

"I do not speak the language of the Roman filth," Jorrit responded, this time in the native tongue of the Britons. The enemy captain was surprised at his knowledge of a language assumed to be unique to Britannia, but Jorrit had taken many slaves from these shores in recent years. These slaves proved useful in teaching him their language.

"Where did you come by the ring?" the captain replied. Jorrit's captor slowly began pressing the point of the blade into Jorrit's stomach, causing him to betray a grunt from the discomfort.

"Shit spills from your mouth, Briton. Why would I know one foolish trinket from any other?" Jorrit shot back as he glared back into the eyes of his enemy. Though he did his utmost to appear defiant, he heard his voice begin to break, and felt the blood rushing away from his legs as the fear in the back of his mind had begun to creep to the forefront.

"Tell... me...," the young man insisted.

Jorrit thought to keep his defiance alive, but the truth seemed just as effective. "I don't know..."

Would this fool truly kill a prisoner before interrogating him? he wondered as he glanced down at the knife pressed to his stomach. *That would certainly be a slow death.*

The apparent sincerity in his confusion provoked the Jorrit's attacker once more as the blade began to gradually plunge its way roughly an inch beneath Jorrit's skin. He gave a hollow gasp as the man gently pushed the dagger ahead before he was checked by another man Jorrit recognized from the battle at sea. The man with the curly hair about his head who did not speak. He gently squeezed his captain's hand as he slowly drew back the knife, all the while the commander was still glaring into Jorrit's eyes. Two more men trudged forth from the ladder, one of which calmly took the blade from his leader before giving Jorrit a nervous look.

"You would do well to answer him," the stranger warned. "Our people have lived in fear of your raiders for decades. We hold no soft spots for your suffering."

Jorrit scoffed. "It is not easy to answer questions which I do not have an answer to."

The captain took a deep breath before removing his hand from Jorrit's arm and reaching into a small pouch at his waist. He found whatever it was he was fishing for and began to lift it right into Jorrit's gaze. After a moment, Jorrit could see it was indeed a ring, and a finely crafted one at that.

Drysten closed his eyes and drew in a deep breath in the pointless effort to calm himself. He had the fleeting thought to question his captive as to how he knew the language of the native Britons but decided it wasn't important in that moment. "Where did your people take my woman?" he demanded in a low voice, still holding the ring into the stranger's face. "*Your* people took her somewhere and robbed her of *this* before they did so. I want her back."

The man in front of him cocked his head to one side, apparently confused by the question. "I have no knowledge of your woman."

Drysten reframed the question. "Then where were you when you found this?" he stated as he deliberately lifted his mother's ring even closer to the man's eye.

The captive glimpsed down at the ring, then back to Drysten. "A vessel from the east. We boarded it at dawn the day before we attempted to take yours. There were only a handful of fighters. Only one worth of worrying about."

Drysten glanced away for a moment. *Well, the lone fighter worth fretting about must have been Bors' son. He'd be the only one these animals would have marked as threatening based on the size of him.*

He took the dagger back from Cynwrig and placed it in its sheath, then peered up at the foul man standing in front of him and resumed the questioning. "Where was the ship going?"

"It was a slave ship; the women have most likely been plowed up and down the coastline by now. I don't think you'll be desiring yours back," he answered with a grin, provoking a booming strike from Drysten's right hand which knocked the prisoner to his knees. The man stood up with a wicked smile from ear to ear and looked Drysten in the eye. "You're indeed more fun than the rest of these lot, or maybe a bit bolder at least. Most are afraid to keep eye contact with me."

Drysten snickered. "I have no reason to fear men like you."

"He has no need to fear mortal men at all should my memory serve me." Cynwrig's remark only gripped the prisoner's attention for a moment, but it was enough for the man to contort his face in obvious confusion. Drysten quickly glared back at his childhood friend, who was getting looks of bewilderment from Diocles as well as the captive.

The prisoner held his perplexed gaze on Cynwrig as he finally spoke. "The man you want is from Frisia and goes by the name of Servius. He paid us a tribute, and we let him journey off. Probably plowed your bitch since then."

Drysten slowly returned his gaze back to the chained man in front of him and calmly smirked for a short moment, drawing a perplexed look from Amiram who was still standing close by. In one motion he pushed the man back to the wall of the basement, prompting a grunt of pain from his prey, then quickly drew his dagger and thrust it to its hilt into the man's side, just far enough away from vital organs to prevent a life threatening wound.

Diocles, Amiram, and Cynwrig were all too late to hinder him. They could merely press Drysten to cease what he was doing, though Drysten was too focused to hear any of their pleas. "Considering you can understand me, it is helpful I'll only have to speak this once. You're going to direct me to where my woman is. You're going to reveal how to get there. You'll even sail me there yourself if I tell you to." Drysten ever so gingerly rotated the knife, causing his prisoner to grit his teeth and whimper something in his native language. "Now, you're going to swear this to me." Drysten's voice suddenly went lower and more ominous, almost reminding him of the new voice which tormented him in his own mind. He ultimately deemed it fitting this man at his mercy was now subjected to it as well. "If you fail me. If I discover my woman is dead. You will be the one to answer for it. I will deliver you to our mute, whose tongue was torn out by your people, and I will permit him to return the favor." Drysten nodded toward Amiram, still standing close by. It was obvious the glaring mute was doing what he could to convince the prisoner he would be capable of inflicting such pain on another human being, though truthfully Drysten would have been rather alarmed at the spectacle. "Now tell me your name, and swear to me you'll do as I command."

"I am called... Jorrit," he explained with a wince. "I will serve you. I swear to you!"

"And what should you swear on, I wonder?" Drysten whispered gently. "What could an individual such as yourself care for more than his own life?"

The man called Jorrit began frantically peering between his captors before eventually noticing the shallow pool of his own blood now growing at his feet. "My boy!" he shrieked. "I swear on my son's life that I will serve you!"

Drysten then gradually withdrew the knife from the man's side, causing him to slump to the floor. He was about to speak once more until he caught the thumping of footsteps overhead.

"Drysten!" someone boomed. Drysten, stop!"

Drysten wheeled around and saw two shapes race from the ladder's base and into the light from Cynwrig's torch. The first of which was clothed in polished Roman armor, instantly familiar to Drysten, while the other wore boiled leather of similar make to Drysten's own.

"Father...," he whispered. He suddenly recognized the extent of the cruelty he had dispensed on the man at his feet. "Father I..." Drysten hesitated as he noticed a third shape begin to creep its way down the ladder. He slowly scanned the room at the disturbed men gazing back.

Next to his father was Bors, both of which were wearing the same expression of shock as Drysten's companions. But the third seemed stoic, and regal in the way he moved into the torchlight.

Because that man was the king.

CHAPTER III

Everyone who bore witness to what Drysten had done now stood in confusion as they glanced amongst themselves. Hall discovered the king had intended to have the prisoner whipped for information mere moments before learning Drysten had begun an interrogation of his own. At present, the monarch was now roaring at Hall about how his valuable captive may have been killed by a child carrying a knife.

"And all you're doing about it is *standing* there!" An exasperated King Ceneus roared.

Hall surmised the most useful thing he could do was quietly stand by and take the verbal onslaught from the monarch. It would be decidedly unwise to try and defend his son at the moment.

Bors obviously did not care for the king's whining any more than Hall did, and rolled his eyes before nonchalantly wandering up to the prisoner to inspect his wound. Hall managed to tune out the king long enough to observe Bors as he used his foot to carefully turn the man over, halting momentarily to watch a pair of rats who crawled up from behind the king.

"Agh! For *fuck's* sake!" A disgusted Bors yelled in response, the two rats ran off toward Amiram, who shuffled his feet to shoo them away toward the ladder. "For fuck's sake, did you see how that one looked at me?" Bors recounted to the mute.

Amiram returned a patronizing smirk to Bors, prompting the man to grunt in dismay and focus his attention back to the prisoner. He glanced down at the man reclining amidst a small pool of his own blood and examined the wound. His face was white, but it fairly clear he hadn't lost enough blood to be the cause. It was likely just fear.

Bors quickly studied the wound, quickly scoffing at what he observed. "Manageable flesh wound, Lord. I'm certain this bastard will live." At that Bors looked at Diocles and ordered him to find some acid vinegar to clean the wound, and boiled woolen cloth to bandage it.

Hall nodded before he trained his attention toward his son, staring him in the eye and examining the strange emotions displayed over his face. He noticed a smattering of guilt mixed with some brand of ambivalence which Hall could only venture a guess at. "So you knocked out the guard upstairs and... *borrowed* his keys. You have never exhibited any tendencies for unprovoked violence, so I must ask you why it was so important for you to speak with this man?" He urged through a hardened tone.

Hall assumed his son was commanded to do so by some mysterious entity speaking inside his mind, but judged it best to ask about that when the king wasn't present. Hall always felt guilty of his suspicious nature toward that aspect of his son. Though these voices had proven to be troublesome at times, Hall had to admit they rarely prompted his son to engage in violence. Even when they did so, it was not an erratic madness which took hold of his son, more like a directed fury which almost always found the right mark.

Drysten turned toward his father, his face mostly expressionless as if nothing had transpired. "Mother's ring," he answered, almost as if that simply explained everything.

Hall remembered giving his son the ring not too long ago. "What *about* the ring?"

"I gave it to Isolde," he answered as he was gazing down at the man he had just cut. "It was in the box from their ship. Somebody took her, father. I... convinced him to show me where."

The king was brooding to himself behind Hall, quietly listening to the exchange between father and son, but quickly elected to reassert his authority over the matter. "Not before we pull what information we can from him. *Certainly* not before you answer for attacking my guard," he commanded. He briefly eyeballed Drysten and his companions before releasing a heavy sigh and shook his head.

Drysten began to object but was abruptly hushed by his father, who rose a finger toward his son in the same manner as their first encounter at the docks. It was apparent to all that the monarch was in no mood to indulge a plea for help. Hall tensely watched as Drysten stepped toward the king, then to his father's surprise, he proceeded to apologize in a hushed tone. "Lord, I apologize for my actions, and I will not challenge any discipline received for bringing harm to your man, but first I need to speak to my father."

Hall watched as the king glared at his son, deciding to step between the two and break the king's gaze. "I could not hear you before, son," he fabricated as an excuse for the movement, "what was it that you needed to say?"

Drysten took a step toward his father, pointing toward the prisoner. "This one's a Frisian named Jorrit. He informed me that a man took some of our people as slaves. This man has sworn an oath to me, vowing to show me where they went." Drysten broke eye contact with his father to gesture for Bors' attention. "I believe he took your son as well, as he mentioned there was only one man worth worrying about on the ship they assailed. Judging by that fact alone, it would be fair to say it was your boy. We all know how few giants we have roaming Burdigala."

Bors cursed under his breath before he glanced at Jorrit, presently sitting with his back to the stone wall while Diocles tended his wound, yet obviously monitoring the conversation closely. "Well, Frisian? Did the man bear any resemblance to the face you see now?" Upon receiving a nod,

Bors angrily turned back to Hall, wearing a pleading expression across his face.

Hall was about to try and reassure the man until he noticed the king look from Drysten to himself, clearly weighing his next words.

After a brief pause, the king cleared his throat. "I... understand the hasty reaction to what has occurred, but as the man you assaulted was not directly under my command, I do not judge it fitting to administer a punishment myself."

Drysten nodded as the black-clad guard stepped closer to Ceneus. "May I ask who the man serves, Lord King?"

The guard scoffed, with Hall immediately discerning the man's foul demeanor. "I serve the *prince*, you—"

"That is quite enough, Vonig," the king commanded, interrupting the angered guard with a smoothly raised hand.

Vonig glanced to Bors, who was giving him a scowl and stepped back a pace behind Ceneus. "Very good, Lord King. I will notify your son as to his duty to deliver a fitting penalty."

The king nodded as the guard called Vonig sprang his way up the ladder, giving Bors a slight moment of amusement. "As for the punishment itself, I can assure you it will not be too... inhumane."

Drysten returned a short bow of the head. "I thank you for your understanding, Lord King."

Bors took a step toward the king, clearly making the man a touch nervous. "I will not allow for my boy to become a *slave*. Especially to the Saxon filth this man deals with." Bors angrily gestured toward the wounded Frisian before quickly turning toward Hall. "I say we let Drysten go hunting and find our people. If we do nothing, or even if we simply wait too long, you know you will lose the support of most of the men. They will go out in search of their families with or without your permission."

King Ceneus produced an irritated grimace as he trained his attention from Bors to Hall. "Before I free a single soul to go in pursuit of this... slaver, I must reiterate the need for you to retake the fortification to our North. Its position is much too strategic to let it remain in the hands of the Picts."

Hall glimpsed toward his son. "I would hardly say my boy is essential to that goal, Lord King," prompting an annoyed look from Drysten, as well as a snicker from Amiram.

"But he would be taking many of your people along with him, would he not?" the king responded, drawing a nod from Hall. "Due to this, I require his punishment be fulfilled, as well as the fort retaken. Those two provisions are not negotiable, Lord Hall."

"If Drysten leaves to find them, we will need to send some of our own to accompany him, of that the king is correct. That will take manpower away from whatever course we take to regain Segedunum. If we do not send him, our people will most likely be lost to us forever whether or not we eventually *do* go looking."

The king stepped forward and placed a hand on Hall's shoulder. "I *assure* you, once that fort is taken..."

"My people will never follow a king who they feel abandoned their families to slavery! That much I can say for certain," Hall interrupted, prompting a staggering look to pass over the king's face. "If you wish for them to fight for you, if you wish for your army to have leadership, you will allow my son to go and find the ones who were taken. If you do not think you can allow that, then you will need to find another man to lead your armies North, as I will be sailing back to the continent to find them myself."

The king was visibly frustrated by the ultimatum, abruptly removing the hand he had kindly placed onto Hall's shoulder and turning away in disgust. Hall knew the king would never be able to rely on his allies to provide extra men for a fight which would not take place within their own borders. If he wanted Segedunum back, he knew he would need Hall's help. "Have it your way, Hall. But understand this, I do not forget those who presume to command a king. Not only that, but your son's punishment is still a condition which I will not forego."

Hall gently bowed his head. "Fair is fair, Lord King. My son will answer for assaulting your guard. As for myself, please forgive my tone."

"All is forgiven. Now speak to our prisoner and find out what he knows." At that, the king turned and started up the ladder, and Hall turned to Drysten's prisoner.

The stranger who completed tending to Jorrit's wound haphazardly supported him to his feet before stepping back to the ladder. Jorrit caught a better glimpse of the man through the torchlight, seeing his face and discerning he was younger than expected, much like his commander. He wore an uneasy expression over his face as he subtly observed the others huddled in the cellar. The suspicious glance was not unlike Jorrit's own, and he couldn't help but wonder what must have transpired to lead him to his current whereabouts. Even with the fewer years attached, Jorrit had to acknowledge he did a respectable job in not only binding the wound but halting the bleeding altogether, leading Jorrit to wonder what sort of background some of these men had. He nodded his head in thanks at the man as he walked toward the ladder leading to the surface, receiving only a dubious glance from the stranger.

That went well, he reflected. *Almost died before I sent them all in the wrong direction. Boy nearly saved his people without even knowing it.*

Jorrit tenderly placed a hand at his side and walked toward his captors, fidgeting with his new dressings as the men began to retreat up the ladder. The man who stabbed him left first, shortly followed by his companions. After another short moment of uncomfortable silence, the man he assumed to be the king moved up the ladder, leaving the big one who questioned him aboard the ship, and someone who presumably held rank over him. He recognized he should have paid more attention to the names being thrown around, but also gave himself credit for keeping himself together despite the unusual moment of violence which transpired.

The unnamed man looked over Jorrit for a moment before he finally decided to wander over, glancing down at the fresh wrappings on his abdomen. "So you swore an oath, did you?" the man inquired.

"Better that than dying with my hands tied behind my back. Not the best way to go. When did the one who helped my wound decide to untie my hands?" Jorrit asked in a slight surprise.

The stranger snickered to himself. "I would imagine when you were rolling around on the ground. He probably assumed you would prove more manageable if you could breathe easier." The man motioned his head toward the ladder, gesturing for the bigger of the two to follow the others to the surface.

Jorrit scoffed as he watched the man slowly climb the ladder. "Don't recall much rolling being done. But to answer your question, I did swear an oath to that... *boy*."

Jorrit surmised vowing an oath could be a blessing in disguise if he could take advantage of it properly. At first, he simply did it to prevent further harm, but upon collecting himself, he realized how to make his next move. If he helped these strangers bring back their people, there was a chance he could find a moment to escape. That or there was the slight possibility he would be set free. Free to join his son back in Frisia, and free to come back with enough men to secure his new home.

Jorrit casually met the man's gaze as his captor approached him. "Do all men from these parts speak to their lord in that way?"

The stranger grinned. "Certainly not, and I probably shouldn't have either." The captor wearily looked back at the ladder. "But I did," he finally said, prompting the Frisian to snicker in amusement.

"Who's the boy?"

The man turned back to face Jorrit, folding his arms as the chilly air of the basement began to seep through the gaps of his armor. "My name is Hall, and the boy was my son, Drysten. The ring he found formerly belonged to my wife. When she passed, I granted it to him. In turn, he presented it to *his* woman."

Jorrit stood there, remembering the day his own wife had passed. The way everyone gazed at him as he walked through the village carrying their son. She was beloved by everyone in their homeland and was mourned by people who Jorrit didn't even know. She was not a delicate beauty like the Romans seemed to prefer, but she had a strange grace which drew people to her. She was the perfect woman for Jorrit, as he was restless and impatient. He looked at his captor and saw the familiar pain in his eyes as well. "How did she die?"

Hall took a moment before answering. "Birth, like many women."

Jorrit grimaced at the thought. "I know of that all too well."

"You have lost someone in that way?" Hall inquired.

Jorrit did his best to hide the sadness of the memories that flooded his mind but was unsure if Hall had seen them anyway. "I did, but I do not wish to converse of it, as it holds no importance here."

"For me, it is the only thing that is important. That much I know for certain," Hall responded in a solemn tone.

The two men gazed off in various directions as footsteps could be heard thumping away from the storage shed. After a moment it was just the two of them in the whole building, and Hall took on a gentler tone than Jorrit was expecting. "I hope my boy did not harm you too severely."

"Because he needs a guide?" Jorrit replied with a

chuckle.

Hall shook his head and wandered toward the torch left in a sconce by the ladder. "Because I fear how drawn to violence he truly is. When your people attempted to raid our home a few years ago, I led my men against them. My boy was to stay back and defend the families."

Jorrit began to smirk. "I take it he neglected his duties then?"

Hall nodded. "He did. The families had been attacked, and some of our loved ones perished. He did his best defending them, but he saw a chance to end some of the attackers and ran off without understanding the consequences."

"Doesn't sound strange to me. Seems he must have been quite young, the young ones always make mistakes," Jorrit put in lightly. "Why would you assume he is drawn to violence from that?"

Hall gave a strangely pained smile as he looked down. "For two nights, he tracked the survivors who managed to evade our patrols, leading only a handful of men. When he found them, he left no survivors."

Jorrit was moderately impressed by the thought. He had not figured the boy to be so determined. "How many were there?"

"About a dozen fighters," Hall responded before glancing back toward the ground.

"Fighters?" Jorrit asked, unsure why Hall felt the need to specify.

After a moment of silence, Hall raised his head. "Saxons should not travel to war with their families." The two men remained silent for some time, each staring off into a separate corner of the dark basement.

Jorrit began to grow uneasy at the lack of conversation. "What will happen to me now... Hall?"

"I expect the king will come back tomorrow with someone to question you. Personally, if I were you, I would answer all those questions now. It should be obvious by this point I prefer to gain information without torture. Along with this, I will guarantee your survival if you indeed help my son find our people."

"Not just yours," Jorrit responded.

"What do you mean? Who else was taken?" Hall inquired.

"Before recently, the last time I saw the slaver was more than a month ago. He had sold off some slaves who were born in this kingdom. Supposedly they were born to the North of here and held knowledge of the roads," Jorrit informed Hall. He knew telling the truth of him owning some of these people would be a horrendous mistake and chose to leave that out.

"I would assume these captives were taken to act as guides and interpreters for anyone trying to attack Britannia," Hall thought out loud. "Well, you're certainly giving me more of a reason to keep you breathing.

Jorrit sighed, envisioning what the Britons would do to a man who attempted to raid their shores, especially one who owned some of their people. The coastlines of Britannia were under constant threat of invasion, so naturally, the Saxons, Jutes, Angles, and Frisians were especially hated. "You want to know about the man who took your people?" he asked.

"Tell me his name," Hall demanded with a nod.

"Marhaus, I believe. But he works with his father."

"Named?"

"Servius," Jorrit responded, prompting Hall to curse under his breath and turn away.

"This man is *known* to you?"

Hall turned back to Jorrit, red in the face. "Yes, he is. The bastard turns up whenever a town is sacked and provides fresh slaves for the labor needed to rebuild. He always seems to turn up at the right moment to make a profit." Hall tilted his head to the side, giving Jorrit the belief he may have been recalling some previous run-in with the man. "We should have killed him," he finally whispered.

"Servius is well known to us. He obtains many of our slaves from the Brythonic speaking peoples. *Very* good at what he does," Jorrit informed.

You're telling me he's been *working* with the very people who raid us, then he sells slave labor to those who have *lost* because of such raids?" Hall demanded.

"Personally, I never paid him much attention, but yes," Jorrit responded.

In truth, he knew a great deal about Servius, as well as his operations across the sea. He was one of the more acclaimed slavers in the area, procuring people from lands further north of his own home, to the lands near the Pillars of Heracles far to the south.

Jorrit noticed how Hall was growing noticeably furious with each answer. "Considering the Saxons have taken a liking to you Frisians, I would assume you hold some knowledge of their plans for us."

Jorrit took a step forward and worked to give the impression he was under some sort of internal struggle. Of course, he already knew what he needed to do. He was commanded to tell his enemy the war would spread from the north, and that their main forces would march from a fort which should have been taken by then. This army then planned on marching all the way down to the city the Britons viewed as a capital. They even gave him the names of towns they would attack along the way, though regrettably Jorrit only remembered a handful of them.

Jorrit pulled in a deep breath. "We were to draw your people toward the coast as the main army gathered at a northern fortress. Once fit, they would march South and take Eboracum from your little king," he revealed. "If we were to be checked along the way, we would simply garrison the most important walled town we could spot and raid the countryside until you ultimately submitted to our dominion."

Hall scoffed, leading Jorrit to believe the thought a Saxon tribe accomplishing something so grand was improbable. "I find that... *challenging* to believe, but nevertheless I have a few more questions for you."

Jorrit understood the crucial part to convince them of was the place the attack would erupt from. They could never identify the real attack would come from the sea. All the knowledge he would produce would lead them to reinforce their garrisons at the opposite end of Ebrauc, leaving its capital vulnerable.

He looked at Hall through the torchlight, and began to lay the trap.

Drysten's heart felt as though it was thumping its way out of his chest. The dull, constant sensation had crept its way into his neck and legs since he had plunged a knife into an unarmed prisoner. He knew the action was wrong, but what disturbed him the most was the idea he did it of his own will, not that of a strange voice venting from the heavens.

"I can't wait too long to set out or I'll never win her back," he told Diocles, who was following Drysten through the courtyard of the villa. "I made her a promise...," he whispered to himself.

"We will find a way," Diocles replied, awkwardly trying to reassure a man who he barely knew, "I do not wish to sound... insensitive, but we cannot forget about the others who were taken as well."

Drysten sighed quietly and replied with a nod. *How do I fix this?* he wondered silently.

The man who stole Isolde away from him was going to turn her into a slave, and worse yet he knew who the man was. When he considered how his woman, the woman who was carrying his child was now at this man's mercy, the dull thudding seemed to turn to a thunderous roar.

Drysten annoyedly flung his hands up. "How the fuck do I get her back without men, or even money for that matter?"

He halted his pacing and peered up into the shadowed sky, trying to urge his mind into creating a plan to get his people back, but most importantly to him, Isolde.

The distant answer of a voice stretching out to him for help was all he heard echoing through his mind, ripping his heartstrings further downward.

"Drysten," a small voice beckoned from behind him, snatching Drysten's attention away from the night sky. He turned to see Aosten approaching with the king not far behind, still bearing a perturbed expression. Out of the corner of his eye, Drysten also noticed the guard, Vonig, speaking to yet another finely trimmed man off in the distance behind the approaching king.

"Lord King," Drysten timidly greeted, shortly followed by a bow of his head. Drysten briefly glanced at Vonig one more time before the king decided to speak, noticing him dab blood off his chin. The man he was speaking to turned and seemed amused at something, though it was too dark for Drysten to see his face.

"Your father just apprised me of the discussion he had with our new guest. The man who stole away your people, we now believe he also took people from my kingdom as well." The king paused and peered up at the sky much in the same way Drysten had done. Drysten watched as he closed his eyes and seemed to be pained and conflicted by what he was about to say. "This matter may be almost as important to my lands as the venture North to Segedunum will be. These captives could guide them through the lightly guarded areas of my lands, something which could prove to be a dangerous advantage for my enemies. If I were to help you, you would need to assure me you'd be bringing back those people as well."

"I would do anything to get my woman back, Lord King," Drysten insisted.

"That is obvious, but what about the others in question?" King Ceneus asked with narrowed eyes.

Drysten was taken aback from the assumption he would simply let others suffer even if he had the means to prevent it. "I was raised to believe in fighting for the people who cannot fight for themselves, Lord King. My mother and father instilled those values in me from a young age."

The king studied Drysten's face before glancing toward Diocles, who was listening closely to the exchange. "Fair enough, boy. How many men do you have? Men that your father would not need marching with him."

Drysten didn't need to put too much thought into the answer. "Only three, Lord King. Myself, Diocles, and Cynwrig here." Drysten gestured a hand to Cynwrig, who appeared uncomfortable in the presence of the king. Drysten wondered why that was, but knew it honestly didn't matter now.

The king peeked over Drysten's shoulder toward Cynwrig. "You are the one who brought news of Segedunum."

"I am, Lord King," Cynwrig quietly answered.

"You would not wish to join Lord Hall as he marched on your family's killers?" the king asked in confusion.

Cynwrig hesitated for a moment, glancing from Drysten to the king. "I... my people are dead, Lord King. I can do no further good for them in the North."

The king sighed heavily as he nodded and turned to Drysten. "You'll be needing more men than that if you plan to lead a raid into Frisia. Not only are there the locals to deal with, but now we've been receiving reports there are Saxons there as well. Traders have ventured into the Northern islands, bringing news back of armies massing under a lone chieftain's banner." The king's voice trailed as he finished his thought.

"The families of the taken would surely offer their assistance," Diocles suggested.

Suddenly, a voice came from the doorway to the villa. "No," it answered.

Hall emerged behind the king with Bors in tow, both men giving a quizzical look to whoever the regal looking man was that still stood next to Vonig as they passed him by. "If there's raiding to be done, then my son will take the Fortuna and her crew. We can find more men needed to reinforce our ranks from the local tribes. Provided you approve of that, Lord King."

The king responded with an irritated glance to Aosten, who shrugged as his sole response. "I believe I made myself clear when I told you of your priorities, Lord Hall."

Hall sighed heavily, leading Drysten to believe his father may have regretted not taking more time before accepting the king's proposal of employment. Had he done so, Drysten was certain his father would have not only seen the kind of person King Ceneus was turning out to be, but he would have also been the unquestionable leader of whatever raid would hopefully occur in Frisia. "I believe we spoke of what would result should my people perceive their families were abandoned, Lord King. With respect, we do not have an option. If my people learn steps are being taken to rescue their loved ones, we shouldn't have issues leading a handful of volunteers from my vessel into the North."

The king opened his mouth to speak until he was cut off by the stranger behind him. "Your people should learn to follow their commander's lead no matter the costs," the newcomer answered sternly. Drysten noticed Aosten hang his head in obvious embarrassment by the remark.

What a bag of shit, Drysten thought with a scoff. *Who the fuck is this?*

Aosten glanced up toward Drysten as though he had read his thoughts, providing a slight tilt of his head with his anxious look.

The man in question held a striking resemblance to King Ceneus, but with the eyes of a wild predator and a grin which instilled Drysten with a natural hatred of the man. As he drew closer, it could be seen there was a Christian Druid not far behind him, seemingly observing the goings on of the gathering. Drysten could scarcely make out the man's appearance, and chose to train his attention on the approaching prince striding toward him with Vonig close behind.

The king glanced behind him. "While I echo your sentiment, son, it is wise to conduct oneself more diplomatically than that. This is the first time Lord Hall has been in your presence."

After an uncomfortable moment of silence in which the newcomer and Hall had locked eyes, Hall finally shook his head. "That was never how I led my people. It is important to me that my people know they are not my slaves or thralls. They are good men, and those who I would gladly let go should they feel their own endeavors will guide them down a better path than I am able to provide for them."

"Seems to me *Lord* Hall does not understand his place in our court, father." The man came closer and paused as he met his gaze with Drysten's. "This is the one Vonig spoke of?"

Drysten looked to his father, who was attempting to stare a hole into the prince's forehead. *The only time I've ever witnessed you irritated by being labeled as a lord, father.*

"This is the one you will judge, son," King Ceneus responded as he gestured a hand toward Drysten. "While he did insult your man, I suggest leniency for our new lords."

The prince gave Hall a condescending glance as he strolled over to Drysten, who stood up a little straighter as he narrowed his eyes to meet his gaze.

"I am Prince Eidion. Shortly, you will be following me into the North," the prince commanded. "As I value my father's council, I will forego any punishments for assaulting my guard, but do not think I will forget the act entirely."

"I thank you, Lord Prince," Drysten respectfully replied with a bow.

Prince Eidion smirked. "As you should." He stared at Drysten for a moment longer as he began to raise his head, then turned his attention to Hall. "You may have experienced a loss, but we cannot neglect our duty to punish the Northmen for the murder of our people."

Bors suddenly stepped forward, now standing in between Hall and Prince Eidion. "That's a load of horseshit—"

"Bors!" Hall roared sternly.

Eidion smirked. "This one also needs a lesson on decorum."

Drysten trained his attention back to the king, who was now angrily whispering to Aosten. "Lord King, are there any men in these lands we could call on which would not deplete your ranks?" Drysten asked.

The king broke from his discussion with Aosten for a moment to think. After a moment's pause, Aosten stepped forward. "I... believe I *may* have an answer to this issue." The group of men all trained their attention onto the man as he stepped in front of the king. "There is a mercenary who we have dealt with in the past; one who leads men seasoned from the wars of Rome. He recently trained some of our own, and I believe he would be available."

King Ceneus glanced toward Drysten before turning his attention back to Hall. "Would this be satisfactory to you, Lord Hall?"

"Hmph, *lord*," the prince said in a hushed tone which only Drysten caught. Drysten glared at the prince as he mockingly whispered something to Vonig, who snickered to the prince as he stepped beside him.

Hall nodded. "It is, Lord King. Where can we find this man?"

Aosten took a step forward. "He is found on the Southern side of Londinium's bridge, only a couple days sailing from here." He looked back to King Ceneus. "We could offer Lord Hall what payment he would have been owed for the first few months of service as a means to procure the mercenary's aid."

"I think that would be a wonderful idea. I get my fighters, and Hall gets his people back. Well, I suppose that would be thinking somewhat optimistically at the moment," King Ceneus responded. He scratched his stubbly chin as he looked back to Hall. "Who would you send to Frisia as leader of the... Fortuna?"

Drysten watched his father lower his head as he ran his hand through his hair, considering the possibilities. He glanced to his longtime second in command, Bors, before he trained his attention onto Drysten. "It will take a day to provision the ship, but you will set out in two at the most."

Drysten glanced to Diocles, who offered a reassuring nod. "I am to lead, father?"

Hall nodded. "You are, but there's one more matter to address." He hesitated for a moment, making Drysten begin to dread what he would say next. "We cannot neglect the funeral for the ones who fell on your last venture."

Drysten's mood was already somber, but somehow it found a way to get worse. He slightly lowered his head as he was reminded he led men to their deaths so close to his journey's destination. The night had felt like it went on forever, but now he was reminded of one of the many responsibilities of leadership.

"Oversee the building of pyres, then we will speak of this other matter."

He slowly raised his head. "I'll see to it, father." At that, he bowed to the king and walked toward the main house of the villa.

CHAPTER IV

King Ceneus took a skeptical look at Hall as the man stepped toward him. "Your boy can see this through?"

"He can," Hall curtly answered. "Whether he succeeds or not may completely depend on this mercenary your man spoke of. I don't know how much faith I can put in a man who fights for coin," Hall added as he peered back to Aosten, silently trailing behind them as they strolled toward the villa's entryway.

"Is that not what most men are willing to die for?" King Ceneus responded with a chuckle.

Hall proudly grinned as he trained his gaze toward the sky. "Not my boy. For all his shortcomings, gluttony was never something he displayed."

Hall always knew his son was a gifted swordsman, but he was still intelligent enough to realize he should worry about the decisions he could find himself making. Hall himself had experienced how these situations test you, and how a person answers to this adversity is everything. Drysten hadn't shyed away from a challenge as he grew up, but Hall still worried whether his sole aim was the rescue of his woman and not the numerous others who were taken alongside her.

Again, the king rubbed his chin in visible disbelief. Hall sensed the monarch was more inclined to offer up the souls of mercenaries rather than Hall's men, who he had just secured as his own. The only risk was sending the sole heir to the newest lord of Ebrauc out on a dangerous mission, but judging by the tone of both the king and the prince it was unlikely it mattered to anyone but Hall.

"Come," the king beckoned, "we must hurry to your crew. They are gathered together at the inn across the way."

Before following the king out of the villa, he stole a glance back to watch his son as the boy entered their new home. He turned back to follow Ceneus as they began plodding across the muddy road toward the inn. Bors and Aosten were trailing behind, both whistling to the uplifting tune of an old Roman marching song. Hall observed a rat being chased off by a feral dog, who stole the rat's small bite of rotten-looking food.

"We need to do something about these feral dogs," King Ceneus noted to Aosten.

"I don't know, Lord King. The dogs appear to keep the rats at bay," Aosten returned, prompting a shrug of indifference from the king.

The hound fixed its gaze onto Bors, who slowly crept up to try and stroke the hair on its back before the animal darted away into the night.

"Hmph, dogs normally love me," Bors reacted in dismay.

"Strange, they normally recognize one of their own," Hall quipped to the entertainment of Aosten and the king.

The midnight air grew chilly as it pressed through the links in Hall's armor, with the accompanying wind beating the last of the rain into the men's faces.

They entered the building to the resounding cheers of about three dozen drunken souls and moved their way to the heart of the room. Bors slowly raised his hand to signal for the cheering to cease, leaving only a blatant groan of displeasure from Amiram, sitting in between two women he had met in the private upstairs area of the tavern.

"Bastard has no tongue and he still gets more women than me," Bors whispered to Hall.

"Helps not to smell like an animal, Bors," Hall returned with a grin.

Bors proceeded to lift an arm and push his nostrils into its pit. "Fair point."

Hall snickered before he looked to his men. "I heard how well all of you fought against the raiders," he began, prompting additional cheers from the men. "I've always said you're the strongest and fiercest group I've ever commanded. Tonight, I just want you commemorating the fact you're all alive." The room exploded with a roar the whole village likely heard. Hall slowly glanced toward his feet as he imagined the different response he would receive from the next, less festive portion of the speech. "But *tomorrow*..." he began, waiting for the noise to gradually die away, "tomorrow, I'll need you to get the ship ready to set out." The room was so quiet a woman could be overheard upstairs. Hall assumed it was likely one of the prostitutes from the docks. "We have an enemy, and he has our people," he revealed through a weary sigh. The men began to shuffle in their seats as a murmur started toward the back of the group. "Those who had hoped to join us here were taken by a Frisian slaver. Anybody whose family was to sail with my son's woman could have been taken. This man's name is Servius, and I'm sure you all know of his reputation."

"That fat fucking pig-man?" a voice in the back screamed.

Hall immediately recognized it as Magnus, the ship's physician. "The very same."

The chorus of men emitted a piercing cry of anger toward Hall, who could only manage to stand there in surprise. He had never seen his people act so frantic in all his days of leading them. Through war and conflict, he could always depend on them to be level-headed and defiant regardless of the dangers they faced. But this was clearly different. For the first time in his life, he realized he did not know how to approach his men in this state. Hall looked over the anxious faces of men throwing questions toward himself and Bors.

"Quiet!" a man yelled from behind Hall. He awkwardly turned to see Aosten gently shuffling forward. "Silence!" he ordered. The men all slowly began to calm as Aosten confidently nodded to Hall as he walked by. "You are now men of Ebrauc, and while you will soon be asked to aid us in the fight to our North—" The roaring once again exploded to drown out whatever Aosten was attempting to say.

Hall quickly paced forward. "Silence!" he repeatedly bellowed. The exasperated group now standing in front of him reluctantly quieted down once more. "We will listen to what our king and his man have to say."

Aosten thankfully nodded as he continued. "While you will soon be asked to fight, we consider your families and friends our people as well." A murmur of assent began through the crowd as Aosten hesitated to glance back to the king, who shrugged nonchalantly to Aosten's speech. "We are going to exercise what measures are needed to recover *our* people. Of that you not only have my word, but you also have the word of your king."

"What measures are those, Lord?" Cyrus questioned from the front of the group.

King Ceneus stepped forward. "I will handle it from here, Aosten," he said as he placed a hand on his shoulder.

Hall wasn't sure how he felt about the king addressing his men considering the tumultuous relationship they had created in the last few hours, but knew he couldn't stop a king from doing anything at all without some sort of consequence. As for the behavior of his people, he knew they likely wouldn't do anything to offend him either. They had little trouble understanding who the man was, even if they had not seen him before. He was wearing some of the most beautiful cloth Hall had ever seen and had rings on most fingers along with a bronze circlet around his head.

"We have the same enemy," Ceneus began, pausing to make sure the men would stay quiet long enough for him to speak. "This... *Servius,* as he's known, has taken some of our people as well. He goes along the coast of Britannia and Gaul, kidnapping men, women, and children so he can sell them as slaves to the very enemy who raids these shores."

"And you'll help us how?" Elias yelled from the back of the group.

King Ceneus nodded toward Hall. "Your commander will stay here, but Drysten is leading a small force to our enemy's home to take our people back."

There was an audible groan of uncertainty as the men learned Hall would not be commanding the rescue. Drysten was certainly well-liked by the Fortuna's crew, but when it came to leadership, they preferred his father. He was more seasoned in both warfare and leadership, but most of all had proven he would be willing to sacrifice himself for his people if the situation demanded it.

The king turned to Hall with a quizzical look. "Your son is supposed to lead men who don't trust his leadership?" he asked.

Hall looked to his men. "I will grant you a choice. The men with families will go, and the ones who choose to join them may do so. If you choose not to accompany your brothers, you will stay here and fight in the North with the king's men." Almost a dozen men then immediately chose to remain with Hall, while the others talked among themselves, discussing the vile things they would do to the "pigman" when they caught him.

"Amiram," Hall called, prompting the mute to begrudgingly stand as he casually stepped away from his two companions.

Amiram marched up, lightly snickering to himself as Bors seemed to be entranced by one of the women the mute had just left behind.

"I need you to go with my son. Bors cannot, as I need him here with me. Your job will be the same as it was before, keep my son alive." Prompting Amiram to display a knowing grin. Hall couldn't help but smirk as he placed a hand on the man's shoulder. "I imagine you already assumed this would be the case, but this time may be more troublesome than the last. The man you took prisoner will be guiding you to this slaver."

Amiram sighed and pointed back toward the two women awaiting his return.

"Go," Hall ordered. "Enjoy yourself. But no more bastards. I'm tired of seeing so many curly headed children running around."

Amiram returned a dissapointed look, one which Hall couldn't figure was genuine dissapointment or a joke, and walked away.

Bors tapped Hall's shoulder to grab his attention. "Final tally from the headcount, boss. Looks like we'll need to find some additional sailing men. Only have seventeen fighters who chose to go with your boy. If Amiram goes, we can count on the rowers joining him, but it is hard to rely on untrained men to crew a ship."

Hall sighed. "All my son requires is enough men to make the journey to Londinium. Once there he will be crewing the ship with mercenaries anyway." Hall glanced toward the king, noticing he bore a conflicted expression as he stared intently into the ground.

For fuck's sake. He's going to go back on his word right after swearing it to me, Hall thought silently.

"I will help with that," the king announced as he deliberately lifted his head. "Both of you take a day to rest and prepare your vessel. I will have Aosten round up who he can. I would also advise sending your scout Dagonet with him as he knows the country your son will be traveling to."

"He's from Frisia?" Hall inquired in surprise.

King Ceneus shook his head. "Not from Frisia, no. He was sold by Servius as a boy back when the Romans still ruled here. My first wife needed help in the kitchens and purchased him. The boy turned out to be an excellent hunter, so

I gave him his freedom and he eventually ended up a scout."

"I'm sure he wouldn't mind skewering the man either then," Bors put in.

"Likely not. In any case, I would assume he remembers enough to aid your boy," the king responded as he slowly drifted toward the exit.

Hall nodded as he looked over the men of the Fortuna. "Let's hope," he whispered to himself. He looked to Bors and beckoned him toward the door with a slight nod.

The clay tiles of the villa's roof were producing a hollow sound as the thick drops of rain floated from the heavens. This pitter-patter was the melody which Drysten awoke to the morning following his run-in with the king's man and his assault of the Frisian prisoner. He slowly stirred from his comfortable bed and immediately detected outside air as it seeped in through a crack in the nearest wall. The aroma reminded him of Ostia Antica, the major port city of the Roman Empire and destination of his first journey at the helm of the Fortuna. He remembered wondering how such a massive city could exist, but then he ventured to Rome herself.

They only lingered for one evening, but Drysten was just as fascinated by Rome's former capital as he was with its port to the West. The legionnaires patrolling the streets made Drysten wonder how an enemy could ever overwhelm such men, then he remembered Britannia. Britannia had thrashed the Romans around for centuries, and almost two decades ago, the Empire had decided it wasn't worth the effort to try and claim her. Drysten remembered the final day he saw a legionnaire patrolling Eboracum. He recalled his tired eyes which seemed to sink deep into the man's head, though at such a young age, Drysten had little understanding of why this was so.

I wonder what happened to him. Drysten thought as he stared up into the ceiling above.

After sitting up in his bed, he slowly rose and pulled his foul-smelling tunic over his head. He strapped his black leather jerkin to his chest, resting it nicely over his once white tunic with the blue embroidering now coming undone. The excellent leather article was a gift from his father, and when Drysten had first seen it, he was impressed by its workmanship. It was mainly comprised of boiled leather but had iron rings sewn all around the front and back with leather cording. The sides were without rings, but Drysten knew if he had an enemy to his immediate left or right, he was most likely in a situation with no favorable outcome anyway.

He then tied his sword belt, comprising his short sword and dagger, around his waist. The sword purchased in Ostia on his previous voyage was touted by a merchant as once being wielded by the great barbarian general, Vercingetorix. Though initially amused by the idea, Drysten believed the chances of that were slim at best. In any case, he favored the weight of it and made the purchase at a fraction of the man's original asking price. The dagger was also a gift from his father, who was outfitted with the blade on the day he signed up for the Roman auxiliary. Finally, he donned each sandal, also hand me downs from his father. Drysten thought it was somewhat comical how many of his belongings were not originally his own.

I suppose this means you had a similar build to my own in your youth, Drysten mused as he thought of his father.

He slowly outstretched his arms in an attempt to further wake himself, failing to do so. He figured he would feel more awake once he filled his belly, and upon finishing with his equipment, he finally made his way to the courtyard.

He noticed some of his father's men standing in a circle, presumably waiting for Hall, and two of the men began walking over to Drysten.

"Lord!" one man pronounced. He was one of the Cretan archers in his father's service known as Paulus. "Lord, the Fortuna is being stocked with supplies as we speak. When do we plan to leave?" he questioned eagerly.

"So far as I know, tomorrow morning," Drysten replied as he walked toward the kitchen. Unbeknownst to Drysten, the whole group was now following him.

"And this prisoner we took is going to show us where?" Paulus asked.

Once Drysten finished yawning he turned to face his crewman and was somewhat startled to see all the others standing behind him as well. "He knows what will happen if he does not," he answered.

The men seemed satisfied with that answer for the moment, with some turning to leave. Three men stayed with Drysten as he made his way into the kitchen.

"No, no, no!" a voice groaned from the corner. Drysten turned to see it was coming from a servant who had been cooking over a fire. "I had no idea there'd be this many! How many of you are actually here to eat?" she asked the group.

Drysten glanced behind him again, then awkwardly turned back. "Uh, all of us if there is enough food to be had," Drysten caught himself speaking as if he wasn't one of the people in charge of the villa. "We could come back when more food is ready."

Looking exasperated, the woman threw her hands up and turned toward the fire where she then began to stir some kind of soup inside a large cast iron pot. "Just don't get mad at me if the portions are too small. I was told there would only be two others living here. Not a small army!" she insisted.

"You do realize this man is the new lord here, don't you?" Paulus lightly inquired.

The woman turned and gave him a scornful look. "Lords come and go, but what happens to the servants? We stay here and cook for whoever else gets thrown into this home!"

The group uncomfortably glanced at each other, weighing if it was worth the wait for food if it meant dealing with this bitter woman. Then, they began to smell whatever was in the pot. It was the most pleasant and enticing aroma of meats and spices any of them had ever breathed in. All at once, the men rounded up any chairs they could find and sat down at the small table in the corner of the room. Though silent at first, they gradually began to tell stories of the people who might have been taken by Servius until a familiar voice interrupted them.

"You know, there's a chance not all of our families were taken. I mean, his ship is only so big," Maurianus put in as he walked into the kitchen.

"Doesn't matter," answered Paulus. "Even if my sister is safe, I still want to make sure the others are too. These are our people."

"It isn't just an issue for the men who've had a wife or child taken," Petras, Paulus' younger brother, added.

"We'll bring them all back," Drysten maintained, "all of them."

Maurianus scoffed at Drysten's enthusiasm. "And how do you know this, *Lord*?

"What I know, is anybody who gets in our way will die," Drysten declared as he locked eyes with Maurianus. "Anyone." Drysten did not bother to hide his dislike of the man, as it was notably shared with every other member of the Fortuna's crew. The man had recently tried to rob the body of a fallen crew member known as Baak, as well as swindle many of Hall's men out of hard-earned gold through various dice games. What baffled so many on the Fortuna was how nobody could figure out how he actually did it.

There was a tense moment of locked eyes between the two, but Maurianus eventually broke first as he stepped away from the table.

Maurianus produced a smirk which angered Drysten for no reason other than he hated the man. "Well, I suppose we'll have to wait and see. Won't we?" He then walked out of the kitchen.

"I hate that fucker," Paulus said quietly as he turned to

Drysten. "The king will send us more men?" he asked in a curious voice.

"He's working on that right now. Probably already has a few ready," Drysten answered.

Before long, the woman came back holding three bowls of soup, while another servant walked up holding one. "Good thing the other one left, there's barely enough for the lot of you as it is!" she stated as she placed each bowl down in front of the men. "I do hope you enjoy pork. It was butchered this morning."

"It will be wonderful, I am sure," Drysten replied with a smile.

The men greatly enjoyed the soup, as none of them said a word until they were finished. It only took a few moments, and once they devoured their meals, they each reclined back and stared into the empty bowls.

Drysten let out a long sigh. "Are the pyres completed yet?"

Paulus glanced to his brother, Petras, who Drysten had put in charge of the construction of the pyres the night before. "They are nearly complete, Lord. I stepped away when I saw a crowd gathering inside the villa."

"Well done," Drysten expressed through a weary voice. "Let's go send off our brothers."

The group rose from their seats, thanked the servants, and marched their way outside.

"Pyres are this way, Lord," Petras stated as he gestured to the easternmost edge of the town.

"Lead on," Drysten replied with a nod.

Paulus glanced over at a group of children playing with a frolicking kitten they stumbled upon. "Thought what you'll say at the funeral, Lord?"

Drysten nodded. "I believe I have something."

Though the truth was, Drysten had no idea what he would say to his remaining crewmembers. He painstakingly dwelled on the upcoming eulogy the night before, but failed to find the necessary words no matter how hard he tried.

The group rounded a few dilapidated buildings as the pyres first came into view. The wooden structures had been constructed by Diocles and Cynwrig, with the help of some locals and a few other men of the Fortuna. They had nearly completed their task when the rain lightly began to fall once more, causing the group to rush through the last couple of pyres as the rest of the crew made their way to the funeral.

Hall led a group containing Elias, Cyrus, Aosten, King Ceneus, and Bors into the front of the men who had gathered. Drysten and Diocles approached the king and bowed. He then stood next to Hall as the pyres were about to be lit.

Drysten glanced toward his father. "What do I tell them?"

"You tell them they died for a purpose," Hall quietly whispered as he gestured his son forward. "You'll find the words, son. Just don't seek to rush it, that's all the advice you need."

After a deep sigh, Drysten started willing himself toward the neatly stacked pyres. Each step felt as though it added additional weight into his legs. He began making his way to the closest pyres before eventually turning toward those gathered to hear his eulogy. There was a total of seven pyres constructed holding multiple men, but thankfully the smell had not become too pungent for Drysten's focus.

Drysten slowly drew in a deep breath as he examined the tired-looking men and women standing on either side of his father. He was surprised by how many of the locals were present, as these people obviously had never known the dead men behind him. "When people wish to understand what it takes to be a hero, they may look to those such as the great kings of Greece or the fallen emperors of Rome, all of whom led great campaigns in an attempt to unify the world we walk through today. But the true heroes are the men and women that fight and support those great lords. They are the ones whose passion makes those conquests possible.

They sacrifice their own well-being for the sake of the men and women they love. These men here, though they did not know it at the time, sacrificed themselves so we could have the information necessary to save those who we are sworn to protect."

Drysten cleared his throat and stole a glance behind him, seeing atop the pyres the many men he led. He truly wished he could find the words to convey his sorrow, but knew even if he had, there would be no place for them. He was purposed with denoting the best qualities of them all, the best qualities of those he wished he had gotten to know better.

Drysten slowly returned his focus to the crowd standing in front of him, moving his glance toward his father to find out if he had chosen his words poorly. To his surprise, he only received a hint of a reassuring smile, along with a nod as if telling him to keep going. "I would trade places with any one of them if I could, but since I cannot I will honor this sacrifice by pledging we will not return without our families and any others we find along the way."

Drysten turned to Amiram, who was standing close by with a torch as he awaited the command to light the first pyre. Drysten solemnly nodded, hearing the sound of thunder rumbling overhead. The dried thatch was nearly waist high to the mute, who lowered his torch into the middle part also containing a fair amount of cooking grease.

As the rest of the pyres were subsequently lit, the rain began to pour forth from the heavens. At first, Drysten believed it would dampen the thatch to the point the pyres would struggle to hold a flame. But after a few moments, they all seemed to burn more fiercely than he predicted.

"Greased up the middle layers of kindling, Lord," a local farmer explained to Drysten's father. "Knew there was rain coming, so we had to be certain it would not hinder the funeral for your people."

"Well done," Hall responded to the farmer as he walked

toward his son. Drysten briefly turned back to the pyres, unsure of what his father wished to tell him. At first, Drysten simply felt a slight pat on his shoulder, bringing him a momentary feeling of relief as he thought his father had simply passed him by.

"You failed them all, son. But for all your many shortcomings, I know that that fact is not lost on you," Hall forcefully seethed.

Drysten's heart sank down to the soles of his feet, wholly terrified to meet his father's gaze.

Hall roused a hollow laugh before continuing his indignant tone. "Always afraid to face the ones you fail the most. Your mother would be disappointed in you. She believed you to be a princely soul, but *I* know better. You are no son of mine, *murderer*."

Drysten slowly lowered his head, feeling something worse than shame which had no words. "Disappointment," was all he heard ringing through his head. "Disappointment. Disappointment. Disappointment."

"Murderer?" Drysten whispered. "How does he know—" Drysten wheeled to face his father only to find he never paused to speak with his son at all. He was speaking with a group of men much too far away for his typically quiet tone of voice to travel.

You will fail him, Drysten, the voice whispered. *You will fail them all.*

The color left Drysten's face as he stared toward his father and their men. One man noticed his odd demeanor and gestured for Hall to wander over to his boy.

Drysten slowly trained his attention back to the pyres as he attempted to shake off the chill along his spine. He remembered how the only other moment in his life he had seen any of that size was after a raid on Burdigala. He remembered how the odor had been much worse than it was at present, and how he had set out to find the surviving band of invaders that fled after their failed attempt at conquering

Burdigala.

"Find them!" he had yelled to his men, all frantically hunting the remnants of the invaders through the dense woods. Had it not been for a small scrap of bloody cloth Amiram had found, they likely would have lost the trail entirely.

"Here, Lord," Amiram had proudly stated. At that point in time, he hadn't had his tongue cut out, and until that moment was known to be difficult to keep quiet. Drysten could see in his eyes how furious he was at the sight of their friends and families lying dead within the city's walls. But what stood out more to Drysten was how Amiram had said little throughout the day of tracking. They finally did catch up, and what Drysten and his small company of men did next still haunted him to this day.

"Drysten," a familiar voice said from behind him, breaking his thoughts. He turned to see his father walking up to him. "You spoke well, albeit somewhat brief."

Drysten slightly turned his head but did not have the will to respond, still quietly reeling from the encounter with the voice.

Hall gently placed a hand on his son's shoulder. "I will oversee the provisioning of the ship. Bors will explain who is accompanying you."

Again, Drysten stayed silent, this time lowering his head.

Hall removed his hand from his son's shoulder and turned to whisper in his ear. "You need to forget what happened. Dwelling on the past is not helpful when needing to focus on the future. You need to—"

"I may have caused these pyres, father, but they will *never* haunt me as much as the first ones did," Drysten interrupted. He glanced toward his father as he slowly began to make his way back into town. Drysten did not need to ask, but he knew his father immediately understood what he meant.

Hall oversaw the provisioning of the Fortuna for its mission to Frisia the rest of the previous day. Due to his crew being undermanned, the journey would likely take about four days in the first leg to Londinium, then another three days going directly East into the Frisian islands across the sea. Once there, Drysten would be relying heavily on Jorrit for navigation. That created a feeling of dread inside Hall which would likely persist until his son's return. Jorrit had so far shown himself to be a reasonable man, but Hall had wondered if the foreigner had some other designs he was hiding. He acknowledged it may simply be as plain as a man doing what he perceives will keep him alive, but nevertheless, he felt uneasy placing the lives of his son and crew on this man's shoulders.

Jorrit briefly spoke to Hall while he was allowed outside for air, expressing his gratitude at influencing the king to forego torture. Hall was surprised, as his prisoner then pledged he would keep his son safe so long as he was awarded his freedom at the journey's end.

"Once we have obtained your people, I will instruct your boy on the safest way to return home. Then, by my estimations, my pledge will be fulfilled," the Frisian had stated.

The bulk of the day was hectic with preparations, meaning Hall didn't rest until well into the night. Right as he started to rest his head, yet another storm began to settle in the clouds above.

Forgot how much it rains in this fucking place, Hall silently thought. Despite the sudden downpour, he had little trouble falling into a dreamless sleep.

Hall wondered what images his son would be seeing, and whether they were messages from unknown deities secretly wandering the world around them. Following what felt like a blink, his eyes opened to the glint of dawn sunlight manifesting itself through a cracked window. He gradually rose from his bed, listening to every joint in his body crack and pop as he did so. His belly grunted and groaned, urging him to quickly make his way to the villa's kitchen for a morning meal. Along the way, he was welcomed by the scout Gawain, who was also shuffling toward the kitchens. Being so early in the morning, the single interaction between the two men was a slight nod. Hall briefly halted to pick a crusty object away from his eyelid, and allowed his scout to pass by as they moved into the dining hall.

"Roads'll be soaked, Lord. It'll slow us," Gawain informed his commander.

Hall lamented the idea of trudging through mud at his age, nearly fifty. "I'm certain the worst thing we'll face on this march won't be a bit of mud." Hall nodded toward the food in front of Gawain. "You should fill your belly up now. We won't be eating this much for a while."

"How long is a while?" the scout asked while rubbing his eyes.

"Until the job is done. That is, assuming it *can* be done," Hall responded.

The two men shared a glance and walked over to a pot containing some kind of wonderfully smelling stew. Two servants were stirring its contents and slicing freshly baked bread on a nearby table. Hall wondered who employed the servants, or if they simply came with the villa. One of the servants was older, roughly about the same number of years as Hall or a few less. It seemed she had come from somewhere outside of Britannia. She was tall with red hair braided down her back, and defined arms showing through the sleeves of her dress. The other was obviously younger and looked much like the other, leading Hall to believe the younger one to be her daughter. They both turned and smiled at the men as they entered.

"Food will be ready very soon, Lord," The younger one said.

"There's a pleasant aroma in here. Why does it smell so familiar?" Hall wondered rumbling suddenly erupted from his stomach.

The older woman grinned. "Garlic, Lord. Bought it m'self in town. Few more traders from Londinium showed up 'ere not too long ago. Had 'nough garlic 'n salt to last a small army on a march."

Hall nodded as he glanced toward the pot, eagerly awaiting the moment when he could fall into his meal. "We'll be sure to take some of it with us then. Doubt there'll be any traders out that way."

Hall then sat down at a beautifully crafted table produced from local yew trees. The very same trees worked to make bows for the king's men as well as the arrows they launched. Gawain relaxed himself down to Hall's left and offered him a hunk of bread he found sitting over a stove, to which Hall gratefully accepted.

The two women were pouring the stew into a pair of bowls when Aosten walked in. "I hear the plan changed."

Hall glanced up from the table as he waited for the moment he could begin shoveling food into his mouth like an animal. "The fort may be too heavily garrisoned to attack it by ourselves. The king notified me that he sent word to Powys for aid a couple of days ago, but we won't know if they're sending help until they actually arrive."

Aosten lifted an eyebrow. "And if they don't?"

"Then we will be forced to fight them the same way they've been fighting us for centuries," Hall answered.

The last remark brought a snicker from Aosten, who seemed to enjoy the possibility of raiding some of the enemy's villages the way they had been invading theirs. "Bet we'd be better at it. What road are we taking?"

Hall took a deep breath. "First, we make our way to Isurium to meet with the king's boy, then on to Cataractonium where we'll rest for a night. *Then* it's on to the fort at Piercebridge, and from there to Luguvalium. North the whole way." Hall did not simply choose the route because it offered the ease of the Roman roads. He picked it due to its passing through a vast forest between Piercebridge and Luguvalium. He had roamed the area in his days as an auxiliary in the Roman army and was more than familiar with it.

Aosten narrowed his eyes. "Sounds easy enough, though I thought we were supposed to be attacking Segedunum, not trying to avoid it."

"Is it easier to attack an enemy's front or to move behind them?" Gawain questioned, prompting Hall to nod to the scout and casually point in his direction.

"Fine by me, Lord, though you'll be needing to hear of a certain issue which may arise. The king's boy believes he is to be the leader of the army. The Bishop Germanus has our king's ear, and he himself decreed it so," Aosten announced as he awkwardly turned to Hall.

Hall shrugged, dismissing the remark and clearly surprising Aosten with his indifference. "If he wants to lead, he can lead us down the path I chose. Makes no difference to me who stands in the front of a march. As for this... Bishop Germanus, I will simply remind him who has more experience in war between the two of us."

Aosten cocked his head to the side. "Well, Lord... that *may* be about even. He was not always a bishop."

"A bishop?" Hall said with a snicker, "I thought that to be his name."

Aosten smirked and shook his head. "A title, Lord. Or maybe a ranking, I have not figured it out for myself. Christians do things differently than most in these lands are accustomed to."

"He's fought in wars even though he is a priest?" Hall inquired, though his interest was mild at most.

Aosten shrugged, "I would not be able to tell you specifics, as all I know about him is that he was once a Roman governor in Gaul."

"Ah," Hall said as he slowly nodded, "much fighting in that role. Or at least commanding men to fight."

"As for the king's boy, you've already met him. I am

certain you understood how much of a twat he is. Just make sure you're watching out for him," Aosten said as the bowls of stew and loaves of bread were put in front of the three men. "The army is almost ready. Your big man is seeing to it," Aosten stated in reference to Bors.

Through his stew, Gawain raised his head. "I'll keep a mile ahead in case we find any trouble. If there happens to be any, you'll have a warning." The scout took his bowl and left the room to fetch his supplies.

Hall nodded and turned to Aosten, who was shoveling his food faster than he could taste it. "There's another reason I chose this route," Hall then turned toward the fire crackling under the cooking pot, "I'm not sure I believe this prisoner of ours. I plan on leaving a small garrison in Isurium. If there's trouble behind us, I want to be protected from a rearward assault.

"You think there could be an attack on Eboracum?" Aosten asked.

"I'm not sure, but if there is, I'd like to leave enough men behind to repel it. Or at least hold out until we're able to return," Hall explained, "I suppose before we worry about that I need to see my son and his men. I still haven't heard from the king how he plans to reinforce their numbers."

"Aren't they *your* men?" Aosten asked.

"Not if he leads them well enough. I'm getting much too old to be fighting. My mind is still good, but my body aches every time I rise from my damn bed. My legs sound like a bundle of twigs being thrown to the ground," Hall explained in frustration.

Aosten chuckled. "Should find you a woman. That'll keep you young."

Hall shook his head. "No other woman could give me what my Fortunata did. Even in death, she is the only woman who will ever matter to me."

Aosten started to reply, then simply shut his mouth slowly nod.

The two men rose from their seats, thanked the servants for the excellent meal, and made their way outside. The streets were nearly flooded due to the last few days of sporadic rain. Aosten briefly explained there was a week-long storm which ended about a day before Hall's arrival from Burdigala. Hall glanced down at the muddy paths and thought it was a wonder they found any wood dry enough for the funeral. The rain had flooded the small farmsteads in the area surrounding the villa, and there was no shortage of farmers doing what they could to save their crop from being submerged under too much water. Hall and Aosten made their way to the docks, walking around the Western side of the villa's compound, then through the marketplace toward the docked Fortuna and its crew. Hall looked on as the men were loading his vessel with the last provisions for the journey to Frisia. A couple of the men nodded to Hall as he walked by. It was obvious the Fortuna's men thought they'd be seeing a small force riding up to join them.

"I don't see any men other than mine," Hall remarked as he glanced around the docks.

"The king's men could still be on their way, I suppose," Aosten clumsily responded. "He's not known to make empty promises, though you should always pay diligent attention to his tone when he promises something."

Hall looked at Aosten with a suspicious glance, then walked toward his son who was overseeing the loading of the ship. Bors and Diocles were with him, and Hall was encouraged to see his boy start to gather his own following, albeit it was still only one newcomer. They made their way to a tired looking Drysten, who turned and greeted them both with a quick smile. As Bors turned around, Hall watched as he cursed under his breath at something over Hall's shoulder and quickly walked by them toward the town.

"The ship will soon be ready, father," Drysten informed him.

"No word from the king?" Hall inquired.

"He made his way here not too long ago. Said we wouldn't be getting any of his *own* men," Drysten said with a disappointed tone.

"That doesn't seem right," an embarrassed Aosten put in as Hall shot him an angry gaze. "Truly, it's not like him to go back on his word. He's a lot of things, but a liar isn't one."

"Don't suppose you paid diligent attention to his *tone* then?" Hall scornfully replied, prompting Aosten to embarrassingly lower his head.

The three men stood near the ship in silence as they watched the men do their best to finish their jobs while the rain was not too heavy. It had started up again as Hall and Aosten were walking toward the ship, but the sparse cloud cover told the men it wouldn't get much worse. Bors was now making his way toward the men from the tavern across the village, helping Amiram stumble beside him.

"Not to worry, Lord!" Bors stammered, "Amiram'll be right as rain in no time! Rough night with those money-grubbin' wenches again." The two men finally made their way to Hall and Aosten, pausing briefly for the mute to empty his stomach out beside a goat standing nearby. The goat slowly turned its head toward Amiram, who met its gaze with a dejected sigh.

Hall and his son snickered at the sight, then turned and saw the king riding his horse down the Northern road from Eboracum. In tow, he had a dozen black-clad men carrying weapons and armor, and on another horse was a small box with a lock.

"Hardly much help," Bors observed with a scoff.

Hall sighed in disappointment. "I suppose they're better than nothing."

Once the king finally reached the group, he dismounted and marched toward Hall while gesturing for the dozen men to board the Fortuna. "I know the numbers aren't overwhelming, but I've brought your boy something else." The king walked to the second horse carrying the box, unstrapped it from the saddle, then carried it toward the men. He plopped it down into the mud and unlocked it for the men to gaze upon its contents. There were gold coins to the brim, and on top was a small necklace with an amulet bearing the depiction of a sun. The chain looked old, and King Ceneus noticed Drysten's gaze.

"You're going to need to look the part of a lord if you're to lead," the king stated in a reluctant tone. He picked up the chain and handed it to Drysten, who gratefully accepted and hung it around his neck. Even Hall had to admit, the chain made his son look particularly regal.

King Ceneus closed the box, hoisted it up and carried it to Bors, who looked as though he considered making a frantic sortie into the wilderness to begin a new life.

"Close your mouth, Bors," Hall said lightly. "Put it below deck."

Bors nodded as he stared down toward the wealth in his hands and began moving toward the Fortuna, glancing back every so often to see the watchful eyes of the king's guards.

"I understand your son indeed means to seek out that mercenary in Londinium," the king began. "That is assuredly sound judgment, though he does not come cheap. As a result, I have placed more coin than we originally agreed upon into this chest. I want you to consider this wealth is a gesture of goodwill between your people and myself. It is important you all understand you can rely on me for aid should you need it while you are here."

Hall watched Drysten bow before rising to meet the king's gaze. "I thank you, Lord King. They will know who is responsible for giving us the means to find our loved ones."

"Where did it come from? " Hall respectfully inquired. "That was an impressive haul you gave us."

King Ceneus nodded in agreement. "As the Romans hurried away, many were unable to bring all of their wealth with them. These coins and baubles are what we were able to keep for ourselves."

"Can I ask this mercenary's name, Lord King?" Drysten asked.

"Titus Octavius Britannicus. He served with the very same legion your father fought beside against the Picts. Victrix or some other...," the king responded, "the banner with the bull. Its name escapes me."

Hall turned once the sight of the king attempting to remember his beloved legion became too unbearable to ignore. "The Victorious Sixth, Lord King," he answered before turning to his son. "I remember him. He was a Roman-born centurion who journeyed here on the same ship as Stilicho. One of the few Roman regulars we had in command during the war and a good man indeed, though I did not know he was made a general."

"He was never formally promoted as such, but was given the cognomen of Britannicus for his constant efforts to safeguard the Britons. I was curious if you would have crossed paths with him," the king replied.

"He served directly under Stilicho, commanding tribesmen from the mainland as well as others trained in Rome. He was a charismatic and honorable man, but he followed Constantine when the man made a move for the crown. Did he desert once his general was defeated?" Hall asked.

The king shook his head. "His twenty-five years were up. He took advantage of the land grant he received from Emperor Constantine, then auctioned it for quite a nice sum. He relocated to Londinium and recruited his own men from the deserters who had fought for Constantine before turning to mercenary work. Very good at what he does. Still acts the part of Roman general quite well."

Hall noticed Drysten was still admiring his new chain during the exchange between his father and King Ceneus. "Where in Londinium will I find him?" Drysten asked.

"He owns a large villa on the South side of the bridge. You should not have any difficulties locating it," the king responded.

Drysten turned to his father. "With how few men we have it could take us almost five days before we arrive. Are you sure there aren't more men willing to join us?"

"Sadly, I am. To keep a decent pace, you will need the fighters to row as well. Amiram will take care of them until they can be replaced," Hall replied.

"Rowing is good for a man," a deep-chested man announced.

The group turned and saw Cynwrig leading Jorrit from the villa. He seemed to be in good spirits, which could be expected from a man who had mostly been confined to a basement for the last few days.

"Why are his hands not fastened?" Hall asked Cynwrig in a riled tone.

Drysten answered for Cynwrig. "Can't point where to go with his hands tied behind his back." After giving his father his response, he then turned to the ship. "Diocles! You're in charge of this one."

"Lucky me!" a voice blared from somewhere on the Fortuna.

The king glanced to Hall with a raised eyebrow and bid the men good luck before making his way back toward his horse. King Ceneus and Aosten both mounted and began to guide their horses north to Eboracum. "Bring your people to the city when ready," he shouted.

Hall nodded as he surveyed the Fortuna one last time. Her crew was getting ready to depart, with Drysten as its captain once again. Everyone was aboard except their leader, who Hall took aside.

"I have one last thing to give you before you leave," Hall stated as he undid the brooch clasping the bearskin cloak about his shoulders. "You have the gold to look the part. Now, if you wear *this*, nobody will question you anywhere." The heavy cloak was both warm and elegant, fitting over Drysten's shoulders much the same as it did on his father's.

Drysten smiled at his father. "Thank you, father. I imagine I look much the same as you did at my age."

Hall smiled and nodded. "Now go and get our people. Most importantly, watch out for the Frisian. I seem to trust him less than you do," Hall noted before he embraced his son one last time before he left.

"I don't have a reason for wanting this little venture to fail," Jorrit began, "if it fails and the crew is killed, I would be willing to bet I would be joining them in the afterlife."

"Then watch out for my son and all will be well," Hall commanded.

Drysten chuckled at the Frisian's tone. "We'll see you soon, father." He then turned to Jorrit. "You never know, you may end up wanting to stay before this is over."

"You stabbed me," Jorrit nonchalantly replied.

"Right," Drysten said in slight embarrassment. "To business then."

King Ceneus truly hoped the boy found his people. He wasn't foolish enough to believe it likely given the lack of faith the Fortuna's men seemed to place in him. But still, hope he did. Hope was something which had left the king in recent years. At first, his reign began with certain assurances of power and wealth he vowed to distribute among his people, but things quickly shifted. Where there were once promises, now laid voids left by deceit from the Christians.

The bishop originally assured him his people were to be cherished by the church, only to see that was quite the contrary. More people of Ebrauc had been put to death in the prior year than in any other year of Ceneus' ten years of reign, something Bishop Germanus likely thought went unnoticed. The man believed all but himself and a select few to be simpletons, but Ceneus believed he was anything but. Tricked, perhaps, but not stupid.

"This trek feels longer than before, Lord King," the priest known as Maewyn complained. The priest reclined back in his saddle as he attempted to outstretch his arms without falling.

Ceneus knew enough about the man to understand he was well-intentioned. But the best intentions seem to have had the worst of consequences in recent years. "We will be in Eboracum before you know it, priest."

Maewyn smiled. "I do hope so, Lord King. How are your children faring in your absence?"

"If I am correct, then my daughter is currently faring well underneath that Powysian prince. My son Gwrast is dutifully seeing to the administration of the city, or what seems to be left of it, and my middle son, Mor, would be preparing for a journey to Gwynedd to... *beseech* their king for aid along our coast," the king responded.

Maewyn wearily glanced back to Bishop Germanus, currently explaining previous wars he fought alongside the Romans of Gaul to Prince Eidion. "That one seems to be... different than the rest of your brood."

King Ceneus chuckled. "Sometimes I wonder whether he is mine or not. My brother was the first lover my wife took before Eidion was born. Were it not for the fact we look very much alike, I would truly wonder..."

"As would I, I expect," Maewyn responded.

"He wasn't always... the way he is," Ceneus blurted out. He felt slightly embarrassed by having to justify the cruelty of his son. "He went to the market as a young boy and was nearly trampled to death by a horse or some such thing. I have not been able to find all the details, as I was off fighting with my father and brother against the Gaels."

Maewyn gave the king a knowing glance, hinting to the king he was already told the story. Likely by a disgruntled servant bound to the royal family.

"The boy spent the better part of a week asleep, and when he awoke..." Ceneus couldn't bear to finish the sentence. He remembered how Eidion had once loved horses, and walking with the king through the fields surrounding Eboracum. *He was no longer my son.*

The two rode silently for a while longer, listening to the bishop ramble on about the various accomplishments during his prime. Maewyn seemed to be humming to an unknown melody, one which Ceneus began to grow curious.

"Where is that from?" the king asked.

"From the village I was born to. My mother would hum it to my baby sister when I was young. For some reason it seemed to come to mind," Maewyn responded.

"Where is it you're from?" Ceneus inquired.

"Ebrauc, Lord King. Right on the Western coast," the priest cheerfully responded.

A surprised King Ceneus turned. "You were once under my rule?"

Maewyn nodded. "I was, Lord King, but I was taken and sold into slavery at sixteen. The man who purchased me took me to Dal Riata."

"Ah," the king responded, "Many are are stolen away from us to those parts."

"Sadly, you are correct, Lord King. Many people I was enslaved alongside had once dwelled in neighboring villages. I was one of the lucky few who escaped and returned home," the priest solemnly responded.

"I apologize, priest. I failed in my duty to protect you," King Ceneus declared as he hung his head.

He truly did feel sorry. Throughout his reign, he sorely wished to be the strong ruler Ebrauc desperately needed. His older brother to the North had the strength in war, but Ceneus knew a king needed to be intelligent as well. His brother's aggressive nature was the reason he took up Bishop Germanus' offer of Ebrauc's throne. *Or so I tell myself,* the king mused.

"You may yet make up for it here, Lord King," Maewyn happily responded. Ceneus noticed the warm smile sweeping across the priest's face. "You have done a good thing in supporting this... Drysten."

Ceneus scoffed. "I never would have guessed when hearing how the bishop saw my decision."

"He is a man of... *singular* goals, Lord King," the priest returned, "he personally has difficulties focusing on multiple tasks, meaning he believes all others do as well."

"And that is why you are present?"

Maewyn nodded. "Indeed, Lord King."

"Then perhaps you could see about stemming the killings near our borders," Ceneus hissed, "Germanus sends his Christian riders from village to village, striking down images of native gods and hanging the ones who defy them."

"I was told those incidents occurred in response to armed raiders. I will address the matter with His Excellency, but I was told this from the men he sent out to secure that portion of your territory," Maewyn responded.

The king grumbled under his breath as he turned to face the far-off walls of Eboracum. The sight of his home caused a momentary shower of relief to wash over him, but that soon was dispelled upon the bishop groaning in response at the very same sight.

"The fucking city of ghosts, Ceneus. You should work to incentivize repopulation of the area," Bishop Germanus tiredly put in.

Must have run through all the whores, King Ceneus silently assumed, prompting a smile to cross his face. He gazed over the countryside sitting in the shadow of his beloved city when he noticed a small entourage containing a dozen riders cantering toward him. *My favored son,* he thought. As Gwrast approached, Ceneus felt yet another small smile begin to cross his face.

Prince Eidion groaned. "This insufferable fool…"

The horses came to a halt on the crumbling road, prompting the king to signal for his party to keep moving toward the city while he addressed his son. "Gwrast!" he began, "what matter brings you out of the city?"

The ragged, blonde-haired prince glanced toward the bishop and spurred his horse forward. "The raids to the West have intensified. Messengers have come with stories of disappearances along the coast."

"A story I am all too familiar with," Maewyn responded.

The king glanced back toward the bishop, who was listening intently to the exchange. In recent months, there were a string of abductions by the Gaels from across the Western sea, meaning there would be occasional refugees seeking the protection of the king in Eboracum. Though, more often than not the families of the victims considered Powys or Gwynedd to be safer and ventured South instead.

"Do not trouble yourself with such trivial matters, Lord King," Bishop Germanus began, "God's grace will guide them through their plights and carry them home, much in the way he did for our dear friend, Patrick."

Ceneus glanced to the priest he knew as Maewyn, briefly witnessing him doing the sign of the cross as he nodded reassuringly back to him. "With all due respect, Your Excellency, I will take care of this matter myself." He slowly trained his attention back to Gwrast, who was giving the bishop a distasteful look as he grumbled under his breath. "Where was it this time?"

"Further South than before, but only a small handful were taken. They left no tracks," Gwrast replied.

"I suppose no tracks would mean they were indeed from across the water," the king responded.

Gwrast nodded. "I would like to take my men West, father. We *must* stop this."

The king nodded. "Take your men, plus fifty more from my guard," he said as he gestured toward the men adorned in royal blue cloaks trailing behind his son.

Ceneus had not journeyed with his own guard since the bishop had arrived from Londinium. Germanus cited he had no need while he traveled with Prince Eidion, as they brought their own black-clad guards who seemed to heed every word out of the king's mouth. They were most certainly acting as spies under the Bishop's orders. King Ceneus was no fool, and understood the bishop and the prince were likely conspiring against him. But thankfully, while Ceneus held the support of Powys and Gwynedd, he knew the bishop would be reluctant to make a move against him.

Gwrast nodded as he eyed Maewyn and turned toward the city.

"I feel as though I am not trusted by your people, Lord King," Maewyn observed.

"Nor myself, priest."

Maewyn gave a dejected glance down toward his saddle, clearly hurt by the king's distrust. Ceneus felt no pity for the man's feelings, as the presence of the Christians had proven to be little more beneficial to him than apostates which originally inhabited his kingdom in greater numbers.

Maewyn glanced toward the king, speaking in a hushed tone only audible to him. "I understand you have little trust for the bishop, but I swear my presence here is only meant to aid you, Lord King."

Ceneus glimpsed toward his son, receiving an indifferent shrug, and looked back to the priest. "If this is true, then do what you can with the raids on my people. They are not criminals simply because they worship The Morrigan, Donn or... Cernunnos." Drumond's image found its way to the forefront of the king's mind, with Gwrast noticeably feeling the same. It made a fair bit of sense to Ceneus, as Drumond was a big part of his children's lives. The man taught them everything from hunting, to fighting, to even dealing well with women.

But none of that mattered now, because as important as the man was to the family of the king, he was still dead.

CHAPTER V

Drysten heard the hail pounding the hull of the Fortuna. To him, it sounded identical to the day the ship was being beaten by hammers when the new hull was repaired. The spring storm that was assailing the southern regions of Britannia had turned from a light rain, which began shortly after Drysten rose that morning, to a wall of wind and ice. The sun had disappeared behind the thick gray clouds and the frigid wind seemed to be cutting right through any layers of clothing and skin. The crew was rowing the ship up the River Tamesis, the dark-watered river flowing through Londinium. A few men had been at work bailing water from the lowest deck since the storm began, occasionally sprinting up the stairway to hurl their buckets' contents into the river.

"I know how *close* we are, but we may have to make camp for the night if this keeps up," Cynwrig put in. The new addition to the crew was sitting next to Drysten near the rowers on the second level of the Fortuna, huddled under a thick blanket of boar pelts sewn together with leather cord. "The winds alone are blowing in the wrong direction. Spells for a short trip if we aren't careful."

"She can hold a bit longer," Drysten responded with a smile.

"I pray you're right," Cynwrig wearily replied as he glanced at the darkened sky.

The two men were then shaken by a loud crash of thunder and a blinding flash from the sky. A startled Drysten sprang up and started giving orders to row the ship toward the riverbank in the chance they would be forced to follow Cynwrig's suggestion. He finished, then turned back to see Jorrit, sitting on the rearmost rower's bench, and Cynwrig speaking about the storms in Jorrit's homeland.

"Waves bigger than our shelters. Granted, most of our dwellings are not that sizeable," Jorrit stated with a chuckle. To Drysten's surprise, the man was somewhat pleasant to talk to, despite Drysten stabbing him when his hands were bound behind his back. He had a rough sense of humor, but nothing like Bors.

"How long will it take us to travel from Londinium to Frisia?" Drysten inquired as he stepped closer.

Jorrit hesitated to consider their route. "Hm... I'd say it would take us about three days if we navigate straight there. Though I doubt this ship could handle open water very well."

Drysten knew this was especially true. Quinquiremes were designed to carry about four hundred souls through shallow water. The Fortuna on the other hand had been refitted to be a trade ship. The standard sized crew for her would be about two hundred, and they had nearly half that number. By Drysten's estimation, this meant their pace would be further slowed if they were forced to row due to lack of wind. "We'll go South to Londinium, then cross to the coast of the mainland straight east of there. Hopefully, we don't run across any more of your people along the way."

Jorrit perked up his head. "By the way, why are we journeying into Londinium? Nobody has bothered to inform me of anything since I have been... *welcomed* aboard."

"You *are* a prisoner, you know. In any case, there are mercenaries we can employ in the city. An old Roman officer leads them," Drysten answered.

"Gah!" Jorrit exclaimed. "Romans might be the most overpraised warriors in the whole world."

Drysten gave him a quizzical look. "You do recall they

conquered most of the mainland, don't you?" Prompting Jorrit to shrug as if it simply wasn't impressive.

"Most, but not all," The Frisian arrogantly replied.

Cynwrig stood up while outstretching his arms to keep his blood moving. "Men or not, I just hope this damn weather calms down. The cold is enough as it is without this *fucking* rain." Drysten couldn't help but smile at the man. Cynwrig revealed before they left Petuaria that he had never been on a boat more substantial than his father's fishing craft.

"There's no way we'll be able to sail into open waters in this storm," Jorrit added.

Drysten nodded and looked on the tired faces of his crew. The Fortuna had been at sea for two days and nights, meaning they would reach their destination toward the end the next day. The men had sailed without stopping since they had departed Petuaria, and Drysten noted they were in good spirits considering what the purpose of their journey was. The men had largely remained optimistic about their chances, but one man had stood out from the others. To nobody's surprise, that lone individual was Maurianus. If it weren't for the fact he saved Hall's life sometime in the years prior, he probably would have been thrown overboard long ago.

Maurianus spent most of the trip on the second deck gambling, and primarily just questioning whether the venture was even possible. He had about thirty winters under his belt, and had a long, crooked nose broken in a bar fight, a prominent brow, and short black hair that seemed as though it was perpetually stuck to his head. The men of the Fortuna knew to mostly stay away from him if he was bored, as he would routinely try to goad them into losing money one way or another. Unlucky for Drysten, this dislikeable man was now coming up to him.

"Hall's boy!" Maurianus called.

Drysten released a heavy sigh as he noticed Jorrit and

Cynwrig both taken aback by how he was addressed. "You will address me as lord or sir, nothing else. Now, what is it?"

Maurianus returned a mocking giggle at the order. "Fair enough, *Lord*. I'm assuming we plan on pillaging bits of Frisia along the way to nabbing our people, are we not?"

"I only have a mind to rescue our people," Drysten replied.

Maurianus cocked his head to the side at the response. "Even though this man took our people?"

Drysten locked eyes with the man, surveying the wicked features across his face. "You have made it known you don't regard them as *your* people, Maurianus. To further answer your question, the only thing I plan on doing once we get our people back is promptly returning to help my father."

Maurianus laughed through his grim smile. "You of all people should relish a little raiding. Drysten, the renowned slayer of innocents!"

Drysten exploded up to his feet and seemed to glide across the deck until he arrived mere inches from Maurianus, glaring into his eyes. Drysten heard two sets of feet shuffle toward him, presumably belonging to Diocles and Cynwrig.

"Lord?" Cynwrig whispered to his captain.

Drysten inched closer, subjecting Maurianus to his piercing gaze. "If there is something you wish to say, then say it," he hissed. Drysten's hand began deliberately moving toward the hilt of his sword, seizing the attention of his prey.

"There is nothing more I wish to say to you," Maurianus declared through his wicked smirk. He began to turn away until Drysten instantly seized his arm.

"You did not understand me before? What are you to call me?" Drysten snarled, squeezing Maurianus' arm progressively tighter.

Maurianus' smile gradually dissolved. "I have nothing else to say, Lord." To which Drysten begrudgingly released the man's arm.

Drysten watched as Maurianus slowly sauntered back toward the entrance to the second deck, not recognizing the crack of thunder vibrating the wooden planks below his feet. A faint chuckle was detected from Jorrit, and Drysten slowly turned to the Frisian.

"He won't be *any* trouble at all," Jorrit put in.

The Frisian's sarcasm somehow managed to slightly ease Drysten's nerves. "When he's with my father he isn't," Drysten replied with a sigh. "He has no trouble keeping him in line. What will most certainly be a problem is the fact he has nobody to rescue, so I would imagine he views this as just one voyage like any other."

Diocles stepped closer to his captain as he watched Maurianus disappear below deck. "If he is truly that much trouble, I would suggest we leave him in Londinium and tell your father he abandoned us. There should be no place for a man who thinks only of himself in this crew."

Drysten nodded. "That is certainly an option."

The two men walked toward the bow of the ship as the storm began to calm. After a short while, the men of the Fortuna finally gazed upon the large city of Londinium. It was located on either side of the River Tamesis, while the smaller settlement was situated on its Southern side. Drysten was told that at its height, the city held sixty thousand people, an amphitheater, a palace, multiple baths and temples to various gods.

The whole Northern portion of the city was surrounded by a massive wall of about twenty feet in height and roughly fifteen feet thick. Drysten guessed the wall was a necessity after the city had been burned to utter ruin during the campaign of the infamous Boudica. Accompanied by many different tribes, she leveled some of the most populated Roman cities or towns in Britannia but was stopped somewhere on the Roman road to the northwest of Londinium.

The city was now inhabited by various tribes of native Britons, wealthy Romans who stayed behind when the Empire left, and a score of other people trying to find work in one form or another. One thing he remembered Bors explaining to him was the presence of Saxons and Angles, descendants of men who once fought against the Romans, but then acted as mercenaries who fought under their former enemy's employ.

The city began to come into view about an hour after reaching the entrance to the river. Drysten stood up near the bow of the ship and was joined by Jorrit, Cynwrig, Diocles, and the two Cretan archers.

Drysten had not chatted very much with the Cretans on their first journey, but Petras and Paulus were both smart men and capable fighters. Due to this, he had ordered them both to join him as he walked through the city.

The crew gathered together as they marveled at the stone bridge connecting each end of Londinium. The craftsmanship was impressive, even to those who had seen other settled areas of the empire in their many days at sea. The ship finally docked on the Northern bank of the river, just to the East of the bridge. They then disembarked and started toward the nearest marketplace.

Drysten briefly turned back to the ship. "The money is locked away?" he asked Amiram and Magnus, who had walked with the men a short distance. Amiram nodded in confirmation.

"Keep it that way. Nobody goes near it except you or one of us when we return. And don't forget to find some more men for the rowing." Again, Drysten's lead rower nodded.

"Lord," Magnus said, catching Drysten's attention before he turned away, "we should consider purchasing another sail. The Fortuna has a unique design, but a different sail could help change her appearance enough to not betray who crews her."

Drysten considered the man's words for a moment, then

looked back to Amiram. "You heard him, get us another sail. Preferably blue, I've always liked blue." Amiram nodded with a smile and turned back to the Fortuna, soon followed by Magnus.

"How do we plan on finding this man?" Diocles inquired as he looked through a crowded street.

Drysten gestured toward the South bank of the river. "King Ceneus informed me to go South of the bridge. Apparently, our Roman owns a very particular villa that way."

Cynwrig chuckled. "I've set foot in more villas in the last week than in the whole rest of my life."

"You mean one?" Diocles asked, prompting a smile and nod from Cynwrig.

The men were now walking through sparse crowds with Drysten and Diocles in the lead, followed by Cynwrig and the Cretans. They finally made it to the bridge and began to cross, just as a couple of stick-wielding children began playing soldier. They briefly clapped their weapons together a few times, then scurried away as Drysten and his men paused to let them pass.

The little ones turn into big ones, Lord, best to stop em' before then, the voice whispered, causing Drysten to shudder before training his attention forward.

The seagulls circled overhead as they waited for some particle of food to be dropped by the many women carrying baskets across the bridge. It was surprising to see the city looking so alive. Drysten's impression was that most places in Britannia were growing more and more deserted now that the Romans had left. In Londinium, it appeared this was far from a reality.

People were wandering in both directions over the bridge, some quickly weaving in and out of the way of others who were walking with a more leisurely pace. It was easy to ascertain who had business on the other side of the city or who was just out admiring the views. Some children were following their mother toward Drysten's group, when one who wasn't watching where she was going bumped into Diocles. The Greek warmly snickered at the girl as she stared wide-eyed at the newcomer. Diocles held up a finger to gesture for her to wait, then tossed her a small silver coin from his belt. The mother graciously thanked him, and continued to usher her children toward the Northern side of the river.

The men finally reached the Southern side and were able to witness two dogs fighting over a loaf of bread that had been dropped by an unknowing passerby. They both gave Cynwrig a brief glance until one suddenly plucked up the food and ran off, with the other struggling to keep up.

"I miss having a dog," Cynwrig sadly stated as he ruffled a hand through his hair.

"You should get to know Bors," Diocles quipped.

The group gazed down the main road until Petras spied a large home with a banner bearing the insignia "VI" for the Sixth Victorious Legion of Rome. Drysten saw the banner swaying with grace at the very top of the villa's entrance.

"What legion was he with?" the younger Cretan asked.

"Same as my father, this must be the place," Drysten stated. "Petras and Cynwrig, stay outside. Go get Amiram if something happens."

Diocles perked his head up. "Expecting trouble? I thought this was who we came to see."

Drysten shrugged. "I just don't want to take any chances. Especially not with people we don't know."

It was agreed there was most likely nothing to worry about when it came to dealing with this mercenary, especially after hearing his father's opinion of him. Nevertheless, Drysten decided after the results of his last foray as captain that he would take no chances. So far on the journey, nothing out of the ordinary had happened, but he grasped things could always turn sour rather suddenly if he weren't cautious.

The men casually strolled up to the gate, immediately finding it locked. Drysten shrugged to Diocles as he stepped up and lightly pounded his fist on the bars. A man fully outfitted in Roman armor approached with his hand on his sword hilt.

"You have business here?" the guard muttered from between his helmet's cheek plates.

"I came to speak with Titus Octavius Britannicus. I have a job for him."

The guard cocked his head to the side. "And who might you be?"

"Drysten ap Hall."

"I'll bring the general word of your arrival."

The guard let go of his sword as he politely nodded and walked through the villa's doors. Drysten and his gathering waited for roughly thirty minutes before the guard eventually marched back. Behind him trailed a man of about fifty years, who was dressed in a finely stitched tunic embroidered with red stitching on the arms. Around his neck were two chains, one gold, and the other silver, and on his fingers were four rings with different insignias on each. The man with short, black hair and a powerful brow approached Drysten as he signaled for the guard to unlock the gate. Drysten looked over the man, seeing the wars he had fought etched into his face, in his eyes, over the slight scar on his forehead, and in his distant stare as it surveyed Drysten's companions.

"You have dealings with me?" The stranger inquired.

"I am in need of soldiers, and I've been told you're the person to talk to," Drysten declared.

The man then looked over the group and decided they were at least worth a conversation before he finally beckoned them all inside.

"Catulla!" Titus called. A woman Drysten guessed to be a slave broke from her discussion with another finely dressed man, this one younger and presumably Titus' son. She looked over the newcomers and gracefully stepped toward her master.

The general turned to Drysten. "The other two won't be joining you?"

Drysten glimpsed back at Cynwrig and Petras. "They have errands to run in the city. They simply wanted to see if your home was as big as people say."

"Judging by what people say of me, they were likely disappointed," the man replied with a grin. "What people have you been talking to?"

Drysten stood up straighter as if revealing his association with a king gave him added authority. "King Ceneus ap Coel, of Ebrauc."

"Ah. That one," Titus stated wearily as he led the group to a room Drysten guessed to be his study. Drysten was slightly concerned for the indifferent tone Titus seemed to take toward the naming of the king. "Please, sit. Be comfortable. There's no shortage of wine or food. I'll just call for a servant if you or your people require anything."

"You're a truly gracious host," Paulus replied with a short bow of the head.

"I do try to be. Manners are hard to come by in these times. Now, let's talk of business," Titus began as he cleared his throat. "It's certainly no secret I lead men for the right price. But what you may not have been told is I don't accept any job that comes our way. I have been asked to fight for Armorican rebels against Rome, the Picts or Gaels against mostly everyone, and for my men to become the personal bodyguards of wealthy aristocrats in town. I declined them all. Why should I be swayed to work for you?"

Drysten shifted awkwardly in his seat as he realized this may not be as easy as just paying out some gold and silver. "You seem to garner quite the reputation if you receive offers from such... diverse groups of clientele."

Titus grinned. "Some Saxon from across the water asked for me to fight in the North as well. I would never work for the fucking *Saxons*. Why he thought I would is simply beyond me."

Diocles scoffed. "You must give him credit. It was certainly a bold request."

"Just what Britannia needs, bold Saxons," Drysten put in before training his attention back to Titus. "Some of my people were taken by a Frisian slaver. I want them back."

Titus smiled. "Well, one can surely understand that."

Drysten nodded as he glanced to Diocles. "They took our families when we were away in Ostia. We were obviously unable to defend them. There is an obligation for us to get them back."

"That there is," Titus replied, still seemingly unswayed by Drysten. "I understand why you must risk your lives, and I even agree with you that you need to. But tell me, why should *we?* And don't say because you'll pay, that is a response I receive to that question every single time I ask it. If I had accepted each time, I would be significantly richer with fewer fighting men under my employ."

Drysten sat in judgment, hesitant with his next choice of words. He subtly glanced at Paulus to his left and Diocles to his right, while shifting in his seat. "Because my father seemed to think you an honorable man," he awkwardly blurted out.

Titus leaned back in his seat and stretched his arms. "So you're Hall's boy," the general finally replied as he studied Drysten's surprised expression. "I have seen many faces in my lifetime, and the sons of those faces rarely stray far from their father's. I liked him for the brief time I knew him. A tragedy what happened to your mother and sister. I always thought Fortunata was a good woman to your father." He stood and walked to a table under a tall window, considering what his choice should be.

Diocles leaned toward Drysten. "Is this fucker going to fight with us or not?" he whispered, prompting Drysten to shush him before returning an unknowing shake of the head.

"Yes!" Titus abruptly proclaimed. "This fucker will fight indeed!"

Diocles slunk down in his seat, causing Drysten and Paulus to snicker in amusement.

Titus happily walked over and gave Diocles' shoulder a quick pat. "I was already going to join you once you mentioned your reasoning. I just prefer to see if I can get more information out of someone before I let them hire my people. The fact I remember your father certainly improved your chances as well."

Drysten rose from his seat, and the two men shook hands. "We should discuss your payment. Also how many men can we expect?"

"Well, that wholly depends on what you can afford," Titus replied.

"Let me speak with my people for a moment," Drysten requested.

"Of course." Titus then bowed his head and left the room with the guard stationed near the door.

Drysten then turned to his men. "Go outside and tell Cynwrig and Petras to go back to the ship. Have them tell Amiram to take half of the gold out of the box and to send it here."

"I'll tell them to hurry," Paulus replied as he rose from his seat and moved through the door.

Diocles slyly glanced to see if anyone could hear them then turned to his captain. "Only using half the gold would mean quite a few men would be left unhired."

Drysten nodded. "You are correct, but contrary to what the king and my father believed, hiring a whole army would be counterproductive to what we are trying to accomplish."

"Care to let me in on what you're planning?" Diocles asked.

Drysten smiled. "I can't say I have a plan. I simply know it would serve us better not to march into Servius' lands with an army."

Diocles leaned back and shrugged. "I suppose knowing what not to do can be just as critical."

Drysten and Diocles waited for roughly an hour until the Cynwrig and the Cretans returned with the gold. Amiram had done what Drysten directed and emptied half of the wealth into a separate bag to be saved aboard the ship. Upon gaining entry to Titus' villa, the guard at the gate led them into the back room. Titus was instructing Drysten on the soundest method to beat a phalanx by using an old lamp and bundles of parchment as his props.

"Pinch the *sides,* boy! Hit them there and the whole thing collapses unto itself." Titus imitated something shriveling by bringing his hands closer together.

Drysten leaned forward. "You do recall the Romans had elephants when they fought the Greeks, do you not?"

Titus leaned back in his chair. "A student of history, are you?" he responded with an impressed grin. "Your father must have spoken much of ancient battles between Rome and her enemies."

"Not my father, no. Truthfully, I don't think he even knew of a great many. It was my mother," he responded with a smile.

"Ah," Titus replied solemnly, "I recall her being a bright one. The children of nobles typically are."

Drysten was about to ask precisely what Titus remembered about his mother until Cynwrig thumped the chest down onto the desk, slowly lifting its lid to reveal the contents.

Titus' eyes widened for a fleeting moment. "Money is the soul of war."

"Spoken like a true Roman," Drysten responded. He had heard such expressions from other soldiers fighting for Rome in the last few years of their occupation in Britannia. He may have been very young at the time, but anything a true Roman legionnaire said always carried weight to him.

"Judging by how much I see…" Titus slid his hands of the assortment of wealth in the chest. "I would guess this could amount to roughly fifty of my fighters."

"You would be commanding them?" Drysten inquired.

Titus nodded and pointed a finger to his chest. "I go wherever my men do. A good commander always does, and while I am not a good commander, I may as well act the part."

The men in the room all smiled at Titus' jest. Everyone silently understood this man was not only a good leader but a man worthy of their trust, something which Drysten knew was just as essential.

The negotiations took much less time than Drysten and his companions anticipated. It was ultimately decided that Titus would have fifty men, as well as himself, sail with them. To Drysten's delight, the general appeared excited at the prospect of fighting beside the son of somebody he served with.

Titus proceeded to his nearby barracks to inform his people of their new employment. "They'll be happy to hear they won't need to drill for a little while. You can head to your vessel and we'll join you there at sunup," Titus declared.

Drysten stood and happily nodded, then left for the Fortuna with his company in tow. Diocles was skeptical of Drysten's plan to not take additional men and save half of the gold for themselves, but his doubts were put to rest when he finally goaded Drysten into explaining himself.

"The man is a merchant, is he not?" Drysten asked him, prompting the Greek to nod. "Since he's a *merchant,* he wouldn't be alarmed by a ship containing only a small force making port on his shores. We will simply state we are looking for... his merchandise."

"So, we're going to trick them?"

"The one thing I know of the man is he happens to be a greedy slob of a man. He's going to see the oppurtunity to make himself that much richer, then invite us into his home. *That* is when we end him," Drysten declared.

Cynwrig moved up alongside Diocles. "What if they have more men than we do?"

"I doubt that." Drysten responded with a shake of his head. "In Burdigala, he always arrived with about fifty men of his own, and that was only after my father made it known he was unwelcome. He thought he needed protection."

"Did he?" An interested Diocles asked.

"My father simply didn't want any more of his slave markets popping up. He had no intention of killing him, though he should have."

The group followed the main road to the bridge where they began to cross to the northern side of the river. The sun was setting over the water, manifesting an orange sheen across the waves. The men all stopped and marveled at the sight when they reached the halfway point on the bridge. This section consisted of a draw bridge which could be lifted to bar an enemy from making it across the river should the need arise. One of the many protections built into the city's defenses to prevent another sacking.

After the group had finished taking in the sights, they kept moving North and eventually crossed to the other side. The Fortuna was to the east, docked on a bank near some old Roman baths that had been built a couple centuries prior.

They turned right, after which Cynwrig tapped Drysten on the shoulder. "Crew could use a break, Lord. I thought since we have a night here, we should encourage them to walk the city," Cynwrig suggested.

"Let the men have their fun. Just make sure they're back by sunup," Drysten commanded with a nod.

The five men walked further East toward the ship, slowly making their way through a small, alarmed looking crowd gathered for some unknown reason. Drysten gave Diocles a perplexed look, then began gently moving people aside as he stepped through. When they had arrived within sight of the Fortuna, they saw two bodies of King Ceneus' black-clad men laying on the ground near the foot of the ramp leading onto the ship.

"Gods above...," Drysten whispered as he drew his weapon.

The five men moved quickly toward the now apparent racket of combat coming from the Fortuna. A group of men led by Amiram was fighting two of the rowers, the names of which Drysten did not know. Drysten watched as Amiram parried a blow from one man before hitting him in the chin with his off hand, spiraling him back a step before Amiram thrust his sword into the man's chest from the side. The man screamed in pain as Amiram slowly drew his blade back, withdrawing it and spattering blood onto the Fortuna's deck.

Another one of his foes noticed the mute was turned away from him, and swiped lower into Amiram's side. Amiram never noticed the man coming toward him until he was already within striking distance. The blade swept across his rib, grazing him well enough to draw a grunt, along with some blood from the wound. The mute fell to a knee, but to Drysten's surprise was saved by Jorrit, who lifted Amiram's sword and plunged it down as the shocked traitor moved forward to finish off Amiram. The dying man gave the Frisian a horrified look of surprise as he began to say something, yet was finished off with a stroke through the side of his head. Jorrit sent him down to the ground near a new bright blue sail that had yet to replace the old white one, spraying droplets of fresh blood across its edges.

At the time of the exchange, Drysten and his five companions had just rushed aboard, leaping over the handful of bodies in their way. Amiram's group consisted of fifty or so men, but most were unarmed and looking to avoid a fight. The men Drysten presumed to be the traitors numbered at about two dozen frantic-looking rowers and a handful of Ceneus' guards. All of them glanced at Drysten as he made his way onto the ship, then chose to jump over the side to avoid him.

"What's happened!?" Drysten bellowed as the traitors were still leaping into the water.

Amiram walked forward, holding his side as a small trickle of blood ran through his fingers. He slightly lurched forward from the pain as he nodded his head toward Magnus, beckoning him over.

"Speak, Magnus," Drysten ordered.

The man eyed Amiram's fresh wound as he walked toward Drysten. "Lord, that bastard talked Ceneus' men into stealing our coin and making off with it. Most of the men who joined him left moments before you returned."

"That bastard?" Drysten said in confusion. He glanced around until he finally understood who the man in question could be. The one person who every single person on the crew hated above all. "Maurianus," Drysten whispered angrily.

Jorrit slowly stepped up to Drysten. "Your king's men followed him. They killed the ones put in charge of guarding your wealth, then began threatening others who seemed to consider checking them."

Drysten cursed under his breath then looked to Amiram. "Which way did Maurianus and his little following take our coin?"

Amiram reflected for a moment, then pointed North toward the city's old forum which had once been used by the Roman military governors who dwelled there in the past.

Drysten looked over the men who had stayed loyal, then told the bulk of them to remain with the ship before turning back to Amiram. "You're in charge here," he ordered, prompting the man to shake his head in disagreement before being hushed by Drysten. "You're already wounded. I don't want to lose you before the real fight begins." Drysten looked through his men to figure out which man could track someone through a city, and then the wilderness if he was not found in time. "Dagonet, where are you?" Prompting the scout to step forward carrying a bloody sword.

"Find him?" The scout enthusiastically suggested.

"Take Petras and Paulus with you. You're to go North outside the city and prevent him from escaping altogether. Diocles and Magnus, come with me. We're going to try to stop him from getting that far. Amiram, take another group of four and send them with Cynwrig across the river." Drysten turned to his childhood friend. "You're to go back across and request for Titus to watch that side of the river." Drysten's three groups quickly left the Fortuna, with each turning in a separate direction depending on their instructions.

At least we may make it hard for him to escape. Drysten thought as he began rushing through the streets. It must have been a strange sight for the residents of the city, as armed strangers were frantically storming past them. Before long, the three men made their way into the large open area of the forum, which was teeming with people apparently celebrating the start of spring. Despite Drysten, Magnus, and Diocles all being armed, the people still managed to obstruct them from moving freely through the crowds.

"Anyone from the crew we can trust is on the ship. Anyone else is with Maurianus!" Drysten shouted. "If you see a familiar face then go after him!"

The three men forced their way into the crowd, where Diocles pointed out a stairway leading up to into the basilica positioned in the central area of the forum. Drysten dashed up the stairs with his two companions, trying their best not to push over the many locals in their way.

The men lingered for a few moments as they each thoroughly scanned the crowd. Despite their hope of spotting something from a higher vantage point, they came up empty and decided to move to the Western parts of the city. The three men briefly paused outside the forum, glancing around through the joyous faces of revelers.

"Could be hiding by the temples. There are a few two streets over," Diocles said.

Drysten cocked an eyebrow. "How do you know that?"

"Overheard someone speaking of them in the crowd earlier. Apparently, some bishop recently visited the city and riled up a few mobs against the gods of the islands."

"Lovely," Drysten replied in frustration. "More fucking people to wade through."

The outer streets were significantly easier to move through due to the festivities attracting most of the locals to the forum. The men dashed madly through alleyways and courtyards, eventually finding their way to the temple of Mithras, a god from Persia that was popular with Roman soldiers throughout the empire many years ago. The temple was an underground building known as a Mithraeum, hiding below a more substantial building which seemed to be in the process of being converted into a Christian church. Some Christian priests were preaching in the front, but upon Diocles approaching them, they halted their preaching, with one pointing toward the newcomers.

"You!" the man said as he pointed to Drysten. "Give up your dangerous practices of immorality and worship the one true God!" the priest exclaimed. In response, the three men awkwardly glanced to one another.

"What...?" Drysten simply returned.

The priest grew louder as he tried to make his voice reach a small crowd of people standing nearby. "You *glorify* false idols! Your soul will be doomed to the infinite abyss of hell for all eternity unless you repent! Repent and feel our Lord's grace." The man held both hands toward the sky as if he were a child waiting to be picked up by his mother. All Drysten thought to do was give a ponderous look to an equally confused Diocles.

"Did you see a man running through here carrying a large bag of coins?" Magnus calmly inquired.

The priest turned and noticed a crucifix hanging around Magnus' neck. "You serve this man though he carries the symbol of a false god?"

"The pay is good," Magnus replied with a shrug.

The priest gasped at the response. "Then your greed will be the cause of your soul following *his* into the pits of hell!" The man jabbed a finger toward Drysten.

Diocles half drew his weapon and calmly stepped toward the priest. "Did you see anyone or not?" he demanded sternly.

The priest glanced down at Diocles' weapon and looked to his companion for help. Surprisingly, the other priest merely stared back at him as though he was alone in the matter. "I... will embrace the chance to gaze upon the Lord with mine own eyes," he responded, his voice trailing off.

The additional priest quietly smirked as he stepped in front of his companion. "Ignore him, Lord. He's simply mesmerized by our Lord and savior." Drysten was surprised to hear the sarcasm in this priest's voice. "It is either that or he is trying to behave while the good Bishop Germanus' people are near. We saw a small group of men moving toward the Ludgate, looking over their shoulders as if being chased not long ago. I'd be happy to show you if you do not know the way."

"Was that so difficult?" Diocles said to the priest who was obviously still trying to think of a way to protest the situation.

"Follow me, Lord," the priest kindly said as he motioned for Drysten and his company to follow. "My name is Matthew by the way."

"A pleasure, I'm Drysten ap Hall."

"Don't take the man's tone personal, Lord. I was told he followed Mithras when he served the empire," Matthew began. "They kicked him out of the temple one day. I think he was stealing offerings or some such thing."

Diocles scoffed from behind the two. "Hold's a bit of a vendetta then?"

Matthew nodded. "Seems to."

"Ironic," Drysten put in.

The priest cocked his head to the side. "Ironic, Lord?"

"Mithras is the god of brotherhood. Doesn't sound as though the man was particularly brotherly," Drysten replied.

Matthew showed a slight grin. "Ironic, indeed. Spends most of his day trying to prevent people from entering the temple. He got worse once Bishop Germanus arrived to shout down the Pelagians."

Drysten was about to inquire who the Pelagians were until his thoughts were interrupted by Magnus. "Lord!" he whispered as he pointed toward a tavern. In the middle of the crowd were Maurianus, a couple of the other crew members, and the rest of King Ceneus' men.

Drysten turned and slowly backed into an alleyway, followed by his companions and the priest. "Magnus, go find Dagonet by the North gate and tell him where we are." Drysten then turned to Diocles. "Go get Cynwrig and his men and bring them here. They are likely awaiting nightfall before making a move out of the city."

The two men nodded and proceeded down the parallel street to avoid being seen by the traitors. That just left Drysten and the priest who guided him to his prize.

"Thank you for the help, priest," Drysten said as he glanced at Matthew.

"You're very welcome, Lord. This is the most exciting thing that's happened to me since my arrival to this city. Other than the occasional scuffle in a tavern," Matthew stated.

Drysten chuckled. "You don't really remind me of other priests I've met."

"I'm still studying to become one, though not by choice," Matthew replied. "I'm the youngest of four sons. The chance of inheriting anything from my father is next to nothing, as it was all taken long ago. This was simply the only occupation with the guarantee of a meal and shelter."

"That's unfortunate. How was it all taken from your family?" Drysten inquired.

Matthew sighed. "We followed the usurper." Drysten knew he meant Constantine, who had attempted to take the imperial throne about twenty years prior. He was elevated to the position of emperor, going from soldier to monarch with the support of the legions stationed in Britannia. Drysten's father and a handful of his men had followed the man to war shortly thereafter.

This was obviously a sore subject for the priest, so Drysten decided not to press him any further. The two men stood in an alleyway while they observed the traitors' movements. Maurianus had gone inside but was peeking out of a window in the tavern every so often. The others in his following were wandering around the courtyard to alert him if they had been found. Unlucky for them, they had been found for about fifteen minutes before Drysten's full group of companions had returned. With them, was Titus.

Once Drysten noticed the group, he sent Matthew through the crowded street to warn them about being seen, and instructed them to stay out of sight one alley away from the tavern.

Upon seeing Drysten, Titus smiled and greeted him, wearing full war gear and trailed by a dozen of his own men dressed in the same manner. "Drysten!" Titus said with a smile.

Drysten was surprised by the band of men he had brought with him. "You are a welcome surprise, Titus."

Titus patted Drysten on the back. "Don't worry, I posted sentries outside each gate but this one. The guards employed to watch the city know to be on the lookout as well. Also, you may want to talk to your man about divulging too much information. If he had told anyone else but me there was gold to be taken…" he let his voice trail off.

Drysten wheeled around to an embarrassed Cynwrig. "You told him *everything?*" To which the man nodded. "Cynwrig…"

Titus interrupted him by putting his hand on Drysten's

shoulder. "All is well, boy. I don't steal. Though I wouldn't be opposed to maybe renegotiating our arrangement to account for our services being utilized in advance."

"Deal," Drysten agreed, though he had little choice otherwise.

The men under Titus' command were now getting ready for a potential fight when one accidentally stepped within sight of the tavern, causing Maurianus to catch a quick glimpse of a fully armored soldier. He sprang out of the tavern window and yelled for his small band of men to follow.

Upon seeing this, Drysten just pointed and shouted, "Go!"

The large group of men began their pursuit, startling everyone who was near enough to witness it. Drysten was weighed down because of the bear cloak draped over his shoulders, but even so was having an easier time keeping up with Maurianus than Titus, whose age was starting to show as he immediately fell behind. Drysten heard the clanking of swords and armor behind him and wondered if they stood a chance at overcoming the lighter-footed Maurianus.

None of our people can move fast enough to catch them, he thought.

Drysten was running through a crowded street toward the Ludgate when suddenly he was passed by Diocles and Matthew. "You're still here?" he shouted as he ran through the streets.

Matthew panted as he ran ahead. "Yes, Lord. Thought I would help you a bit longer!"

"Catch him, and you gain a spot on my crew! You won't need to worry about becoming a priest any longer." Drysten shouted, spurring his new acquaintance onward.

Eventually, the group found their way to the Ludgate, where Maurianus and his men had killed the guards stationed there and run through. Drysten turned and instructed Dagonet to find their tracks, which he quickly detected running North, parallel to the wall.

"Odd choice of direction," Dagonet declared as he continued onward, though Drysten did not know why he believed this.

The two men were soon joined by the rest of their companions as they ran beside the wall of the city. They were quickly aware why the traitors had chosen the area. The grounds had winding paths which were overgrown in the spaces without headstones, giving them ample cover to hide behind. What's more, the tracks split up once they touched the edges of the graveyard.

"They must be trying to blend the tracks with those belonging to the people visiting their dead," Dagonet observed. The scout kneeled and touched the edge of the closest track.

"Will this make it harder to find them?" Drysten asked as they paused near a monument dedicated to a prominent Roman centurion. While awaiting the scout's answer, Drysten glanced over the ornate piece of stone and the man must have died fighting near the city long ago. "The stalwart defender," Drysten whispered aloud. The Latin inscription was worn, but still readable.

Dagonet finally stood and smiled. "This won't help them. Or maybe it would if *I* wasn't the one hunting them."

Cynwrig, Matthew and Diocles then approached. Upon joining together, the five men set off northward after telling the others to spread out and find anyone they could. Soon, Dagonet ran across the tracks of four people running in the direction of a farmstead not far from the walls. Although it was about a hundred yards away, Drysten was sure he spotted a man looking out through a window in a barn.

"There," Drysten announced as he gestured toward the home.

Diocles stepped forward and moved toward a group of bushes most likely used to designate property boundaries. "I'll circle round. Cynwrig, come with me," he whispered.

"Stay behind cover whenever possible."

Drysten agreed. "Keep low and out of sight. Once everyone else catches up, we'll move on the barn." He then turned to Matthew. "Round up anyone you can find and tell them where we are."

"Yes, Lord," the priest replied.

The three men moved off in their respective directions, leaving Drysten and Dagonet to watch over the area where they expected to find their prey.

CHAPTER VI

The warmness of the sun was now beginning to dissipate as it slowly set behind the Western hills. Drysten and Dagonet had been laying low beneath the branches reaching out from a cluster of trees when they were joined by the rest of the men. It had been roughly an hour since they found the barn where they suspected Maurianus and his fellow traitors held their gold. Just to be sure nobody had crept out the back, Dagonet had circled around to look for tracks. None were found, and Dagonet returned to Drysten with news of Cynwrig and Diocles being able to see if anyone would try and leave through that area. The flatness of the fields would make it easy to spot anyone trying to escape, provided the sun was still up.

"We should be able to see them from here until they get behind those hills," Dagonet pointed out as he gestured West.

Drysten nodded. "I would prefer to wait for them to come out into the open before we make a move on them. Though, I suspect they will hide behind whoever owns that home if it comes to it." Drysten peered behind him as he noticed the thumping of approaching footsteps.

"Ran back to the ship and brought our bows, Lord," a man announced from behind Drysten.

Drysten shifted in the dirt as he trained his attention to the men behind him. He was pleased to see Petras and Paulus crouched down behind him. "Don't miss," he replied with a grin.

Both Cretans scoffed and moved in beside Drysten and Dagonet, waiting for their opportunity to rain arrows down on the traitors if they tried to flee.

"Works better if we can *see* them," an annoyed Petras stated.

"We'll need to move on them before the sun goes down, Lord," Dagonet suggested. "I'm a good tracker, but it's easier during the day than the night."

Drysten glanced over his shoulder at the men waiting for his orders, then back to the farmhouse. "Bring me Titus," he commanded.

Matthew took a moment when he realized everyone was assuming he would be the one to go fetch the general. He finally moved back behind the bushes and shortly after, Titus crawled up beside Drysten, who turned back to give him his orders. "Take your men and surround the barn. Use the other men I haven't placed anywhere as well. Nobody leaves."

Titus beamed. "Such excitement from a man I've only just met today!"

Drysten chuckled. "Send someone back when your men are in place. Also, I do not want any innocents they may have in their grasp to be harmed for any reason. Especially not for gold."

Titus gave an approving nod. "I will let our people know."

The general nodded and left, leaving only Drysten and Dagonet near the trees just South of the barn. A brisk wind had begun to pick up, making the leaves above them dance and sway. Drysten knew this would typically be favorable weather for an evening of merriment and was sad it was spoiled by the actions of a few. He would have preferred for his men to be spending their only night of rest inside Londinium's taverns or old Roman baths, but was hopeful the situation would be over with enough time left over for such activities.

The two men waited for no more than ten minutes and were then alerted by Titus' second in command that the men were now in place. "They call me Bastakas, Lord. We're ready for whatever you're about to do."

Drysten wearily turned and nodded, then glanced at Dagonet before standing up, unbuckling his father's bear cloak, and walking toward the barn. "Petras, Paulus, follow us until you reach a distance you think you can hit your targets from." Dagonet and Bastakas both joined him with their hands on their weapons, ready to draw them for a fight if the need arose.

As they walked, Drysten saw a faint, dark figure peek through an open window on the South side of the home. "Whoever's in there knows we're coming," he warned. As he got within about fifty yards from the farmstead, he glanced back and noticed both Cretans had vanished. "Did they even follow us?" he asked Dagonet in surprise.

Dagonet smiled in amusement. "Most likely just walked with us to hear what your order was. Quite gifted with a bow they are. Also, the priest picked up your cloak and brought it behind the bushes."

"Seems I accidentally hired a servant," Drysten said sarcastically.

Dagonet chuckled. "I believe he wants you to save him from whatever life he has here. I would do so, if I were you. Men like that typically serve a lord well."

"I have certainly been giving it thought, as I'm sure you could guess," Drysten responded. "He would need to learn to fight properly."

"I'm certain the general would be happy to help along the way to Frisia. He taught many of the king's men."

Drysten chuckled. "I'm beginning to enjoy Matthew's presence. I wouldn't want anyone teaching him to be a traitor." Dagonet smirked as he slowly glanced from Drysten to the barn.

The men were now thirty yards off when they could

detect a faint shuffling noise coming from the house. Drysten met Dagonet's gaze for a brief moment before turning back to eyeball the building as they stopped. They were now roughly twenty yards off from the noise of shuffling feet.

Get them to turn on each other, a voice hummed. Drysten instantly recognized it was not the malevolent one which had been plaguing him recently. Instead, it was a gentler one resembling that of his father.

Drysten glanced to the ground as he tried to comprehend what the voice was instructing. "Get them to turn...," he whispered. "Wait here," he commanded as he raised his head and stole a few extra steps forward. "Maurianus! Give me the gold and leave with your life."

For a few moments, there was an eerie silence in which nothing was heard from the home. Drysten began to wonder whether they had been mistaken and were merely stalking some poor family who had to be terrified at the sight of armed men encircling their home. Just when Drysten was about to turn back and order up Dagonet and Bastakas to join him, there came a woman's scream, and the front door sprang open. A frantic, blood-covered woman ran out toward Drysten waving a knife. In response, he held up his hand in the direction he assumed the Cretans were hiding, signaling not to loose any arrows. The woman ran almost right up to Drysten before finally dropping the knife and nearly collapsing into his arms.

"The man sought to kill me!" she screeched.

Drysten held her up gently. "What man?" He asked.

The woman began to cry as Drysten began inspecting her to find where the blood had come from. To his surprise, he found no wound, understanding then it was not from her.

"What man!?" Drysten insisted.

She peered up into Drysten's eyes. "One'oo took your gold," she finally explained. "Broke in 'n wanted to hide. Killed me father and tied me brother and sister up with me. I got away when one cut me loose to…" her voice trailed off.

Drysten sneered at what the woman worked to say, then shouted loud enough for anyone nearby to hear him. "They're in the house!" As he shouted, he listened to the thunderous footsteps of his men converging on the home. "Nobody enters! They have more captives!" Drysten's men got close enough to prevent anyone from leaving, but far enough away to prevent spooking Maurianus into harming his captives. He gestured for Dagonet to care for the woman, then moved to about ten feet from the front entrance of the home.

"Maurianus, I can't let you leave here alive," Drysten began, "but if your men surrender now, I will allow them to leave here freely. Nobody will stop them, but only if you've been given up."

Upon presenting the offer, there was an eerie pause. Drysten overheard frantic muttering from inside the house, soon followed by shouting. Drysten knew he would be dooming the innocents still inside if his men rushed in to try and take the gold back, and decided following the voice's advice was the surest way to try and prevent that.

"Make your decision!"

After a few moments, he heard a great deal of shuffling, grunting, and a clearly audible struggle emanating from inside the house, shortly followed by yet another woman's scream.

"Don't kill us, Lord. We'll come out," an unfamiliar and unmistakably frightened voice announced as the door began to open.

Drysten elevated his hand once more to prevent any arrows from the Cretans. "Slowly," he commanded, as three men gradually emerged from the home. All three were darting their eyes between the many men circling the home as they walked toward Drysten with their hands raised.

"We surrender, Lord," one stated before slowly taking out his sword and laying it on the ground. Drysten recognized him as the rower who jumped overboard when he had first returned to the Fortuna. The second man, clad in black, followed suit. Then the third, also one of Ceneus' men, was gripping Maurianus by the hair as he led him toward Drysten. The traitor wore a calm, yet disgruntled expression as blood gushed from his nose. Evidently a product of whatever struggle took place within the home. Drysten glared into the traitor's eyes as he was violently forced down to his knees by the man leading him.

"Which one of you killed the girl's father?" Drysten demanded from the group. The three men responded by motioning toward their leader, who merely shrugged and smiled back.

"Which one of you murdered a guard?" Drysten followed.

The second man to leave the house took on a wide-eyed look of panic as he began to gaze from his companions to Drysten. Upon realizing he would have to fight his way out to have any chance of surviving, he clumsily snatched up his sword and attempted to hack into Drysten's neck. Drysten quickly drew his blade and easily deflected the blow away. As he was trying to strike downward into his attacker's leg, an arrow tore through the air and embedded itself to the fletching through the man's neck.

The man's eyes went even wider as he dropped his sword and thrust a hand up to cover the wound. He locked eyes with Drysten, who felt no pity, until he slowly dropped to his knees. The blood trickled through his fingers onto the black cloak before the man slumped over, gagging and groaning. Drysten had a brief thought of easing the man's journey into the afterlife, but ultimately decided a man guilty of murder wasn't worth any kind of mercy. The man slowly bled out on his knees, and the gasping stopped entirely as he gently fell all the way forward.

"Lord, what are we to do with the others?" Dagonet inquired.

Drysten pondered for a moment. He understood he gave

them his word they would not be punished should they turn over their leader, but he also understood a handful of them were now murderers. Drysten turned to Bastakas. "Untie their other hostages and have them brought to me."

"Yes, Lord," Bastakas returned.

The two captives were brought forward right as the hostages emerged from the house. The woman who was lucky enough to escape dashed toward her siblings and lovingly embraced them both.

Drysten walked toward the family, attempting to speak through a calm tone in the hopes they understood his sympathy. "Can you tell me which ones are murderers? Who tried to keep their hands clean?"

The lone male of the three children moved forward. "The man with the arrow in his neck bragged about killing a pair of guards. Another man said he killed a man on a boat, but he ran off North after the leader... the leader..." The boy began to cry as he pointed to Maurianus, the man that killed his father.

"I lost a parent too, once. My mother," Drysten whispered, placing a hand on the young man's shoulder. "I lost my mother when I was ten. All we can do for our parents is to honor their memory when they pass." The boy peered up at Drysten before he sorrowfully hung his head.

"Your mother was a fucking *whore,* boy! Mother to a murdering bastard!" yelled a seemingly crazed Maurianus.

"The opinions of dead men hold no weight with me," Drysten coolly responded.

"Aye, and what of the opinions of your *own* victims? The ones from the forests," Maurianus whispered with a smile.

Drysten felt a pit form in his stomach. Most of the men around him had no idea what was done in response to their home being raided by barbarians, but Drysten knew. He knew because he led the reprisals against them. Something he would prefer stayed between him and the handful of others who joined him.

"Struck a soft spot, have I?" Maurianus quietly uttered with a smirk. "I wonder, does the wailing still trouble you? The women were unquestionably the loudest, but it was good we kept some of the men alive to watch."

Drysten glanced down at his feet, almost unable to speak as the memories of that day flared up in his mind.

Maurianus' eyes tightly closed as he threw his head back and began to madly cackle. He knew he was a dead man, but he also knew he could still cause Drysten a small measure of grief before he was ultimately flung into the afterlife. "So proud you were. Drenched in *blood* and *guts* like a true warrior. How long was it before your father was able to look you in the eye?"

Magnus moved up beside Drysten. "Lord, just take the fucker's head and be done with it!"

Drysten was disgusted with himself as he remembered the look on his father's face when he returned. The sight of his loyal men covered in the blood of unarmed and defenseless people clearly made him nauseous. The few fighters the Saxon families had defending them that day were no match for Drysten and his men. Their husbands and fathers had almost taken the city until Hall's defense had been rallied and the attackers had been driven back. A small group of the raiders attempted an escape into the woods surrounding the city, prompting many of Hall's men to follow Drysten in pursuit.

He led them to the forests in an effort to deter further raiding by other tribes. If word got out about Burdigala's shoddy defenses, others would surely come to rape and plunder. And that was something Drysten obviously wished to prevent. He expected to find warriors to kill, not families of those who died in the city. But his own men had just watched their friends perish at the hands of the raiders. In a fit of fury, they erupted out of the woods and flooded into the camp to end the life of anyone they saw.

Maurianus played a role in the worst moment he had

ever seen, a sight which haunted him every time he closed his eyes. Drysten, Amiram, and a few others had both been hacking their way through the few combatants worth worrying about as the rest of the company converged on the families. One man fought savagely to protect a pile of blankets for some odd reason. Upon Drysten cutting into his leg and Amiram slicing down the back of his neck, the two slowly sauntered over to have a look.

"Whatever he hid there must be precious to him if he died defending it," Amiram observed. He was still the happy owner of a working tongue at that time. The soon-to-be mute cautiously glanced around before finally pulling the blankets aside to reveal the only treasure worth protecting to the now fallen Saxon. A young boy, teary-eyed from witnessing his father brutally cut down, slowly began crawling backward.

Drysten remembered the shocked expression on Amiram's face as the two men each paused to witness the carnage around them. Hall always prided himself for hiring good souls, but those good souls were now engaging in a massacre, annihilating the innocent families of the people who had assaulted the city. Most of their own families suffered the same treatment from the Saxons, but before that moment there was a sense of their people being better than the barbaric invaders. Now, that sense of worth was utterly abandoned as the men hacked down the defenseless women and children. Each of their screams seemed to take a piece of Drysten with them as they all gradually faded away into nothingness.

"Lord...," Amiram had whispered to Drysten. "Lord, we... we need to..."

Drysten turned back to the boy, who was now as pale as the snow beneath his feet. He slowly lowered his weapon and began to gently walk toward the boy, unsure of what to do next. He simply understood this boy did not deserve a fate like the one befallen his people who were madly wailing for mercy all around them.

"Lord!" Amiram had screamed, though Drysten was in a state of shock and scarcely heard him. The voices in his mind were screaming of his shame, drowning Amiram or the dead and dying.

Drysten dropped his blade to the snowy dirt and held out a hand to the boy, who seemed to understand his only option was to walk forward. Then the axe struck him in the back of the head, and his body slumped forward. Drysten must have stared into the bloodied snow around the young boy for quite a long time before he finally raised his eyes to meet the gaze of the man who had done the deed.

"The small ones turn into big ones, Lord. Much easier to kill them before then," Maurianus had stated through a blood-soaked grin before jubilantly running off to further satiate his appetite for death. Drysten knew from that moment on, the day would haunt him. He knew he would forever be staring into the eyes of a young boy searching for mercy.

Maurianus had continued his berating of Drysten for a few moments, but his target was lost in the flashbacks of his actions. Drysten heard little of what was said, just knew he wished to end the man in front of him. Maurianus had played a role in stoking the wish for vengeance that day in the forest and Drysten simply wished to see him turned into nothing more than another corpse.

Give him death, the malicious voice demanded.

Drysten finally broke from the painful memory and raised his head. Maurianus' smile began to fade as he understood what was going to happen next. Drysten took slow, deliberate steps forward, never breaking eye contact until he was right over the man. The Roman blade in his hand slowly began to raise as Maurianus closed his eyes.

"No!" screamed the young voice from behind him. "I have to kill him!"

Drysten abruptly turned. "You don't have to do anything, boy!" Drysten turned back, ready to strike when the boy began to protest once again.

He was now stepping toward Drysten, fidgeting with his white tunic as he moved. "He killed my father, Lord. It should be me."

Drysten considered ignoring the boy and simply finishing the job himself, but found his sword arm lowering. He glanced around, then closed his eyes for a moment before finally walking over to the boy, who took the blade in his hand. "Slice his throat if you want him to bleed out quickly. If not, simply start poking him until he stops screaming," Drysten instructed as he stepped back to watch.

The boy tensely looked from Maurianus to his sisters as he understood what he was about to do. It was clear to everyone around them the boy had never taken a soul, which wasn't surprising considering his age. His movements seemed careful and deliberate. He hoisted the sword up over his head, pausing for a moment to glance at Drysten, then brought it down into the base of his prey's neck, causing Maurianus to shriek in agony. The wail made the boy spring back in fright until he understood he couldn't stop. After a nod from Drysten, he again moved toward his victim, and awkwardly raised the sword up before violently hacking it down. After about seven or eight swings into various parts of his body, Maurianus' screaming began to turn to stomach-churning gurgles. The man was reduced to a mangled pool of blood, while the boy kept swinging through his tears. Each scream awoke the frantic memories of the wailing innocents from the forests of Burdigala in Drysten's mind. Each time Maurianus gurgled for a merciful end, a woman or child could be heard beckoning for the justice to continue.

Drysten allowed the boy to go on for a moment after the gurgles ceased. Diocles noticed as well and crept up next to him. "He is dead, Lord," the Greek whispered. "I gathered he has an unfavorable history with your people, but he is gone now."

Drysten calmly nodded and stepped toward the butchery taking place. "Boy," Drysten called. "That's enough," he asserted in a calming tone. The boy paused and dropped the sword at his feet, then slowly walked over to his sisters, who both brought him into their arms.

Drysten picked up his sword and walked inside the home, accompanied by Dagonet and Diocles, all in search of the wealth which had been temporarily stolen from them. The home was modest, and had various cooking utensils hanging from rafters below the thatch roof. The interior smelled like a combination of thatch from the roofing, smoke from the recently stoked cooking fire, and death from the old man whose body now lay near its entrance. Drysten gazed around and was instantly reminded of his home in Burdigala. While it had been much bigger than his current surroundings, it had the same feeling of warmth, which seemed to grip you upon stepping inside.

"This had been a happy home but a few short hours ago," Drysten said to no one in particular.

"Wealth, Lord. Wealth does this to people," Dagonet responded as he looked on the corpse of the old man.

The bag was quickly discovered behind a table which had been knocked over. Some of its contents had spilled just behind it. Diocles slowly walked around the dead man and began to pick up the mess of gold and silver that now lay on the packed dirt floor.

"Wait," Drysten stated as he raised a hand, "give the people here what was scattered about."

Diocles nodded and used his hands to sweep the coins into a neat pile before placing them on the table after Drysten stood it back on its legs. It was not much of the bag's original amount, but it would certainly help the family for the near future.

Drysten and Dagonet walked outside to see one of the women being held by Magnus, who looked somewhat awkward in his response. Drysten slowly walked over to Titus as the people around all stole glances of the hacked-up body on the ground. "Get your men ready to depart tomorrow. We leave at sunup."

Titus nodded and relayed the news to his men, then turned and bid the family farewell. Titus turned to Drysten with a quizzical look as he shuffled toward him. "What was the traitor speaking of? I typically do not miss the mark on my judgments of a person, but I heard him speak of murder."

Drysten awkwardly looked from Titus to the still oozing corpse near the house. "When I was young, my home was attacked. We were nearly overwhelmed until my father forced them back. I chased after the stragglers through the surrounding forests. Their families were with them."

"What happened next?" Titus inquired, appearing as though he both knew the answer and did not wish to hear it.

"A mistake."

Titus stiffly gazed at Drysten, who he could see was ashamed of whatever had been done. "I am no stranger to those, my boy. Sadly, I made them often enough under the Roman banner, but no more," Titus replied quietly.

Drysten nodded before looking at the men who were being held captive. "Dig a grave," he sternly commanded as he began to walk away. "One grave. Not for the traitor, but for the old man inside. Then you are to throw the traitor's body into the river, and pray you never cross paths with me or these people again." Drysten turned to his men and instructed Magnus and the Cretans to linger until the traitors were finished, then return to the ship.

Drysten was leading his men away from the scene when he began to hear the shouting of a woman and turned back. One of the prisoners had requested tools to dig the old man's grave and was instead given a gash along his cheek from the oldest sister. She had picked the knife back up from the ground and done the damage as Drysten's three men watched in amusement.

"Dig with your hands!" the woman screamed as she

waved the knife.

Drysten chuckled as he returned to walk back toward the city when Matthew sauntered up carrying his cloak. "Saved it for you, Lord," Matthew stated as he helped Drysten clasp it around his shoulders. "Very nice piece, indeed, Lord."

"It belongs to my father. Never realized how heavy it was until I began wearing it myself," Drysten replied as they all kept moving.

"I was hoping, Lord—"

"Grab your things; you're leaving with us tomorrow."

"Thank you, Lord!" Matthew replied through a broad smile.

The group silently traveled back through the city and eventually reached the Fortuna to see the crew awaiting to hear what occurred. Diocles wasted no time in relaying all that happened to the crew, who for the most part was happy with the way things turned out. Though there were undoubtedly some who believed every one of the men should have been executed, Drysten explained he made them a deal and felt it necessary to honor his end.

"Honorable men are easy to betray, Drysten," Jorrit said cautiously.

Drysten smirked as he looked to the Frisian. "Good thing you will find none of those where we're headed."

Accompanied by sparse rain spreading from the West, daybreak finally arrived to rouse the men aboard the Fortuna. Though it was a slight rain, the wind which accompanied it proved to be a huge development. With a wind blowing directly East, it would mean the crew could reach their destination that much sooner, and hopefully liberate their people.

The Cretans were especially happy with the good omen. Despite Drysten being friendly enough with the pair, he had only just found out the night before that they were only half-brothers despite their resemblance. The two of them were there under the assumption their sister had been taken along with Isolde.

Another element Drysten discovered on the first leg of their journey was just how many of the men were present based on a hunch. Nobody but Drysten knew for sure whether their spouse or sibling was in danger, something Drysten hadn't even considered. Many of the men here were simply coming along on a guess. It made Drysten wonder how many would still be there at all if they knew their families were actually safe.

When Jorrit had first been brought on board, he had to field questions about whether he had seen specific loved ones. Each crewman tried their best to describe the one they were looking for, down to nearly undetectable scars or birthmarks. Despite the thorough descriptions, the only individuals he remembered with any amount of certainty had been Isolde, due to her beauty, a man presumed to be Bors the Younger, and a woman with a birthmark both Cretans seemed to believe was their sister. Drysten had been present for a handful of the despairing and anxious men drilling questions into the Frisian. Never interfering with the questioning, he noticed the gradual amount of discomfort building with each encounter. The man was originally cordial, and even welcoming to some extent. But after a few series of the inquiries, he began to occasionally stumble over his speech and apologize more and more for not being able to render any useful information.

"Saw him speaking with a few of the rowers this morning," Diocles mentioned to Drysten. "The man looked conflicted."

Drysten shrugged. "Could be that he's taking a liking to some of the men aboard. Maybe doesn't wish to cause further angst while he's here."

Diocles eyed the Frisian as he spoke to Amiram toward the bow of the vessel. "If that's indeed the case, then maybe we should find out more about his *internal* struggles."

Cynwrig glanced toward Jorrit. "I do not believe him when he says he means to help us. To what end would he wish to aid people who imprisoned him?"

"And stabbed him," Drysten awkwardly put in.

The three men stood silently as they each contemplated the presence of the Frisian. Diocles was noticeably hung over from a festive night in a tavern across from the Fortuna, while Cynwrig was fumbling over the straps in the leather armor he purchased shortly after waking.

Most of the men were working to make room for the additional souls that were expected to arrive when Titus and his men finally marched up in a column. He was accompanied by the agreed upon number of men, who all moved in an orderly fashion behind him. "Good morning!" he cheerfully roared.

"Fucking hell," Diocles whispered, shortly before dry-heaving over the side of the vessel.

"Greetings to you, Titus," replied Cynwrig from the top deck.

After grinning to Diocles, now voiding his stomach of the booze he imbibed the night before, Drysten walked out to meet the general until he was quickly stopped by Dagonet. "The priest never showed," he alerted Drysten.

Drysten glanced toward the road leading from the city's center. "He was supposed to join us last night, was he not?"

"That was what you commanded, Lord," Dagonet replied.

Drysten sighed. "Alright, let's see if we can find him. We can't take too long, but hopefully he just waited until morning to join us."

The two men grabbed their weapons as a precaution and moved above deck.

Drysten was greeted by Titus as he had just come aboard. "The son of Hall! Bright and early I see."

Drysten was just as amused by the general's enthusiasm as everyone else. "Welcome aboard, Titus. I have to take care of a small matter, but when I come back, I'll describe our plans for rescuing our people."

Titus clapped his hands together. "Very good! It should take some time before we're settled anyway. The wagon carrying our provisions is still behind us on the bridge. Can I ask where you're off to?"

"The priest didn't come to the ship last night. I just want to find him and see if he still intends to join us or not," Drysten replied.

Titus briefly scratched his chin in thought. "Bastakas! Albic!" he called behind him. Two men stepped forward, both looking in the same sickly condition as Diocles. "These two are good men, but every damn time we leave to *fight* someone they end up getting sloshed the night before. Do me a favor and run them around with you so they can sweat some of the ale out!"

Drysten chuckled and instructed Petras and Magnus to follow as well. At Magnus' recommendation, the six men set off to the Temple of Mithras in the hopes of finding Matthew, or at the very least an individual who might know where to find him.

It only took the men a brief period of sauntering through the Londinium streets until they arrived at the temple, and immediately caught a look from the unpleasant priest they had encountered the day before.

"The heathen devils have come once more!" the priest shouted, much to the annoyance of the nearby onlookers. "Have you come to reconsider my offer of redemption?"

Drysten was already growing more annoyed by the man's tone than he was in their previous encounter. "Where's Matthew?" he demanded in a cold voice.

"I... what?" the priest stammered in a surprised tone.

"Matthew! Where is he?" Drysten began again.

The priest worked to display further confusion, but he clearly understood. "I... have no knowledge of a Matthew," he emphatically proclaimed to anyone within earshot.

Drysten was unwilling to indulge this man's strange actions and drew his blade. "I would rather not hurt you, but I will if you don't give me a straight fucking answer."

The priest glanced around him, not to seek out aid, but by Drysten's perception, it was to make certain he was not being watched. After a moment in which Drysten slowly lowered his blade and the priest finally looked back to the group, he skittishly moved closer for him to whisper. "The Pelagian was cast into chains when he told the bishop's men he was to leave. He may be misguided, but he is a good and honorable man. I may have secured my own escape, but I cannot leave until I am certain of his fate."

Petras glanced at Magnus. "Pelagian?"

"They believe something different than other Christians. Though, I have no understanding of it myself," Magnus responded with a shrug.

Drysten gently placed his blade back in its dark leather sheath. "What is happening to you and your people? And what is your name?"

"It is James, Lord. They call me James here, though the name of my birth is Victorianus," the priest began. "There is not one sole way of thinking in our grand church, there are a great many."

"Pelagians are one?" Dagonet inquired.

James nodded. "It is not my own preference, though I see certain... *agreeable* aspects in its reasoning."

"Why did you change your name?" Petras asked in confusion.

James sighed heavily. "When I was made a priest, they changed my name to that of an apostle under Christ. I was being reborn in a way, and the changing of my name signified this."

Drysten suddenly began feeling an ounce of pity for the priest. While he did not seem as though he was not taken care of, there also appeared to be certain aspects of his old life which he may have dearly missed. "Why do you never leave?"

"Some can, I will grant you. But then there are others who cannot, for various reasons. I am one of those," James said sadly. "The people here do take care of one another, regardless of how this sounds. We are our own kind of family." James was about to continue until his eyes grew wide as he looked over Drysten's shoulder, obviously deterred as two other priests came marching down the street. "You must go, Lord!" James whispered. "Matthew is being held under the church to the East. It's right next to the baths, with only one guard on the front door. There's an entrance to the basement around the back of the building. But beware of the Bishop Germanus and his men!" He then reopened his customary tirades of how Drysten lived a heathen life and would burn upon his eventual death.

Drysten slowly turned and walked back the way he came.

"What's the plan?" Bastakas asked through vomit stinking breath.

"Wouldn't be a good leader if I abandoned a man to die in chains. I imagine we should rescue the man," Drysten responded in frustration. "Magnus, go back and let the crew know where we are and where we will be going. Should we fail to return, tell Amiram to lead a group to search for us."

Magnus nodded and remained with the group until the ship was within eyeshot. Drysten, Petras, and Dagonet were now in the lead with Titus' two men behind them. After a few moments of walking, Drysten noticed a wealthy looking individual walking toward a building while beginning to prematurely shed his tunic. "Found the baths," he announced to his men before stopping to look around for the church in question. There were only two buildings made of stone across the street from the baths, each looking much like normal homes to well-off Londiniuns. After peering at both, he chose to send Bastakas and Albic to one and lead Dagonet to the other, leaving Petras near the bathhouse in case he saw anything significant.

Drysten strolled along a stone pathway up into a small courtyard of grass and flowers before glancing behind him. Making sure he was not seen by any citizens who would know he was out of place, he briskly walked around to the rear of the dilapidated structure.

"You know if this is the wrong building, we could be hung as thieves," Dagonet stated cautiously.

"How exciting."

Upon reaching the back of the house he heard a shout from the other building. Drysten and Dagonet perked their heads up to see Bastakas vomiting in the street near a woman who had been walking by, with Albic apparently trying to apologize to her for the sight.

"They're attracting attention before they even do anything wrong," Drysten said to Dagonet, who simply groaned and shook his head.

The two men returned to the task at hand, and eventually found a hatch leading down into the earth. Dagonet checked to see if it was secured, with both men being pleasantly surprised that it was not.

"Who leaves an entrance to their home unfastened?" Dagonet wondered aloud.

Drysten shrugged. "Likely those who would assume people do not steal from priests."

"Does it count if we are stealing a priest from the priests?" Dagonet retorted in a joking tone.

Drysten quietly chuckled as he lifted the lid, doing so as carefully and quietly as he could. The darkness gave way to the morning sunlight as a short stairway was dimly illuminated, with both men slowly making their way down into a scarcely lit room.

In the corner, there sat a highly stacked pile of rags along with short boxes placed atop one another. The unsettling scratch of mice could be heard all around them, causing Drysten to groan as a shiver of disgust ran its way down his spine. The smell of stale air was rampant, to which Drysten was about to mention, until footsteps were suddenly heard approaching from a stairway across the room. Dagonet quickly closed the hatch leading to fresh air, and both men quietly ran to the right in an effort to stay out of sight. They found a niche in the stone wall of the cellar behind a cluster of old boxes to hide behind. Drysten sensed he would be undetectable considering the amount of dust and cobwebs layered over his hiding spot.

"Thought I heard something," one man uttered.

"Check on him then," answered another.

Two shadows passed their way down the stairs into the room shared by Drysten and Dagonet. One man in front carried a torch, while the other stood by as he waited for his companion to walk across the room. As the torch illuminated the room, Drysten could see the pile of rags in the corner was actually a bloodied Matthew, who stirred when he saw the light of the torch through his swollen eyelids.

"Still here," announced the man with the torch, who slowly turned back to move up the stairs. "Told you it was nothing. Probably just some rats eyeing their dinner."

The two men made their way back up the stairs, leaving Matthew behind. Drysten peeped back toward Dagonet. "Were either of them armed?" he whispered.

Dagonet shrugged. "I couldn't see anything. Didn't see any robes on them either," he suspiciously noted.

"I don't think they were priests," Drysten replied as he gradually began to creep from his hiding spot. "Priest!" Drysten whispered.

Matthew began to frantically stir. "Who's there?" he answered in a panic.

Drysten stifled a laugh as he finally reached him. "Your god has come to rescue you."

"Lord! The keys are upstairs with the big one," Matthew informed him as he anxiously displayed his chains.

"How do we get him out without alerting anyone?"

Dagonet wondered.

Drysten turned to Matthew. "Are any of them even priests? They certainly did not appear so."

"Only one, but I don't think he's here," Matthew answered.

Drysten turned toward the stairway, pondering for a moment before turning back at Matthew. "Make noise," he commanded.

"Forgive me, Lord, but I was under the assumption that would be the *wrong* thing to do," the stunned priest replied.

Drysten beckoned Dagonet back to their hiding spot. When they were both settled carefully behind cover, he drew in a deep breath. "Fuckers!" he boomed.

Suddenly two sets of footsteps trudged down the stairs until a man with a torch appeared near Matthew. "What did you say, you piss-soaked priest?"

"Just cut his throat and be done with it," the other said as he soon followed the first.

"Boss wouldn't want us doing that," the man with the torch exclaimed, "but it doesn't mean we can't rough em up a bit."

Drysten nudged Dagonet, who nodded and began to draw his dagger, pointing at the smaller of the two. Drysten rapidly rose to stalk toward the bigger one. When he arrived within arm's length, he erupted forward and plunged his blade deep into the back of the man's neck, sending him down to the ground. The second man turned toward Drysten, cocking his head in startled confusion right before Dagonet plunged his knife between the guard's shoulder blades. Both men were now dealt with, giving Drysten and Dagonet the chance to search for the keys to Matthew's restraints.

The keys were eventually found on Drysten's kill, and after a moment of fumbling to find the lock, the priest was free.

"Thank you, Lord!" he graciously responded as Drysten

helped him up through the hatch. He found his way into the waiting arms of Bastakas and Albic, who had been waiting overhead.

"We didn't find a basement at the other place," Albic explained.

Bastakas nodded. "Almost came down until we heard two voices we couldn't recognize. Figured we'd do better to wait."

"Worked out well," Drysten cheerfully stated as Petras jogged up.

After a few moments of rushing toward the Fortuna, the six men eventually made their way through the empty morning streets of the city and back to their vessel. The men were greeted by Titus' soldiers, who were just then starting to board the ship. They made room for the wounded man to be brought aboard. Matthew was then handed over to Diocles, who took him to be cleaned up before they set off.

"Left my things in the church, Lord," Matthew wistfully stated before Diocles took him away.

Drysten smiled reassuringly. "You had more important things to worry about. We'll find you some new clothes on board."

"I brought some he can use," announced Titus, who upon seeing the injured priest walked up beside him.

After a few moments, the men were all loaded onto the ship.

And now, the real journey was to begin.

"The men left with my brother as you ordered, father," Mor announced as he entered the dining hall. "Fifty of yours, plus his own gives him roughly a hundred souls to send against the Gaels."

"Pray we need no more," King Ceneus responded.

Mor sauntered over toward his father, dining alone where his family had once held joyous feasts in their family's name. King Ceneus always considered his youngest son to be the closest to Eidion in ferocity, but gentle in some ways like his sister. It was a strange combination, but occasionally the king wondered if his youngest boy could indeed become a good ruler should the opportunity arise. The likelihood of such an occurrence happening was next to nothing when considering how he would not only have to come to an understanding with Gwrast, but likely win a war against Eidion.

"These kidnappings are... *strange,* father," Mor remarked as he lowered himself next to King Ceneus.

The king tilted his head to the side as he sipped his cup of wine. "How so?" he wondered, though he'd heard similar stories at various times in the past.

"The lack of remains is slightly off-putting," Mor responded. "Normally, there are at least tracks to follow."

King Ceneus chuckled. "It would be a truly remarkable thing to be able to track a boat in the water, son." Mor grinned as he reached to pour himself a cup of his father's wine, nearly oblivious to the entrance of Bishop Germanus and his priest into the dimly lit hall.

The king could not tell if he remained oblivious, or was merely doing his utmost to try and ignore the guests. *I suppose it matters little,* the king thought.

"Lord King," Maewyn greeted as he sat across from Mor, who grunted in disgust and attempted to rise from his seat before being pressed back down by the king.

Bishop Germanus smirked. "A shame your other children do not relish the light of the Lord like your eldest, Ceneus."

The king chuckled. "It is not the Lord he has issues with, Your Excellency."

Bishop Germanus dismissively waved a hand as he glanced around the room, lifting his robes to sit. He snapped his fingers toward a servant to signal he was hungry, and the man dutifully nodded and left to fetch the bishop his dinner. "We are making great progress against the apostates and heretics in your realm," he happily stated.

King Ceneus glanced into his cup as the image of his childhood friend, Drumond, flashed in his mind. "The sooner your job is finished here, the sooner you can journey back to Rome."

"Ha!" the bishop roared. "A wonderful thought!"

The king noticed Mor glance toward him as a silent request to depart from the uncomfortable setting. He glanced over at his son, nodded, then looked back to the bishop before he could protest Mor's exit. "What exactly are your plans thus far, Your Excellency?"

The bishop seemed surprised at the question, almost as if he did not think Ceneus interested enough to ask. "I... well, once your kingdom is placed in God's hands, I believe I will instruct Patrick here to venture to the land of his confinement."

For fuck's sake, the king thought silently, *what purpose would he have in sending the only good man in his employ back into chains?*

"I am to help facilitate the converting of the Gaels, Lord King," an excited Maewyn exclaimed, seemingly reading Ceneus' mind.

"And you volunteered for this?" King Ceneus asked in surprise.

Maewyn happily nodded. "It is my purpose, Lord King. The church preaches forgiveness, and I can think of no better way to forgive the Gaels for my time as a slave than to bring them closer to God."

The king glanced down toward the table. *These people seem to believe they can turn the whole world to their side,* he concluded. *It would be a dangerous thing indeed should this come to pass.*

"In time, I expect the other kingdoms of Britannia will follow suit," Bishop Germanus added as his meal was placed in front of him.

The fire in the hearth began to fade until a slave strolled

over to stoke the flames. The smoke seemed to grab at Ceneus' lungs as he stared off toward the entrance to the dining hall. The light of the candles illuminated just enough of Bishop Germanus' face to alert the king to his gaze, with his bloodshot eyes seemingly hovering over him from under the man's wrinkled brow.

"What are your plans for the newcomers?" the bishop finally asked.

The king peered toward the flames before training his attention back to the bishop. "I am in need of generals for my army. I will support Hall to the North as best as I can, and hopefully his boy, should he even return."

"I could have simply called on the ranking general in Gaul for aid should you require it. He would no doubt have officers he could spare, and he certainly *would* have spared them given our relationship," Bishop Germanus responded.

The king grimaced with the thought of Romans returning to govern his lands. The general the bishop alluded to was known as Flavius Aetius, and his current whereabouts were known to be far to the East as he attempted to seat a usurper on the throne of the Western Roman Empire. Some of his men were already in the service of the bishop, with them being the riders sent across Ebrauc to strike down images of the old gods. The king knew more of such men would spell ruin for him, as a dangerous shift of power could occur. One which would see his rule all but replaced.

"I prefer to call on the services of my own people to that of the Romans," The king said wearily.

The bishop smirked. "You seemed fine dealing with the man from Londinium."

"As did you, until you found he worshiped more than one god," King Ceneus replied.

The king couldn't tell whether the bishop heard his remark, as the portly man was loudly wrenching the meat off the bone once belonging to some type of bird.

Eats like an animal, the king thought in amusement.

"That may be so, but I feel it would be more beneficial to cast them aside once their job to the North is completed," the Bishop finally remarked. "The boy is volatile, and his father seems to be too... *competent* to allow him to remain."

The king looked over the bishop's face in shock. "You would have me toss aside a good man because he's capable? That seems rather counterproductive."

Bishop Germanus chuckled. "I would have those who could inspire loyalty and pull your people further from their king cast out."

"Hall was known by my father to be—" the king began.

"Your *apostate* father," the bishop interrupted as he pointed the meatless bone toward the king before dropping it back to his plate.

"And the high king of Britannia," King Ceneus responded harshly.

The king glanced toward Maewyn, who was looking back to him with sympathy in his eyes as the king erupted up from the table and proceeded toward the entrance to the dining hall. The bishop began to cackle behind him, chiding him for his weak stomach to do what needed to be done.

But does this need to be done? the king wondered.

Hall was a gifted military commander, and the only reason for the bishop to want him out of Ebrauc would be he saw the same thing.

Likely believes he could offer resistance should the bishop subjugate his people as he does mine.

The king finally made his way outside to his decaying capital. It was night in Eboracum, and the only street to be illuminated was that of the main roadway leading from the front gate to the Roman-built fort across the river. The king attempted to peer through the darkness all around him, wondering if there would ever be a day where this city would once again be teeming with life.

CHAPTER VII

The additional men hired to crew the ship were a boon to the Fortuna's crew. Most of the men felt they had been constantly on the move for the last couple months, so to have additional pairs of hands to keep the ship in order provided welcome relief. Titus himself was neither concerned nor shy about lending aid himself. To the amusement of the oarsmen, he plucked Amiram up out of his seat and began leading the rowers himself. After a rather strenuous moment of work, he threw his hands up in the air and motioned for the mute to retake his post, getting jeered at by the rest of the rowers as he smiled his way up the stairs.

The rainy weather had also given way to a mostly cloudless sky. The only rain to be seen was off to the South, a direction the men would thankfully not be traveling. After a day of sailing without pause, there was little more for the crew posted above deck to do than to lean over a railing and either watch the Southeast coast of Britannia grow smaller or watch the Western coast of the mainland grow larger.

Upon leaving Londinium, the Fortuna reached open water and proceeded directly East. Drysten was following the advice of Jorrit, a man born to the sea. Drysten was relieved when the Frisian advised open water would be quite doable, citing lack of rain as well as the wind blowing in a favorable direction.

Jorrit was in a strange position at this point. The crew understood he had once been an enemy who killed their brothers, but Drysten was told it was Jorrit who first alerted the men to Maurianus' betrayal. On top of that, Drysten witnessed him killing the traitor who had almost sent Amiram to the afterlife. That and the fact he was seemingly doing his utmost to provide reliable advice for the trip meant the Fortuna's crew was beginning to view him in a more favorable light.

"What do you think of him?" Diocles had asked Drysten as they stared over the stern of the ship.

Drysten shrugged. "I still don't know if we can trust him. I *did* stab him."

Diocles snorted out a quick laugh. "People get stabbed all the time. At least you had the decency not to kill him."

Drysten smiled before glancing back to the recent, and likely temporary addition to the crew. "Either way, if he continues being this helpful, he won't have an issue with me when the journey is over."

"An issue?" Diocles inquired.

Drysten turned to the man who had started to become his closest friend. "We'll take him home instead of leaving him once we're done with Servius."

"Ah, the land of the terps."

Drysten nodded.

"You know, there *is* another option as well." Diocles slowly turned around and began to whisper. "The men have started getting used to the big ugly bastard. Maybe there's a way we could talk him into staying once this is over. I know you would need a man who understands the seas as well as him."

Drysten started to consider the idea. On the one hand, Jorrit had been a valuable asset thus far. If he had not notified the rest of the crew to Maurianus' betrayal, there's no telling how far they could have gotten before the money was eventually discovered missing. On the other, Drysten stabbed him while the man was tied up and defenseless, something most people hold a grudge against. "Something to consider, I suppose. Let's just worry about it if we even get that far."

After a moment's pause in which Diocles looked as though he wished to speak, Drysten finally nudged him lightly. "Something troubles you. The Frisian?"

Diocles shook his head. "I have heard... rumblings, Lord."

Drysten slowly turned to face the Greek. "What rumblings?" He assumed Diocles would have questions about what occurred in Burdigala, likely due to the traitor's final moments a few days prior.

"Do they truly speak to you?" Diocles asked awkwardly, clearly referring to the voices. The very same which Hall's people knew strangely echoed through Drysten's mind.

Drysten sighed. "I'm... not certain I have an answer to that."

"I meant no disres—"

"The truth is, I do not understand it myself," Drysten replied in a solemn tone. "Some mornings I wake and hear a chorus of pained voices screaming messages of ruin. Then, there are some days I wake to the loving embrace of my mother. It always seems to change depending on my present circumstances."

Diocles turned back to face the sea. "Why would the gods wish to torture someone in that manner?"

"I have learned to ignore those voices. Of that, you need not concern yourself," Drysten said reassuringly.

Diocles shook his head. "I meant your mother. I would lament any time I heard the voice of my mother. She was a loving woman, but hearing her speak of who her son has become..."

"A good man?" Drysten remarked thoughtfully.

The two men stood in silence for a short while, watching the birds off in the distance grow smaller and smaller before eventually disappearing altogether. Occasionally, there would be a small fishing boat spotted toward the mainland, but no ships of any real size worth noting. So far, Drysten was pleased with how quiet the trip from Londinium had been.

He was even more delighted to see Matthew up and around. Jorrit was helping the man up the stairs as Drysten and Diocles were speaking. Other than Matthew's limp, he was only sporting a swollen cheekbone and a black eye. Titus had given him a new assortment of clothes and armor, so other than the crucifix around his neck, one would hardly figure him to be a priest. Somehow, he even got his hands on a new sword to strap around his waist.

"You nearly resemble a genuine fighter!" Drysten said through a wide grin.

Diocles smirked at the sight. "With that face and limp, he looks more like he lost."

Matthew offered a half smile and gently made his way over to the two. "Glad to see you don't have a reason to throw me overboard yet, Lord."

"*You're* here for if we run out of food!" Jorrit whispered to the priest.

Matthew wearily laughed but looked to Drysten and Diocles for assurance. "I've heard his kind do that. He's joking, isn't he?"

Drysten leaned closer. "Pray we don't run out of meat and you'll never need to find out."

The priest nervously smiled and hobbled his way toward a group of Titus' men talking amongst themselves on the port side of the vessel, leaving Drysten, Jorrit and Diocles alone on the Fortuna's stern.

"How long until we arrive?" Diocles asked the Frisian.

Jorrit glanced over the approaching coastline of the mainland. "From this point, and at this speed, we could be there by midday tomorrow. I have never been there myself, but it's right on the coast from my understanding."

"How did you come by this knowledge if you've never been there?" Drysten inquired.

"Our chieftain bought many of our slaves from this man. One of my men sailed there with his son for the purchases," Jorrit responded.

Drysten nodded his head and turned his attention back to the sea. "Might as well waste the rest of the day below deck."

The three men agreed, and made their way down to the second level, where Drysten noticed how relaxed everyone down below looked. Most of the rowers were leaning against the hull due to the sails being in use and their labor being unneeded.

Amiram stood up and walked to Drysten, who beckoned the mute to follow them to the room once used for the worshipping of various faiths. The men belonging to Titus had left almost no space next to the supplies the ship carried, so this room would be shared by him and Drysten until the journey was over. Drysten did not like sleeping separately from his men, but it was nothing other captains would not do. The men entered to overhear Titus attempting to teach Cynwrig strategies he employed in previous wars, although the Briton clearly didn't understand any of it.

Drysten entered first and was followed by Amiram, Diocles, and Jorrit. The three men greeted Titus and dragged over nearby boxes to be used as seats while they spoke.

"To what do I owe the pleasure?" Titus chirped as he glanced around the room. As he did so, Dagonet also entered before leaning himself against the doorway. Drysten guessed the men around the second deck thought they would be going over some sort of plan and began to feel slightly on edge. "Thought our Cynwrig here could use a break from the war-talk," Drysten said with a grin.

"Agh! The boy has potential, Drysten, just you wait. He'll be leading men to war before you know it," Titus declared with a jovial laugh.

"That would be... something," Diocles put in.

Titus nodded before directing his attention to Drysten. "I was thinking about your idea to gain entry to Servius' estate. I understand that if we sail up to his docks as traders in search of labor, it would not be cause for alarm." Drysten nodded as Titus paused for a moment. "Now what we need to know is the layout of his villa, which I believe our scout and the Frisian could help us with."

Titus gestured toward Dagonet, who scratched his head and stepped forward. "To start, I have not been there for many years. What I do know for certain is he does not have just one place to rest his head should he choose. He has two, with one being much more formidable than the other."

The group let out a collective groan of frustration as they realized they may need to split their forces. Drysten knew splitting them into two separate groups could easily mean both parties would be at a disadvantage.

"Tell us of them both," Titus requested as he leaned forward. Drysten noticed he seemed to be intrigued by the prospect of a challenge.

"One of the estates is an island he lovingly dubbed his *farm*," Dagonet said with a sigh.

"That's where he keeps his captives, isn't it?" Bastakas said wearily.

Dagonet nodded. "He brings them there before he either sells them or takes them deeper inland to his villa."

"Who does he take to his home?" Drysten wondered aloud.

"Women worth his bed," Dagonet replied. Sensing Drysten's discomfort, he turned to his captain. "I do not wish to alarm you, but many who were taken there during my time as a slave did not return. My sister was one of them. He took her when the rest of us had disembarked on the island. I never saw her again." The group sat in silence for a moment, understanding they may not be able to save as many as they had hoped. The two Cretans must have been listening from the other side of the doorway, as each slowly walked into the room and settled in behind Dagonet with grim looks on their faces. "*But* we should not assume your loved ones met the same fate as my sister. Servius was a younger man in those days and I doubt he could spend much of his time with that many women these days."

"Too old, or too fat?" Diocles inquired.

"Both," Drysten put in, "he would let his crew go whoring ahead of him in Burdigala before he made his way to the taverns. We all wondered if he did so to prevent the women from telling his crew how he couldn't... *perform*." The last comment drew a few smirks from the group, all thinking of the wealthy and powerful Servius unable to please a woman. Amiram glanced at Diocles and held out his hands in front of his stomach as if to show how fat the man was, causing even the Cretans to cast small grins.

Jorrit gained everyone's attention. "I can guide you to the island. It has shallows nearby which beached one of our chieftain's boats. His boy came back and complained about the repairs for weeks."

"But what of the island's *defenses*?" Titus responded. "As much as I would like to hear more of your chieftain's boy, the defenses are certainly much more to my interest."

Jorrit grinned and nodded. "Fair enough, Roman. The small fortress on the island is located on the Western end, shaped much like a triangle. The chief's boy mentioned it was heavily defended. Unless I missed my guess, I would assume that was because it was a *planned* visit. The slaver was present for the sales, as was his son."

"Servius has a son?" Drysten said in surprise.

Jorrit nodded. "Nearly the same age as you."

"Take his boy hostage?" Diocles happily recommended with a smirk.

"Aye," Amiram said through a grin. Although without a tongue, his speech sounded odd to anyone who wasn't used to it.

Titus eyed Diocles as he leaned forward. "That's one option, though I am normally not one for a kidnapping."

"Better that than allowing them time to warn the second estate. At least this way we could make our intentions known. They could second-guess killing any prisoners,"

Drysten wearily mentioned.

Titus nodded. "True, this will not be as simple as raiding one place and then the other. Any prisoners not kept on the island would surely be killed rather than taken elsewhere. Regardless of who we have in chains."

"It would seem our only option is to attack them both at the same time," Drysten declared. "I will take a handful of men ashore at midday tomorrow. Titus, you will lead the raid to the island in my stead."

The group sat for a short while longer, with many attempting to talk their way into the small band of men accompanying Drysten ashore. It was finally decided the men accompanying Drysten would be Diocles, Cynwrig, Dagonet, and the Cretans, while the rest would stay with Titus for the raid on the island. To ensure the island's assault would begin at nightfall, the Fortuna anchored near the shore for the remainder of the day and would resume its course at sunup. Drysten and his small band of men would disembark from the closest dock to the mainland estate, by the guidance of Dagonet.

The men all accepted the plan and slowly began to rise from their seats. Diocles and Amiram were still enthralled with their sense of humor, and mimicked a fat man attempting to bed a woman by lifting rolls of skin along their stomachs. To Cynwrig's dismay, Titus gestured for the man to return to his seat for further explanations of the decisions made during battles he'd fought. The only men who left the room were Drysten, Dagonet, and the Cretans, who all went back above deck to watch the sun as it began moving far off into the West.

The sun rose the next morning to reveal a beautiful cloudless sky, a good omen to the men of the Fortuna. Some of the more faith-driven individuals decided whatever gods were watching wanted to be able to determine how their trials eventually played out, while many of the others were simply happy to know there would be no rain while they were fighting.

Titus briefed his men on the plan of attack, and simultaneously talked a reluctant Drysten into taking three additional men with him. One was a big brute of a man nicknamed Heraclius, who resembled Bors in size, yet had long, golden hair down to the middle of his shoulder blades. The second man was named Lucius, who was a smaller man than Heraclius but with similar traits. The last was Bastakas, Titus' second-in-command who was greatly respected among Titus' men, and widely considered the best fighter among them.

The coast of Gaul was now within two hundred or so yards to the ship's starboard side. Rows of small huts belonging to salt makers were scattered along the beach and under squawking seagulls. Drysten was walking through the men, while trying to speak small words of encouragement to each of them. Titus' men needed little, if any. They were all battle-tested veterans of previous Roman wars, and thus were not unfamiliar to raids such as these. When Heraclius saw Drysten, he rose his gigantic frame up from the floor and walked over to introduce himself.

"Lord, I was told I'd be joining you," the Greek said.

"A pleasure," Drysten replied as he took a moment to marvel at how truly huge the man was. The strangest thing about the man which Drysten easily noticed was the look of his eyes. Where many big men Drysten had known growing up had intimidating eyes, this man's were gentle somehow.

"To you as well. How many prisoners are we expecting to find in this place?" the giant asked.

Drysten shrugged. "There are only a few we know are there for certain. My plan is to free them all, then sort out where to take them after we're gone."

Heraclius nodded. "Best we can do without being certain. They really kidnap *Roman* citizens?"

Drysten sighed. "Not sure Britons count as being Roman

anymore, although I'm sure many would count themselves as such."

"Can't hardly blame them. Born living under the greatness of Rome only to be cast aside by a child-emperor. I suppose that would be the main reason I chose to stay there. Figured they would need people like me," Heraclius stated.

"You're too right about that."

The two men chatted for a while longer, mainly about problems they may encounter ashore, or other more trivial matters. Heraclius seemed like a capable fighter and Drysten wondered of the quality of the other new additions to his group. He was about to inquire about them until voices began ringing out above them on the top deck.

"It would seem something is amiss, Lord," an excited Heraclius observed as he began to jog his way to the top deck. "Let's have us a look!"

Drysten snickered at the large man's enthusiasm and followed him up, where he was met by Cynwrig and a few of Titus' men. In the distance, there could be seen two boats heading South from the direction of Servius' island.

I know those ships, Drysten thought. "Fetch Titus," he ordered.

Cynwrig nodded and disappeared below deck, leaving Drysten and the others gathering around to observe the oncoming vessels. Cynwrig eventually reappeared from the stairs with the general, then gestured Titus toward Drysten.

"What's the issue?" the sleepy-eyed general requested.

Drysten pointed to the ships off in the distance. "Those vessels belong to Servius."

Titus strained his eyes to see them. "How can you be sure?"

"I remember them docking in Burdigala. An old Roman vessel he served on and one more he stole from Armorica a few years ago. Fucker bragged about it to everyone who would listen," Drysten replied.

"The conceited ones always take any chance to gloat,"

Titus concluded. The two men stood staring North, both unable to discern how many people were aboard each vessel.

"We could try intercepting them," Diocles suggested as he slowly approached. "Both of them are smaller than us, not to mention they won't be able to defend themselves very well if they're packed with slaves."

Drysten stood in silence as he considered both options. If he decided to assault the ships, there was a very good chance one could be able to slip away. If he didn't attack, then that could mean two ships worth of slaves dissapeared forever. "Let's just try to get close enough to talk to them. We'll attack if need be. If not, then we press onward."

"I'll have someone signal something once we're close enough," Titus responded, "Might also be wise to ask them how to find Servius' estate if we're to be acting as merchants."

Drysten nodded. "See if you can draw their attention without betraying our purpose. Put most of the men below and only use half the oars, pull the others in."

The commands were quickly relayed as Titus began to call them out. Half of the ship's oars were brought back into its hull, and half of the men who had been above deck moved out of sight If Servius saw their superior numbers, there would be a good chance he would simply ignore any attempt to speak. Not wanting to be seen due to the slight chance he would be recognized, Drysten made his way down below with the others. He handed off the role of captain to Titus, who was obviously more than capable of filling it.

As the ships drew closer, Titus called for one of his men to bring up an old Roman buccina, a long, circular musical instrument used for centuries by Roman commanders to relay orders to their men. It had a very distinct note. With the oncoming ship being Roman, Titus hoped it meant there may be someone on board who would recognize it.

After a few moments, the ships began to turn away from the Fortuna, slowly moving off toward the West. Titus looked to his man carrying the buccina and nodded his head. The bugler played the note used for signaling troops on land to form up, with the tone reverberating the eardrums of the Fortuna's crew. The man played well, as Drysten expected from a former Roman, yet the repetitiveness of the note quickly began to become a slight annoyance to those nearby. Even Titus was growing annoyed by the constant assault on his ears, running his fingers over his stubbly beard in frustration.

He was about to signal for the worn-out bugler to stop altogether until, to his surprise, the two vessels suddenly changed course toward the Fortuna. The ships were close enough to communicate with each other for a short time, then after a few moments, one began to sail from the Fortuna's port to her starboard.

"That's certainly fortunate," Titus happily announced.

Drysten poked his head up from the stairwell, catching the ships come up alongside the Fortuna. He also glanced to Titus, who was getting his first look at the man who had caused so much pain and suffering to so many. Servius was easy to spot, as he was the most rotund individual aboard the nearest ship. Showing again that he was the master, he stood on their starboard side near the bow, moving his garments to make certain his golden chains were on full display.

Titus cheerfully walked to the port side of the Fortuna and cleared his throat. "Salvè, friend! Nice day for sailing isn't it?"

A suspicious Servius muttered something to the man standing next to him before returning the stranger's pleasantries. "I suppose so. To whom am I speaking?"

"I am Titus Octavius Britannicus of the Victorius Sixth Legion," Titus declared proudly. "And your name, friend?"

Servius seemed moderately impressed and indeed surprised by the appearance of a legionnaire so far from Roman shores. "My name is Servius the Merciful, I served in the Classis Britannica," he returned, referring his old naval group in the Roman navy, and an accomplished one at that. "What are you doing in these parts?"

"The merciful? The fuck does he know about mercy?" Drysten murmured as he nudged two oarsmen out of his way, moving to a gap in the hull of the Fortuna. Amiram began to follow as they each slowly crept into a better position to survey the enemy vessel nearby. Drysten noticed a few men in chains, but for the most part the crew was unbound and watching intently.

"As a matter of fact, I am here to meet you!" Drysten heard from Titus. "Praise the Gods, the luck I have in meeting you now."

Servius suspiciously glanced over the Fortuna, but even he could not turn away from Titus' charismatic demeanor and the chance for easy gold. "Seems to me, you could use some more men to crew this impressive vessel of yours."

Titus let out a fake, full bellied laugh. "Indeed! I was told you procure the *finest* in this region."

"I suppose that would be true. I also happen to be the *only* slaver in these parts, as I do not tolerate any competition. You want workers? Women?" Servius asked.

"A bit of both, I suspect. I largely need some who speak the languages of the Britons, as well as a few others to replenish my crew," Titus responded.

Servius turned back to the nearest man standing behind him, clearly giving some type of command. "I have a handful with me here," he shouted. "If you wish, you can look on them now, but I cannot go back to the larger group. A busy man such as I has a tight schedule to keep."

Drysten was relieved Titus saw the opportunity to get more information for their assault. Even if the slaves Servius had with him were not from the main group they intended to save, they would certainly know where the others were being held.

"Good deal!" Titus said with a laugh. "Give me a moment to grab my son, I want him learning how to do business like a gentleman. Shall we come to your ship or will we be playing the role of the hospitable host?" He turned to Bastakas, who had been standing nearby and whispered Drysten couldn't hear."

"You will come to mine," Servius ordered.

"Very good! I'll bring wine along! Bring your ship close, as we have a boarding ramp available when you're ready." Titus peered behind him as Bastakas made his way to the stairs.

"Swords at the ready!" Drysten hissed to the closest men around him. He sprang up and grabbed the nearest skin of wine he saw before running to meet Bastakas at the foot of the stairs.

"Up, Lord. General wants you."

Drysten nodded and moved to the top deck to be met by Titus.

"Do nothing to betray our intentions, my boy. He's going to take the two of us onto their ships. We are here —"

Drysten held up the skin of wine. "I heard. It's a good plan." What Drysten neglected to tell Titus was how there were now about forty armed men waiting at the base of the stairway, ready to pounce on Servius at a moment's notice.

Titus gave Drysten a skeptical look. "If you see your woman or anyone you know, we'll simply buy them. Either way, this is our chance to find his compound undermanned. Do nothing to start a fight."

Drysten grinned. "There's no reason to attack them at the moment. I would prefer us to get what we want *without* doing anything dangerous." Drysten knew Titus could sense his true intentions, but was relieved he either did not care or silently agreed with attacking them depending on the situation.

After a few moments, Servius instructed his oarsmen to row their vessel close enough to tie a line to the Fortuna. Once secured, Titus oversaw the boarding ramp as it was brought down and secured to the other ship. Bastakas checked to make sure it was steady enough to safely traverse, then gave the okay as Drysten and Titus made their way down.

"Well, I must confess, this isn't the usual way I conduct my business," the slaver began. "On *this* ship, we only have four worth looking at, but on the other, we have near ten."

Titus leaned down and inspected the men dragged in front of him. Drysten followed him a few paces as he got his first up-close look at Servius' business prospects. Standing in a line with their heads facing down to the deck, were a handful of the most miserable looking men he had ever laid eyes on.

"Hm..." Titus mumbled as he inspected the slaves. "They look healthy enough. You said there were others?"

"Give my other ship a moment to come around," Servius responded.

Titus tenderly lifted the arm of one of the slaves and inspected his brand of FVG, then turned to see each one was carrying an identical brand in the same space on each of their forearms. "Are these your troublemakers?"

Servius displayed a grim smirk toward Titus and Drysten. "I suppose that would be accurate."

Titus chuckled. "One more thing, before you said there were four worth looking at."

Servius' eyebrow twitched as he returned a slight nod.

"Judging by the *state* of the ones I see here..." Titus turned to Drysten. "Always pay close attention to a merchant's words, son."

Drysten did his best to look uninterested. "Yes, father."

Servius scrunched his face tighter in inconvenience, but reluctantly motioned for his closest man to return below deck. "The few I have down below are a scrawnier bunch, but I am certain you could find a use for them if it came down to it." The individual sent to fetch the remainder of the slaves returned with five more men in chains trailing behind him. He violently tugged them toward the slaves already lined up, and proceeded to force them each down to their knees.

Titus walked over to the newly displayed slaves and began to inspect each one, looking at teeth and eyes. One was much younger than the rest and looked him right in the eye.

"What's your name?" Titus asked the youngest of the group. The only response Titus received was a simple smirk with a raucous stare. "I asked you your name, boy!" The boy's smile grew slightly wider, causing Titus to slowly turn to Servius.

In response, Servius hobbled over to the boy and violently grabbed his slave by the hair, wrenching his neck to the side as he screamed directly into his ear. "You *will* answer him, or I will feed you your own eyeballs and turn you to pig feed!"

What kind of man dreams that up off the top of their head? Drysten thought as he and Titus each glanced to one another. Both were clearly disturbed by the sight, but neither broke their act.

"It's... Virico," the boy eventually responded.

Titus again looked at the boy. "I like him. He's got spirit. How much?"

Servius must have been moderately confused by the offer, as he simply gazed up and blinked for a moment before reacting. "Seeing as how you would have to tame him yourself... I would say eighteen-hundred Sestertii."

"Bah!" Titus exclaimed as he threw up his hands. "Better toss in another one for that amount."

Servius mumbled to himself and let the slave go free from his grasp. Just then, the second ship drifted its way around the Fortuna to be secured to Servius' own vessel. "The more... *alluring* alternatives are available on my second vessel."

"I pray you're right," Titus dubiously replied.

The captain and lead rower of the second ship arrived

to find out what the situation was. Upon understanding there were possible customers to deal with, their demeanor became considerably more cordial. The sailor went back to his own vessel and proceeded to quickly return with every slave he held aboard his ship, marching them toward the two potential customers.

In the rear of the line, two men were leading a hulking man in chains up from the bowels of Servius' personal ship.

"Fuck off!" the bulky man warned. "You better pray to whatever gods watch over you I don't get free. I'll kill the lot of you when I—" And then he saw Drysten.

Drysten peered out of the corner of his eye toward Servius, making sure the man would not be able to see his subtle nod of reassurance. Bors glimpsed behind him and returned Drysten's gaze with the hollowest stare he had ever seen.

What did they do to you? Drysten wondered.

Drysten stepped forward from behind Titus. "That one!" he stated cheerily as he pointed in the direction of the outburst. "That one looks as though he could be very, *very* useful," he said as he turned to Titus.

Titus lifted an eyebrow as he glanced toward Drysten, understanding the man was known to him. "The man looks like he'd just as likely to try and kill you as one of those savages from Caledonia."

Drysten shrugged. "We could use him for a bit of sport in the fighting pits back home, father."

Titus turned to Servius. "How much for the big man?"

Servius walked over and inspected him. "Three thousand Sestertii. Not negotiable for this one. He could fetch just as much or more from the markets of Armorica."

Titus quickly glanced at Drysten, who subtly nodded his head. Titus then looked behind him toward Bastakas. "Fetch the coin."

Drysten stepped toward Servius, doing his best not to glare into his eyes with too much fervor. "You mentioned women?"

Servius patted Drysten on the shoulder. "A *horny* one!" He cakcled and motioned for another group to be brought up from below deck of the second ship. Drysten noticed the brands on their arms had been recently burned into their skin. The group was comprised of six women, all of which had black hair like that of Isolde, but none happened to be her. One did look vaguely familiar to him and he calmly walked toward her. All the while she was staring back at him in disbelief.

"Your name," Drysten commanded.

The girl nervously peered from Drysten to Servius, who moved his hand to the whip he kept at his waist as a warning not to disobey. "Petronela, Lord," she finally responded in an uneasy tone.

"You're very beautiful, Petronela. I'm sure you would do nicely," Drysten said as he winked at the woman, then turned to her captor. "The price?"

Servius snorted in disbelief that Titus could afford so much at one time. "She's Greek, not to mention beautiful. That would drive the price up considerably."

She's Greek? Drysten thought. *She could be the sister to the Cretans.* He glanced back toward the ship before finally training his gaze toward the portly slaver.

"The price, Servius," Drysten stated in a more authoritative tone.

Servius sneered, obviously not used to being commanded. "Twelve thousand Sestertii."

Drysten smiled, then turned to Bastakas who freshly returned with the first payment in hand. "Grab it."

Bastakas glanced at Titus, who nodded in approval, then made his way back below deck.

Drysten turned to Titus. "I will see to the payment, father. Don't want the help to miscount it." Then made his way up the ramp to the Fortuna where he was greeted by Magnus.

"The girl is the sister of Petras and Paulus!" Magnus

whispered.

Drysten nodded. "I gathered as much. I'm assuming you noticed Bors the Younger in the vessel as well."

Magnus nodded. "What course are we—?"

"We're going to kill all but the fat one."

Magnus smiled as he followed Drysten down to the second deck of the ship. "Titus did not intend to fight, Lord."

"Titus isn't in charge."

Bleed them! the voice wailed.

Drysten shook off the sudden outburst. "Besides, he knows how much I hate this man. There's no way he thinks I simply wanted to resolve this peacefully."

Petras and Paulus walked up besides Drysten and Magnus, bows in hand. "We'll keep them from cutting the ropes or moving the ramps away. We were able to see the faces of the others he brought from below deck. Isolde is not with him."

Drysten nodded and continued his way to the large group of men huddled near the stairway. In all, about forty men were waiting there with their weapons in hand. All Drysten had to do was survey the group and nod his head.

There was a thunder of feet as armored men erupted from the stairs of the ship and made their way to the ramp. One of Servius' guards saw the oncoming enemy first and tried to shift the ramp into the water, but was then struck in the chest with an arrow fired through a porthole of the second deck. Servius himself started to draw his sword but was quickly grabbed and thrown to the ground by Titus. Six men had made their way onto the enemy ship and formed a shield wall while the rest were now forming up behind them. Two enemy guards were now running back onto the second ship when each was struck in the back by arrows coming from the Fortuna.

"You are *Roman!* Have you no honor for business?" Servius yelled as he squirmed on the ground with Titus' sword on his throat.

Titus smiled at his new captive. "You capture and sell Roman citizens into slavery. The punishment for that is death. Don't talk to me of honor."

The first dozen men of the Fortuna were outnumbered by both of Servius' crews, who had formed their own shield wall to stop the advance of the boarders. Diocles was in the middle of the front row, bellowing out a command to push. He was now joined in the front of the shield wall by Drysten and Amiram, the former sounding the same command.

Men were cramming themselves into the rearward portions of the shield wall as it advanced onto the vessel, bobbing side to side due to the extra weight. Swords clanged together and the sound of screaming men and shields being beat rang loudly over the water. Drysten pushed a man's iron shield up high enough for Amiram to slip his blade under, cutting into the man's groin and sending him down to the wooden deck of the ship. Every so often, an arrow flew overhead and embedded itself into the neck or chest of a man attempting to cut the rope tying Servius' ships together.

Drysten could hear Bastakas ordering men to push, but the only ones who obeyed were Titus' men. Drysten's people were mostly ramming themselves into the enemy line and hacking at the tops of heads or below raised shields. Drysten quickly glanced around and noticed Titus' men had a more cohesive approach to the boarding.

Are we slowing them down? Drysten wondered. As he looked on his force, he noticed the men under Titus' command all wore annoyed expressions and glanced between each other as if waiting for the Fortuna's men to fall in line.

Titus and Servius were now behind Drysten's shield wall. With the slaver being cut off from his men, Drysten knew there was now an easier way to resolving the conflict, one which would likely spare the exposed men of the Fortuna who frantically swiped from side to side. He pointed to Titus, who understood immediately what was to be done. He slowly drew his knife from the sheath on his right hip and dragged the fat slaver up from the deck before placing the blade at his neck. "Tell your men to cease," he commanded.

Servius attempted a feeble and pointless struggle, but failed once Titus put enough force into his neck to draw a small amount of blood. "Stop!" Servius squealed at the top of his lungs. "Lower your weapons!" Upon hearing their leader, the enemy crews backed away from the shield wall and dropped their weapons to the deck.

Titus uttered with a smile. "That turned out well."

"Lost a man," Bastakas said as he walked up to the general, wiping sticky blood from his cheek.

"You'll lose them *all* once word of this gets back to my people," Servius hissed.

Drysten stepped forward from the shield wall and looked over the bodies. After the fighting was over, the only man they had lost was one of Titus', of which Drysten had not known his name. He turned to Diocles. "Grab their weapons and bring the slaves to the Fortuna."

Diocles nodded and delivered the order. Servius' men had now dropped their blades and shields, and raised their hands as to not agitate any of their attackers into killing them. Servius was still in Titus' firm grip and Drysten proudly oversaw the prisoners being freed and sent aboard his vessel. After the slaves had been moved, the enemy crews were put onto the second ship. The second vessel was then tethered to Servius', and a guard of ten men stood across from them on the boat that had once been commanded by Servius. When that was all arranged, he was brought into the second level of the Fortuna by Diocles and Bastakas to be interrogated by Drysten. The slaves were mostly crying tears of joy upon being rescued, and each one made it a point to thank every man they could when they too were brought aboard.

Bors the Younger sought out Drysten through the now crowded upper level of the ship. "Knew I smelled something when they were bringing me up."

Drysten smiled, and the two men shared a brief hug before making their way down to interrogate the enemy captain.

"When was the last time you saw Isolde?" Drysten asked as they walked by the two Cretans, who were overjoyed by the presence of their sister.

Bors sighed. "She was taken to his villa straight away. Most of the women were."

Drysten felt himself turning red in the face as his mind was conjuring images of what could have been done to her in such a place. "Do you know if she's still there?"

Bors shook his head. "Sorry, brother."

"I guess I'll just have to ask him myself," Drysten murmured. He gave his friend a pat on the shoulder and turned towards the entrance to the middle level of the Fortuna. Shortly, he found his way into the room containing the foul-mouthed captain, currently in the middle of spitting curses toward his attackers.

Drysten stood above him, staring into the eyes of the man who had taken his woman. "Leave," he commanded the nearby men. He waited until the shuffle of feet quietly disappeared and knelt down to the man. 'Do you recognize me, piggy?"

Servius spat toward Drysten, hitting him in the chest. "I don't give a rat's ass who you are you worthless fucking—"

Drysten cut the man off mid-sentence with a quick strike from his right hand. "I'm going to ask you a series of questions. You're going to answer them. If you don't, I will open your fat *belly* and throw your still-squirming corpse to the fish."

Servius' nose was now bleeding, but still, he remained defiant. "I'd bet you wouldn't last an hour in my care," he said with a smile.

Drysten smirked as he leaned closer. "Maybe. Maybe not. That is not the situation we find ourselves in. Is it, *piggy*?" He leaned back and walked toward the doorway.

There was a strong smell of filth in the room, leading Drysten to wonder if his new prisoner had voided his bowels. "*You* took my woman. Maybe in return, I'll make you into one." Drysten slowly began to remove his knife from its sheath.

Servius' tone turned more agreeable at the threat. It was apparent from everything Drysten knew of the man, he enjoyed his time with women. "What is it, then?"

Drysten pulled a box up and made himself comfortable. "My woman was taken by you near the town of Burdigala a couple months ago. Raven colored hair, fair skin, and by now it would be obvious she's pregnant. You're going to tell me where I can find her."

Servius chuckled. "In a man's bed most likely. She may be pregnant, but there are still uses for her." Drysten placed his dagger on his lap, catching Servius' gaze. "We wait for the pregnant ones to give birth before we sell them. Young ones can fetch quite the price as well as the women."

"I asked you where I can find her. Answer me quick, or I'll burn down everything you have, and leave you with no eyes and *cockless* in the streets," Drysten hissed.

"My home," Servius responded. "Take the bitch and be done with it. I have prettier ones I can sell off in her place."

"So, she *isn't* on your island?" Drysten asked.

Servius shook his head. "Can't trust most of my men to keep their hands off the women. Keep the fairer ones in my villa."

"How many guards are in your villa?" Drysten questioned.

"Twenty when I'm away," Servius reluctantly answered.

Drysten rose and sheathed his dagger before sarcastically thanking the man, and made his way to the top deck.

"Find out anything useful?" Titus inquired.

Drysten nodded. "I know where my woman is as well as how many men to cut through to get to her."

"Guess that means we're done posing as merchants,"

Diocles guessed.

Drysten shook his head. "Actually, no it doesn't. Our original plan will still work, especially now that we know there are fewer fighters to deal with."

Titus nodded. "I agree. Tomorrow we leave you and your group off on the coast. It should only take you a couple hours to walk to Rodanum if the Frisian is correct. I will lead the raid on the island."

A voice came from behind Drysten. "And what of us?"

Drysten turned and saw Bors walking up in front of four others from Servius' ship, then turned to Titus. "Bors is a good fighter, I can't vouch for the others."

"If they want to fight, I say we let them," Titus said with a smile. "What of the prisoners?"

Drysten thought of the rabble on the far ship. "The punishment for enslaving Romans is death, or so says imperial law."

Titus sighed. "You're quite right." He walked toward Bastakas, then gestured toward the prisoners. "Make their deaths quick."

Bastakas nodded obediently. "Yes, sir." Then turned to relay the order. Drysten felt it was his duty to watch, considering it was ultimately his command that sealed their fates. Along with Diocles and Amiram, he leaned over the starboard side of the Fortuna and witnessed the slaughter. One man had gotten free of his bonds and made a run at one of Titus' men, but was cut down with little effort. The swipe of the sword came from overhead and landed into the side of his neck, sending him to the ground screaming before he was finished off by a short stab into his heart. The rest were now moving backwards, begging for their lives when the rest of Titus' men moved on them. Two managed to jump overboard to avoid being stabbed, but their hands being bound meant they had little hope to stay afloat in a full suit of Roman leather. Most simply fell to their knees, shrieking for mercy as their lives were quickly ended.

Drysten felt little guilt for dooming these men. He knew they were usually on the other end of exchanges such as these. The only difference was the men and women they murdered were civilians, most likely incapable of putting up a fight or defending themselves. One man tried to persuade his killer by mentioning his family, something Drysten found quite ironic.

How many families have your people broken up in the name of making some coin? Drysten thought to himself as he watched the sword cut the man's throat. *This will be how all of you meet your end. I'll do it myself if I must.*

"I don't like killing prisoners," Titus said as he walked up to stand next to Drysten.

Drysten sighed. "This is the punishment for their crimes. The Romans may not hold influence here, but *we* do. They made their mistakes."

Titus nodded his head. "Aye. What do you want to do with the bodies?"

Drysten thought for a moment. "Put them all on one of the ships and then burn it at sea. We can't risk someone washing up ashore and alerting the people here of what's happened. Try and see if you can fish out the two that jumped overboard if you can."

"And our man?" Titus inquired in reference to the lone casualty Drysten's crew incurred.

Drysten turned. "Who did we lose?"

Titus sighed. "His name was Alexius. He was young. Young but noble beyond his years."

Drysten grimaced. The sight of the prisoners being killed did not rattle him in the slightest, but losing a man under his command was painful. Even if he had not known him. "Wrap him in linen. Use the old sail. We'll take him ashore in Rodanum once this is over and burn the body."

Titus glanced to his feet. "It's a nice thought, but he didn't worship the old gods. I believe the Christians are asked to be buried."

"Then we bury him with what honors we can. Have one of the other Christians say a prayer for him as well," Drysten said quietly. "Perhaps Matthew could be of help? Did he have family?"

"Only the ones you see here."

"Then we will send him off as a brother."

Titus nodded and moved to Bastakas to relay the order.

CHAPTER VIII

The clash with Servius lasted roughly an hour, meaning it would be another hour added onto the trip toward Rodanum. Once the fighting was over and the prisoners had been executed, their bodies were promptly thrown onto the top deck of Servius' second vessel to be set ablaze. Any food discovered among their belongings was carried onto the ship Servius himself had captained, which was then moored on the nearby beach. A small group of men was left to guard it, along with the former captives rescued so far. The plan for after the journey through Frisia was to take Titus and his men back to the vessel, help them return it to the water, then the two groups would go their separate ways.

Men were cramming themselves into any space they could find to try and grab some last-minute rest, while a skeleton crew remained to man the ship. Drysten strolled through his men, seeing Diocles and Heraclius speaking amongst themselves on the top deck, while Dagonet was explaining the layout of the area they would traverse to Bastakas and Lucius. Drysten briefly listened until he was satisfied he knew what to expect, and walked to the Fortuna's bow once he spied his old friend, Bors.

"The Greek seems a good fighter," Bors stated in a mildly impressed tone.

Drysten nodded. "Doesn't scare easy. The men have quickly learned to respect him."

"But what of the Frisian?"

Drysten was reminded how the only interaction Bors had with Jorrit was the moment their belongings were stolen from Servius, an occurrence Drysten still did not know much about. "I understand you've encountered him during your time in captivity."

Bors nodded. "Bastard stole all of our belongings from the ones who stole them from *us*. I wouldn't trust him. There was some kind of acquaintanceship amongst him and the slaver."

Drysten glanced behind him to make sure Jorrit was out of earshot. "What *kind* of familiarity?"

Bors shook his head. "I don't know exactly, but I could say they were somewhat kind with one another until Jorrit moved to steal from him."

A mindful Drysten turned to Bors. "Tell me what happened the day you were captured."

Bors let out a long sigh. It was apparent touching on this subject made him feel uneasy. "When your father left, a man named Marhaus offered to take us all to Britannia. I knew in my heart it was too good to be true, as all the families struggled to find passage before your father ventured off. Then, one day, this *savior* shows up promising us all the one thing we needed," he began. "He said he was traveling to Eboracum, and anyone who wanted to go with him just had to pay what they could to purchase crossing. Most of the people who were with us were families of the crew, or those who wished to remain employed by your father." Bors paused and looked out to sea. "We sailed a few miles out when his guards killed two elderly men to send a message to the rest. I managed to kill the fucker who went after Baak's father, but they chose to punish me by making me kill him... myself."

Drysten hadn't encountered such cruel souls before. Even knowing the rumors associated with Servius' people, he still had a strange feeling of dread when dealing with them. He could not tell if this was simply because he was new to commanding men into battle, or if he truly was unprepared.

Bors hung his head low and drew in a heavy breath. "They lined up five of our people and told me if I didn't kill him myself, they would cut their throats one by one until I was... convinced I should play along with their little game. They took such enjoyment from it all..."

"That's how they control their captives. Through fear," Drysten responded.

Bors nodded. "I did what the fuckers wanted, and I looked into his fucking eyes while I did it." Bors' eyes momentarily shut as tears began to well up.

"I don't need to hear—"

"They made me do it slow..."

"Bors..."

"I—"

"We'll kill them all! I promise." Drysten gently placed a hand on his friend's shoulder. "Now, tell me of where you were taken."

"They brought us all to an island to the North after they stopped off in the port we're heading to now. That's where most of the women left us, along with Isolde," Bors answered.

Drysten grimaced. "Was she injured at all?"

Bors shook his head. "Not that I saw. She was with me and a few others down below deck when it started. I don't think he'd hurt the women, just men."

"I guess men are easier to replace than a beautiful woman," Drysten observed.

Bors nodded once again. "We were separated into two groups once we arrived at the island. One was made up of the children or the elderly, the other, comprising the men they felt could resist them."

"Which one were you in?" Drysten asked sarcastically.

Bors betrayed a brief smile at Drysten's attempt for humor, but that smile slowly faded as he glanced down to the fresh brand of enslavement burned into his left arm. "We were only made to march to Servius' villa once during the time we were separated. We were ordered to deliver supplies brought from further North."

"How long ago was that?" Drysten asked.

Bors glanced into the sky as he considered his answer. "Only about a week. And before you ask, yes, she was still there."

Until that moment, Drysten was only operating under the hope his woman was still alive. The idea he now knew of her whereabouts made his heart leap with elation. If his plan worked, it could all be over by the time the sun came up the next morning. "Thank you, brother. Should you wish to fight, you will need to speak with Titus."

Bors smirked. "And miss a chance to gut those whoresons?"

Drysten gave his friend a reassuring nod and began making his way below deck to collect his items. He waded through the men on the second level, and to his surprise, they were mostly excited for the fight they would face. It seemed to Drysten the tales of Servius' cruelty moved them, who now saw it as their responsibility to make sure more men and women weren't the subject of kidnappings in the future. Servius made the mistake of bringing his business into the lives of his father's people, and they would be the ones who would make him pay.

"You ready for tonight?" a voice spoke behind him.

Drysten turned and saw Petras and Paulus standing behind him. "I am. Although, I'd say I'm more ready to get this over with."

"I know how you feel," Paulus replied.

"We wanted to thank you for helping us get our sister back," Petras stated as he inched forward.

Drysten smiled. "That is truly not necessary."

"Once the empire abandoned the Western regions, it seemed they took the concept of order with them," Paulus stated.

Drysten solemnly nodded. "I suspect it falls to people like us to enforce the virtues of a once-great empire."

And Drysten was right. For centuries, the Roman Empire had provided security for the Britons and other tribes in the Southwest portions of the continent. Drysten understood this was quite ironic when considering his ancestors most likely played some type of role in the uncountable number of wars against Rome. But nevertheless, when their legions began to withdraw from these territories, the pirates and raiders saw the opportunity to more freely take advantage of these unprotected areas. The responsibility of protection went to local lords who routinely used their new influence to make themselves wealthier at their people's expense.

"Promise us we'll burn it all down when we leave," Paulus emphatically requested.

Drysten smiled again and made sure his next remark was audible enough for Servius at the far end of the ship to hear. "When we leave this place, we'll take everything these people have with us! The only thing we'll leave him will be ashes and dead men!" There was a resounding cry of approval from the Fortuna's men, but what satisfied Drysten more than any of it was the dark scowl across the face of the slovenly man in chains.

Drysten looked back at the smiling Cretans and patted Paulus on the shoulder before he returned to donning his boiled leather tunic. He looped his arm through and secured it to his chest, capturing the slight odor of the leather as it was wafted into his nose. It fit looser on him than it had when they first set out, a side effect of eating smaller meals. The vambraces and greaves fit him in the same manner as he was used to, with the vambrace on his left arm still slightly scratched where arrows would scrape against his arm during hunts with Bors or his father. Finally, he slung his brown cloak over his shoulders, and overlaid it with his father's bearskin.

"You look like a lord," Jorrit observantly stated as Drysten was finishing up. The Frisian glanced behind him where Bors the Younger was attempting to stare a hole into the back of his head. "The big man looks a lot like his father."

Drysten chuckled. "The last time I saw him, he was a bit bigger around the waist. But yes, I suppose he still resembles him quite a lot."

Jorrit walked closer to Drysten. "I kept my word. I led you here. When will you let me go?"

"Once it's over and done with, you will have your freedom," Drysten answered.

A frustrated Jorrit looked Drysten in the eye. "You sought to kill me when I was defenseless, but still, I chose to trust you."

"And now you're wondering if that was a mistake," Drysten indifferently replied as he clasped the bearskin and cloak together with a tin brooch.

"I am," Jorrit coldly replied.

Drysten chuckled. "Jorrit, the men have gotten used to you. Killing you would bring them no satisfaction. Once the journey is over, and there is no opportunity for you to impede it in any way, we will take you home."

Jorrit grumbled something under his breath before turning away in annoyance.

"One more thing," Drysten said, causing the Frisian to turn back. "How do you know him?"

Jorrit slowly turned back, wearing an apprehensive expression. "Who?"

Drysten nodded toward Servius, clearly doing his best to try and figure out what conversation was being had between his captor and the only other prisoner on the ship.

"The fat man?" Jorrit asked with a raised eyebrow.

Drysten nodded as he stared into the Frisian's eyes, doing his best to make the man uncomfortable.

"I told you—" Jorrit began.

"I want the truth this time, Jorrit." Drysten slowly inched his hand toward the hilt of his knife.

Jorrit grumbled something to himself, but this time he returned with a different answer. "I know him."

"How?" Drysten questioned in a harsh tone.

"My chieftain bought slaves from him. I sailed to make the deals with his son," Jorrit explained.

Drysten took a step forward. "There's more, isn't there?"

Jorrit shook his head. "That is all. I swear it on my father's grave."

"So if I ask him—?" Drysten began.

"He will say the same. What does this have to do with our deal? Will you, or will you *not* honor your word?"

Drysten nodded. "I will. I promised it." At that, Drysten walked by Jorrit toward the stairs, giving a reassuring nod to the Frisian.

As he made his way up, he saw the small group of men he would be leading into Rodanum. It consisted of both Cretans, Dagonet as their guide, Bastakas, Heraclius, Diocles, Cynwrig, and another one of Titus' men named Lucius. Cynwrig was initially going to aid Titus in the attack on the island, but was able to talk his way into Drysten's group once Bors the Younger and his four slave companions offered to join the battle on the island. Drysten knew under most circumstances he should be the one leading his crew, but Titus' experience in war was an invaluable addition he knew he was lucky to have.

All Drysten's men were ready to go, dressed casually enough to avoid suspicion but still bearing swords. Both Cretans and Dagonet were also carrying their bows but knew if anyone asked, to simply explain they were ashore to find food for their crew.

"Tonight we find the rest of them," Cynwrig optimistically stated to Drysten.

Drysten chuckled. "Remember when I said your wealth

lay ahead of you?"

"I suppose so, yes," Cynwrig replied.

"Well, here's your chance to steal it." Drysten gave his smiling friend a pat on the back and stepped toward the bow.

The dock they would be disembarking to was now off in the distance. The spiritual men said last-minute prayers to whatever gods they believed, touching medallions they had hung around their necks. An interesting detail Drysten was surprised to see was Heraclius and Lucius both worshipped the god Mithras.

Matthew himself was unsure of his role to play in the battle, but was put at ease when Titus told him he was not ready for fighting yet. "Your time for fighting will come, lad," Drysten heard him say to the priest. "There's no need to rush such things."

"I feel like I should be helping. Lord Drysten saved my life. It's only right I should repay him now," Matthew protested through a swollen cheek. His limp had subsided, but his face was taking longer to mend. Magnus, the ship's expert with medicine, had concluded he was given several broken bones that would take longer to heal than the two days it had been since he was rescued.

"You *will* repay him, my boy. You'll just have to wait for the chance," Titus told him as he placed a hand on his shoulder. "If you serve him, you'll be one of those close enough to watch out for him in the future. There's no finer way to repay a man than that." Matthew had sullenly nodded before making his way back down below deck.

The dock was now close enough to see the fishermen searching through their fish traps near the beach. There were only a handful of them, and each one stopped to stare at the oncoming vessel. To them, the Fortuna was an odd sight indeed. The Romans had rarely ventured through these parts for any reason, and the sight of a Roman ship would be startling to the men and women who worried continuously about raiding parties.

"You think they'll tell anyone?" Diocles asked Drysten.

"Tell them what? They saw a ship pass through?" he responded.

Diocles shrugged. "I mean it may look odd to have a ship only dock for a moment to drop a few men off, then leave immediately."

"I doubt there'll be any cause for concern. Don't forget, Servius' ships were of Roman design as well," Drysten replied, silently hoping he was right. The only men he was going to have with him weren't fitted for war, just a quick skirmish should the need arise.

The Fortuna began to slow as Titus was giving the order to prepare for docking. After the ship slowed, then eventually stopped, the ramp was set and Drysten's company made their way ashore. Immediately to the left of the dock was an old Roman building with a thatch roof and cracked walls, but for the most part, the inhabited structures were those found on the beach. They were an odd sight, all of which being made with mud.

Drysten was first ashore and walked to the other end of the dock as he waited for the rest of his men. Once they were assembled and everyone was satisfied nothing was forgotten, he waved Titus off and the Fortuna began to depart.

"We're standing at the very edge of an Empire, boys," Heraclius commented. "It's hard to believe there were ever *Romans* here."

Dagonet scoffed. "Even Rome couldn't find a reason to stay here long."

"Let's get to it. We have a few hours of walking to get through," Drysten ordered.

The company began making its way through the small village. Out of curiosity, Dagonet asked a local what name was bestowed on the area. To everyone's surprise, they found out it was never bestowed a name by its own people. The fifty or so individuals who remained there simply called it home.

"Hard to believe anybody wants to call *this* home," Diocles mentioned.

Drysten laughed. "Not everyone got to grow up near Achaia, Diocles."

"Neither did I," the Greek responded. "I grew up near the place Alexander was born."

Drysten was about to ask the name of his home until he was interrupted by an old woman carrying a basket over her head. She bumped into Drysten when he wasn't looking and proceeded to hurl what Drysten would assume to be curses at him, though nobody could understand the obscure language she spoke. Trying to avoid attention, he held up his hand to signal her to stop the commotion and gave her a silver coin from his coin pouch. In response, the woman gave him a toothless smile and proceeded to lift her tattered gown up, causing the men to create a small commotion of their own as they quickly walked in the other direction.

Dagonet couldn't help but laugh at Drysten. "Really know your way around a woman, don't you, Lord?"

Drysten, white in the face, simply stared straight ahead. "Nobody speaks of this. *Ever.*"

Command was nothing new to Titus. He led soldiers into battle for the Empire during the best years of his life, even met two emperors during his time under their banner. Though for as privileged as those experiences were, his favorite company to keep would always be that of his own men. People thought he used his influence to become wealthy in the empire's absence, but truthfully, Titus never had any aspirations to become rich. He simply knew how. When the Empire left Britannia, he recruited men who had fought in its legions but decided to stay behind. These men had fought for various self-proclaimed emperors against other Romans and raiders, so by the time the Empire officially left, they chose to remain with the only people who had consistently been present in their lives.

Titus was one such soldier. He met a high-ranking aristocrat when he was first stationed in Eboracum. Her name was Marivonna Glannder, and soon after the empire left the shores of Britannia, they married. They relocated to Londinium, the city with the largest number of defectors, and began to put together a group of men to turn into a small legion. Once he recruited a significant enough force, they then turned to mercenary work for the various lords of Britannia, and even the king of Armorica across the Oceanus Britannicus. He helped defend their borders from raiders such as the Saxons, Gaels, and Picts. He made a name for himself and made his men rich and prosperous in the process. The very same men he would now lead into battle this coming night.

"It'll be dark soon," a voice said from behind Titus.

Titus nodded. "We'll be there right when we need to be."

"And what do you think of this plan?"

Titus chuckled. "I think it's not your concern, Frisian."

Jorrit stepped up beside Titus on the bow. "From my point of view, I believe it is. If you lose, then I have a harder time getting myself home."

"That may be so," Titus responded indifferently.

Jorrit grumbled. "What assurance do I have that you will honor the boy's word?"

"You're not to leave the ship until this is over. That is not negotiable," Titus sternly replied.

"I will not be denied my freedom, *Roman,*" the Frisian hissed before walking away in frustration.

Titus looked up into the sky toward the flocks of birds hovering above, wondering if this was some sort of omen from his god. He was raised to be a Christian, but still understood there were others who shaped the world he lived in. Mithras awarded traits such as bravery, Neptune guided men on the sea, and the Christian god rewarded those who embraced compassion. These were the three which Titus concluded influenced his life the most, and thus, worshipped them differently.

He guessed Mithras was probably the most powerful of the three, as it had become a favorite of the Roman soldiers stationed in Britannia long before he was even born. It was also one reason he embraced Drysten's employment so quickly. The boy walked into his villa wearing a medallion around his neck of a sun, Mithras' symbol, though Titus could not figure out if Drysten understood it.

"Bors!" Titus called to the men behind him.

The largest man aboard the Fortuna walked toward his new commander. "Sir?"

Titus turned to face him. "What can we expect from the island?"

"When we left, there were no more than fifty men at the island. Servius takes the best fighters with him, so now that you've killed *them,* the only people left to worry about are the scrawny or old," Bors answered.

Titus raised an eyebrow. "What purpose does he have for weak old men?"

Bors sighed. "They're very often the cruelest. They know how to crack a whip and use them more than the newer men."

Titus grimaced at the idea of Roman citizens being sold into slavery and treated so horribly. It was one thing for men to sell themselves into the service of someone to pay their debts, it was another not to have a say in your own fate even though you were given these rights by being a Roman. To Titus, there almost seemed no point to being born a Roman anymore. "How high are the walls?" he asked while massaging the space between his eyes.

Bors pondered for a moment. "Eight feet or so. Two towers on the North and Southwest corners and no ramparts."

Titus rubbed his chin. "Only two towers? What happened to the third?"

Bors shrugged. "I imagine it was ruined by a storm sometime in the past. The sole protection on the Eastern wall is a canal of about five feet in depth."

"Its width?" Titus asked.

"All of about five, but the main reason to avoid it would be the spikes at its base. It is also where they toss the ones who... perish in their care," Bors responded.

Titus grimaced in frustration. "Then tell me of the layout inside the compound."

"The cages they kept us in are on the Southern wall," Bors answered. "The Northern corner is where the guardhouse is located."

Titus stood in thought for a moment. He now knew any assault against the walls would have to be directed toward the Southern or Western walls. The ditch in front of the Eastern wall could halt any progress in an eye blink if enough men fell in. Not to mention with the abundance of dead bodies at its base, any small wound could spell a gruesome death later on. That left the South and West sides to consider. "Where are the docks in relation to the compound?"

"To the Southeast, about a hundred paces or so. The main entrance is on the Western wall," Bors answered.

A frustrated Titus ran his hands through his hair. "I suppose that means we'll be running around the compound from the dock."

Bors nodded. "We do have another option."

Titus' frustrated expression turned to that of interest. "Explain."

"Servius' second in command, his son, sleeps outside the walls," Bors said with a smile, "If we show the men we have both of the people responsible for paying them, they may simply do as we ask."

Titus betrayed a smile as he pondered aloud. "We could also attempt this with Servius when we arrive, negating the need to waste time with a kidnapping."

Bors nodded. "Good thought."

CHAPTER IX

D rysten's band made it to the town of Rodanum almost the moment the sun had begun to slide away behind the hills. To Drysten's surprise, it was a fairly Roman looking town, including stone buildings which still boasted their tiled roofing. They entered through a wooden gateway on the Northwest side of the city, where they were stopped by two ineffectual-looking guards who questioned their business.

"Just passing through. Looking to stay the night," Drysten told them. Both guards seemed suspicious, yet satisfied as the response seemed adequate. They let them pass into the town and recommended one of the taverns straight down the road. Drysten and his men thanked the guards for the recommendation and slowly proceeded their way down the street.

"Dagonet, take us by the villa," Drysten directed.

It was still too early to make any kind of move on Servius' estate, but the men knew it would be wise for all of them to see it while there was still sunlight. They made their way down a road that gradually turned left from the gate, where they spied a cluster of wooden homes and a tavern. "We'll wait for darkness in there," Drysten declared as they passed by. On the other side of the inn, there was a stone wall of about eight feet, typical for Roman villas in much the same way as Petuaria's.

Dagonet halted and motioned toward the wall. "Other side of this is where we want to be."

Drysten nodded and led the men toward the front of the villa, hoping to see through any gates or cracks in the stone wall. The only opening was being watched by three guards between the road and a small guard post. Each man was clad in a faded red tunic and mail.

"Looks like they wear uniforms here," Diocles whispered in surprise.

Heraclius glanced behind him toward the Cretans. "Lord, there's a two-story building overlooking the villa's courtyard. If we put the two Greeks up in one of those windows, they can thin the lot out before we even get inside."

Drysten turned to Petras and Paulus. "Take Lucius with you. You'll loose on them once we've set a fire inside." The two Cretans nodded and moved to the back of the group to inform Lucius of his task.

The group picked the pace up once more and began to pass by the guards of Servius' estate, who eyed them suspiciously as they went. He managed to get a quick look through the metal bars of the gates and saw two more guards standing next to a statue centered in the courtyard. As much as he wanted to strain his neck and see more, he fought the urge and continued on.

The men eventually made it to the end of the street, clearly marked by the rubble of the old Roman fort. Most of the fort had been knocked down when the Romans finally left the area. Dagonet explained how at one time, it was taken by a kingdom made up of local barbarian tribes, but Rome later retook the fort about seventy years later. However, when Rome decided the area was to be abandoned, they reduced the fort to ash and rubble.

In its place, there stood a wooden palisade roughly half the dimensions of the original fort, and presently garrisoned by some of the most useless looking guards Drysten had ever laid eyes on. It was apparent they had about half the amount of gear they needed for a full garrison, meaning what weapons were in use could probably be found on the guards currently patrolling the city. Only a handful appeared to wear any armor, leading Drysten to guess it must have been reserved for displaying rank.

"Gods above, we could capture this whole fucking town if we wanted to," Diocles noted in surprise.

Dagonet chuckled. "Servius is the one who really runs it. These men just let everyone feel like they have protection from him. In reality, that couldn't be further from the truth." The men passed by the front of the fort and made a loop toward the entrance they had arrived through.

"We'll go back to that tavern we spotted and wait until nightfall," Drysten commanded.

The group made their way back, cutting through some alleyways instead of taking the main road to avoid suspicion from any guards patrolling the area.

They soon arrived at the modest-looking tavern and slowly made their way inside. "Well, this is inconvenient," Diocles said as he gazed over the room. Sitting at every one of the tables inside the tavern, were men wearing red.

Drysten awkwardly cleared his throat and moved toward the strangely familiar looking man he presumed was the owner, counting as he walked. *One, two, three...* he counted silently as he kept weaving through the chairs and tables. The occupants had all began gazing on the newcomers as they piled inside. Drysten finally counted to a total of fifteen men seated at the tables.

"Greetings," he said to the tavern-keeper. "I would like to rent rooms enough for my men before we leave in the morning.

The man eyed Drysten suspiciously and looked as though he was about to decline until he saw the golden necklace hiding underneath his father's bearskin cloak. Once he noticed the fine piece of jewelry, his eyes widened and he became much more hospitable. "And how many are with you, Lord?"

"We're nine, and we'll sleep in one room if we have to.

We must be off early tomorrow," Drysten responded in an authoritative tone.

The owner looked over Drysten's men. "And where might ye be goin, Lord?"

Drysten gazed over the man's face. For some unknown reason, he genuinely disliked this stranger from the start. "That is of no concern to you. Do you have a room available or not? I'm sure somebody in this town will."

"Our rooms are small, but I'll get two fixed up for you. Won't take but a minute, Lord" At that, the man moved upstairs. Drysten turned around and gazed over the silent men clad in red, who plainly sized Drysten up as if wondering whether they could get away with robbing him. In response, Heraclius slowly sauntered over to Drysten's side and banged on a countertop for service, followed soon by the others. After the huge Greek walked through the strangers, they clearly decided it wasn't worth the trouble that they could find themselves in.

"Service!" Heraclius yelled to the back room as he pounded his fist on the counter.

"Give them a minute, you dullard. They probably only have one or two people working this whole room," Bastakas said to him as he moved in beside him.

"I have a whole building full of people to take care of!" a woman screamed back.

"Gah! I haven't had any ale in me for a long enough spell," Heraclius complained as he again pounded his fist on the counter. "I can hear somebody back there moving cups —"

"Just a *moment!*"

Heraclius grumbled something Drysten couldn't hear to the girl, who poked her head out of the back room and hissed something to the big Greek without betraying the slightest hint of intimidation.

Drysten looked toward the kitchen but only caught a glimpse of the girl's shadow as she walked away.

"Just get me an ale before my throat dries up, and stop your staring!"

"Odd one," Bastakas quipped to Heraclius as the woman apparently walked away.

"Most beautiful ones are in some way," Heraclius noted.

Bastakas let out a low laugh. "Even pupped, she's a rare thing."

Drysten had not paid much attention to the exchange until that moment. He had been turned with his back to the countertop as he fidgeted with his medallion and stared out the window. He did his best to look as bored as possible, but in reality, he was doing his utmost to try and listen in on the conversations around him. He managed to learn the leader of the men located on the island was Marhaus, seemingly the very same man which Bors spoke of. Other than that single piece of information, nothing was relevant or interesting enough to listen in on. But when he heard Bastakas speak of the rare beauty who happened to be pregnant, he suddenly stopped caring about anyone else in the room.

He slowly turned his head, craning his neck to try and peer his way into the kitchen. He saw a woman with dark, unkempt hair standing with her back turned as she began filling wooden cups with ale and placing them on a tray. He almost lost his balance when his elbow slipped out from underneath him on the bar, causing one of Marhaus' men to snicker in amusement.

"Somethin' caught yer fancy, Lord?" the man asked. "Sorry to say, but you can't have that one. Our boss has first dibs once she's done wit her babe. Says it's bad luck for her to be touched b'fore then."

Drysten awkwardly turned and smiled to the man before returning his gaze to the doorway leading to the kitchen. Standing there with a cup of ale in her hand, looking just as happy to see Drysten as he was to see her, was Isolde. Drysten felt his heart stop as he had to quickly devise a plan for her freedom. She began to smile, but was stopped once

Drysten subtly shook his head. Isolde lowered her gaze as she understood what Drysten was thinking, and shuffled away as if she had never seen him.

"Girl!" Heraclius began until he was quickly shushed quietly by Bastakas, who noticed the way she was looking at Drysten.

"You really are a simpleton, brother," Bastakas jokingly whispered to his friend.

Drysten saw Bastakas gesture at him after tapping Heraclius' arm. Heraclius' face showed the new understanding of the situation. "For fuck's sake, you had to find her *here*? In a tavern with *all* of the bastard's men?" he whispered.

Drysten snapped out of his surprised state and beckoned Isolde over as if they had never met. "Girl, come here," he said in an authoritative voice.

Isolde produced a disgruntled expression, making it clear she wasn't amused by his tone and slowly began walking over. "Can I get you something, *Lord*?" she said in a sarcastic tone before beginning to whisper. "Speak to me like that again, and I'll poison your drink."

Diocles, who apparently was not as observant as Bastakas, slowly spit the ale Isolde had just delivered back into his cup before glaring at her in confusion.

Drysten smirked as he glanced to his men. Most of them were still unaware of who Isolde was and were still talking amongst themselves. "Think we can make a move on them here?" he asked Diocles.

Diocles subtly turned and surveyed the room. Of the fifteen men, only two were without a weapon. The rest were keeping their blades close in light of the group of strangers who walked through the door. "If we tried them, there's a good chance only a few men would walk away from it, and I don't know which side they'd be on."

"Let the men know to be ready," Drysten commanded in a whisper. Diocles moved off down the line and quietly instructed each man to keep their swords ready, all the while acting as though he was trying to find somebody to gamble with.

Drysten looked outside to make sure it was getting dark, then turned back to Isolde, who had been listening in on his order.

"These men are *yours?*" she whispered in surprise.

Drysten nodded and began to whisper. "Where are the others who were taken?"

Isolde glanced at Servius' men behind Drysten. "A handful were sold immediately. Most are on the island. The only people here are another girl who spends most of her days in the villa with Servius' wife and myself."

"And how many men will we have to fight through in there?" Drysten asked.

Isolde paused for a moment, clearly waiting for a moment to respond when none of Servius' men were watching. "Most of them are here. I would be surprised if there were more than half a dozen inside the villa. You showed up at a good time."

Drysten nodded. "Go about your business as you normally would. Don't forget, we have never met before."

Isolde nodded and went back into the kitchen after taking nearby empty cups. Drysten could not be sure, but he thought he could hear her crying in the back. Whether they were tears of happiness or fear, he could not tell. He turned back to Diocles, who had just returned from informing the men of the situation. They all quietly tensed as they stared at their leader.

"Not the best at being subtle, are we?" he jokingly remarked to Diocles.

"Eh, maybe not, but at least we know we can fight well enough."

Drysten chuckled. "Tell the Cretans to string their bows and tell Heraclius and Bastakas to block the door. You and Lucius are to keep men away from Petras and Paulus so we can let them do their work. Cynwrig, Dagonet, and I will kill anyone we can."

Diocles let out a nervous sigh. "Alright then, let's get this started." With a slight grin, he walked through the men once more and relayed the new orders.

Drysten watched as the Cretans strung their bows out-of-view of the men they would soon send their arrows into. Shortly after the group was instructed on their plans, Diocles returned. Heraclius and Bastakas acted as though Heraclius was searching for a woman for the night and walked toward the door. Upon their arrival, they became silent and glanced toward Drysten.

Drysten knew it would fall to him to start the fight, and he slowly undid the brooch clasping his cloak over his shoulders. To fight so many men in such a small space would require mobility, which he wouldn't have under the weight of the impressive cloak draped over his shoulders. He set it down on the counter right as Isolde nervously poked her head out from the kitchen. Drysten nodded to her and smirked before turning toward the nearest table. He glanced once more to his right to make sure his men were ready, then in one movement drew his dagger and drove it through the back of the closest man's neck.

The man was given a quick death. He had been laughing one moment, and in the next he was meeting his ancestors in whatever afterlife the people of this area chose to believe in. Blood spattered onto the face of the man sitting to the deceased enemy's right, causing him to fumble with his sword belt before being stabbed in the stomach by Dagonet. The man let out a wail, causing anyone who had not seen the bloodshed to turn and stand as they drew their swords. Drysten managed to kick the table over into the lap of the man sitting across from him, then drew his sword to parry a blow from another as he stood to his left.

The Cretans had loosed two arrows into men sitting across the room before the first one to challenge him ran from their left, only to be stopped by Lucius. He cut low into the attacker's leg, causing him to fall to his wounded side where he was finished off by a stab in the chest from Diocles. Blood was spurting out onto the floor of the tavern when the owner ran down the stairs to check on the commotion. He was about to yell something when Paulus sent an arrow into the wall next to him, causing him to turn tail and run back up the stairs. On that shot, Paulus' bowstring snapped. With wide eyes, he glanced to his brother and drew his blade.

Two men rushed the door and were met by Heraclius and Bastakas. The first was driven back into the other by Heraclius' massive swings of his sword before Bastakas swiped his blade right, narrowly missing them both. The second man stumbled down to the ground, while the first parried a blow from Heraclius and was able to draw blood with a quick stab to the Greek's side. Heraclius grunted in pain, signaling Bastakas to rush him. Doing so, he grabbed the collar of the man's tunic and dragged him away from Heraclius, who stabbed forward and embedded his blade into the man's stomach.

The second man was now up off the ground and charging at Bastakas, who was turned and unable to defend himself. The man plunged his blade through his chest, sending him to the ground with a low groan before his killer was struck in the neck with an arrow from Petras.

Eight men were now left for Drysten's company to deal with. Now without Bastakas, and Heraclius injured or dead, Drysten yelled for Diocles to move to the door, leaving Lucius and Paulus to protect their only remaining archer in Petras. Bastakas was now dead in front of the men, sending Heraclius into a rage. He rushed forward into a group of two men still unsure of who to attack first. The nearest man put his sword up to parry the heavy blow from the Greek, but was unable to stop the force of the overhand swing. Heraclius' blade met with his and was still able to drive its way down into the man's face. There was a scream and spatter of blood as Heraclius again drew his blade up and forced it down, embedding itself halfway through the man's head before he let it go. The second man attempted to swipe into the Greek's neck, but was stopped when Heraclius grabbed his arm tight enough for Servius' man to drop his sword. The Greek plucked the fallen blade from the ground and plunged it downward into the side of the man's neck.

The biggest of Servius' men ran from the back of the room toward Drysten and swung wildly down toward Drysten's head. Drysten nimbly hopped to the side, narrowly avoiding the blade as he brought his own up to stab the man. He was stopped when an elbow connected into his temple, sending him to the ground in a haze. Spots and stars were dancing around in his vision as he looked up to see the man getting ready to finish him. Just then, a shadow danced through the air and plunged itself through the man's left ribs, going feather deep through his heart.

He fell to the ground as Diocles rushed over to pick up his commander. "Up!" the man shouted. He scooped up Drysten's sword and placed it into his hand at the same time another was thrust a few inches into the thigh of his right leg. He screamed in pain and swiped behind him, missing the man who had drawn blood. The sword was quickly pulled free and brought back as the man was getting ready to stab once more.

Drysten's daze had finally subsided well enough for him to lurch forward with all his might, pushing his blade up through the groin of his friend's assailant and forcing it up toward his stomach. The man screamed wildly as he fell backwards onto the floor, blood surging out from between his legs.

Drysten helped up Diocles, who was cursing under his breath the whole way before he looked on the rest of the room. He saw Bastakas laying in a pool of blood produced from an open chest wound, Cynwrig a few feet away holding his own side on the ground, and Lucius' head lying near his torso a foot away. The last four men to deal with were now huddled in a group at the far end of the tavern as Heraclius was stepping toward them, brandishing his own weapon and that of one of the men he had killed. All at once, they tossed their weapons in front of them and went down to their knees. Each man was desperately pleading for mercy as they knelt down to surrender. Drysten stood and leaned Diocles onto the countertop.

"I will take care of him," Isolde said as she slowly walked out from the back room, visibly shaken by what she just witnessed.

Drysten looked at Diocles, who nodded for him to press on, then turned toward the prisoners. "Bind their hands," he ordered his men before walking toward Cynwrig. "How bad is it?"

Cynwrig gasped for a moment. "I think I may need to get to Magnus soon."

Drysten nodded and ordered the Cretans to take care of him before once again moving his attention to the men on the other side of the room.

Heraclius moved in next to him once the weapons were all put into a pile. "They killed Bastakas."

Drysten put a hand on the Greek's shoulder. "They will pay. But first, I have a use for them," he said as he walked toward him. He slowly shifted his attention toward the captives, now clearly unsure of what was about to befall them. "My name is Drysten ap Hall of Ebrauc." He was unsure why he added the last part to his name, but decided it couldn't hurt. "If you want to live, you will help me. If not, you and anyone else I have to kill will die."

The frightened men stared wide-eyed at one another before one nodded and stood up. "I will help you, Lord."

Drysten nodded and gestured for the man to follow him toward the entrance. "Dagonet, with me." The scout nodded and followed Drysten as he led the prisoner through the doorway. They were met by ten ill-equipped and petrified town guards, as well as the remaining men from Servius' estate.

"Lay down your arms!" the ranking guard yelled as Drysten left the tavern. Of the group standing in front of Drysten, it was apparent the only real threats would be the five men belonging to Servius and the man yelling the warning.

Drysten surveyed the men standing in front of him. "I will give you a choice. The first one is you get out of my way and I have no reason to kill any of you or my prisoners. The second option, and one I would personally prefer, is you do not remove yourself from my path, and every one of you will die. Choose."

The guards looked at each other, unsure of what the next move would be. "You don't know who owns this tavern do you, boy?" one of Servius' men snidely asked.

Drysten laughed. "I don't care who owns it. It changes nothing." Drysten dragged his prisoner forward. "See if you can talk them into getting out of my way."

The man looked from Drysten to the men assembled to oppose him. "He came to take his woman back. Just let him leave."

The ranking guard stepped forward. "He knows what will happen to him if he kills any more of our people. Do not worry, boy."

Drysten smiled. "You seem to think I have reason to fear you. Let me describe your present situation. I have your employer bound aboard my vessel, and all but nine of his men are dead. Should I not return from my journey to reclaim my woman, the rest of my men will come through here and slaughter the lot of you. As well as *your* people, you would be dooming the people of this shit-stinking village to the same fate that befell my own people by your employer's hands. Your choice in this very moment would prevent that."

The leader of the guards sneered. "He's bluffing."

"He's not," the prisoner stammered. "He leads hundreds of men. *Roman* men."

The idea that a powerful war band made their way into

these parts was scary enough for the rabble of guards. The only thing more terrifying to them would be fighting against the might of Rome itself. The stories of Rome's conquests and the way their prisoners were sold into slavery was obviously not appealing, as a handful began to slowly walk away from the confrontation.

"Cowards!" the guard yelled, "get back here!"

Drysten smiled at his prisoner. "Good guess about our numbers."

"Just doing what I can to survive, Lord," the prisoner responded.

Drysten chuckled once again. "I suppose that's all anyone can do." He gave the prisoner a pat on the back and looked toward the group of men still intending to resist him. "Your friends made the right choice. What will you do?"

The men still standing in the group opposing Drysten began to look to each other for their decision until the five men belonging to Servius made it for them. They each began to charge the thirty or so foot gap toward their enemy when two arrows came from the window and doorway leading into the tavern. One man was hit in his right eye, and another on the left end of the group was hit square in the chest, knocking him backwards to the dirt. The group froze in shock as two more arrows were sent forth with low, yet audible twangs, hitting two more men in the chest and neck. The whole group stopped, with the town guards turning to flee, and the lone survivor of Servius' men dropping his blade and gently raising his hands.

Drysten watched the remainder of the men bolt away as he led the prisoner back inside, seeing Diocles approach as he turned.

"They'll certainly bring more, and seeing as how we're down two men, I don't like our chances," Diocles warned.

"They likely don't have any more men in the actual town for us to contend with," Drysten responded. He slowed his pace as he looked on the two bloody bodies of Lucius and

Bastakas, both covered with linen purloined from upstairs. "We'll be gone before any arrive. We'll take everything of value that Servius has, then burn what we can't carry."

The men silently agreed, each understanding this conflict was becoming more and more personal with each small interaction between them and Servius' people. Their families were taken, their friends were dying, and more could follow should they fail. Each man slowly marched through the entrance to the tavern, all staring down at the bodies of their comrades.

The streets were now dark, lit only by torches near houses across the street. The courtyard was pitch black, as servants and guards employed in the villa were either dead or running as fast as they could toward the fort at the other end of the town. Heraclius walked toward the villa's gate and slowly nudged it open before walking through with Drysten, Dagonet, and Paulus.

"This way," Dagonet announced as he motioned toward the main building. "Anything of value is going to be here. He hides gold under the floor of his bed when he's away."

Drysten chuckled. "Wouldn't that be the first place someone looked?"

"You would think," the scout replied.

The courtyard was well taken care of, with a fountain in the middle shaped to portray Mercurius, the Roman deity of commerce. The pool of water was now still as the men walked by, quickly admiring the craftsmanship.

"Amiram would ogle at this for hours," Paulus lightly noted.

They then ventured into the entryway, and were greeted by an old man; a servant by the looks of his ragged grey colored tunic, brandishing a thick broom in his defense.

Drysten walked forwards, putting his sword in its sheath. "We mean you no harm. You can leave if you wish it."

The old man acted as though he could not understand what had been said, then gently lowered the broom. "You...

Servius is not here, Lord."

Drysten smiled. "That's because he's tied up on my ship. Go peacefully and find yourself a place to live out the remainder of your days." The man looked shocked as he slowly made his way toward the gate, then departed.

The men pressed forward into the main building. Its ceiling was higher than it looked from the outside, with murals painted on every wall. Most portrayed a man doing some sort of brave deed or flaunting his wealth in some magnificent pose.

"That... *cannot* be Servius," Paulus stated in surprise.

Drysten scoffed. "The man certainly sees himself differently than the rest of us do."

The men continued until Dagonet led the way into Servius' bedroom. There was a large bed at the far wall, many elaborate fabrics hanging from the roof and strangely crafted murals portraying Servius' fictional self throughout the room. Only these were different. These depicted wars and slaughter, with blood being painted spewing out of his victims.

"This is where he fucks?" Heraclius wondered aloud. "The man has strange tastes."

Dagonet went to push the bed until Heraclius decided to overturn it by throwing it nearly halfway across the room, prompting Dagonet to glance at the giant with a slightly surprised, yet amused expression.

"What? We're burning the place anyway," Heraclius cheerfully stated as he began to tap his foot at the wooden floor underneath.

"Wait," Dagonet said while pointing to a handle jutting up from the floor. Heraclius finally understood the instruction and lifted it to reveal a stairway leading down to a dark room. Drysten immediately understood what he would find. He remembered the rumors he heard about Servius' sadistic tendencies. Yet all the same, he knew he had no choice but to lower himself down the stairway. He clutched onto a candle that had been lit in a corner and slowly led the way down.

The room initially looked empty until Drysten lifted the candle and walked further inside. Before he was able to lay his eyes on his surroundings, he felt the scars in the background, left from the immense suffering inflicted on likely undeserving people. He smelled it and even tasted it in the musty, stale air of the basement. His gaze first strayed over a wooden table with hooks hanging overhead, and a series of knives and strangely shaped metal objects dangling from above. He took a knife down from a hook, hearing screams from the forests near Burdigala ringing through his mind as he turned it over in his hand. Upon further examination, he discovered it was rusty and crusted from its handle to its tip with blood. "Sick bastard," he muttered to himself.

"Lord," Dagonet called.

Drysten gently laid the knife on the table before shifting to see Dagonet gesture toward a door at the other end of the room, directly across from the stairway. "That's where he stores everything?"

Dagonet responded with a grin before yanking the door ajar.

What Drysten saw next transcended every expectation he had made on the journey. Dagonet had unveiled a room crowded with wooden boxes stacked on top of one another. He slowly brought the candle toward them when he noticed a torch sconce inside the room near the doorway and moved to light it instead. The torch's brilliant glow danced over the boxes, some of which were already opened to reveal the most extraordinary sight Drysten could have hoped to see. Gold was everywhere.

"That's... wow..." Heraclius whispered as he walked through the doorway.

Drysten turned back to his men. "We need to find a way to take as much as possible."

"I can help with that," a woman's voice announced from the stairs. Drysten turned to see an unknown woman standing there with the old man he had set free upon entering the villa. "My husband keeps horses in the back of the villa. There's a wagon there too."

Drysten skeptically studied the woman before turning to Paulus. "Instruct the men to fetch them. Our dead take priority, but pile on as much as we can." The Cretan suspiciously nodded while staring at the beautiful woman in front of him, only briefly meeting her eyes before he finally disappeared up the stairs.

"Start bringing it all up," Drysten commanded as he lifted the lid of one box to find old Roman coins scattered inside. "They must have been preying on villages the empire left behind. Stealing their wealth and then taking them as slaves."

"I think I was Roman once," Dagonet quietly remarked. He held the gaze of the woman, much like Paulus, but this time she returned it in kind. "What is your name, woman?"

She slowly walked forward, the torch illuminating her face enough to reveal scars on the left side of her cheek. "What is it to you? Are you not going to kill me like my husband's men?"

Drysten turned around to watch the complex interaction between the two. Dagonet had seemed to forget about every box of wealth laying by his feet to stare at the woman.

"Dag?" Drysten called.

Drysten's lead scout slowly walked toward the woman by the torchlight, looking as though he was examining every piece of her scarred face. It seemed to Drysten he knew the woman, yet the woman clearly stared at Dagonet as though she was confused at his presence. "Atestatia…"

"What are you doing?" the woman awkwardly asked.

Dagonet stopped and glanced at Drysten. "Lord, I think that's my sister."

"Antipho!?" the woman suddenly cried.

Dagonet looked down to the ground for a moment before slowly nodding and raising his head. "They took my name from me when I was sold. I... I had not heard it in so long I almost forgot it." The woman hurried across and held Dagonet so tightly Drysten wondered if he could breathe. She began quietly sobbing on the man's shoulder, while to Drysten's surprise Dagonet shed tears as well.

"Dag... Antipho, whoever, she can come with us, but we have to get moving," Drysten softly put in. "Go with Heraclius and make sure nobody else is here. I don't want to leave anyone behind." Dagonet nodded and began to move toward the stairway, halting for a moment upon noticing Atestatia gazing over the boxes.

"What he has in here; these boxes contain the only items Servius likely cares for," Atestatia indicated through a hushed tone. "I had only been down here once before. I forgot how many there were."

"*You* were down here?" Drysten asked in shock. He assumed anyone taken into the basement of this villa would not be alive when they came out.

"I was," the woman answered. "When he gave me this." She pointed toward the scars on her cheek before turning her attention to her brother. "Servius told me he killed you for being troublesome. I thought you were dead all these years."

Dagonet smiled warmly. "Not dead. Just a slave in Britannia."

"What was this about your name?" Atestatia asked. Drysten was surprised by the question, as he assumed Servius would be the one to prevent his slaves from using their names from birth.

"The one I serve." Dagonet replied. "He was the one who would not allow me to use my name."

'King Ceneus?" Drysten asked in surprise.

Dagonet nodded. "The very same. It's not favorable for a Christian king to condone the procurement of slaves. He changed our names and fabricated a story of liberating us from a slaver off the coast when I was young. Obviously, this was false, but he needed stories of his prowess and noble deeds to help gain reputation if he wished to become king. Most of this was done on that fucking *bishop's* order"

Drysten glanced back to the doorway as footsteps were heard. "This king we are sworn to seems to have two faces and may not even be the person in charge of Ebrauc."

Atestatia, who had remained silent during the discussion suddenly chuckled. "This man seems almost as bad as my husband." Both Dagonet and Drysten glanced at her as if waiting to hear her resist the idea of killing him. "He enjoyed the scars he gave me so much he gave me my son, Marhaus."

"You know we will have to kill them both, do you not?" Drysten said skeptically. "Your son played a prominent role in taking my people."

To his surprise, Atestatia modestly shrugged as if it did not matter that her son and husband would soon be dead. "He always took more after his father than he did me. It should also come as no surprise I have a very strong hatred for my husband. I was beautiful once before these." She gestured toward her scarred face with obvious disdain.

Drysten smiled. "You still are, my lady," which caused a blush from Atestatia.

"Thank you, Lord. Now steal my husband's wealth and use it for something worthy," Atestatia commanded.

Drysten happily nodded, and turned to pick up a box.

The stars glittered overhead as the Fortuna arrived within sight of the island. The docks were well lit off in the distance, giving the crew an easy path as they navigated the waters near the coastline. Titus would lead his men to the docks as Drysten had planned, but he was going to attempt to resolve this without bloodshed if possible. He knew men would not fight if the person who pays them is dead, so he ordered Servius to be brought up from the second level of the ship. The fat man was blindfolded and gagged to mitigate the vexatious tone of his speech.

"Take the blindfold off him," Titus ordered Magnus.

As the blindfold was removed, the fat around Servius' neck prominently shook, almost making an audible sound and causing Magnus to chuckle. "I'll turn you into a mute like your rower, *filth*," Servius hissed toward Magnus once his gag was removed.

"How *merciful* of you," Magnus replied with a grin.

"You can strike him if you desire. I care not," Titus offered to Magnus. The man graciously declined and took his laughter back down to the stern of the vessel where he struck up a conversation with two of Titus' men.

"My people will ruin anyone who sets a hand on me," Servius stated as he turned to Titus.

Titus laughed in the man's face. "After this is all over, I can guarantee you two things. The first being you will have no slaves, and the second being you will have no treasures to your name."

Servius' face turned white. "What are you saying, Roman?"

"I'm saying you're about to become irrelevant," Titus said with a grin. "The only thing I can offer you is your life."

Servius stood in thought for a moment. "What is it you ask of me, Roman?"

Titus clapped his hands together. "Excellent! I hoped you would be a reasonable businessman!" He turned toward the oncoming dock, now only moments from the Fortuna's arrival. "Your men will have cause to fight us should we decide to go about this the way my employer wanted. However, I think we can achieve our goals through a more... peaceful process."

Servius grumbled to himself. "I rarely ask twice, now what is it you wish of me?"

"Do not kid yourself. You will ask a third, fourth, or fifth time should I demand it." Titus turned back and pointed a finger to Servius. "*You* will go to the men on the island, under guard mind you, and you will tell them to take all the captives they have in their care onto my ship. You will do this on the condition that I let you keep a small portion of whatever my employer looted from your home."

Servius chuckled. "You know I have no choice but to take this offer of yours, provided you can give me an assurance of my safety."

Titus nodded. "I will. That I can guarantee you."

"Fine, Roman. You have a deal," Servius murmured as he looked toward the dock. Titus wondered why the man chose to address him as a Roman, especially considering he supposedly was one himself. Either way, to Titus it did not matter.

The Fortuna finally made port a few moments later. The men on the island had originally stood in defiance of the intruders, but upon their leader commanding them not to resist, they slinked their way back to let Titus and his men pass to the gate on the Western side of the enclosure.

"Open the gate, you bunch of pisspots!" Servius yelled. A few moments later the gates slowly opened, and a man stepped forward.

"Father? We thought you would be in Gaul by nightfall," the leader stated.

Servius waved the man off as he led Titus and his men inside. "I was delayed."

Marhaus cautiously looked at Titus, who calmly nodded and pointed to himself. "That was my doing."

"Swords!" Marhaus yelled to his men, who followed the command and made themselves ready for a fight.

Servius obviously considered letting it all play out, but after a tug at his collar by Titus, he decided the chance of him losing his own life was too high. "No! Let them take what they want and leave, boy."

Marhaus' face contorted in confusion as Servius spoke. "They'll take them all!"

"They solely wish to take the slaves. This man is supposedly an honorable Roman and he's given me his word as such," Servius responded.

Upon being given his orders once more, Marhaus finally relented and allowed Titus and his men to take the slaves. Each one was quickly brought out of the pens and placed in the care of the Fortuna's crew. Most were men but there were a few women who Titus guessed their captor didn't find attractive enough to send to his villa. Aside from their confusion, the one consistent trait between them was the sight of their ribs poking through their tattered clothes. It was painfully obvious they were greatly malnourished and in need of care.

"Where are we going, lord?" one man nervously asked of Titus.

Titus smiled and put a hand on his shoulder. "We're taking you away from this place. You're going home."

The man's eyes lit up as he began to grasp what he had been told. His smile grew wider and he turned to relay the news to the people coming out of the enclosure.

"You're a Roman?" Marhaus inquired.

Titus nodded.

"Then what do you have against slavery? The Empire has long been the biggest procurer of slaves for centuries," the slaver protested.

"Maybe. Yet I don't believe I was ever told of Romans kidnapping their own citizens to be sold as though they were worthless," Titus replied angrily, causing the slaver to take a step back. "I suggest you don't try to justify your little venture to *me*, boy."

Marhaus grumbled and walked away toward the men he had lined up across from the Fortuna. Once Titus was satisfied everyone had been taken, he walked back to Servius.

"You'll honor our deal, Roman?" Servius hissed.

Titus smiled. "*No.* I won't." He then drew his sword and swiped it through Servius' neck before turning back and racing toward the ship. An arrow clipped the side of his neck, but did no real damage, and his men formed a line with their shields to ensure he made it to safety.

"You fucking pig shit Roman!" Marhaus yelled as he tried to usher his men toward the shield wall before they were able to make their escape. "We'll hunt you wherever you go! You will never outrun us!"

Titus turned back, satisfied he was out of range of the bowmen. "My name is Titus Octavius Britannicus. I live in Londinium. Come and find me!" Then ordered the ship to push off. "Let's move! Get us back to the port!"

Just then, Jorrit began screaming curses toward the Fortuna's crew, knocked a man down, and leapt into the water beside the ship. A confused Titus could only keep running toward the Fortuna as Jorrit waded his way toward the line of men under Marhaus' leadership.

"You're all swine!" the Frisian yelled.

With a lurch, the ship steadily began to move back the way it had come. All the while, the men had lined up in a shield wall over the starboard side of the ship to prevent any arrows from hitting the people huddled behind it. Titus looked through the shields for a moment to see what his enemy was doing. To his surprise, the men had largely given up the chase altogether.

Must have been confused by the Frisian, he thought to himself before turning to see Magnus grinning as he approached.

"We let him go, Sir. We figured Lord Drysten would steal everything of value from the pig's villa, meaning he would undoubtedly be chased wherever he went. Would've made it much more troublesome taking the Frisian to his home before returning to ours unnoticed," Magnus explained.

Titus was briefly angered at not being consulted, but ultimately decided leaving Jorrit behind held no real consequences. He simply nodded, patted Magnus on the shoulder, and ordered the ship back toward the port.

The wagons obtained at Servius' villa proved to be more

than enough to carry the treasure. Most of the two dozen chests were filled to the brim with old Roman coin, tribal jewels, and various other trinkets of value. Drysten had guessed them to be trophies taken from scores of helpless people Servius had kidnapped, but there was no way of knowing for certain. One wagon held the bodies of Bastakas and Lucius along with the chests, while the other carried the wounded Cynwrig, who had begun to lose the color in his face. Isolde, the strange old man from the villa, and Atestatia were with him attempting to tend to his wounds. Along with the wagons, the group found enough horses in the villa's stables to both pull the carts and transport them all North to the port where they had disembarked.

One peculiar addition was a puppy which Isolde had taken a liking to during her stay in captivity. It was a small, brown, stocky looking thing with big brown eyes which seemed to follow her wherever she went before their journey. "He is Maebh, and he comes with us," Isolde emphatically stated as she clutched the beast. Drysten saw no harm in its presence, and decided it was best not to cross his future wife.

Drysten rode in front of the wagons with Heraclius and Diocles, while the others brought up the rear. To Drysten's surprise, they had come across no resistance to that point, a trend he hoped would continue until they reached their destination.

Wait, the voice commanded.

Drysten halted his mount and stared off in the distance, making sure the way was safe. He grew annoyed by the darkness, attributing it to a thick, black sheet being placed over his eyes.

Diocles halted as well, beginning to scan the area around them. "What is it?" the Greek began, "I don't see—"

Arrows pelted the side of the cart containing their fallen, with one finding the space where Lucius' head had once occupied. Heraclius' mount was hit in its rump, rearing upward in pain as the shock of the ambush set in.

They weren't going for reinforcements, Drysten realized. *They were setting an ambush on the road.*

Men began pouring from the darkness, only illuminated by the torchlight emitting from the wagon containing the living. Dagonet glanced to Drysten before drawing his blade and riding off in the darkness, spurring on toward the direction the arrows had come.

"Antipho!" his sister screamed, clearly nervous she would gain her baby brother back only to watch him die shortly after.

"Heraclius! Go with him!" Drysten commanded. The Greek had just gotten his mount under control enough to steer her toward the direction their scout had disappeared into. "Petras, Paulus, keep them moving," he commanded once more. Drysten drew his blade and rushed to the aid of Diocles, the first man of their company to meet their steel with the enemy. One man was working to unseat the Greek from his horse, but was quickly halted upon Drysten rushing over and slicing down into the man's spine. The howl of agony startled another, who was distracted long enough for Diocles to slice into the man's neck and send him to the ground.

Dagonet and Heraclius erupted from the darkness, each taking out a man before forming up alongside Drysten and Diocles. Drysten could hear more footsteps around him, but instead of attacking they were moving further down the road toward the fleeing wagon and their people.

"Keep moving!" Drysten commanded.

The group spurred forth into the darkness, their only guide being the faint light of the cart off in the distance. A pair of men came into view, both quickly diving into opposite sides of the road to prevent themselves from being ridden down by Drysten and Diocles. Heraclius started to pull up for a confrontation, but was stopped on Drysten's order.

"We have more pressing concerns than two *fools* in the

dirt. Press on!"

And press on they did. Each man weaved in and out of the assailants they came across, only one of which made an attempt on their lives. He wheeled around when the thundering of hooves came upon him, and attempted to strike the legs of Heraclius' horse until Dagonet inched ahead and sliced into the back of the man's neck, nearly decapitating him.

Drysten wondered if these men were from Rodanum, or whether they happened upon a group of highwaymen. He hadn't seen a man wearing red in the few who were visible enough to be seen plainly. The ones they passed were all armed better than the guards who he had threatened inside the city.

"Rid the cart of the torches!" Dagonet yelled as the group neared the wagon. "The only way they will be able to shoot us is by using the light of the torches."

As he spoke, an arrow whispered through the air and embedded itself into the old man's neck, quickly toppling him over the side of the wagon into the darkness of the roadside brush.

"Lord, do we stop for him?" Diocles asked frantically.

Drysten cursed under his breath as they rode on. "If he still lives, he won't for long. Keep going," he commanded. He did not need to look at the faces of his men to know their expressions. They were now within mere feet of where the old man had fallen, but the company pressed forward toward their wagon. As Drysten rode by, he caught the faint sounds of frantic gasping coming from the roadside.

A few short moments went by until the group finally reached the wagon. The sloshing sound of muddy feet had since disappeared as they raced forth, with one of the wagon's wheels clearly making a grinding noise indicating it would soon need repair.

"Slow up," Drysten ordered. "Dagonet, stay a few paces behind and let us know if you hear anything worth worrying about." The scout nodded and halted his horse, soon vanishing from view into the night's air. He then trained his attention to the wagon and the wounded Cynwrig resting on its bed. "How is he?" he asked his woman.

Isolde looked at Drysten with clear sadness in her eyes. "I don't know. If we get his wounds dressed, he could live, but until then…"

"We'll get him the help he needs on the ship," Drysten assured her.

"How many men do you actually have?" Isolde asked as she played with one of Maebh's ears, causing him to try and nibble her finger.

Drysten thought for a moment. "Currently, I would guess around a hundred and fifty."

"A far cry from the number your prisoner boasted," Isolde said with a smirk.

Drysten nodded. "If it weren't for his deception, then we may not have left Rodanum."

"Is that why you left them all alive?" Isolde asked. She turned to Drysten with a strange, antsy look to her. Her eyes seemed hollowed out, much like Bors' had when he first encountered him aboard Servius' ship. She seemed to have trouble holding eye contact and her voice noticeably cracked, causing her to stutter as she spoke.

Drysten initially intended to kill any prisoners he had taken, but the man cooperated. Drysten turned away from Isolde as he reflected on his decision. He now understood the mark left by her time in captivity, and wondered whether it would have been better to simply kill every prisoner regardless of what he promised him. "He did what was asked of him—"

"You should have killed them *all*," Isolde interrupted. "He was one of their *worst*."

Drysten was surprised by Isolde's icy tone. "I'm… sorry."

Isolde herself seemed startled by her own response. She quickly broke eye contact with Drysten and began rubbing

Maebh's head as Drysten decided to ride ahead of the wagon.

The group had been riding for about an hour to that point, all of it through total darkness. Even in the dark, it was still possible to find their way. The road they had taken was paved near the city and had few turns to worry about. Drysten guessed the original plans for the area had been to pave the road from Rodanum to the coast and use the port they arrived at as a trading post. There were other towns nearby where the Romans had once resided, but they did not stay long enough for any of those plans to come to fruition.

The Northernmost territories the Romans endeavored to settle were always in a state of war, with raiders coming from the Northern parts as well as rebellions starting up in far off areas away from any real imperial authority. That and the simple fact it was difficult to get resources to these areas spelled for disaster, and many places were partially built only to be abandoned before completion.

"Should be there shortly, Lord," Heraclius noted. "I remember walking over a similar hill to this a couple miles after we departed.

Drysten nodded. "Let's pick up the pace. If all went well with Titus, then they could very well be waiting for us already."

The group kept moving through the thick darkness of a mostly barren countryside. Occasionally, they would slow upon hearing some small animal scurry out of the path of their horses and wagons. Once the attackers had vanished, the foggy night over Northern Gaul provided a peaceful respite from the hectic day of war and loss. The men Drysten had led were largely successful, but only a handful came away from it unscathed. He had not lost any of the Fortuna's men, but Titus had incurred two losses.

Lucius was made whole and placed into a wagon with care, and next to him was lying Bastakas. Both bodies were covered in beautiful white linen taken from somewhere in Servius' villa, and Drysten made sure to hide one more strip of linen should Cynwrig require it. To Drysten's disappointment, the wounded man indeed looked as though he may indeed join Titus' two warriors in the afterlife.

Not long after the men crossed over the hill, they began to hear seagulls and smell the salt of the sea. Off in the distance, there could be seen small fires poking out from windows of mud huts lined across the beach. The Fortuna was at the dock, comforting them all to see their ship awaiting their return.

"Petras, spur forward and let Titus know we're coming. Have him clear space near the shrines for the boxes," Drysten ordered. The Cretan nodded, clicked his tongue to signal his horse to go from a walk to a canter and road ahead into the darkness.

"How are we splitting it all up?" Diocles inquired, referring to the treasure looted from Servius' villa.

Drysten tilted his head to the side until he found his answer. "We save two chests, then divide up the rest evenly between the men."

Diocles nodded. "Sounds fair enough. Although I worry some might consider the two chests to be your personal take from the trip."

Drysten nodded before spurring his horse forward.

The group finally made it to the Fortuna where they were greeted by Titus and Magnus, the latter of which looked over Cynwrig on the wagon. "He may yet live, Lord. I will see to his care myself," he said in a reassuring tone.

"See to it," Titus commanded before looking at Drysten. "Did they suffer?" he asked, referring to his dead wrapped in linen.

Drysten shook his head. "Not from what I saw. Bastakas saved Heraclius from a similar fate. Lucius died quickly."

Titus hung his head for a moment before noticing the two beautiful women hopping down from the wagon. "This must be your woman," he said gesturing toward Isolde, who smiled warmly at the man. "Who is the other?" he asked

Drysten.

"Servius' wife," Drysten responded, "and she seems to be Dagonet's sister."

Titus gave Drysten a surprised look. "Well, I suppose that's some good news then."

"She hates both her husband and her son. She will be no trouble," Drysten said with a nod.

After a few short moments, the chests and their dead were loaded onto the Fortuna, followed by Drysten and his company. They pushed off as Drysten made his way through the freed captives, all of whom were thanking him. "I don't deserve the thanks. Titus was the one who saved you," he replied, though few heeded his words. In his first real taste of leadership out from under the watch of his father, he set out to free them and had succeeded.

Titus informed him of Servius' fate, as well as the threats bellowed from Marhaus.

"That one may be trouble when they find a way to get back on their feet," the general warned.

"We'll worry when we get home," Drysten replied before looking over the crew. "Where's our Frisian? We're to take him further North." Titus chuckled as he relayed what occurred on the island. Drysten found some amusement in the act, but still felt as though he had not kept his word. "I promised him I would take him to his home."

Titus shook his head. "I know what you promised him, but you cannot deny how difficult it would be to watch over all these people in an even more dangerous part of the world than this one. It worked out better this way. Not just for us."

Drysten nodded and patted Titus' shoulder. "I could not have achieved any of this without you," he declared as he watched Isolde playing with Maebh by the Fortuna.

Titus chuckled. "You're more capable than you know, boy. It's obvious from what I remember of your father he did well in raising you."

Drysten smiled and looked out to sea. "I have one more

proposition for you."

Titus turned with a mildly interested expression. "That is?" he said with a chuckle. "More wars to fight? More blood for the gods above?

Drysten turned back to the man. "What we reclaimed from Maurianus and the two chests I took from Servius, in exchange for a more permanent form of employment. I expect we'll be needing men to protect our people from one man or another."

Titus tilted his head back as the thought ran through his head. "That's enticing. I'm assuming you mean for me to serve the king of Ebrauc?"

Drysten shook his head. "As a matter of fact, I meant myself," he answered with a smile.

And with that, Drysten had found his first army.

CHAPTER X

To everyone's relief, the journey home to Petuaria was largely uneventful. Once the Fortuna was underway from the port outside Rodanum, the only task left was to leave Titus and his men off at the vessel they had beached the day before. When they reached the ship, the first group who had been liberated, as well as the few left behind to protect them, finally had a chance to meet with loved ones who had been taken. As his crew mingled with their loved ones on the beach, Drysten oversaw the transfer of rations and payment onto Titus' new ship.

Thankfully, the venture to free the captives taken by Servius had only resulted in a small number of deaths or injuries. The first casualties came from Maurianus' treachery in Londinium, which were then followed by Bastakas and Lucius' deaths inside the city of Rodanum. Titus took the linen-wrapped bodies of his two men aboard his new vessel with his second payment from Drysten. It was then a new agreement was struck between Titus and Drysten. Titus would relocate most of his men to Petuaria to serve under Drysten, with a small number left behind in Londinium to aid the locals in keeping the peace.

Even with the voyage being an overall success, there was still a small number of men who had found out their wives or children were taken and sold before they had arrived to save them. Drysten allowed about a dozen of these sullen men to remain in Gaul to continue searching for them. However, he ordered them to attempt to find a way to return once their loved ones were either found or hope was abandoned that they could be located.

Most people quietly understood an unlucky few would never be recovered, but it would be hard to find anyone willing to say it openly. Even considering that, Drysten and his men decided the rescue was an overall success, and celebrated it as such. One night was spent on the beach with everyone who had been involved in the journey drinking and merrymaking, with some briefly disappearing with their spouse or a stranger they had just met. The next morning Drysten and Titus both bid each other farewell, and sailed to their respective destinations.

As Diocles and Drysten leaned over the stern of the vessel, reaping the rewards of the festivities the night before, Diocles watched Titus' ship venture off.

"I don't trust most new acquaintances very easily, but I believe that man would never simply take his payment and remain in Londinium," a dreary-eyed Diocles stated.

Drysten nodded as he noticed Isolde walking toward him. "I agree. My own judgment is telling me the same, and the impression he left on my father so long ago leads me to believe he will be a very welcome addition to our people."

"Your morning resembles most of mine recently," a smiling Isolde put in.

Diocles slowly turned to face his captain's woman. "I promise if he is pregnant too, it is *not* mine." Prompting Isolde to laugh and Drysten to once again lurch forward and spill out the contents of his stomach.

Clear skies and an easterly wind meant the voyage to Petuaria only cost the Fortuna three days of sea travel. As the men disembarked upon their arrival, they noticed the changes that had begun to take place in the small town. People were tearing down old, dilapidated, and even decaying buildings to make way for new homes for Hall and Drysten's people. The roughly two weeks Drysten had been gone was enough time for people to clear build plots, lay their foundations, and in some cases begin construction.

"Drysten!" the king shouted as he saw The Fortuna's crew disembarking in the early morning hours.

"This fucking king is a halfwit. We would do well to find someone else to serve," Diocles noted wearily.

Drysten sighed heavily as he watched King Ceneus walking toward the dock. "The thought has certainly crossed my mind since speaking more of him with Dagonet."

"I take it by all the new faces you were successful?" Ceneus happily inquired.

Drysten nodded as he walked toward the king, who was accompanied by his guards and an older man with a wrinkled brow adorned in a priest's robe. "We were, Lord King."

Drysten watched as King Ceneus examined the people disembarking, and slowly realized the only one to be his was Dagonet, who was now standing beside Drysten as if he was sworn to him. "Where are the men I sent to aid you? Surely they could not have all been killed?" he asked quizzically.

Drysten stepped forward, prompting the king's guards to tensely glance toward one another. "The majority were, Lord King."

"How?" the king inquired as he slowly became aware of the small glint of anger in Drysten's eyes.

Drysten took a small pace forward and started to talk in a low, grave tone which seemed to disturb the king. "Your *son's* men endeavored to betray me, and murdered a handful of my men along with local guards."

The king nervously glanced back toward his priest, unsure of how angry Drysten truly was. "I... My apologies, Drysten. I meant to send you the most capable men I had available."

Kill him now! the voice commanded. *He lies!*

"*Clearly*, they were not, Lord King," Drysten glanced toward the Fortuna. He tried not to show it, but sensing the king's discomfort gave him a slight feeling of happiness. Not to mention this was one of the rare occasions in which he and the voices in his mind agreed on something. Drysten returned the king's gaze. "No matter. The worst of them were dealt with and the few others I let live will no doubt be in hiding or rotting in a noose above Londinium."

"You mentioned murder?" the king inquired.

Drysten regaled the tail of the mutiny, led by one of his own but supported by the men the king had sent to help him regain his people. In the end, the presence of the king's men was unnecessary, as their goals were accomplished without them. Drysten chose to leave out the fact Titus was going to be preparing all his people for the move North to Petuaria. He was unsure how the king would respond to a significant force being in his land, yet not necessarily sworn to him. In truth, Drysten didn't care. He had grown to understand King Ceneus was nothing more than an untrustworthy man born to privilege.

"That is... an unfortunate story, Drysten. I will attempt to make things right by you and your father. I would also like you to understand I am happy to hear the men I sent were punished. I also think the punishment fair," the king remarked, though Drysten did not recognize much sincerity in his voice. "I will allow your people to log and farm this area without being taxed until such time as you can sustain yourselves well enough to afford it. I will also garrison a small guard force that I will pay for until you, again, can afford being taxed."

Drysten could detect the uneasy grimaces of Dagonet and Diocles standing behind him. Not a single person of the Fortuna liked the idea of more traitors sleeping nearby, and Drysten clearly shared that sentiment.

"That is very generous, Lord King, but there is little need of a guard force," Drysten replied.

The king raised an eyebrow. "This is the first village which would be raided if a force chose to enter the Abus, or should someone row across the river from the now occupied kingdom of Rheged. Yet you're telling me that you do *not* require protection?"

Drysten turned back to the Fortuna. "You misunderstand, Lord King. We most certainly require security, but we are more than capable of providing it for ourselves. These are no longer the only men I have under my command."

The king was noticeably taken aback by the comment, peering back toward the priest who wore a confused expression. "And where would the rest of your forces be?"

Drysten turned back and smiled. "They will all be here soon, Lord King. They are currently organizing themselves for the journey North."

"North, you say?" the king said as he thought for a moment. "If they are coming North, then surely you must be speaking of Titus! This is a marvelous day indeed!" the king said as he clapped his hands together excitedly. "I am unsure what you had to say to the man to garner his support, but well done, Drysten. *Well* done, indeed."

Drysten glanced back to Dagonet, who was wearing a knowing smile that the men relocating to Petuaria were, in fact, Drysten's, and not the king's. "One thing I must request, Lord King. I require a scout, one who knows these parts as well as those on the mainland. Dagonet has proved himself to be loyal as well as effective. I would like to keep him in my service."

The king nodded at Drysten. "I think that is a fine idea. Though he is under your father's command and the decision lies with him. Until he is back, I do not see an issue."

"And what would my duties be in the meantime, Lord King?" Drysten inquired.

King Ceneus gestured toward the town. "Rest for a few days and oversee construction. It is my hope to have a bustling trade hub by the beginning of the next year. Once your men are rested and ready to move, I want you reinforcing your father's numbers to the North."

Drysten gave the king a slight bow of the head, and made his way back to his father's ship. The men had almost entirely unloaded its contents by the end of the conversation with the king, leaving small groups of men standing nearby as they anxiously awaited their first free moments with their loved ones in their new home.

"May be wise to leave the work for tomorrow, Lord," Dagonet suggested as he followed closely. "The men could use more time with their families."

Drysten nodded. "My thoughts exactly. Bring them all together for a moment."

Dagonet walked toward the men milling around the vessel and told them to join Drysten on the other side of the dock. The only two men to stay with the ship were Cynwrig and his caretaker, Magnus.

Drysten waited for the men to assemble in front of him, then commenced to speak. "It is no secret the last two weeks were tiresome and taxing on us all," he began, "that being said, you should all be proud of what we accomplished. You made the region safer for not only ourselves, but other innocents who would be preyed upon by Servius and his bastard son. The only remaining order I have for you now is to be with your loved ones and celebrate them being with us once again. We can leave the work to the locals for a day."

The group cheered as Drysten began to turn away. Most now had families to go to, while others made their way to the tavern to celebrate. Drysten paused for a moment and reflected on the time he spent away in search of Isolde, when she walked up behind him.

"*This* is our new home?" she asked with a smile.

Drysten felt a smile beam across his face as he joyfully turned to face his woman. "It is."

Isolde looked around her, taking in the meager, yet promising sights of the town. "It's certainly different than I expected. Where do we live?"

Drysten held out his hand and upon her grasping it, he slowly led her around the walls of the villa in the town's center. He made his way to the front gate where he stopped and turned to her with a smile. "Here. It was gifted to my father once he accepted payment from King Ceneus, but it is certainly big enough for us as well."

Drysten watched as Isolde's eyes began to widen. Her home in Burdigala was made of simple wood and thatch, having a dirt floor much like most of the other buildings in Petuaria. To her, living in a villa was something she had never even dared to dream of. "Surely you're joking…"

Drysten laughed as he led her inside, closely followed by the alert pup, Maebh, at her heels. Like Amiram, she stopped and stared at the extravagant murals painted on the walls of the entryway, then made her way into the courtyard. "These paintings are heavenly, Drysten!"

"It certainly has its own charm," he responded with a wink. "Make yourself at home, I want to walk through the town and see what work needs to be done."

Isolde smiled widely before lovingly kissing him, then began making her way from room to room. Drysten watched her momentarily before leaving, then made his way back into the now-crowded streets of Petuaria. He spied the Cretans showing the space across from the villa to their sister, describing how they would tear down the old, uninhabited building to replace it with one of their own makings. Petronela seemed pleased with the location of the plot, but was slightly put off by the sight of drunken men wobbling away from the tavern close by.

"I was very pleased to hear you found your people, Lord," a voice rustled from behind Drysten. He turned to see another priest standing behind him, wearing similar, yet less ornate robes to the man who walked with Ceneus. Drysten surveyed the man's face, as he believed all Christians to either be inherently good or powerfully wicked at heart, with rather few being in between. This one had eyes of a deep green and a warm smile of kindness which emanated off his face. "Slavery is no laughing matter, and I am happy to know more innocents will not meet the same fate as your loved ones, or myself for that matter."

"I suppose being sworn to a god you have never seen could be its own type of slavery, I'll grant you. But I have never heard a follower speak of—" Drysten awkwardly began until the priest began to snicker in amusement.

"I do not mean my Lord and Savior, Lord. When I was all of sixteen years, I was taken by the Gaels to Dal Riata, and made to tend their sheep," the priest explained. "My name is Maewyn, and I take care of the clerical work for Bishop Germanus."

Drysten stepped forward and outstretched his hand. "It is a pleasure to meet you. They call me Drysten. The two shook hands when Drysten suddenly recalled his conversation with James near Londinium's temple of Mithras. "What was the name given upon your conversion?"

Maewyn gave an impressed look as stared back at Drysten. "It is true Maewyn was the name of my birth, and during that time I was not known as brimming with faith. When I made my journey home and finally settled upon the path I'm on now, I was ordained as Patrick."

"And is it customary to introduce yourself with your birth name as opposed to your... *Christian* name?" Drysten wondered aloud.

Maewyn shook his head. "It is not, Lord, but I was not speaking as a Christian. I was simply introducing myself as a former slave who was overjoyed to hear the chains of bondage were broken by your people."

"How poetic." Drysten gave the priest a skeptical look as he gazed over at the king and his departing entourage. "I have heard some troubling rumors about your bishop. I am hoping they are unfounded, but I have a man below deck of the Fortuna who seems to be living proof of them."

Maewyn adopted an uncomfortable expression as he subtly glanced behind him toward Bishop Germanus, who was currently staring into the backside of a woman bent over to play with her child. "They are all true, Lord," he responded sadly.

"Are you speaking as a Briton, or as a Christian?" Drysten probed.

The priest slowly turned to depart toward the bishop. "Both," he quietly replied.

Drysten stood and watched Maewyn shuffle off toward the king and his men until he saw Bors the Younger slowly pace through the market stalls near the villa. "Drysten!" his friend called upon meeting his gaze.

"Need someone to show you around?" Drysten asked as the two walked toward each other.

"As a matter of fact, I do. Where's the tavern?" Bors said with a smile.

Drysten grinned and waved a hand for Bors to follow, stealing one last look toward Maewyn. The priest met his gaze from atop his horse and nodded before spurring his horse forward. The two men walked across the narrow road, past the Cretans now arguing about the location of their soon-to-be home, and entered the tavern to the thunderous cheers of the Fortuna's men.

"I don't think that was for me," Bors jokingly whispered in Drysten's ear.

Drysten felt himself turning red in the face from the unexpected attention, and decided the only way for the awkward feeling to subside was to find the space furthest from the bar and in the darkest corner. The two slowly made their way through the crowd of men between them and the far corner of the room. The whole way, men tried to sway Drysten to either gamble or settle down at their table for a drink, but each time Drysten graciously declined. The two finally reached an empty table and fell into their seats.

For the first time in what felt like an eternity, Drysten began to relax. He listened to Bors blab on about the various things he hoped to do once he had the money, and mainly just watched his men enjoying their time of leisure.

After what felt like hours of listening to Bors get progressively drunker as he continued to talk, Drysten's heart leaped when he saw his woman being led into the tavern by Dagonet, who smiled as he pointed her toward the far end of the room and the table Drysten was seated at.

"Where is the little Maebh hiding?' Bors inquired as he glanced toward Isolde's feet. "I do love seeing them as little ones."

Isolde laughed. "You are the strangest *big* man I have ever met. He is playing with a servant girl at the villa."

"Speaking of villas, this one says she can get used to the life of a noblewoman," Dagonet stated as the two settled in on either side of Drysten.

Drysten took Isolde's hand in his own. "Not sure we count as nobles, love."

Isolde let out a quiet laugh. "Who else lives in villas but the great nobles of Rome?"

"I am still not certain of what this king wishes for us, love. I would not assume my father is a noble in the man's court, nor myself for that matter," Drysten responded, before shifting his attention to Dagonet. "Who owned the villa before my father?"

Dagonet sighed heavily as he eyed the men in the room before slowly leaning closer to prevent himself from being overheard. "His name was Drumond, Lord. He was a good man. Had your father's position."

Drysten noticed the uneasy tone of his scout. "Where is he now?"

"Dead, Lord. He betrayed the new customs of worship enforced by the king... or rather the bishop. He was executed by Prince Eidion a few months before your arrival," Dagonet sadly replied.

Just then, a drunk Heraclius stumbled up from the next table. Raising his mug toward them. "This petty king wouldn't dare turn on us, Lord!" he said jokingly.

Isolde uncomfortably turned to Drysten. "Where did this one come from?"

Heraclius laughed and raised his mug before glancing at Drysten. "Titus ordered me to facilitate the building of a barracks before everyone's arrival."

"Looks like you've gotten off to a good start," Dagonet sarcastically replied as he glanced around. Obviously unsure if anyone else was able to hear his conversation, and upon being satisfied the Greek simply had phenomenal hearing, he trained his attention back to Drysten. "I would not worry about King Ceneus at the present, but I would recommend keeping an eye on him in the future. I have seen him cast those aside once they have fulfilled their use to him."

Drysten gave a knowing nod as he glanced at Isolde, wide-eyed and ghost-faced from worry. She was running her fingers over the newly healed "FVG" brand on her forearm, staring into the mark as she relived the moment she received it. "I will not make the same mistakes as my father's predecessor. I will watch myself in our dealings with him."

"That would be wise, Lord," Dagonet began, "I would like you to know if I had to choose, I would choose to serve you rather than him. You will never worry about my allegiance, I swear it."

Drysten smiled and raised his wooden mug toward his scout. "I believe you. Now go find yourself a woman to spend the night with."

"In normal circumstances, I would, though at present, I would rather catch up with my sister," Dagonet responded happily.

"How is she faring?" Isolde asked. "She was kind to me once I was taken to the villa."

Dagonet smiled. "She is in good spirits, though worried considering we have no place to rest our heads at the moment."

Drysten noticed Isolde staring at him and took the hint. "You both will be welcome to reside with us in the villa, provided you can deal with my woman's new ferocious beast."

Dagonet smiled and returned a grateful nod. "That is

most generous, Lord."

The tavern-goers continued their drinking well into the night, some not managing to vacate the building at all before the following morning. Most were spending their time together, while a lucky few managed to find a cheap enough woman to waste the rest of their day-long break with. Drysten and Heraclius sat and spoke of where Titus and his men would build their new barracks and homes, while Isolde sat and spoke with Diocles who had managed to limp his way toward their table. All the men and women were taking advantage of the day without work, and Drysten suspected it would be the last day of leisure for quite some time.

"There's a good chance you'll be the strongest warlord in Northern Britannia after the rest of the men show up," Heraclius cheerfully put in.

Drysten chuckled. "If that ends up being the case, then maybe I should find a different King to serve. This one rubs me the wrong way."

Heraclius drank what was left in his cup. "He seems ambitious and rich. Rich and ambitious kings either make their men wealthy or get them all killed."

"I haven't been able to tell which one would happen to us," Drysten responded. "Either way, I intend to take a force to join my father once we are able."

"How many men did your father leave with?" Diocles asked.

Drysten shrugged. "I don't know. All I heard was he took some of the king's, a few of ours who chose not to accompany us, and then there were some men from Powys as well. A few hundred in total."

"Seems awfully shorthanded for advancing on a fortress," Heraclius observed.

Drysten nodded. "If I know my father, he'll probably try to draw them out to *him*. Fight them somewhere of his choosing."

"Always smarter to fight them on your terms," Heraclius agreed.

"He will most likely fight them the same way our enemy's ancestors fought the Romans. Small groups attacking weak points. Large groups ambushing at night. Things of that nature," Drysten explained.

The men remained in conversation for a short while longer, discussing the best way to defend the coasts from raiders. Once the men grew tired of debating, they each made their way to wherever it was they would be sleeping that night. Drysten was somewhat surprised to see a handful of men using the ship as a barracks and decided the next day they would begin construction of a more permanent residence capable of housing the Fortuna's fighters. He made his way to the villa with Isolde and Diocles to check on Cynwrig, who miraculously had started to regain the color in his face, but was still at risk for succumbing to his wounds if he was not closely watched. Magnus greeted them from the man's bedside along with Matthew, who had taken a liking to learning medicine.

"Lord!" the former priest greeted him. "He seems to be doing... better."

Drysten smiled at the news. "All your prayers, I'm sure."

Matthew turned back to Cynwrig. "Or his stubbornness. Could be either."

The group stayed and spoke with the newest member of the crew for a few moments before departing for the lounging area toward the front of the home. The merriment largely began to quiet down, giving way to the sounds of the insects and birds cawing overhead. All seemed to be peaceful in that moment and Drysten sat there silently with his woman, wondering how long it would last.

"They did not know of all the locations we hid our wealth. If your people agree to fight for me, I can promise to pay you well for it," Marhaus hissed to the chieftain. "They made us look *weak,* this insult cannot go unpunished."

That's because you are weak, you gangly little shit.

Jorrit observed Chieftain Dieuwer as he sat quietly in the dimly lit hall, tenderly cradling his cheek in hand. He knew the news of the aggressive nature of the Britons was confusing to the man, especially considering his declining intelligence. The Britons were widely considered to be feeble in their strength since they were no longer under the jurisdiction of the Roman Empire. However, these new hostile Britons showed the initiative to aggressively lash out from their own lands.

The chieftain was currently aiding Colgrin on the finishing touches of their fleet destined for raiding of the Briton's shores. He would have to remove some of his people from building boats to aid Marhaus if he truly wanted the wealth he would receive from him. Something Jorrit knew was very unlikely. The Frisians had long been the ableist boatbuilders of the continent, and they were already being handsomely compensated for their talents by the Saxons planning to raid further into Britannia. It was unclear if the Frisian chief would gain anything from the venture.

"Lord?" Marhaus said as he tried to gain the chieftains attention once more. "Did you hear me?"

The chieftain scoffed. "You're only a few steps in front of me, of course I heard you. I'm trying to figure out if this would be worth the trouble. I've never done business with a Roman bastard before." The chieftain was referring to Marhaus' very Etruscan appearance, a gift from his mother's side.

Marhaus began to grow visibly frustrated. He had brought the Frisian held prisoner by Drysten back to his village in the hopes he could recruit enough men for revenge, but so far all he had achieved was half of their leader's attention. "Like I said before, I will make it worth your while. I will pay very, *very* well."

Jorrit stepped forward from the corner as he noticed Colgrin walk in from a back entrance. "Lord, if I may have a word," he said to the Saxon.

Colgrin nonchalantly glanced toward Marhaus as he made his way to Jorrit. "What's all this then?"

Jorrit gestured toward Marhaus. "The slaver's bastard."

"Ah, that's the man with the little vendetta then." Colgrin looked over toward Marhaus, sizing him up. He clearly wasn't impressed by what he saw. The man was a scrawny looking ghoul, wearing gold and silver on every finger as well as around his neck. His patchy beard and unkempt hair were a strange contrast to the wealth he was attempting to flaunt. "Doesn't look like much. Of course, you cannot expect much of a Roman."

Jorrit chuckled. "He *isn't* much, but he certainly served his use."

"And what use was that?" Colgrin asked.

"He's the one I convinced to bring me back. Wasn't at all difficult really," Jorrit answered with a slight smirk. "All I had to do was tell him my people could be paid to help him kill the man who held me prisoner. The same man who stole his wealth."

Colgrin laughed and patted Jorrit on the back. "Clever! I can appreciate a man who thinks quickly on his feet, one more reason it was you who I sent to Britannia."

Jorrit nodded, though internally, he knew Colgrin had sent out many of the men who could be seen as his equals, of which it seemed Jorrit was the sole survivor. "Now, down to business."

"Business?" Inquired an interested Colgrin.

Jorrit faced the Saxon. He did not understand why, but what he was about to say felt like it held more weight than anything he had spoken in his life. "What I want to tell you has to do with your invasion," which caused Colgrin to turn slightly more toward Jorrit, clearly hinting curiosity. "I have seen the North. Ebrauc would be an easy prize, but the one more worthwhile lay further South."

Colgrin adopted a perplexed expression as he subtly

raised an eyebrow toward Jorrit. "How much further?"

"Londinium would be the true prize. Better yet, it is also easily accessible by a river joining the sea." Jorrit answered enthusiastically.

Colgrin ran his hand through his beard as he considered Jorrit's new information. "Why would Londinium be more favorable? We have already amassed the support of the tribes to our enemy's North, as well as the cannibal-king from the island to their West."

"Cannibal-king?" Jorrit asked in surprise. He thought the practice of eating other human beings was abhorrent, further enforcing his belief Colgrin should forsake the tribesmen of Britannia in favor of Jorrit's plan.

Colgrin nodded. "His name is Abhartach. I have only dealt with his emissaries as of yet, but he appears to be rather fearsome."

"We *could* make good on our deal," Jorrit acknowledged, "or we could strike out on our own. The king of Ebrauc is a weak fool. He will not send aid to the South with enemies to his North. The only other kingdom on the islands which could oppose us would be Powys, who is also sending aid to Ebrauc. Londinium has no standing military force at the moment, other than an old Roman general named Titus Octavius Britannicus."

Colgrin began to smile. "So you're suggesting we leave the tribes to their own devices, and march on Londinium instead. Why would this area be more favorable?"

"The land is much more suited for our needs and there are far fewer people there to defend it. It lies directly on a river much like Eboracum, except with no military. We won't have to be worried about defending it when we arrive," Jorrit explained.

"It would sound more enticing if we did not already hold an agreement with multiple tribes." Colgrin said with a grin.

Jorrit nodded and returned the smile. "The best part is

that it's surrounded by thick Roman walls. All we have to do is raid by way of the river and we'll be able to defend it easily once we possess it."

The two men were interrupted by Marhaus walking through them, noticeably angered by the chieftain's inattentiveness. He grumbled the whole way out the door, where he was met by two of his men, and kept going toward their vessel. Colgrin and Jorrit walked outside after him, overhearing him complain of the smell of the village. In truth, he couldn't blame him. During this time of the year, it wasn't uncommon for the scent of livestock to drift from the fields to the town. The smell proved to be rather unpleasant to people returning from long voyages or outsiders not accustomed to its sting.

"I'll be going now, best not leave the boat builders unattended for too long. You've given me much to think about, Jorrit. Well done," Colgrin said as he began to make his way to the small shipyards.

Jorrit nodded and looked out over the village. He was not sure why he felt so compelled to turn Colgrin's attention from Ebrauc to Londinium. Everything he had told the man was the truth, but there was some other reason behind his enthusiasm. He ran his hand through his hair and turned back to the chieftain's hall, watching children run by as he made his way inside.

It was a welcome sight considering his recent journey. Like anyone else, his home had always been his haven for respite, though in the past it was due to the presence of his wife. Now, the only family he had was his son, Lanzo, who was currently sleeping in a back room of the Chieftain's hall near Colgrin's wife, Inka.

After a moment of soaking in the warmth of the hall and the smell of cooked meat, he made his way to his boy, weaving through the chieftain's grandchildren playing in the large room. He walked down the hallway until he spotted his son in the arms of Inka, who upon noticing him smiled and laid him back down in his small bed.

"I'll leave you to him," she said as she left.

Jorrit was always struck by the sight of her. She was the twin of his late wife, Elke. Every time he laid eyes on her, he longed for his wife more than he ever had when she was still alive. He loved her dearly, but not being able to hold her was more tortuous than long journeys away from home.

Suddenly he caught himself wondering how Drysten was faring. He knew from Marhaus he had not only found his woman, but he killed a score of men and stole a sizable portion of the late Servius' wealth.

"Definitely misjudged that one," Jorrit mused with a chuckle.

At first, he had hated the man with a burning passion. Something even Drysten himself could not blame him for. The man stabbed him while Jorrit had his hands tied behind his back, then was forced to act as his navigator. Jorrit knew the best way to get his revenge on the boy was to ultimately play the role he was forced into, and wait for Colgrin's plan to come to fruition. However, now he found himself missing the boy and the men he led. He proved himself to be an effective leader. Not only was he respected by his men, but from what Jorrit overheard he also had the admiration of gods as well.

Colgrin was a stark contrast to Drysten in many ways. Whereas they both lead effectively, only one did it with the reverence of his men. Colgrin led through creating fear in those who served him, and Jorrit only followed because he shared that fear. Jorrit had seen his cruelty firsthand multiple times and knew it was extremely unwise to challenge him. Whereas Colgrin demanded loyalty and obedience from his followers, Drysten was continually trying to prove to his own that they could put their trust in him. For Jorrit, it was odd to see at first.

"No wonder the Roman followed him," he whispered.

Titus was a hard man for Jorrit to read when they first

met. Once they shared their first conversation, he knew to respect him, even if they were to eventually become enemies. Jorrit gathered it must have been his actions the day of the mutiny that gained the respect of the Fortuna's crew, despite it being himself that caused it. He was able to quickly pick out the most selfish, antagonistic, conniving, and unreliable person on the crew in Maurianus. The moment the man heard of the bag containing half the wealth of the Fortuna, he desperately wanted to steal it. Jorrit even let him believe he would help. In truth, he just wanted to create some discord under Drysten's watch and discredit any influence he may have had over the crew.

Jorrit chuckled when he recalled how Maurianus had stared in shock as Jorrit killed one of the traitors. He never considered the possibility that Jorrit was tricking him into serving his purpose. But in all fairness, why would he? Until that point, all Jorrit was to anyone on that ship was a means to find their people. But then something began to change for the Frisian. The crew started offering conversation and more food than he expected during their meals. They slowly started to respect him for the role they believed he had played in trying to stop the Maurianus' traitors. In reality, he was the first one to notice anything because he had been speaking with them right when Maurianus grabbed the coin.

"Greedy fool," he whispered to himself, causing his one-year-old Lanzo to stir slightly in his sleep. Jorrit reached down and touched a finger to his son's cheek, calming him enough to prevent him from waking.

"I see you found the boy!" a voice said from the doorway. Jorrit turned and saw his leader, Chieftain Dieuwer, smiling as he entered. "You are certainly no fool, Jorrit. I know you simply brought the slaver to our lands as a means to return."

Jorrit chuckled softly. "I did, Lord."

Chieftain Dieuwer stepped around Jorrit toward the cradle containing Lanzo. "What I wish to know now is what

Colgrin was speaking to you about. His men were here in greater force than we were told to expect, then you returned and all of them returned to their camps outside the village. I would assume you had something to do with that?"

A confused Jorrit simply glanced into the chieftain's eyes. "Whatever he had planned, I assure you it did not involve me. If I were you, I would not trust him."

Dieuwer stared Jorrit in the eye, trying to figure out whether to believe him. "Hmph. No matter. In any case, they will be gone soon enough." He walked back toward Jorrit, glancing at Lanzo as he slept. "What was this I heard about Londinium?"

"I was attempting to convince Colgrin there are more favorable lands we should focus on," Jorrit explained.

Chieftain Dieuwer folded his arms in anticipation. "I wish to know of these lands as well. It would seem your words carried weight with the Saxon. He was speaking to his navigator of a different course. Now speak."

Jorrit smiled widely. He did not mean to, but there was a noticeable feeling of relief in knowing Drysten and his people could be saved.

King Ceneus took a rare stroll through his city the night the messenger arrived. He led a handful of his personal guards into the market square to look on the state of the citizens of Eboracum. He assumed he would find men and women who would look fondly upon their king. What he ended up finding, was nothing.

The only familiar sights were a few whores roaming the streets, moving from tavern to tavern until they ran out of prospective customers, and a few fishermen leading a horse-drawn cart out the city gates. The life in Eboracum had all but disappeared since his last visit into the nighttime streets of the city. "The Christians!" one man said, while another mentioned the bishop specifically. Ceneus presumed it was invariably a bit of both which drove his people into the wilderness.

After a moment of staring into the vacant streets once teeming with life, he decided it best to send his guards forward to the taverns in the hopes they could find the whores who had been roaming about, and slowly made his way back to the Roman baths of his fort. King Ceneus stole a glance toward his banners hanging above the main gates of the city, seeing them wave in the slight breeze moving its way around them.

The anchor now rests over a vacant city. My father would be... disappointed, King Ceneus sadly mused. He moved slower than he had on the walk into the city. For the first time since his reign began, he truly didn't wish to be king.

What's the point in being a king if your people flee from your lands? Ceneus wondered as he walked through the gate to the fort. He slowly wiped a hand over his brow as footsteps began nearing him from the baths.

"Lord King," Maewyn greeted, "I was hoping to catch you in your time of leisure."

"I suppose this would certainly count," the king replied. As much as the king tried to, for some reason, he could not find a reason to dislike the bishop's companion. Maewyn smiled and glanced behind him, waving another man forward. This newcomer was quite obviously a scout, and an exceedingly well traveled one at that.

King Ceneus waved the tired man forward and got a better look at the man with jet-black hair and bags under his eyes.

"News from Londinium, Lord King," the messenger stated. "Lord Hall's son managed to secure the aid of Titus' people."

Good, the king thought with a sigh of relief. *Perhaps the boy will challenge the bishop.*

"I've another message from Prince Gwrast as well, Lord King. Just arrived this morning before I came to report to you," the messenger continued. "He encountered a small group of men from over the Western waters. They were indeed the individuals behind the disappearances."

"Wonderful news!" Maewyn excitedly stated from the other end of the baths.

The king glanced at the priest and happily nodded. At first, when he had met the man both known as Maewyn and Patrick, he was not sure he could trust him. But ever since he began distancing himself from Bishop Germanus, the man had shown himself to be rather pleasant and kind.

"I would agree were it not for the rest of my message, Lord King," the messenger solemnly stated.

King Ceneus sat up straighter as he prepared himself for the news. "Tell me what has happened."

The messenger nodded. "The intruders served a king from across the water. They were not petty raiders as we once thought them to be. The king's name is Abhartach, and he also sent a sizeable force to aid the effort against you to the North. We have this information courtesy of a prisoner who seemed... content with divulging everything to us."

Damn, the king thought as he glanced to the water, *the whole of the islands seem to be against me.*

"I know of the man he speaks, Lord King," Maewyn gravely put in. "He once ruled a kingdom in the Northern region of Hibernia before being cast out by his people because of his insanity."

"How strong is this man?" King Ceneus inquired, sitting up straighter.

Maewyn shrugged. "I cannot tell you of his strength, simply what I was told of him by my former master in Dal Riata."

"Speak then," the king said with a nod.

Maewyn sighed before finding his words. "He feasted on his own people, drinking their blood in the belief it would keep him alive forever. I believe the ones he took from your shores were sent back to him for that purpose."

"He... you're saying... my people were *cattle* to him? Cattle to be raised and eaten?" the king stammered. He'd heard tales of the Gaelic cannibal king in the past, but never heard of the man's identity, nor did he consider these tales to be true.

"Indeed," Maewyn uncomfortably replied.

The king shifted his attention back to the messenger, who like him was startled by the realization that their people could possibly have been consumed by a Gaelic invader. "Raise levies from the villages along our Western coastline and instruct them to patrol the waters until these disappearances cease. Send another message North to warn Lord Hall of the added threats and recall Gwrast back to Eboracum. I wish to speak with this prisoner."

The messenger nodded and exited the bathhouse. King Ceneus sunk down into the warm water of the Roman bath, wondering what else could possibly be thrown his way.

CHAPTER XI

Hall touched the crucifix dangling around his neck as the messenger appeared with word of Drysten's return. The man had ridden hard for three days without rest, only stopping to exchange horses in whatever city or village he found himself in.

"He arrived with a small hoard he stole from the slaver. The Frisian was not with him," he had said. Hall was beyond proud of his son, especially because he somehow achieved freeing their people without losing anyone.

"Thank you for the report. Stay the night in camp, but return with orders for him to join me here," Hall commanded the messenger.

The messenger nodded and left the old Roman tent with the insignia of a bull on its flap, leaving only Hall and Aosten. The two men had crossed the Northern wall into Caledonia the previous day, then chose to make camp in a forest about a mile away from a small village. Their goal was to attack small towns in an effort to draw out the current occupiers of Segedunum. He knew it would take time to do enough damage to the surrounding countryside before that happened, so he encouraged his men to get what rest they could before they were discovered. That was a couple of hours ago, as the sun had started to go down behind some hills to the West.

Aosten broke Hall's thought. "How many should we send to the village?"

"I didn't see many of fighting stock. I will lead fifty men

from the Northern side, and surround the tree line and the fields on the other side. Instruct your men to be ready for runners," Hall responded.

Aosten nodded. "The boy from Powys was concerned for the village's women and children."

"Those who are not a threat will be left to themselves until whatever fighting there is to be done is over. Once that time comes, we will send those who did not run off down South," Hall commanded. "It's no different than how the Romans treated their prisoners." It appeared he was trying to convince Aosten their tactics were not cruel. In reality, Hall was trying to convince himself of the very same thing. He never liked seeing innocents in fear, no matter the side of a conflict they happened to be on.

"I'll tell the boy," Aosten announced as he stood up and walked toward the entryway.

As he stood and outstretched his arms before slowly following Aosten out of the tent, Hall wondered whether the boy in question was the prince of Powys or the one from Ebrauc.

"Get some rest before tomorrow. We attack at dawn," he added to Aosten as the man wandered off.

Hall looked around at the men under his command, slowly beginning to question how long his weary fighters would be able to survive in the harsh North. The men were all ill-fitted and only lightly trained, meaning they were best suited for the assignment they were currently on; scaring women and children. Most of them were either too old or too young to be relied upon.

At least the Powysians look capable enough, he thought to himself. He looked off toward their camp and saw Bors sitting with a handful of men from the allied kingdom, listening to stories of their most recent war with the Gaels.

War was nothing new to this part of the world. The Romans had attempted to extend their rule North on numerous occasions. Always pushed back, this led to centuries of raids and skirmishes between them and the Caledonians. It was obvious the people living above Hadrian's Wall could not be conquered, so they decided to try and extend their reach by buying off high ranking tribesman in an effort to broker peace. Some played along, understanding they could become wealthy by taking Rome's money and serving as an occasional buffer between Rome's territory and that of the more aggressive peoples to the North.

The area they were presently camping in belonged to the half-brother of King Ceneus. One would assume they were allies, but there was only a tentative peace agreement between the two kingdoms. This land was named Bryneich. In truth, they were no more Briton than anywhere else north of Hadrian's wall. The people had Brythonic ancestry, but their proximity to the Caledonians meant they were forced into friendly arrangements once their Roman protectors abandoned Britannia. King Garbonian ap Coel, who ruled from the ancient tribal hill-mount at Din Guayrdi on the coast of his northern border, preferred not to acknowledge his family to the South for fear of incurring the wrath of his neighbors. This meant many tribes raiding into these Briton-ruled lands would go unhindered through his territory.

After hearing a few voices in the tent next to his, Hall was reminded he had the luxury of being accompanied by *two* princes on his trip North. The first was Prince Eidion ap Ceneus of Ebrauc and the other being Prince Ambrosius Aurelianus of Powys. Eidion had proved himself to be a nuisance to Hall during their travels North, but Ambrosius was more in line with what a soldier, and more importantly, what a prince should be. When the men first departed, Eidion had held up his group of fifty men so he could get a quick session with a town whore. All the while, Ambrosius was speaking with Hall about their strategies against the Northmen they would be facing.

It was strange to see, as Eidion was the one with the

actual royal blood in his veins. Ambrosius was merely the nephew of a rich man who succeeded in a power grab once the Roman Empire decided to leave Britannia. That being said, the boy showed a real gift for his new leadership role, something which was widely known to be an effect of having a good man and a true Roman as a father. Hall observed as he strolled through the men encamped around him, trying to learn their names and get to know them. Things Hall learned when he served under Stilicho against the Picts so long ago. The boy was no older than Drysten, but somehow carried himself as though he was a seasoned veteran.

"Lord," a voice said from behind him. Hall turned and thanked a servant who had brought him his meal from the small cooking fire before waving him off. Gawain had gone out earlier and found a couple of wild birds worth cooking. Upon killing them, he kept one for himself and took the other to Hall. Eidion had noticed and began muttering something under his breath until Gawain finally relented and handed his bird off to the prince.

"Fucking *pissant*," Gawain said quietly as the prince proudly shuffled away. Where Ambrosius was a pleasure to have in camp, Eidion had begun to prove himself quite a detriment.

The night had begun to set in as the last rays of sunlight began to disappear behind the hills. The men all began to claim small plots of dirt they would sleep on for a few hours before they would begin the raid of the village. Hall began to move back toward his tent when the voice of the Powysian Prince called for him. "Lord," he said.

Hall turned to greet the young man of about eighteen years as he walked toward him. "Prince Aurelianus," he said with a slight bow. "To what do I owe the pleasure?"

The Prince smiled warmly as he got closer. "Aosten informed me of the plan tomorrow."

"And it's to your liking?" Hall inquired.

The Prince nodded. "So long as the ones who don't fight

us are spared."

Hall looked toward Eidion's tent as the noise from inside grew louder. The prince from Ebrauc had tried to convince Hall they should kill anyone they met in the village, then burn it. He was too fond of killing for Hall's liking, and not fond enough of planning. To him, any issue could be solved with enough force applied indiscriminately in all directions. He had none of the nobility typically required to inherit a kingdom. For that reason, Hall knew he would never swear his loyalty to the current ruling family. He would remain as a mercenary until he chose otherwise, but never more than that.

"Others don't share that sentiment, Lord Prince," Hall returned with a sigh.

Ambrosius glanced toward Eidion's tent. "He knows he will lose the support of my people should he go against my wishes. I told him as much when we arrived."

Hall scoffed. "Was he sober enough to remember?"

The Prince shrugged. "Is he ever?"

The two men laughed for a moment before bidding each other farewell for the night. Hall plodded his way into his tent to arrange his belongings, then to eventually get some rest.

These marches are much more taxing on you than they once were, Hall thought to himself.

He drew the skins back on his hammock and sat himself down. As he did so, he unstrapped his leather boots to reveal his blistered feet. A small streak of blood flowed from an open sore on his heel. "Ugh," he let out as he withdrew his foot before leaning back. The noises of the men began to fade, slowly giving way to the sounds of insects and birds. Even Ebrauc's prince had decided to retire for the evening, as Hall could hear the men who had drank with him drunkenly swaying back to their own tents. Hall wondered why they had chosen to retire earlier than they had the previous nights, but decided even a royal entourage could grow weary from too much drink.

All were beginning to quiet down in preparation for the raid the next morning. Most of the men would not be taking part in it, but the fifty or so accompanying Hall were mostly asleep in the middle of their camp, while the rest were watching the nearby hills for any movement. Hall was uncertain if his force had crossed the wall undetected, but knew if anyone saw them, they would assume they were moving on one of the larger cities to the North rather than moving East toward Segedunum. The army managed to find its way to a forest and moved through the concealment of the trees toward the general area where they intended to raid. The princes led the column from horseback the whole way there. Hall marched close behind on foot with Bors, Cyrus, and Elias, each of whom would be leading their own groups of about thirty men. The soldiers themselves were little more than militias by Hall's standard. Should they find themselves in a proper fight, Hall knew enough about the land near Segedunum to lead them to safety considering a full-on fight wasn't an ideal situation to find himself in.

The village they were about to attack was chosen due to its proximity to Segedunum, being no more than a five-hour march West-Northwest. Hall was not familiar with its name, only that at one point many years ago the Romans built something on the same site. Judging by the buildings Gawain reported, the older Roman structures were long gone, as everything was built from the ancient favorite of the locals, mud, wood, and thatch. Gawain also reported back the lack of fighting-aged males living in the town. Something which clearly indicated the men were off at war, most likely in Segedunum.

Hall finally began to slowly fade out of consciousness as the silence of the camp slowly lulled him to sleep. This was the strange time Hall always thought to be rather soothing. There could be thousands of men encamped around him, but each soul knew they could meet their end the next day, and all figured they would have a better chance of avoiding such a fate if they were blessed with better rest than their enemy. Slowly but surely, the pain in his aching feet began to subside, and soon he was asleep.

Dawn came with the agonizing dins of screams coming from the camp. Hall awoke with a start and burst out of the tent with his weapon drawn. He frantically looked around him in confusion as every man he was intending to lead during the raid looked back at him. "What the fuck is going on?" he yelled. The only responses he received were drowsy expressions, indicating the men knew as much as he did. "Make ready!" Hall shouted as he thrust the flaps of his tent aside and donned his armor, slowly bringing his boots over his raw heels.

"Lord!" a voice said from outside. Bors burst in with Prince Aurelianus, both in shock of what they saw. "Hall…" He began before trailing off.

The Prince stepped forward. "Eidion led a small raid of his own before dawn. He slaughtered everyone but the women he wanted to claim and burned everything to the ground."

"That *fucking* animal," Hall said with a sigh. He understood people would die. He just hoped if he led the raid the way he intended that some would also be able to escape. "Where is he?"

The Prince glanced at Bors. "He's… with a woman in his tent."

"A woman?" Hall asked angrily.

"One he took," the Prince responded. "Others are being guarded over by his man, Vonig, by their campsite."

An enraged Hall burst out of his tent and made his way across the camp, weaving through the men who were beginning to assemble outside. "Move!" he roared. Soon he found himself outside of the Prince's tent, where he found multiple battered women tied to a post and being watched over by guards in black, all looking to Vonig.

"Go," Vonig commanded. "My lord is busy." He slowly began to cackle at the sight of Hall grimly staring into the swollen face of a woman near death.

Hall took a firm stride toward the guard, slowly placing his thumb on the cross guard of his blade. "You will move," he commanded in a calm tone.

The other guards took notice of Hall's subtle action and stood shoulder to shoulder with their leader. Hall, Bors, and Prince Aurelianus found themselves outnumbered three to one should anything happen.

Hall took another step forward. "As I said, you will move," speaking in a more stern and commanding tone.

The guards drew their weapons and began moving toward Hall and his companions when the tent burst open, and Prince Eidion happily strolled out. "What's this then?" he asked with a smirk, "I thought *I* was in charge here, am I not?"

One of the guards stepped forward. "You are, Lord Prince. Though *this* one seems to think otherwise."

Eidion raised an eyebrow. "Does he now? And why is that, *my lord*?"

"I *am* in charge, because of all the people in this camp, I am the only one who had the wealth to be. Not wealth in money, but the wealth of *power,* you miserable shit. You led a raid on a defenseless village with every man you have. How many is that again? Twenty? I have *many* times your number, and that number will only fight in my name. Do not forget who I am, *boy,* because if I wished it, you would be dead for disobeying my orders and engaging in a senseless slaughter." Hall turned to the guards. "You will untie these women, and every one of them will be given the needed care and set free. If you disobey me, I will make each one of your deaths worse than the last." Hall turned to Prince Aurelianus. "I was telling you the truth when I said I didn't like killing innocents."

The Prince nodded at Hall before angrily turning to Eidion. "You will follow his commands. If you choose not to, you will be the reason your father loses the support of

Powys," then followed Hall as they began to walk back to Hall's area of the encampment.

"What power do you think you have over me?" Eidion bellowed as they walked away, none of them bothering to turn around. "You're just a hired sword! We will soon have no need of you!"

Hall kept walking, unshaken by the prince's words. The men Prince Eidion commanded had little discipline, and their savagery made Hall uneasy at their presence. They were what Hall used to see from local tribes when he fought for Rome. Farmers and craftsmen who were not soldiers by trade, but were called upon nonetheless to defend their homes. Due to this lack of training, it was a common sight to see them act cruel when they realized there would be people at their mercy.

"Told you the boy was a twat," a voice said as Hall entered his tent. "Been like most his life."

Hall turned and saw Aosten sitting in the corner with a skin filled with either wine or water, of that Hall could only guess.

"You definitely warned me, though I confess I didn't quite expect this," a tired Hall responded.

Aosten chuckled. "I was wondering how long it would take for him to do something like this. Even asked me for my men to join him."

"I'm assuming you said no," Hall asked.

Aosten laughed through his sarcasm. "Of *course*, Lord Prince! I will see you at *dawn*, Lord Prince!" Aosten paused to drink more from his skin. "I agreed, waited for him to leave, then told my men to sleep as long as they pleased. I will not lead my men behind a cruel, spoiled boy. The only reason I didn't warn you is the bastard left one of his men near your tent to alert him if I had tried."

Hall sat himself down on top of the trunk which generally would contain his armor. "You were right. That *boy* will be trouble."

"Especially when he takes the crown. It's a shame it won't pass to one of the other two," Aosten said while shaking his head.

Hall turned to Aosten. "Seems like he would do well to remember there are options."

"Not if the whelp kills those options," Bors put in.

Aosten nodded. "None of the brothers have ever gotten along well. Though the other two at least put their people before their... amusement. They're the ones in charge of the territory we claimed further North toward Hadrian's Wall."

"Don't all of a king's sons receive equal shares of the land and wealth upon his death?" Bors inquired.

Aosten nodded. "That is normally the custom, though with Eidion I cannot imagine a world where he would let that happen. Has his father's dream of a united Britannia. A united kingdom under one ruler."

Prince Aurelianus sighed heavily. "The idea of that man reigning over my people turns my stomach."

"How do you think *we* feel?" Aosten asked sarcastically, leading the prince to return a pitiful smirk.

"It's too bad the best of them is a woman," Aurelianus said shyly. "She has none of her brother's cruelty or ambition."

The three men sat there for a moment as each tried to predict how Ebrauc's future king could end up being a cruel and sloppy child of a man. One who cared little for his own people and even less for people who did not live within his borders. Hall knew he had made an enemy out of the boy, a fact he knew his own son may pay for some time in the future. One thing he clearly understood was the future could wait for a while. This destructive massacre by the boy-prince, though small in numbers, built a pressing need to relocate.

It had been almost a week since Drysten had returned home from his voyage. In that time, the town had begun to construct a handful of homes as well as a new temple with a surrounding graveyard. All the buildings they would build would be wood and thatch, as there were no more people available who knew how to work stone well enough for habitable buildings. Or rather, they did not know how to keep them from falling apart with its occupants inside. Drysten had spent his days helping lay foundations and keep his men out of trouble with the local tribesman they were now dwelling alongside.

These men and women were part of the Parisii tribe, a group who had dwelled in this area dating back to well before the Romans first invaded. They told stories of how their tribe originated somewhere across the water, far to the East. They made their way to their current home over the course of centuries, though Drysten had no way of knowing how accurate their stories really were.

Currently, the Parisii lived under the rule of King Ceneus. the king's father had married a Parisii woman, unifying the tribe with his own Brigantes tribe. Most people believe this marriage was orchestrated by the Romans in yet another attempt at finding some way to bring Britannia deeper into their grasp. As of right now, these people mainly consisted of fishermen and hunters in the Southeast portion of Ebrauc's territory.

Drysten walked with Bors and Diocles through the streets now bustling with activity. Another ship had arrived, carrying the very last group of families belonging to the Fortuna's crew. Everyone was now in one place, something Drysten had looked forward to since he first left Isolde back in Burdigala so long ago.

"Strange to see this place so busy after seeing it as it was before," Diocles observed as they walked through groups of men resting from work. "I suppose the locals will have to get used to more of us now."

Drysten looked around at the people heading toward the woods in search of suitable timber for more homes.

"This whole place will be much bigger by wintertime. I doubt anybody will recognize it."

"Speak for yourself. You'll be living in the *villa*. Doubt that will look much different by wintertime," Bors the Younger put in with a laugh.

Drysten smiled. "I told Isolde to do what she wishes with it, but she told me she would prefer to wait for my father's permission."

"Sensible, I suppose. Any word from him?" Diocles inquired.

Drysten shook his head. "Not even a peep, and neither have I heard anything from the king as to where he is located."

"Here's to hoping we don't need to rescue anyone else!" Bors drew a look from Drysten as he raised a cup of ale in the air and downed it almost as fast as his father could.

"I'm sure he's fine, Lord," Diocles said. "The man seemed like he was no fool."

The men continued toward the docks to observe the unloading of goods from the newly arrived ship. Drysten spied crates and barrels being placed in the corner of the pier next to some feral cats that had recently taken up residence under the wooden planks of one of the villa's buildings. The kittens would playfully run toward someone as they were about to put down a crate, then run off when they were satisfied they had gotten their attention.

"When should we be expecting Titus to arrive?" Diocles asked Drysten.

Drysten glanced East toward the sea. "I would say another couple of weeks."

Bors scoffed. "Unless he took the payment with no intention of delivering on it."

"I doubt it. He seemed honorable enough," Drysten replied as he shook his head.

"He's a *Roman*. I don't trust the Romans. They left the people here to fend for themselves when they figured out their Empire was dying," Bors noted.

Drysten shrugged. "Titus stayed. That counts for something, doesn't it?"

The three men stood and watched the ship being unloaded for a little while longer, then turned back toward the town. They made their way around the western wall of the villa and stopped in the center of the small market square. Stalls were being built to help fill the needs for the newer occupants of the town, mainly selling food and cloth. There was also a metalworker who took up residence in one of the abandoned buildings on the Northern end of the town, who was currently hard at work making armor repairs as well as producing horseshoes for the farms nearby.

"Handy having him here," Diocles mentioned. "Not sure how a town could have gotten by without someone to make horseshoes or nails."

"These tribesmen know how to live with much less than the Romans," Drysten added, "but to answer your question, the king would occasionally send supplies to the towns near its borders."

"Speaking of which, who exactly owns the Southern bank of the river?" Bors questioned.

The group turned around to see if they could spot anyone moving across the water, but decided it must have been free of any people in the immediate vicinity.

Drysten turned to Diocles. "Find Dagonet and the Cretans. We should have a look over there soon."

"There's an old ferry still in use just outside of town," Diocles informed the men. "A farmer told me when I asked him about buying some horses."

"Horses?" Drysten asked. "Didn't the king grant us some?"

Diocles nodded. "He did, but they're weak. You can see their ribs too clearly."

"Of *course* they are. I'm beginning to wonder if we should leave this king sooner rather than later. He seems to be… inadequate," Drysten said with a sigh.

"Nevertheless, we should get to know our borders while we *are* here," Diocles said. "I'll find Dagonet and we can go meet with the farmer." At that, Diocles walked off toward the tavern, leaving Drysten and Bors to themselves near the market square.

The market was slowly growing day by day as more men and women were relocating into Petuaria. The tavern had already been filled with people as they awaited the moment for their homes to be built. That would be a few months more, considering there were still crops to be tended and livestock to be cared for. Typically, this was not the time for people to build a new home, but the vast majority of people who had just arrived in Petuaria had limited options available. Drysten and his men were currently doing what they could to help the building of these homes, as they would be able to live in the villa's barracks during the winter months anyway.

"Lord," a voice said from behind the two men. Drysten turned and saw Matthew and Dagonet walking up with Diocles. "Cynwrig is doing better. I feel as though I can step away, and it would do no harm. What's this about going across the river?"

"If we're going to be living here, we'll need to know the surroundings. I have seen no people across the water, so if we can find building supplies, we should be able to ferry them across and use them here," Drysten said.

Matthew nodded. "Does anyone live out there?" he asked Dagonet.

Dagonet shrugged. "When King Ceneus claimed much of Rheged he drove off many of the locals in that area. I have not been told if they returned."

Drysten stood in thought for a moment. "If they have not come back then we could find much to use in the abandoned villages."

"True, though I would caution you to not take anything

too valuable. King Ceneus may have driven them off, but he has no way of enforcing his reign in those parts. Rheged is still its own kingdom whether he claims it or not," Dagonet informed Drysten.

Drysten nodded. "We'll have to be careful then. What kingdoms lay further South?"

Dagonet paused in thought. "Further South would be the kingdom of Linnuis. Wouldn't venture that far if I were you."

"Why's that?" Diocles inquired.

Dagonet turned to the Greek. "They may be employing Saxons to defend them. Although I'm not sure if it's true or simply rumor."

Diocles led as the men crossed a weakly made bridge supported over a small ditch, with each man eyeing it suspiciously as they tested to make sure it was structurally sound. The farm sat on the opposite end. To Drysten's surprise, it looked more substantial than the others nearby. There was a sizeable field of wheat being harvested by workers who likely couldn't care less who ran the town across the ditch. As they moved closer to the main home, some of the workers stopped what they were doing and pointed at them. After a moment, the men shrugged at their presence and went back to work.

"Hail, Lord," a man said from the home, "I'll be out in one moment. This pail won't fill itself!"

"Pail?" Drysten whispered, "pail of what?"

As he spoke, a man walked through the door of the home and tossed the pail's contents onto the ground near a small ditch, filling the area with the foul smell of its contents.

"Oh. That's what he was filling it with," Diocles whispered with a chuckle.

After a moment, the smell dissipated, and the man made his way toward Drysten. "How are you, Lord? People call me Conway. You're here about those horses your man spoke of?"

Drysten nodded. "I am. The horses we received from the king are *not* what we expected."

Conway laughed. "That's because he doesn't have anyone who knows how to care for them properly! Come this way, and you can see how they're supposed to be bred."

Drysten nodded and followed the man to a reasonably sized barn beside the bridge. Conway opened it to reveal a dozen or so horses of a larger stock than the ones granted by King Ceneus.

"These would serve a lord such as yourself quite nicely. King Ceneus may try to *breed* horses, but I am the only one in these parts who knows how to *care* for them," Conway said in a cheerful tone.

"They're indeed beautiful beasts," Drysten said as he walked in front of the stalls. The horses were taller and more muscular than the ones granted to him by King Ceneus, and overall, they seemed much healthier. "Where did you learn to care for them?"

"Served with the legion at Derventio. My job was to care for their beasts before they departed," Conway responded. "A real shame they decided to leave."

Drysten stood marveling at one of the horses who seemed to be fixed on him. Its large eyes watched him as he walked, seemingly ignoring the others in his company. "How much would you want for them?"

Conway's eyes widened. "*All* of them, Lord? I could not part with them all. I care for them so they can help me manage my fields."

Drysten walked closer to the horse, still tracking him as he moved. "What if we traded the ones we received from the king for them?"

Conway stood in thought for a moment. "I... I suppose that could help us both. How many did he send you, Lord?"

"Twenty, though by my count only a handful are strong," Diocles answered.

Conway stood and rubbed his chin as he considered the offer. "May I see them before I make any decisions, Lord?"

Drysten nodded. "They are being kept near my villa. Come, I would like to make a deal as soon as we are able. We have need to ride across the river."

"Lead on, Lord!" Conway responded.

The men walked out of the barn and made their way back into the town. Conway regaled them with tales from his youth and his service with Rome's legions. To Drysten's surprise, he briefly served with a group of Arabs at Arbeia, the fort across the river from the one his father was moving to retake.

"Though by the time we abandoned it, the fortress was little more than a storage depot," the former legionnaire put in.

Apparently, some of the men the Empire sent to Arbeia had come back following Constantine III's defeat in Gaul. Conway knew of a small number who were still dwelling in that area, but could not guess whether they would have been there when the fort across the river was taken.

The group continued toward the villa, crossing the market's square and waiting for a group of men carrying boxes toward the tavern to cross by. They entered the villa's front gate and walked to the right, moving to the stables.

Conway suddenly gasped at the look of the horses inside. "They're not the best quality stock... You certainly should not be able to keep so many in such a small space this easily," he observed. "How did he manage to make such majestic beasts so lethargic?"

"The king seems to find a way for such things," Dagonet muttered.

"Ugh... look at you," Conway whispered, rubbing the nose of one of the horses. The gangly beast seemed to plea for help.

After much haggling between Drysten and Conway, the deal was struck. Drysten would receive ten of Conway's horses as well as grain from his harvest. In return, Conway would receive all the horses given to Drysten by King Ceneus, as well as a sum one thousand sestertii. Both men shook on the deal and Conway departed to bring the horses back to the villa.

As the men spoke, they could hear hooves coming closer to the villa's entrance. A man dismounted and made his way through the gate. Upon noticing, Drysten made his way over. "Lord," he began, "I've come with a message from your father."

Drysten perked up at the news. "Let's hear it."

The messenger nodded. "He said you are to bring what men you have and make your way north. He's encamped not far from the wall."

Drysten glanced at Diocles, then back to the messenger. "How many is he expecting?"

"He did not say, Lord," the messenger responded, "but he says he needs you to hurry. I have the specific instruction written here."

"How long ago was this?" Drysten asked as he was given a rolled parchment.

The messenger paused for a moment. "A little more than two days, Lord.

Drysten turned to Diocles. "All we can bring is about a hundred until Titus arrives. You stay here and brief him when he arrives. Get everyone ready to move out tomorrow morning."

Diocles began to protest at the thought of staying behind, but decided against it and left the villa. Drysten handed the messenger two coins and instructed the servants in the kitchen to cook him a meal. He found out the man's name was Phelan, and that he actually lived in Petuaria with his uncle, Conway.

"The horses you purchased will serve you well, Lord," Phelan said. "Oldest one is only about four years of age; you'll have them for quite some time if you care for them well."

"That's the idea," Drysten said with a nod. He patted Phelan on the back and walked back outside to join Bors and Dagonet, who were discussing the route they would take to join Drysten's father.

"Best to follow Dere Street," Dagonet mentioned. "We can cross north near Coria, about a half a day's march to Segedunum. I can't imagine he would be much further away than that."

Drysten nodded his approval and the men went to explain the plans to the rest of the Fortuna's crew. Though Drysten knew he should probably go with him, he knew he had an obligation to disclose these plans to Isolde, as she was still becoming accustomed to the new living conditions. Drysten knew she may not look fondly on the idea of him being away from her again, especially after the situation with Servius.

Drysten found her laughing with a servant in the main greeting area of the villa, and upon seeing Drysten entering, she politely excused herself. Drysten met her with a kiss, and the two walked near the small pool.

"We're to leave tomorrow," Drysten explained. "My father asked for more men."

Isolde looked away, failing to hide her disappointment. "I understand. Just try to hurry back this time."

Drysten wrapped his arms around her. "I promised you we would be married. I intend to follow through on that promise."

Isolde looked up. "I know. Just hurry back."

The two kissed, and Drysten went to prepare himself for a long march North.

CHAPTER XII

Drysten awoke the next morning to the sounds of Isolde slipping out from under the furs of the bed. He pawed at her to prevent her from leaving, but after a short giggle from her, she keeled over and began to vomit all over the floor beside the bed. Maebh abruptly shot out from the pile of rags he had been given the night before and proceeded to dart his way underneath Drysten's side of the bed.

"Scared the little one," Drysten said with a laugh. He slowly leaned over the edge of the bed and gently scooped up Maebh, placing him gently beside him on the top of the bed. "Are you sick *every* morning?" Drysten asked of his woman.

"The joys of bearing children," she said as she smiled up at Drysten, who was somewhat shocked by the sight of something so disgusting coming out of such a beautiful woman. "Happens most mornings now. You just don't normally wake."

"I will find a servant who can care for you while I am away," Drysten said as he walked around the bed toward Isolde. "I would feel better if I knew you were not dealing with sickness by yourself."

Isolde giggled. "It is hardly a sickness, *Lord*." She drew out the word lord to annoy Drysten, who upon hearing it threw his hands up in the air.

Drysten fumbled through the darkness to find his trunk. He had donned a tunic and his pants before applying cloth footwraps to his feet as well as strapping his peros in place.

The pero was a type of winter sandal worn by Romans made of a cork sole and rawhide lacing. Drysten had grown up almost exclusively wearing this type of shoe, though many others he had known chose to wear more traditional sandals.

Isolde left the room to grab some fresher air away from the vomit, and allowing time for Drysten to get himself ready for a two-day march north to join his father. He ruffled the short hair at the top of Maebh's head and slowly began to place his armor on the bed when he heard voices outside.

Isolde came running back into the bedroom. "Ships!" she said through a troubled tone. Drysten also noticed her slowly running her fingers over the "FVG" brand now burned into her arm.

Drysten sprang up and rushed through the villa, out the gates, and around the western side toward the docks. There were small groups of men running from the tavern or other buildings dotting the town to check on the commotion. Off in the distance to the East, Drysten could just make out the shapes of masts being illuminated by torchlight.

"Get ready for a fight. We won't know if they're friendly until they arrive," Drysten commanded the men standing around him. By Drysten's guess, there would be a long enough time for the men to grab their weapons and armor before they needed to form a shield wall in defense of the dock.

Drysten himself ran back to the villa to finish applying his armor when he found Isolde crying. "You should have killed them all. I knew that man would find us," she said as Drysten walked over to hold her.

"Servius is dead, love. There's no reason to be afraid of him anymore," Drysten said as he gently pushed her head into his chest.

Isolde lightly sobbed as she gazed into the ground. "I meant *Marhaus*, his son."

Drysten was taken by surprise. He had not spoken to Isolde of the people she encountered in Frisia. There had been no need, as she was currently safe with her people. He also had forgotten there could be someone left who could be harboring a grudge against him. "Atestatia seems to believe he is not strong enough to attempt anything against us."

Isolde nodded. "But what if she is wrong."

Drysten held Isolde as he considered his next move. If the ships did indeed belong to Marhaus, he would undoubtedly be looking for anyone bearing his signature slave brand. "Hush now. If this man has indeed come for us, I will simply kill him myself."

Isolde looked up into Drysten's eyes. "He's a cruel man you would do well not to underestimate."

"He will die if he ventures here, that is certain," Drysten responded with a smile. He then stood up and made his way to his armor, still neatly set out on the bed. Isolde helped him get strapped into the leather jerkin while he took care of his greaves and vambraces. Soon, all that was left was his sword belt containing the sword rumored to have once belonged to Vercingetorix, and his father's dagger. Hall's bearskin cloak was left behind, as there was no need of looking like a lord for the potential invaders. He checked everything one last time, kissed Isolde, then walked out of the villa.

Men from the tavern fell in behind Drysten as he made his way toward the docks. Most had been asleep not long before and had to be roused before a formidable enough shield wall could be formed along the dock. Bors and Heraclius had situated the men in a line curving down the length of the wooden planks of the pier. Drysten surveyed the men and decided they would be ready enough to offer up a fight to whoever it was that was coming.

As they waited, the sun had slowly begun to rise. Off in the distance, Drysten could now see there were three vessels in total. All three were full of people.

"Fucking hell," a voice whispered from behind Drysten.

The ships began to grow closer as the sun started to

shine over the water. As it did, he recognized one of the ships as once belonging to Servius. He walked closer to the edge of the dock and began to make out the shapes of men standing on the bow, waving their arms and pointing to the other two ships trailing them.

"Shit," Drysten whispered softly.

"What is it?" Diocles said as he walked up from the shield wall.

Drysten turned. "The vessel in the lead is with Titus. The two trailing him are not."

Diocles strained his tired eyes and gradually started to realize the situation. Titus was being chased by Saxon raiders from the east and was trying urgently to grab the attention of the men in Petuaria. "They're catching up to him," Diocles observed.

"We don't have any options but to stay and hope they don't get caught," Bors put in. "Not unless we try to sail to them."

Drysten shook his head. "There's not enough time. We wait." Drysten turned to the line of people awaiting their orders. "That vessel has the rest of our people aboard. The two behind seem to be raiders in pursuit of her. Our job is to stand here and pray they don't get caught. When they get here, it will be up to us to defend them and drive their attackers off."

The men looked from side to side as they began to understand what was happening. Most were seasoned warriors who had fought for Hall or served on his crew, but some were new recruits King Ceneus had sent for training. Like the horses he sent, they were not the ideal sort of men. Most were too young or too old. One was even missing a few of his fingers, but they had all volunteered to fight and Drysten knew they were about to.

Drysten turned back toward the water and watched as the ship moved closer, with the two in pursuit catching up. Drysten and his men were all worried they would soon see their people caught and slaughtered in front of them, helpless to prevent it. Diocles began pacing in front of the shield wall, acting like he was inspecting the men. In actuality, it was evident to anybody who knew him that he was merely antsy. Waiting was not something that was easily done by a person like Diocles. Bors too was nervous, though he was much better at hiding it. One would assume he was calm as could be were it not for his fingers feverishly tapping the hilt of his sword as he rested them atop its pommel.

Drysten stood by until the faint voices of the men aboard Titus' vessel could be heard screaming for help and protection. The one voice Drysten expected to hear was either not audible or he was not yelling. Titus could not be seen from the dock, making Drysten nervous as to his fate. He turned to his men. "Diocles, order half of the men to hide out of sight of the other two vessels. I want them to land thinking we won't put up much of a fight. We'll need prisoners and I am not convinced they will give us a fight if they see we likely have an equal number to them."

"I'll put them in the villa. Give the word, and we'll come running." Diocles turned and took half of the men on the western side of the dock back into the market square, where they soon disappeared into the villa.

"Petras, Paulus," Drysten yelled, "get on the roof." Drysten gestured to the roof of the villa, then heard two sets of footsteps run off toward the front gate.

Titus' vessel was now about a hundred yards from the dock, with the two ships in pursuit only twenty yards behind them. Drysten could see spears being thrown from the attackers onto the deck of Titus' ship, but could not tell if they were hitting their marks.

"Shields up!" Drysten commanded as he made his way back toward the line. Drysten hated fighting with a shield, as the extra weight on his left side occasionally threw him off balance. However, he knew at this moment he would need to. He walked up to the outer wall of the villa, which was only about eight feet in height. "Somebody throw a shield over," he yelled. A moment later, a shield came flying over the wall, landing by his feet. He picked up the shield bearing the golden anchor of Ebrauc over its front, looped his hand through the leather, then walked to stand in the first row.

The men aboard Titus' ship were doing their best to keep their assailants at bay, hurling spears and firing arrows behind them. From what Drysten could see they had little effect, landing harmlessly into shields or falling into the water. There seemed to be about thirty men on both enemy vessels, all of them armed for war and ready for a fight. Drysten glanced from side to side to make sure his half of the men were ready. There were about seventy men with him at that moment, and he knew the others waiting around the villa would assure them of their victory. He would wait until the enemy had mostly left their ships when he gave the order for Diocles to strike.

Titus' vessel finally reached the dock directly in front of Drysten. Ten bloodied men ran off toward him, one supporting Titus' weight as he limped.

"Drysten..." Titus began before gasping for breath. He took a short moment to collect himself, glanced behind him at the two ships, then continued. "They took Londinium." Drysten tried to open his mouth to speak but was too thrown by the news coming from a bloodied Titus. "They killed most of my men. Took their families as slaves."

"I...," Drysten managed to croak out, as the sound of the enemy ships hitting the dock boomed forth. "Get your people behind us!" he commanded Titus. He turned and shouted for the Cretans to direct their attention toward the men still aboard Titus' vessel in the hopes of preventing it from being boarded, though thankfully the assailants chose to ignore it upon docking. Drysten joined his men in the center of their shield wall, about forty paces from either end.

Men were now wildly rushing forward toward

Petuaria's defenders. The first few to make contact with the shield wall were heavily armed axemen who did so on its left-most side, most likely in an attempt to make it fold inward unto itself. Drysten watched as the axes came down onto shields, splintering them or wrenching them away from the men who carried them. More men were now running from the other ship, this time using the same maneuver on the opposite side of the line.

"Call the rest of the men, Lord!" a frightened voice screamed from behind Drysten.

Drysten glanced behind him. "Quiet! Not yet," he bellowed.

Most of the two enemy ships were now vacant, with the nearest containing men who had been picked off by Petras and Paulus. The seventy men Drysten had started the battle with had quickly dwindled to fifty due to the flanks being comprised of the less seasoned men. Once the axemen made it to the men who had a history of war, they were mostly halted. They then moved back to their own men and formed their own shield wall.

The Saxons had formed a wall three men deep when they rushed forward as one, all screaming and cursing toward the Britons. The crashing sound generated by the wooden shields meeting was deafening to Drysten, who had never experienced fighting in a shield wall before. He was thrown back with such a force his head began to ring. He instinctively raised his shield and blocked the downward swing from an axe. "Diocles!" he screamed, though he doubted anyone could hear him over the grunts and screams of the battle. "Call for Diocles!" he was yelling back to anyone who could hear him.

The man directly in front of Drysten managed to hook his axe around Drysten's shield and wrench it away, exposing him to a powerful stab from the man on Drysten's right. Luckily it only scratched the leather jerkin and tore a couple of iron rings free, dealing no real damage to Drysten himself when he repositioned his shield. Heraclius saw him in a vulnerable position and thrust his shield into Drysten's attacker with all his strength, sending him back into the man behind him.

Two arrows struck the men in front of Drysten, giving him just enough time to look behind him. "Call for Diocles!" He yelled to the Cretans, who were still shooting from the tiled roof of the villa. After Petras fired off the arrow he had readied before nodding, Drysten was slightly comforted by the sight of him yelling to the men below. Drysten turned back to fend off the next man who had taken the place of the first, now gasping for air beneath them with an arrow pierced through his throat.

The wall held long enough for Diocles' men to rush around the enemy's right flank and push their way into the Saxon line. The Saxons hadn't expected to deal with another force, causing enough confusion for Drysten's line to move them back toward their ships.

"Push!" Drysten yelled.

The men from Diocles' group were now adding men to the right side of Drysten's shield wall, closing the space the Saxons had first tried to open.

The wooden planks of the dock were now slick with blood. Men of both sides were lying all around the fight, screaming in pain for help. Drysten stepped into a stomach wound of a man who was still gasping for air below him, causing him to release a scream of agony. "Push the bastards back to their ships!" he commanded. To his surprise, a small group of men had leapt from Titus' vessel and attacked the men from behind. The Saxons were now down to about fifty men, half of the number they appeared to enter the fight with. Drysten's men had suffered the first casualties, but now their numbers had swollen to a hundred strong, plus whatever men were attacking the Saxon's rear.

A small opening emerged to Drysten's left when Bors the Younger was able to pull a man's shield away. Bors and the men behind him rushed forward, splitting the Saxon line in half. They were now prevented from retreating by Titus's men in their rear and encircled by either Drysten's men or water. Saxons were now falling quickly under the swords and spears of Drysten's men. When the number went down to about thirty, they decided to try their luck at being taken alive.

One man with a long brown beard and bright blue eyes yelled for the remaining Saxons to surrender, then threw his sword and shield down before walking toward Drysten. "Do what you will, Briton. It is over."

Drysten lowered his sword and walked forward, wiping the blood from his brow as he did so. He calmly eyed the man in front of him, then turned to Bors. "Chain them and then put the leaders below the villa. Find another place to store the others. Make sure they are not within sight of their leaders." He turned toward Titus, who had spent the duration of the battle in the protection of two of his men on either side of him. "What happened?"

A weary Titus glanced around him, took a deep breath, then began to tell his story.

CHAPTER XIII

The sun shone over the waters around Londinium's stone bridge. Titus was proud of helping the boy from the North. He was even more excited about the new ship he dubbed the Victoria, or Victory in the Briton tongue. He stood on the bow of the Victrix, staring up at the birds and watching the city as they sailed through. They would dock on the Southern bank, just a short walk away from his villa.

The bireme was a standard enough vessel in the Roman Empire, first used by the Greeks so many centuries ago. Titus believed the ancient Greeks to be the best sailors of history, and he was proud to be aboard such a vessel.

"Row!" he yelled excitedly from the bow. "Row as if your wives miss you!"

The men laughed as if they had not just lost two of their most beloved men. Bastakas was Titus' second, and had a closer relationship to the men than Titus did. Lucius was also loved, as he had a sense of humor for any situation. The men missed their presence dearly and were certainly not looking forward to burying two people they considered family.

The bridge of Londinium passed overhead with people stopping to take a look at the ship. *Must think Rome is returning,* Titus thought to himself.

He looked behind him to all the men wearing their Roman armor, and wondered if there would be a day when the people could see such a sight. Legions gallantly marching up the roads of Londinium to reclaim their lands won by war and bloodshed. If it ever did happen, Titus assumed he would not be alive to see it.

The Victrix finally made its way to the docks of Londinium's Southern bank. The lines were tied off and the men walked into the loving arms of their wives and families. Titus always enjoyed this sight. Anytime a man went to war, he knew he may not be coming back. Such a sight had a true and lasting meaning to those men. They left, fought, and lived to see their loved ones once more. He made his way down the loading ramp and passed through the group of people gathered by the ship.

"Where do you think you're off to?" a woman said behind him.

Titus smiled as he recognized the voice. "I'm going to find a woman for the night. Maybe two if I can afford it," he said as he turned.

The golden-haired woman in front of him smiled. "Well, in that case maybe you can find me a *real* man while you're out."

Titus walked toward the woman. "Marivonna..."

The two smiled at each other as they embraced, with Titus gently kissing her on the forehead. She looked toward the ship. "Where'd you take *that* from?"

Titus chuckled. "Stole it."

Marivonna turned toward Titus with a shocked look. "It's Roman! Surely you're not fighting against *Rome* now?"

Titus laughed and shook his head. "I took it from *a* Roman, at least I think he was, but he most definitely was not working *with* Rome."

His wife glanced back to the ship, then gestured for Titus to walk her home. The two made their way down a short street leading to their villa, all the while Titus explaining what had happened on the voyage.

"Bastakas," she whispered sadly.

Titus lowered his head. "I know."

They continued around the outside of the villa until they found themselves at the entrance. "Where are my children?" Titus inquired.

"Oana is inside; Gaius went into town to the temple," Marivonna responded.

Titus turned. "The Christian temple or the Mithraeum?"

Marivonna shrugged. "I don't know."

The Mithraeum was the underground temple dedicated to the Eastern god, Mithras. Though the Romans had left, many of their religious traditions lived on. The temple was built below a larger, grander building used as administrative buildings by the conglomerate of people who ran Londinium. The region around the city was dubbed Londein by the locals upon Rome's exit, and boasted of being the only region run by its citizens and not a monarchy. It was a practical arrangement due to the diversity of the people who lived there. You could find people from every province once belonging to Rome, a trait the residents of the city were quite proud of.

Titus made his way to the atrium of his home, accepting a cup of water from a smiling servant as she walked by. The servant was a beautiful girl of about twenty years, one who Titus' son Gaius had taken a liking to. Titus knew men forced themselves onto their slaves in other parts of the world, but made sure to raise his son better than that. The love they had for each other was sincere and genuine, meaning Titus knew to treat her as more than just a simple servant-girl.

She walked by him, giving a casual "Lord" before returning to her duties. Titus smiled back as he found a chair to rest in before he took off his armor and bathed, relishing his comfort and how good it felt to be home.

"You know she's pregnant," a woman said behind him.

Titus chuckled. "Was beginning to wonder if his prick even worked. They have surely tried enough." Titus turned and looked on the face of his wife, only about twenty years younger. His daughter was almost as beautiful as Marivonna had been when he first met her. "My ears are still ringing from when they first started their little relationship. Does he really believe we don't know about it?"

Oana laughed. "I was clearly born with all the knowledge of our parents. The least you could have done is leave some for him."

"Had to reserve more room to be a *fighter!*" Titus responded. He leaned forward to receive a kiss on the cheek from his daughter, then downed the contents left in his cup. "How long has she been with child?"

Oana paused in thought for a moment. "Well, she has been vomiting up everything she eats in the morning for about a month now."

Titus nodded. "So our little family will be getting a bit bigger. Fine by me. I always missed seeing you both as young ones, running around with the other children."

"Mother still does not know," Oana noted.

Titus laughed. "Well, she will!"

Oana smiled and bid her father farewell before leaving the atrium.

A grandchild?" Titus thought happily. *I never believed I would live long enough to see myself become a grandparent.* Titus slowly eased himself back into his chair. *What's one more mouth to feed?*

The birds had built nests in the tiles of his roof and flew over the atrium as they brought food to their young ones. The weather was calm and peaceful, allowing Titus to slowly doze off to the sounds of the birds and the voices of his men in their nearby homes. Life was good at that moment, but Titus knew there was always the chance for things to change.

It had been about two weeks since Titus and his men made their return to Londinium. The few pounds he had lost on the voyage had been quickly regained by the more consistent meals he had the luxury of when he was home. The men had been instructed to prepare for the move North to Petuaria, with some swayed by a more generous share of the wealth looted from Servius' estate. A few of the men decided they would rather stay, as they had procured enough money to live out the rest of their lives peacefully and had no more need for fighting.

Titus was jealous of these men. He wanted desperately to grow old with his wife, and knew every time he left, he ran the risk of ruining that desire. One problem he consistently ran into upon Bastakas' death was the idea of not having a man fit to lead such loyal men into battle. He felt as though he would be betraying them if he stepped down with no suitable replacement. Bastakas was the only real choice who could have taken over and was now buried in a cemetery on the North side of the river. The funeral turned out more people than Titus had expected. It seemed he was just as loved by others around the city as Titus was. It was something that made Titus sad, yet unspeakably proud.

It was dawn in the city. People were now waking and readying themselves for yet another day of trade, or for Titus and his men, the move North. In Drysten, Titus had found another man who seemed to have similar qualities of Bastakas. He believed cruelty should be punished, and honor should be rewarded and defended. The gold he had paid for Titus to bring his men North was only a bonus in Titus' eyes. If Drysten had asked him to move without payment, he would have still considered it.

Maybe the boy in the north would lead them, Titus thought quietly, *he certainly has most of the qualities, if little experience.*

At the moment, he was making his way to the homes designated for his men when they first took up residence in the city so long ago. There was a wagon train forming, as most of the men would journey North through Linnuis, then through Rheged, before they reached Ebrauc. Titus would be taking men without families aboard the Victrix to sail the vessel North, most likely reaching Drysten's town a few days before the rest of his people arrived. Upon gazing up and down the column of wagons, he turned and made his way to the dock a short distance north of his villa. The ship was currently being loaded by a few of his men under the leadership of his son, Gaius.

"Son," Titus called, "we must be off soon, try and hurry this up as best you can."

Gaius faced his father and nodded, then turned away to grumble something to a collection of men who were doing more watching than helping. Titus turned and walked back to his villa to make sure his wife and daughter were almost ready to depart. They would be sailing with Titus aboard the Victrix, and staying in the ship's cabin that had been constructed toward the stern of the ship's second level. It was small, but Titus hoped it would provide his wife, daughter, and two female servants enough privacy to feel comfortable.

He entered the villa he had recently sold to a wealthy Briton of the Catuvellauni tribe. The tribe had fared well under Roman occupation, engaging in trade and fighting under the Romans on various occasions. Still, they were not disappointed by Rome's exit as it created opportunities to fill voids that had been created by the Empire's abandonment. All in all, Titus was content in the knowledge the villa would be taken care of.

"Marivonna?" Titus called, finally receiving an answer from one of the side rooms.

"We're coming, love! Find someone to help us with two more chests, would you? They are the last ones we will be taking," his wife shouted back.

Titus turned and waved two male kitchen servants over, signaling for them to go and help his wife. The two disappeared into the room and eventually emerged with a big chest in each of their grasps.

"Take it to the ship if you would be so kind." The servants each nodded and disappeared out the front gate. Marivonna and Oana appeared, each carrying two bags in their arms.

"Traveling lightly, my dears?" Titus quipped, receiving a scoff from his wife and a smile from his daughter.

"All of my things are already aboard the ship. All of this belongs to your wife," Oana explained as she passed by.

Titus laughed, gazed around the villa one last time to make sure nothing had been forgotten, then made his way out of his home for the last time. He followed his wife and daughter in the direction of the ship, hearing voices off in the distance. The trio kept walking, before a man swiftly came racing down the street, rushing toward him from the Northern side of the river.

Titus had witnessed similar displays while living in the city and was about to make a quick joke until Oana suddenly gasped and turned to look behind them. "Father?" she said in a nervous tone.

Titus stopped and listened. At first, he heard nothing but the usual sounds of a populated city, but soon, those familiar echoes turned to screams of panic. "Run! Get to the ship!" Titus yelled to his wife and daughter. "Tell them to be ready to cast off." Titus turned and drew his sword at his hip and ran back one street over to the baggage train.

"Sir! Men are coming from the hills!" one man yelled as Titus arrived.

He turned and looked in the direction of the shouting. "Get your families to the Victrix! Leave everything!"

The sound of men drew closer, now accompanied by panicked screams and people running to reach the north side of the river. Titus and his men escorted the families as they ran toward the docks, many tripping over each other in panic. Titus stopped to help a woman up who had fallen, then ushered her and the others forward. "To the ship!" he yelled.

The group finally reached the dock to find others had come seeking refuge from the attackers. Titus knew he had a difficult choice to make. He could allow the newcomers, people he had seen around his home for years, onto the ship. Or he could push them away in favor of his men and their families.

Morrigan's tits, this is bad, he thought to himself.

"Sir, they're coming!" a man screamed from behind Titus.

He turned and saw a small horde of men rushing them from the other end of the street. "Shield wall!" he screamed, though he really had no need. His men had been trained well and had begun forming a defense before he even gave the order.

His men stood between the families and their attackers, a wall three men deep from one side of the street to the other. Titus knew he had about two hundred men with him and had no room aboard the ship for both them and their families. His only choice now would be to fight.

His men had the traditional Roman pila with them as well as a shield and short sword, so Titus knew there was at least a chance at repelling the invaders if there weren't many more than he presently saw.

"Pila at the ready!" Titus yelled, prompting his men to ready their weapons. The pila were six-foot spears used by Roman armies for centuries to deter a frontal assault or break a shield wall. The metal tip at the top would get stuck into an enemy shield and make it almost impossible to use. Titus knew his men had about two per man, as was the custom for Roman soldiers.

The enemy was now about a hundred feet away when Titus gave the order. "Pila!" he yelled.

A handful of them fell short but most hit their mark. Men were now trying to pry them out of their shields or tripping over someone who received a pilum in the chest or stomach. Men were now rolling around on the ground in agony as the blood began to pool beneath them. The enemy halted and created a shield wall between their wounded and Titus' men, with more still coming to join them from the streets nearby. Titus' men were now up against about two hundred men just in that single area by the docks, and more screaming could be heard from the North side of the river as smoke began to plume up around the city.

The enemy had been temporarily halted by the first volley of spears thrown by Titus' men, yet slowly began to start forward once more. "Pila!" Titus yelled, prompting the second and final volley to be thrown. Again they stuck into shields and flesh, causing men to drop or stumble. "Forward!" Titus commanded. His men slowly marched to meet their enemy, now about sixty feet away.

The two sides finally met with a clash of wood and metal banging into each other. Screams could be heard from both lines as men were being pushed by the people behind them into the walls in front of them. Titus glanced behind him to see his family safely aboard the ship, as well as most of the others who had been waiting to board. The families belonging to his men were the last ones to reach the ship, yet they too were now making their way over the loading ramp. He looked back to see the enemy line pushing his back toward the Victrix.

"Shit," he muttered to himself. "Halt them here!" he yelled to his men.

The dirt road underneath them was now slick with blood. Titus had lost about forty men when the enemy finally drew itself back to regroup.

"Halt! Do not follow them. Reform the line!" Titus yelled from the rear. His prowess was as a commander, not as a fighter. He knew at his age he would be more of a detriment to his men if he chose to lead from the front.

"Father!" Gaius called from the ship. "Father, we're ready to leave!"

Titus looked back at the ship that was filled with their

families. He knew he would not be able to fit the rest of his people aboard. He calmly shook his head and gestured for the ship to leave.

The die is cast, Titus thought. He knew the words of Rome's first emperor fit perfectly for his current situation. *Not even a Caesar could find a way out of this.*

Titus could hear his family screaming for him to join them, wrenching at his heart. He wanted to be there with them with every fiber of his being, but knew to do that would mean abandoning his men to their fate at the hands of the barbarians. He calmly looked back to his men lined up ahead of him, waiting for the second advance of the enemy.

"Sir," One man said as he stepped away from the third rank of the shield wall.

"What is it, Citrio?" Titus asked him in a sullen tone.

The man stepped closer. "Sir, there's room enough for a few. Go be with your family and the wounded."

"I will die with my men." Tears began to well under Titus' eyes. In one short moment, he remembered raising his children, marrying his wife, fighting in the front lines as a young man, and watching Rome abandon his home. Everything he had lived through passed in front of him.

Citrio solemnly nodded and hurried back to line up with the others. Titus took one more look back at the Victrix, which was idle in anticipation of the warriors joining them. He drew his sword and picked up a shield discarded by a fallen man, then made his way into the front rank with the men. "Boys, today will be the last day I have the privilege of leading you. Should you seek to leave, I will not stop you. The ship can hold but a few more souls." Two men turned to look behind them, then turned back satisfied that their families would be safe.

"This *Drysten* will take them in?" a voice said from behind him.

Titus turned around to try and place the voice to a face, but failed. He just nodded and faced the enemy, now making its way toward him in a reformed wall of shields and metal. More had come from the outskirts of the town to reinforce their numbers. "Make them scream, boys. Make them earn it," he said to the man next to him.

With a shout, the enemy charged forward and banged into Titus and his men in the front. The force jarred the line and pushed Titus back a pace into the man behind him. He quickly found his footing and pushed forward, matching the strength of the man across from him. The smells of battle were all too familiar to him. The stale breath of the panting men around him, the blood caked to the ground, and the sweat of men pushing with all their might created a smell Titus had never found in any other moment.

After a few moments of struggling to push forward, a burst of pain erupted from the bottom of his left leg up toward his calf. A man had reached down and sliced into him, ignoring the shield altogether. This was done by the long knife Saxons typically used in battle for just such a purpose. Titus let out a shriek of pain and his position in the line began to wane. The man behind him sensed what had happened and pulled him out of the way to take his place, but was too late. The breach in the line had already been exploited by a group of men swinging wildly to drive a wedge down the center of Titus' shield wall.

"No!" Titus screamed as hands pulled him away from the front rank of the wall. The men in the back finally were able to pull him away, and the two began to drag him toward the boat. "Go back," he begged. He could not bear the idea of his men dying without him. "I can't abandon them."

"Sorry, sir. Take care of our people," the man said. Titus looked on the face of the man who had dragged him to the ramp leading to the boat and could only manage a nod of his head as a response.

His savior turned and grabbed Citrio by the collar and shoved him toward Titus. "Get him to the ship! Come back for any wounded you can get to."

Citrio nodded and took Titus' weight onto his arm.

Titus felt like a small boy being commanded to do something by his father. Two men calmly nodded to him, then turned back to face the enemy who had broken their shield wall.

As the Victrix began to sail downriver, Titus watched in horror as his men were slowly overwhelmed and slaughtered at the hands of the Saxons. Women and children were crying all around him as they too watched the fates of their loved ones unfold.

All Titus could do was watch the massacre happen as the Victrix sailed away.

CHAPTER XIV

Drysten stood in front of Titus, utterly stunned by the prospect of a mass invasion from the mainland. If Londinium had been taken by the Saxons, then Eboracum could very well be next. Should an attack come to the North, it would go right through Petuaria.

"And where did you find your pursuers?" Drysten asked Titus, who was now being supported by his son.

"When we left the docks and sailed East, we found their ships. They left a few guards with their families, but by my count, they could have as many as a thousand warriors if we go by the number of ships we saw. These two bastards followed us from the city the last couple of days. We thought we'd lost them numerous times, but they always showed up ahead of us or right on us," Titus responded with his head hung low, a sight Drysten never thought possible. He had only seen him in his usual optimistic form, perpetually wearing a smile.

"There's another thing," Titus said as he lifted his head, "Jorrit was with them." Diocles, who had been listening to the explanation as the bodies were being either looted or prepared for burial cursed under his breath.

Drysten turned to the Greek. "If he's with them, then he knows where to find *us*." After turning back to Titus, he asked. "Where did you see him?"

Titus wiped some sweat from his brow. "He was standing on a ship near where they docked as we were leaving. He even waved to me, the bastard. I let him go free and this is what he does."

Drysten put a hand on Titus' shoulder, then beckoned for a pair of his men to help the newcomers into the villa. Petras and Paulus had just jumped down from the roof and were reclaiming the arrows they had shot. Many had been damaged, but most of the arrowheads themselves could be reused. One man was still alive as Paulus pulled an arrow free from his chest, causing a cry of pain until Petras drove a blade down into his neck. The sight startled some of the women and children, as most had been disembarking the Victrix. Some of them were sobbing and crying as they did so.

"Make them suffer!" a woman yelled.

Titus turned to glance behind him as if he wished to say something, but instead chose to hang his head once more while he peered at the walls of Drysten's home.

"He'll need a while," Drysten whispered to Diocles.

Diocles cocked his head to the side. "His wound is not fatal. He will surely—"

"I mean he'll need time to himself. He just lost everyone he cared for, save his family. He probably thinks he failed his men," Drysten replied quietly.

Diocles sighed. "From the sound of it, he did what he could. The only victory to be had from that is to save who you can and fuck off to somewhere safer." Diocles moved over to Titus and gently placed a hand on the man's shoulder.

"I agree." Drysten ran his hand over his head as he turned to watch the families of Titus' fallen walk through the market, unsure of what to do next. "We need to find shelter for them."

"The villa is the only real choice. The walls should keep them feeling safe while we're away." Diocles turned and looked over the Victrix, now vacant and tied to the pier, with blood soaking into the wooden deck. "That is, if we still *should* go away."

Titus trained his attention back to Drysten, making

him feel slightly uncomfortable when meeting his frantic gaze. "I beg you, Drysten, do *not* abandon what is left of my people. I will do anything—"

"I do not intend to abandon *anyone*," Drysten sullenly replied. To see such a proud man begging for anything nearly made Drysten sick.

Titus' eyes slowly began to well. "All the gold you paid me is *still* aboard my—"

"That's enough, Titus! I promise you; I will not abandon *anyone*. My father taught me better than that," Drysten interrupted as he glanced to Diocles, clearly as surprised to see the state of Titus as Drysten was.

Drysten began to pace. "We cannot leave our people undefended. If we leave, there's little chance of them surviving an attack. The Saxons could be coming for us as we speak. We can only guess what Jorrit would tell them."

"It's possible they are not far behind this first group," Diocles said wearily.

Titus glanced toward the water. "We only saw the two ships behind us, but word certainly travels fast when a port is left unprotected. Not to mention many saw us depart, and the Frisian knows where we went."

The men stopped speaking as they noticed Dagonet coming to join them. He was glancing at the bodies nearby and dabbing his forehead to check if a cut he had received was still bleeding. "Lord, we don't have enough food to feed them all for very long. Not unless we're taking some North with us."

Drysten stood, staring out toward the sea as he pondered his next move. This new Saxon army to their South could very quickly make its way North and sack every city along the way. He understood the newcomers needed to be defended, but he also knew he had an obligation, even a need to help his father. If he left, he knew the people would be forced to fend for themselves in any sort of attack. If he stayed, he had no idea if he would be dooming his father to be burned alive as the Roman prisoners centuries ago had been.

"What we need... is more friends," Drysten declared through a tired voice. Dagonet looked at Diocles, who glanced back and shrugged. "We need more men, more horses. We need another ally now that the one we thought we had is no longer... at full strength." Drysten hated saying the last statement in front of Titus but knew it was a harsh reality. Titus' value came from the fact he could field a formidable force. Without one, he could only be used as a commander, and not even that until he was healed enough to travel.

Drysten looked over his newest friend as he visibly favored his wounded leg. The man was a proven commander and realistic in matters of war, so it made sense the comment had no effect on him. He simply nodded and stared into the ground before slowly raising his head with a half-hearted smirk. "What kingdom lies to our North?"

"Bryneich," Dagonet tilted his head to the side as he answered.

"What do you know of Bryneich?" Drysten asked.

Dagonet scoffed. "They're supposed to be our Northern allies, but they mostly choose to keep to themselves. Your father briefly considered calling on them for aid, but decided the chances of them helping us were too slim."

"Bring three horses from Conway. We ride to Ebrauc," Drysten commanded before turning to Titus. "You have been through enough. Go inside and be with your people."

"What could the fucking *king* help us with that he hasn't already fucked us with?" Diocles asked.

Drysten shrugged. "We need a way to convince the lord at Bryneich to help. With a territory so vast we must have something they would want."

At the moment, Drysten had no idea what he would offer to the ruler of Bryneich in return for aid, but he was hoping he would have something by the time he arrived in

Eboracum.

King Ceneus reclined into the fresh water of the Roman bathhouse when the bishop entered, quickly sullying the relaxing mood of the environment. The king rolled his eyes and sat up straighter as the man wiped the sleep from his eyes and walked closer.

"The boy was spotted on the road," Bishop Germanus began, "along with and a small party of riders. They were spotted by my scouts not long ago."

King Ceneus shrugged. "A lord wishes to speak to his king. What of it?"

"This lord assaulted one of *your* guards. Do not forget that."

"The boy was not in a right state of mind, and do not forget the man he assaulted was my *son's*," King Ceneus indifferently replied.

"I was under the impression you believe all under your rule to be your people. Was that not the reason you desired me to cease the incarceration of the apostates?" Bishop Germanus returned with a smirk.

"I do not consider criminals under my son's employ to be worth the time it would take to punish a man for their maltreatment," the king angrily responded.

Bishop Germanus grumbled under his breath as Maewyn sauntered in through the main entrance of the bathhouse. The sleepy-eyed priest nodded to the king before bringing some sort of message to the bishop. Germanus glanced down and peeled the wax from the brown parchment before sleepily reading the message.

"It would seem Prince Eidion has grown to dislike the new lord of your court, Lord King," Germanus explained with a smirk. "Perhaps now you will consider removing the man upon his... Oh, this news could prove to be *most* troubling."

King Ceneus perked his head up upon hearing the frustration in the bishop's voice. *Any inconvenience to this bastard could be good for me,* he cheerfully thought.

Bishop Germanus turned. "It would seem Lord Hall has befriended the prince of Powys."

"I would hardly say improving the ties between my allies is an inconvenience, Your Excellency," King Ceneus replied with a boisterous laugh.

"Then you are a simple-minded *fool,* Keneu!" the bishop roared while he referred to the king with his birth name. "The people of Powys stress the misguided values of religious *tolerance* as the old Romans had. Look what that got them!"

"It got them an empire, and if memory serves, it was misguided generals and squabbling priests who brought about the discord which now plagues them," King Ceneus responded.

Bishop Germanus' face contorted in disgust. "Our Lord and Savior is the *only* path to salvation. We cannot allow their beliefs to muddy the waters of our own."

Maewyn stepped forward. "I was always shown it best to approach nonbelievers with kindness, and openness. We are to show them a better way, not force them to convert under penalty of incarceration or death."

"Maewyn...," Bishop Germanus said softly, "you are so naive in your early years of priesthood. We must indeed show them kindness, but when we are shown none in return certain strategies must be adjusted."

A guard adorned in a royal blue cloak marched in through the entrance as Maewyn began to speak. "Lord King," the guard greeted with a bow, "Lord Hall's son has entered the city. Found trouble by the looks of it."

The king nodded. "Thank you. That will be all."

The guard nodded as he gave an uneasy glance toward guards in the service of the bishop, each man adorned in polished lorica segmentata resting under black cloaks of a fine material. He grimaced before departing, leaving King Ceneus and the two priests by themselves once more.

"It would be best to sever ties with them while they are weakest," Bishop Germanus began.

The king shook his head. "I have no intentions of doing so."

"How are we to make a refuge for the followers of Christ should you open your doors to the common rabble of the apostates?" Bishop Germanus roared.

King Ceneus erupted from the baths and stepped toward a startled bishop. "Half of his men wear a fucking crucifix around their necks, you *miserable* fool!"

"I... you would do well to remember who is truly in charge here—" the bishop stammered.

King Ceneus raised his hand as if he would strike the bishop, ceasing the bishop's thought mid-sentence. "It is the *fucking* king! *That* is who." He turned his attention to Maewyn, startled by the exchange and attempting to slowly hover away toward the door. "Leave!" he commanded.

"And order my guards to cease them at the door! They are not to enter here!" Bishop Germanus added.

A ghost faced Maewyn quickly nodded and shuffled his way out of the room. The bishop relaxed his shoulders and signaled for his guards near the door to move back, leading the king to believe the fear was feigned in the attempt to look vulnerable in front of his protege.

"You do so much as blink before I am done speaking and I will have you torn to pieces in your own dungeons. I have people in every major city in these miserable islands. If you go against my will, I will not only pull my support for your reign and install your son, I will instruct those men to slowly choke the life from your kingdom. You are an insect under a boot. It is important you understand that all I have to do to end you is press down on your miserable throat."

The king wanted nothing more than to shove the bishop's head as far underwater as he could. Sadly, his guards understood this as well and began slowly shifting toward them. Both stopped as they turned toward the doorway, hearing voices which caught Ceneus' ears as well.

King Ceneus glanced back to the bishop. "They are coming. Slink your way back into the darkness where you belong. A king must speak with his people."

Drysten made his way through Ebrauc with Dagonet and Diocles trailing behind him. He made a point to show the golden sun amulet around his neck to prevent anyone from stopping him. That amulet and the bearskin cloak he donned made him look as much like a local lord as he could manage. A handful of the guards even bowed their heads upon his passing, causing Diocles to scoff in amusement.

The city was in a strange stage of its life. Most of the people who dwelled there lived along the main road running from the Southwestern gate, and over the river to the old legionary fortress across the water. It made sense, considering the most structurally sound homes were along that very road, although there was still an eerie feeling emanating from the score of abandoned homes deeper in the city. The old market square was largely abandoned in favor of stalls set up along the main road, meaning there was just a big empty space with stores going unused. Drysten and his two companions could catch a glimpse of these areas as they gazed down alleyways and empty streets. The ominous clouds cast shadows that created a strange feeling for them as they ventured through the city, looking on the depressing sights of the run-down buildings.

"It's certainly different than I remember," Drysten announced to the group.

Diocles looked around them. "Was it always so dreary?"

Drysten shook his head. "Last time I was here, there was a market with people walking in every direction. It still wasn't as busy as it was in it's prime, but there was certainly more life to it than there is now."

"The king hasn't exactly been inviting to the locals living outside the walls," Dagonet mentioned.

Drysten cocked his head to the side. "How do you mean?"

"He views any local as a threat to his reign and Christianity. Bishop Germanus has taken hold of him and made him fear the ones who worship the old ways. When the Romans left, their people were then thrust into the minority. Most people living outside his walls still worship the old gods of their ancestors," Dagonet explained.

Drysten sighed. "I have never understood the divisions religion can cause."

The three men crossed the river and began to make their way to the old legion fortress in the Northwest part of the city to meet the king. Drysten was surprised at how abandoned the Southern bank had looked as he passed through. It almost seemed like the only people on that side of the river were people squatting in abandoned homes, or the guards along the road. Nevertheless, the men pressed on, winding their way through the streets.

"Hardly much of a city, really," Diocles mentioned, "not even any whores nearby."

Drysten chuckled. "You do more thinking with what's between your legs than anyone I've ever met."

They eventually found their way to the front of the fortress, where two guards with black cloaks stopped them. "What do you want?" the first asked before noticing the gold around Drysten's neck. He caught a glimpse of it as Drysten turned to speak. "My apologies, Lord, the king is inside the old bathhouse."

Drysten nodded and rode further toward the stone walls on the Southeastern side of the old fortress. They dismounted and gazed upon the combination of old Roman stonework mixed with a new, shoddy repair made more recently.

Drysten gazed upon the strange mix of different stone. "Did something happen to the bathhouse?"

Dagonet shook his head. "He remade the old bathhouse into a private residence. He favored its comfort over that of the Principia."

The Principia was the old administration building used by the Roman legion. It held the rooms of the higher-ranking officers and city administrators in charge of governing the Northernmost province of Britannia. As well as the offices, it contained shrines dedicated to the various gods and goddesses worshipped by the troops stationed in the city.

Drysten dismounted and walked toward the entrance of the comfortable looking residence. Again, there were two guards in black cloaks stationed on either side of the doorway. "Can I help you, Lord?" one politely asked.

Drysten did his best to hold his head high enough to convince the man he held some sort of authority over him. "I need to speak with King Ceneus."

The guard glanced to his companion, who shrugged before returning his gaze to Drysten's company. The guard awkwardly cleared his throat as Drysten did his utmost to not break eye contact. "I apologize, Lord, but the king does not wish for visitors at the present."

"The king does not wish for visitors? I did not wish for malnourished horses or a Saxon raid on my people. Now *move*." Drysten sternly replied.

The guard stiffened as he again glanced to his friend, who was trying to subtly signal for more guards to wander over. "I... Lord, I have been given orders for—"

"Damn your orders," Drysten began, "my people need safety, and I need an audience with Ceneus to—"

"Lord Drysten?" a voice called from the dim interior of the baths. "What has happened?" Maewyn questioned as he neared the guard.

Drysten briefly glanced to the priest before returning his gaze to the eyes of the nearest guard. "My people were attacked, and this guard seems to believe the matter not important enough to notify the king."

"Lord, no—," the guard began until hushed by Maewyn gently resting a hand on his shoulder.

"Follow me, Lord," the priest calmly beckoned.

Drysten walked forward as Maewyn led the small group into the baths. Drysten was trailed by Diocles and Dagonet, and all walked into a large room with a steaming pool of water as Maewyn turned and nodded to them all before departing. In the very center of the pool sat King Ceneus, sitting alone with a servant nearby awaiting his beck and call.

"Drysten!" the king said in surprise. "To what do I owe the pleasure of this visit? And why are you all bloody?"

"We were attacked, Lord King," Drysten responded. He did not know why, but referring to the king by his title made him feel slightly disappointed.

The king stood, accidentally exposing his nether regions to the frigid air, prompting a quiet chuckle from Diocles. "By whom?" he answered.

Drysten took a step forward, eyeing the inviting water. "Saxons attacked Londinium. They killed many of the people coming to join me at Petuaria."

The king took a step forward, ignoring the fact he was on full display to the guests. "How many men did you lose?"

"Not many of mine, but all except a few of the men coming to join me," Drysten responded.

The king cursed under his breath. "Do you still have the men needed to march to your father?"

Drysten turned and slowly paced as he considered his next words. "In some capacity, I suppose that I do. Though I don't like the idea of leaving refugees and my home unprotected in case the new Saxon invaders come North."

King Ceneus pointed to Drysten. "Segedunum is the priority. You must reclaim it from the Picts. That fortress is more valuable than you realize."

Drysten turned. "Than I realize? What is it that's so important about this fortress so far North? I've learned there is one a short distance across the river called Arbeia.

Surely keeping that one garrisoned for the time being would dissuade any Northern invaders." Drysten then turned to Dagonet, who had an equally perplexed look on his face.

The king lowered his finger. "It is not the *fortress,* per se, but what it holds inside which interests me."

Drysten further pressed the king, which obviously annoyed him. "And what else is there?"

"We found word of an old Roman stockpile under the fortress. It looked as though it was hidden with the intention of someone coming back to claim it," the king began. "The more interesting fact is there are silver ingots as well as iron most likely intended to make weapons. We were in the process of bringing it South when they were attacked. The supply train had not even entered the gates when the Picts took the fortress."

Drysten scoffed. "You're telling me you sent men to die for the hope you could recover some old Roman stockpile?"

"Drysten!" Dagonet whispered in the hopes of calming his friend.

The king's eyes narrowed. "Watch your tone with me, boy. I have been very kind to you thus far."

Drysten matched Ceneus' gaze. "My men will stay to defend their families and the refugees we just took in."

"I caution you not to go against my wishes, boy," the king hissed.

Drysten took a step forward as two guards entered the room upon hearing the change in the king's tone. "I will not be going against your wishes." Drysten then walked toward the door, before turning and giving Ceneus a sarcastic *"Lord King."*

Drysten stormed out of the bathhouse with his two companions in tow. "Greedy bastard," he whispered as he walked between the two guards stationed by the doorway.

"What do we intend to do?" Dagonet inquired.

Drysten turned. "The official order he gave his men was to recover the fortress."

Dagonet and Diocles glanced at each other. "So we intend to help them do it regardless of his true intentions?" Diocles asked through a disappointed voice.

Drysten turned and mounted his horse. "We go to help my father, nothing more. To do so, we will need to go to Bryneich and secure reinforcements from their lord."

"You know, they have not been much use thus far," Dagonet warned.

"They will be," Drysten said before clicking his tongue to his mount, ushering it forth. "The king gave me what I needed."

Again, Diocles and Dagonet glanced to each other. "What would that be exactly?"

Drysten turned and smiled. "I'm going to offer their lord a portion of the stockpile he spoke of."

"I'm not sure King Ceneus would agree to that," Dagonet cautioned.

"One problem at a time," Drysten commented, "I could not care less of the wealth, I intend to save my father. We'll go back to Petuaria and use one of the Saxon boats to make our way to Din Guayrdi." Drysten then urged his horse forward and began to make his way South.

CHAPTER XV

It had been two tiresome days since Hall ordered his men to break camp. He immediately recognized the kind of response he would get for the actions of the boy-prince, and knew he had to get his men as far away from neighboring villages as he possibly could.

Since then, Gawain had scouted out the surrounding forest to the West, and found a sizeable force moving toward them at a rapid pace. The sacking of a presumedly peaceful village seemed to be enough for a handful of tribes to send their warriors out in a joint effort to remove what they saw as an invasion. A frustrated Hall reflected on the passing of events from the last few days and wished more than anything he had listened to Aosten's warning of the prince. If he had, he could have prevented Eidion's raid altogether. Now however, there were only six survivors of the village, all of which were set free on Hall's order.

"If that prick of a prince hadn't killed them all, we may not have a thousand fucking men hounding us," Bors mentioned. "I doubt they would see us as such a threat if we acted more like looters than *murderers*."

Hall nodded. "Eidion's actions probably unified multiple tribes, something that isn't easy to do in these parts. They're normally too busy fighting each other to worry about us."

"What's our plan?" Prince Ambrosius inquired.

The three men were riding in the front of the march as they moved their way further North. The enemy had been seen moving in such a way to make Hall believe they were trying to cut off their escape to the South, meaning they were after blood, not just their removal.

Hall rubbed the scruff of his slightly longer beard. "Dere Street runs North toward the Antonine Wall. If we really need to find a place to defend ourselves, then I believe that may be our best bet. We should be able to reach it undetected if we stick to the valleys and march through the night."

"And if we *don't* reach it before someone catches us?" the prince from Powys asked.

Hall shrugged. "Then we try and find a hill fort. The old people made them all across Britannia."

Bors leaned forward on his horse. "We could ask any locals we come across."

Hall shook his head. "We need to keep ourselves away from any villages. Especially considering what the good prince decided to do to the last one."

The three men glanced behind them toward Eidion, who was riding his own horse in the middle of the marching column with a handful of his followers. Most were the sons of wealthy Brigantes, the favored tribe of King Ceneus. The Parisii were also present in the army, but in much lower numbers. The Brigantes had a long history of warfare, whether it be against Rome or neighboring tribes. As a result, they were more adept in a fight and more useful to a king who liked to believe he was capable at playing war. The prince was currently laughing about one thing or another with his entourage and drinking the last of the army's wine. He noticed the three men glance back toward him and raised the skin of wine with a wink.

Hall turned back around. "I hate him," he said quietly, prompting a chuckle from both Bors and Ambrosius.

They continued North toward the border between Bryneich and the new kingdom, just over its Northwestern border. Hall had no knowledge of this place, aside from it recently having won a civil war. It had apparently separated itself from the kingdom of Strathclyde, which briefly held the majority of the lands north of Hadrian's Wall. To reach the Antonine Wall, Hall would have to lead his men through valleys and bogs in the center of their territory. This would prove difficult if he hoped to stay away from any onlookers.

"Where are we exactly?" Bors said as he looked around through the trees.

Hall thought for a moment. "I'm fairly certain we're somewhere directly East of Din Guayrdi."

Bors scoffed. "Don't suppose the prince's uncle would give us shelter for a night."

"From my understanding, he has little love for his brother to the South," Hall answered while shaking his head. "Our best bet is making a journey North in the hopes of losing our pursuers, then swooping down behind them back to the wall."

"Might be best to leave the wagons behind soon," Ambrosius suggested.

Hall nodded. "We'll keep them for one more night. Once we find a suitable place to camp, we can take what we need from them and march through the forests."

The men continued North until the sun began to recede behind the western tree line. They were in a forest as the light started to fade, convincing Hall it was as good a place as any to make camp. The men were ordered not to light fires in the hopes of remaining undetected by the locals. As the tents were being constructed and men were claiming their patch of land for the night, Hall witnessed the stark contrast between the two nobles he had in his company. Ambrosius was walking through groups of men that didn't even serve him, asking whether he could aid in the tent construction or if they needed anything he could provide.

Hall then turned and witnessed Eidion mocking a small group of men in their evening prayers to the local gods that were worshipped by the Britons. He jeered and mocked them relentlessly, all the while he was sitting with his back up against a stone with the ancient carving of one such god at its highest point. As the days went on, there seemed to be enough reasons mounting to justify leaving the boy to his own devices, but Hall knew he was too honorable of a man to entertain the idea.

"Have everything you need, Lord?" a familiar voice rang out, interrupting Hall's thoughts.

Hall turned to the Powysian. "I'm fine, Lord Prince. I was just trying to find a solution for the dilemma we find ourselves in."

Ambrosius chuckled and walked toward Hall. "If I were not so forgiving, I would have killed him by now."

Hall was taken aback by the comment. "Kill him?"

"Indeed. Not because I desire to, plainly because he has repeatedly shown himself a liability. The sole reason we're being tracked around unfamiliar territory is because he elected to raze a village. What *he* did made us look like a full-scale invasion." Hall nodded as the words sunk in. "Furthermore, his presence is like a dark cloud over our men. I would never follow a lord like him into war under *any* circumstances."

"Everything you stated is true, but I cannot allow you to kill him. As much as I do think it would help," Hall replied as he ran his hand over his head.

"I know," the Prince replied with a sigh.

The two men stood in front of Hall's tent, as the nearby men rummaged through their bags for food or small idols dedicated to their gods. Many men in the army were Christian, but most still maintained their beliefs in the gods of their forefathers. Hall could never understand the local customs of the Britons. To him, they seemed to worship the same god differently, all depending on where they were born. The gods themselves never changed and mostly had the same name, but people in different tribes sometimes showed their devotion differently.

"Are you Christian?" Hall asked the Prince. It was a good question considering the man's lineage. He was the son of a Roman of the same name, who had been an aristocrat living under Roman rule in Britannia. Their family had been well respected and admired by both Romans and Britons, making it very easy for them to fill the void left behind by Rome. Though Ambrosius' father was not the king, his uncle was the one who ruled over Powys.

The Prince shrugged. "I was baptized."

"But are you a Christian? It makes no difference to me, I was simply curious," Hall responded.

The Prince thought for a moment. "I am what my people need me to be."

Hall smiled. "You'll make a good king someday, boy," then patted him on the back.

The Prince smiled. "I doubt I will ever be King. My uncle is only ten years older than I, and he has his own son already."

"That's a shame," Hall said as he shook his head. "You'll have to lead in some way. It would be a waste of nobility if you chose not to."

Hall saw the prince smile proudly as he turned his attention back to their army. It was at that moment that Hall understood he'd found a man worth following.

"Run!" Hall screamed to his men. They had camped in a rather dense forest the night before, but despite his strict orders not to light any fires it seemed there was one just bright enough to attract the attention of their pursuers. "Leave everything! Take only what you can run with!" he yelled across the camp. Gawain was scouting to their West when he came under attack by Pict scouts on horseback. He managed to kill one before seeing a dozen others converging on him and hastened his way back to camp. The camp was in utter chaos. Men were trying to stuff their packs with what food and water they could carry before they would be forced to march either East or further North.

Ambrosius ran from his tent, still strapping on his black leather jerkin. "Where are they?" he asked in a nervous voice.

Hall gestured West as he was attempting to finish strapping his lorica segmentata armor over his shoulders, which was made easier by the prince's help. "We have no choice. We will have to fight them soon, *very* soon."

"But where?" Ambrosius inquired.

Hall moved his arms and turned his torso from side to side to make sure the armor was applied well enough to run, but not so loose that it would sway from side to side with each step. "I know of an ancient hillfort far to our North. Dere Street runs close to it, so we should be able to use the road for a while longer, then eventually cut over. What worries me is the location of a town a couple miles further."

"We have about twenty horses. Let me ride out ahead and make sure it's secure before we commit to anything," the prince requested.

Hall considered the prince's offer. On the one hand, it could alert any locals to their presence before they would be able to set up a defense of the hilltop. On the other hand, if he marched there as it was, they would be blind to anyone who may occupy it themselves. "Stay a safe distance away from the town. The hill will not be hard to miss, as there are three connecting to one another, forming a ridge. It was once a great village of some importance during the old days."

Prince Ambrosius glanced at Bors before turning back to Hall, nodded, and departed to rally his men for their ride North. Hall followed him outside to find how long it would take before they would be ready to march.

Gawain saw him emerge from his tent and marched over. "Lord, they have about five hundred men. If we leave now, we can find more concealment to the East, but it won't be hard for them to track us."

"We cannot run from them forever," Hall replied as he watched Bors move off to help facilitate the army's movements.

A nervous Gawain began itching the back of his neck as he glanced around. "They have twice our number, Lord. Running seems to be our only option."

Hall slowly shook his head. "We're marching to a hillfort to the North. Once we reach its summit, we can set up defenses. Hopefully, we can stall them long enough for allow reinforcements to arrive."

"Your son will make it in time?" the scout asked nervously.

Hall nodded. "My boy has enough seasoned men to make this more than an even fight." Hall then turned to the large group of men massing around him. "Leave the tents and wagons. We go North!"

He mounted his horse and started toward the front of the marching column Bors was still in the process of assembling. After a moment of frustration, he gave up and just pointed North and for the men to follow. As usual, Prince Eidion was riding with his men toward the rear.

"Shouldn't take us very long to get there," Hall mentioned.

"Are you sure this is the best course?" Bors asked.

Hall turned to look behind him. "These men cannot win against the numbers chasing us . Not to mention the men chasing us are fucking *killers.* Our only hope is to find the fort near Trimontium."

Bors hung his head. "You know that fort has been destroyed for longer than we've been alive, don't you?"

Hall shook his head. "Trimontium was built near an ancient hillfort just to its South. It once held a signal station on the highest peak. That's where I intend to fight them."

Bors shook his head. "Gods...," then turned to yell for the army to hurry.

Hall began his ride North, silently begging whatever gods were watching to allow him and his army safe passage.

CHAPTER XVI

Drysten returned to Petuaria with his two companions at dusk, riding in on the Roman road known as Ermine Street. It was the main road joining Petuaria to Eboracum and Drysten guessed it must have carried merchants from the port to the city in droves in its prime. It ran all the way North from Londinium, which gave Drysten the idea it could be used by the Saxon invaders should they choose to attack by land. He recognized it as a possibility, although he thought the chances of that would be slim when considering the ships they brought.

On Drysten's orders, the refugees who journeyed with Titus had taken up refuge in the villa. They were also given enough food to tide them over before more could be bought or harvested at the end of the season. Drysten knew it would be a stretch to say they had enough for everyone.

"Lord!" Matthew called as Drysten entered the villa's front gate, "the people here are unharmed, but I fear we run the risk of sickness if we keep so many in one place."

Drysten nodded as he entered the villa to find Titus, who was sitting by Cynwrig's bedside, detailing the situation in Londinium. "What's this then? Aren't you dead yet?" he joked at Cynwrig.

"Feels like it, Lord," the wounded man replied. It seemed an infection had set in in recent days.

Drysten was somewhat taken aback by his friend calling him lord. He awkwardly smiled before looking to Titus. "A word when you have a moment."

Titus nodded before quickly finishing up the discussion with Cynwrig and followed Drysten to the greeting area of the villa, the only place away from all the eyes and ears of its residents.

"I don't know how to help," the general started. "Drysten, I have no men. I have no way to help you other than giving you the coin you paid me with."

Drysten put a hand on Titus' shoulder. "What I need from you is not men. Not directly."

Titus raised an eyebrow. "Not *directly?*"

Drysten nodded. "The people I came to these lands with were trained by Bors and my father. They were trained well, and I would have no trepidations going into a war with them. What worries me is the group the king sent us. They are unseasoned at best. I need you to turn them into soldiers I would feel comfortable with leaving our people under the guard of."

"I will train them. That's certainly something I know to do well enough," Titus answered without hesitation.

Drysten thanked Titus and walked back through the entryway to find Isolde. She was helping the servants distribute the food and water throughout the overflowing villa. Drysten walked up to her and put his hands on either side of her as she was speaking with a woman from Londinium. "Drysten!" she said in surprise. "I didn't know you returned."

Drysten kissed her on the forehead. "I will be off again tomorrow, as I have to go North for a time. This will not be like the last time, as I may be gone for a bit longer."

Isolde's smile faded as she looked away for a quick moment, attempting to hide the disappointment. Drysten felt extremely guilty. He had rescued her from slavery, but upon their return, they had only brief moments of happiness with each other. In his mind, he was not doing enough to care for her and their unborn child. He was unbelievably excited at the prospect of being a father, and whether it was a boy or girl, he knew he would love the child dearly. Drysten's heart ached from the pain he felt he was causing Isolde, and he knew that he needed to try and make it right. He picked his head up and looked around the villa. "A priest!" he yelled, startling the people in their vicinity.

Isolde's eyes opened wide. "Drysten what—"

"A priest! Find Matthew!" he commanded Heraclius, who was walking around the atrium with a limping Titus.

Heraclius glanced at Titus with a confused expression, prompting Titus to lightly slap him on the back and point to the entrance. The Greek hurried outside to find Matthew as Drysten turned back to Isolde, who still did not understand what he was doing. "We will wait no longer!" He then looked to the woman who had been speaking with her. "I need you to find me the ring with a green stone in the middle. It is in our bedroom in a small chest at the foot of the bed," prompting Isolde to smile as wide as he had ever seen.

The woman looked slightly annoyed by being ordered around but decided she owed it to the man who's home she was now residing in. She glanced to Titus, who smiled and gestured to a back room before departing with a perturbed expression.

"She's not a *servant*, Drysten," Isolde said with a giggle.

Drysten turned back. "Who is she then?"

"Her name is Oana Octavian. She's Titus' daughter," Isolde said as the woman returned.

Drysten awkwardly looked back to Titus, who seemed very amused by the exchange. Drysten looked back to the villa's entryway as Heraclius came back, almost dragging Matthew by the collar to the atrium. "Found him, sir!"

"Thank you, brother," Drysten said with a chuckle.

Matthew looked back to the large Greek, then to Drysten. "Lord, I don't understand—"

"I wish to marry this woman," Drysten said as he gestured at Isolde.

Matthew's expression lit up. "Excellent, Lord! Am I to

have the honor of officiating?"

Drysten shook his head. "No, we need a sacrifice," prompting the priest's face to go white, and Isolde to elbow him in the ribs. "Yes, you will officiate."

Matthew sighed in relief. "There has not been a single day since our arrival where someone has not threatened to eat me or sacrifice me..."

The ceremony itself was most likely the quickest and most lackluster of any marriage ceremony in Britannia's history. Drysten and Isolde were both eager to see the service over, so they could enjoy a brief wedding night before Drysten set off the next morning. They started by standing across from one another, with Matthew instructing them to join both of their right hands together. Drysten stared into Isolde's eyes, and only remembered having a faint idea that the priest was babbling something about a sacred ceremony, a wedding night, and then he made a joke to invoke a bit of laughter from the people standing nearby. Afterward, he spoke to the crowd, looked to them both, and offered them a moment to say their vows.

Drysten had not thought about vows to that point, so he simply took a deep breath and hoped his short speech would have enough meaning in it to be passable. "I love you. I have always loved you. And I always *will* love you. You're going to be the mother of my children, and the only woman I ever come home to." He then looked awkwardly at Matthew, who understood he could think of nothing more to say. The priest looked to Isolde, but she was interrupted by Drysten kissing her deeply and lovingly when she started to speak.

Matthew looked at the two people in front of him, satisfied he would get no more words from either of them, then raised his hands. "Man and Wife!" The crowd cheered and clapped as the ceremony quickly ended. Drysten and Isolde were now married, as Drysten had promised.

Diocles and Dagonet walked back into the entrance of the villa with a handful of perplexed crewmembers from the

Fortuna. The men were still tired from engaging the Saxons on the docks earlier in the day, and were confused as to what possible cheer there could be in the villa filled with refugees. Amiram tapped Diocles on the shoulder and pointed to Drysten and Isolde in the center of the crowd.

"What's all this?" Diocles asked Titus.

Titus nodded his head toward Drysten. "The boy married his woman."

Diocles looked over the heads of the crowd. "I leave for one moment and Drysten sells his soul off." Then he looked back to Amiram, who somehow had gone from curious, to teary-eyed very abruptly. Diocles glanced to Titus, who had also noticed the mute's emotional display, and the two began to silently laugh to each other.

The festivities that occurred after the ceremony were as good as the people of Petuaria could manage. Many of the locals who had taken a liking to Hall and Drysten in their few interactions sent small gifts of food to be distributed to the people around the villa. Conway even offered a calf to sacrifice. Isolde and Drysten both felt ambivalent about killing the animal and politely declined.

Diocles led the rest of the Fortuna's crew in shouting various songs of celebration from his homeland in Greece, and Titus sat with his family near the back of the atrium, just taking in the cheer and merriment after their hard ordeal in Londinium.

The light festivities lasted well into the night, even with Drysten and Isolde retiring to their bedchamber when the moon was at its highest. The men around all jeered at them in the knowledge they wouldn't need to consummate the marriage. "They already did!" a voice yelled out, turning Isolde's face a slight red in embarrassment.

Drysten tugged her hand toward the bedroom and closed the wooden door behind them. "I told you I would keep my promise," to which Isolde kissed him lovingly.

"Please don't die," Isolde said as she drew away. Drysten

smiled and nodded, then ushered her to the bed.

The night went as most wedding nights do, then the two fell asleep wrapped in each other's arms. In the morning, they awoke to the dawn sunrise and a slight knocking on the door. Drysten slipped out from under the furs, careful to keep Isolde covered and undisturbed. He glanced around and donned a pair of breeches, then opened the door to see Titus.

"I trust your wedding night was productive," the general said with a smile.

Drysten laughed. "Not as productive as another night, I suppose. We already started making ourselves a family a few months ago."

Titus laughed and gestured for Drysten to follow. "I have a wedding gift for you."

"The coin is yours, Titus. Pay for the needs of your people with it," Drysten said as he followed his friend.

Titus shook his head. "This gift was originally going to go to my son, but seeing as how he now has no men to lead, I think it would suit you more."

Drysten followed Titus to the room he'd given him and his family upon their arrival. He saw Marivonna, Oana, and Gaius all readying themselves for the day ahead, and each greeted him with a smile and a nod, which Drysten warmly returned.

"Did anyone ever tell you what the people of Londinium dubbed me?" Titus asked.

Drysten glanced to Gaius, who was wearing an embarrassed expression before he shook his head. "No, I was only told your name and where to find you."

Titus smiled and nodded his head toward a chest which had recently been set out on the table. Drysten slowly walked toward it, and upon Titus gesturing once more, he opened it to reveal an elegant suit of armor fit for a Roman general. "The Bull," Titus said proudly, "I received the name from my brief days in Carthage stemming rebellions and fighting barbarians. I was so hated by my enemies that a *bounty* was put on me. The bull is what they named me." Titus glanced to his feet. "The bull..."

"Likely from the standard of your legion as well," Drysten added.

He gazed upon the metal armor, created in the ancient Greek style of a single metal plate on the front of the chest and one more attached by leather wiring to protect the wearer's back. The armor was painted a light brown, bearing the golden crest of a bull in the middle of the chest. Drysten glanced at Titus, who smiled and gestured for him to pick it up.

"It served me well in war. I had wished to give it to my son, but I think it would be more fitting to have one more personal made for him. Thus, I give it to you," Titus stated happily.

Drysten took the armor, and with Titus' help, began to strap it on. There were more pieces than just the metal chest piece, as the shoulders were that of the standard Roman lorica segmentata. Those two pieces as well as the grieves and vambraces were created from steel and all dyed to match.

"Titus..." Drysten managed to croak out despite him being overwhelmed by the gesture.

Titus chuckled. "You'll find it is only armor, though its purpose was to display some sort of nobility, a trait I have sadly come to see in few others."

Drysten looked at Titus, unsure of what to say, and simply nodded. Drysten hoped Titus knew how much this armor would mean to him. Drysten began to don the rest of his new equipment, starting first with the greaves, then the vambraces. A white scarf was placed around his neck to prevent any kind of chafing caused by the metal coming into contact with the skin. It all fit him perfectly, Once the shoulders were attached by their leather connectors, he gazed upon himself in the mirror Titus' wife had managed to pack before the Saxons raided their home. The leather lappets hanging from the bottom of the chest and back pieces were all decorated on their ends with bronze plates of a circle bearing "VI", of the Legio VI Victrix. Drysten thought the blue tunic he had worn that morning matched well with his new armor, as did the brown trousers and peros.

Drysten turned to Titus, almost overcome by the man's kindness. "I swear to you, I will do everything I can to repay this gesture."

Titus smiled. "By promising me you will take care of my people, you already have."

Drysten turned to Titus' son, Gaius. "Before I truly accept this, it is important to me that you also give me permission to have it, as this was once intended for you."

Gaius glanced to his father, then back to Drysten. "Too small for me anyway."

The three men shook hands before Drysten slowly shuffled back outside. The people of the villa all stopped to gaze upon Drysten in his new suit of Roman-forged metal. At first, he was slightly embarrassed by these looks. Many people in Britannia had never seen a Roman, let alone a Roman officer wearing such splendid armor. While Drysten was indeed no Roman officer, he could certainly pass as one. He made his way across the atrium to the bedroom shared with his now wife, and stepped inside.

Isolde's eyes widened as she slowly stood up. After a moment gazing upon her husband, she walked over, slowly extending a hand to feel the plated armor. "Oana told me her father wanted to gift you his armor, but she neglected to describe it. I have never seen something such as this."

Drysten smiled. "I suppose you still want me to run my father's shipping company."

"I worry this armor will make you a target to your enemies," Isolde cautioned. "I would rather you only required it for a brief time."

Drysten smiled and took his wife's hand. "I promise you, I will never join a fight I could have avoided."

Isolde nodded before kissing her husband, and helped him clasp his father's bearskin cloak around his now armored shoulders. The two walked back out of the bedroom, through the atrium and the front gates, then around the Western side of the villa's walls to the docks. Every person who saw Drysten starred in either amazement or jealousy of what they saw.

"Do I get armor like that if I get married?" Diocles asked from the deck of the Saxon ship they would be sailing North.

Drysten smiled. "Knowing your opinion of marriage, I doubt you'll ever find out."

The vessel had been loaded the night before and lay ready the next morning. The crew mainly consisted of men from the Fortuna, with Matthew also in attendance. Dagonet was coming as the group's scout, and Amiram hand-picked twenty of his rowers to work the oars, while Diocles picked ten of the best fighters. In all, thirty-five men were joining them. Drysten was pleased to see his friend Bors, and Titus' man Heraclius coming on the voyage, as the sight of them would make anybody second guess a fight.

Drysten turned to his new wife once more. "We will be back once we find my father and finish with Segedunum. Though now that I know why the king wants it, I almost feel as though I should let the Northmen keep it."

"Titus will be able to take care of things here. We will be fine," Isolde said.

Drysten kissed her one last time, then boarded the ship.

CHAPTER XVII

Hall's men finally made it to the summit of the hillfort just before nightfall. They had rushed North through unfamiliar forests and open fields with their pursuers on their heels the whole way. It seemed to Gawain, whose task it was to observe the pursuers, that their numbers had been reinforced by men from the East. At first, this held no meaning for Hall, then he understood they presumably came from the occupying force at Segedunum.

The old Roman signal station was at the tallest point on the middle hill and Hall took a small group to examine it. The signal station seemed to be made mostly of wood, though at some point there must have been an attempt to rebuild it in stone. By Hall's estimate, the Romans were only about halfway finished upgrading the building when they must have decided to leave, as the stone base looked as though there were never any others piled over the top of it.

Prince Eidion decided to make himself useful for once, and rode around the base of the hill to make sure there were no people camped out waiting for them. Prince Aurelianus did the same, though checking the other sides of the South and East hills, finding no souls to worry about. The villagers living just to their North could be seen going about their days off in the distance, showing Hall their presence in the region had either gone unnoticed, or was less than threatening to the locals.

Groups camping on the hills must be nothing foreign to these people, Hall thought to himself. *This place might be some sort of meeting point for local tribes.*

He assembled his men in a ring at the top of the hill, piling some wood on their side of a shallow ditch which was dug around the summit. The wood had once belonged to buildings occupying the hilltop, and by their look, Hall wondered how long ago that could have been. They were all jutting up from the ground and had to be pried free, with some being rotten to the point they were snapping under little force. The stones from the half built signal station were taken and used as a makeshift wall blocking the most accessible point of entry from the pathway leading up the hill. The wall was only about waist high, but would do a decent enough job of preventing people from climbing over should they attack from the pass. Thankfully, Hall saw the other side of the hill would prove to be a steep climb for their attackers.

"Well, we're dug in about as well as we can be," Bors said upon examining their makeshift fortifications. "Though our numbers dwindled some on the march here."

"How many deserters?" Hall asked.

"Nearly fifty," Bors answered in frustration, "puts our numbers at three hundred. Gawain told me there could be as many as six or seven hundred on our heels."

"Three hundred should be enough to at least hold out for a time," Hall said as he surveyed the men. By his guess, the ones who deserted were the most lightly armed and least seasoned. This was some relief, as he would have less to worry about in terms of a line breaking. "Light presence near the wall to start. Make the line at the crest of the hill."

"I'll see to it," Bors nodded and relayed the orders.

The men obediently lined themselves along the point where the slope met the level parts of the summit, surprising Hall that they could make it three deep all the way around without stationing too many at the wall. He was positive the enemies knew their location and decided the idea of prohibiting campfires was useless. The men built more than they needed to hopefully mislead the enemy into believing their numbers were higher than they actually were. Off to their South, Hall saw their response as the enemy's own fires began to light up the tree line. At first, it seemed Gawain's estimate of their enemy's strength was spot on, but then he began to wonder. The fires were beginning to encircle the hill, and some even began to appear on the summit of the neighboring two hills on either side.

"We could be in for a rough night, Lord," a man mentioned to Hall. He nodded and turned to check the lines once more, satisfied the men were placed as best as he could manage.

Aosten and Eidion oversaw the makeshift barrier erected on the pathway, Aurelianus oversaw the whole Western side of the hill, and Hall and Bors' men would be defending the Southern side. The stars of the night sky loomed overhead, making Hall wonder if there was some god or goddess in attendance to watch the events play out.

Do they already know our fates? he wondered to himself, *or do they simply gather enjoyment by watching us stumble around like blind animals?*

A shout came from the Powysians of the Western section of the line. A mass of men appeared from the darkness, illuminated by the torches set into the ground twenty feet down the slope to provide an early warning.

"Swords!" Hall commanded. His men drew their blades as he rushed to his part of the Southern line. He heard the clash of shields and grunts coming from Aurelianus' men, though none had come to attack his own.

"Should we help them, Lord?" one man said.

Hall shook his head. "The last thing we should do is weaken one part of our line to fortify another."

The Prince from Powys was shouting orders to hold the line from their attackers, who were throwing themselves upon their swords and attempting to force their bodies between the small gaps of their shield wall.

"Don't let them get through!" Aurelianus shouted. The men roared and pushed the attackers down, stabbing as they moved. Men were tripping over bodies and hurling insults into the enemy forces, throwing themselves forward. Then, after a moment, a horn blew from the base of the hill, and the enemy withdrew. The attack lasted all but a few moments before the enemy pulled back into the darkness below the few torches left standing.

Hall knew what would happen next. "They're testing each side of the line," he whispered to the man behind him. He positioned himself into the front rank of his shield wall, moving between Bors and Cyrus. He was about to shout for his men to be ready when the first figures appeared, bursting from the darkness as they had in front of the Powysians. What startled Hall the most was how little they heard from the attackers. They seemed to erupt from the darkness with no warning, meaning there could be hundreds of men creeping around the hill without anyone being able to spot them.

This was the first up-close look Hall had of their pursuers. The man charging at him had a face painted with blue swirls and a blue beast painted on his chest. Behind him, more painted men appeared from the darkness, with some fighting naked as their ancestors had against the Romans. Before Hall knew it, they were leaping up toward the shield wall. "Brace!" he yelled. The force of the man's impact into his shield drove him back a half-step, but he quickly corrected with a push of his own. His Roman-style shield was holding his attacker at bay when Bors stabbed through the gaps of the two, piercing into the man's side and sending him to the ground.

Hall readied himself for the next forceful push as Cyrus stabbed toward the same area and brought a second man down. After a moment, the force of a body being thrown into his shield quickly returned, and he pushed back to preserve his spot in the line. Bors' shield had been wrenched a few inches to the side, exposing his arm to the enemy. A small blade appeared through the gap and nearly pierced Bors' side before Hall stabbed his own weapon through the gap, causing a scream before the blade quickly retreated. Just like before, another horn sounded at the base of the hill, and the attack was over.

The men waited for a third attack on the wall, but were relieved when it never came. Hall withdrew back to the center of the hilltop, where the army's small number of tents were erected. The men on horseback managed to keep four in total when the wagons were abandoned. One was being used to house the wounded, though thankfully there were only a few as of yet. The other three were reserved for the commanders, where Eidion and Aurelianus joined Hall.

"They were testing us," Hall explained. "They only needed moments to find out our strength. How many did we lose?"

Aurelianus glanced behind him at the bodies being lined up outside. "Fifteen of mine."

"They dared not attack the wall," Eidion put in.

Hall nodded. "Eight of mine are dead, three more wounded." Hall rubbed his hand over his head. "Half guard through the night. They will attack us again at dawn."

Aurelianus nodded and left the tent, but Eidion stayed and walked toward Hall. "We should counterattack them."

Hall chuckled. "*Gods* no. No, we most definitely should *not*."

The prince's eyes narrowed. "Do not forget who your lord is. I say we should attack. There is no glory for cowards who sit and wait to be bludgeoned to death."

Hall walked to the prince, keeping eye contact as he stepped forward. The prince shied away as he drew closer. "Of the two of us, which one has led a war?" The prince finally broke eye contact as he looked away. "Answer," Hall insisted.

Eidion looked back. "*You* command *me?*"

"Answer," Hall said with narrowing eyes.

The prince scoffed and finally withdrew from the tent, bumping into Bors as he left.

"Little fucker," Bors whispered as he entered, not sure whether he was heard. Truthfully, he did not care in the slightest.

"That spoiled boy told me we should rush down the hill and attack them," Hall said with a chuckle.

Bors sighed. "Let's just leave him here and go fight for the Powysians. Their prince is much more…princely."

Hall nodded. "Maybe once our dealings with the king are done."

The two men sat in silence as the night drew on. Hall knew once the full attack began there would be no opportunity for escape. He considered trying to move off during the night, but his gut told him the enemy would be well aware of any attempt to retreat. All Hall could do was try and get some sleep before the next attack. He took the first watch with the men and instructed Bors to sleep until he was awoken to take the next. Bors nodded and dozed off as Hall walked outside to the stars, hearing the constant murmurs from nervous voices all around him.

Both princes gave similar orders to each of their respective second-in-commands and retired to their tents for the evening. Hall chose to take the first watch in the event he could think up a different plan of action, though he had already run through every scenario in his head. The only one that did not end up with the army being immediately eviscerated was to stay at the top of the hill and wait for reinforcements. After some time, he woke Bors and leaned up against a sack as a pillow. He slept surprisingly sound until he was awoken by Prince Aurelianus, who explained dawn was coming.

"It's almost time, Hall," the prince wearily noted.

Hall nodded as he got up from the ground, dusting himself off. "Get the men ready. They'll be here soon." He stepped out of the tent to be greeted by Elias, who handed him a small morsel of bread with some water before each of them made their way toward the line.

Hall was stopped by Aosten as he was picking up his shield and trying to shake off the chill of the early morning air. "Hall," he said, gaining his attention, "Eidion was none too happy with you last night."

Hall chuckled. "The brat attempted ordering us into a counterattack."

"A catastrophe is what that would have been," Aosten responded as he shook his head. "In any case, he plans to tell the king you did not conduct yourself in an honorable fashion."

Elias smirked. "That man *knows* the meaning of honor?"

Aosten shook his head. "I imagine he'll make something up. I just wanted to warn you should we live this out."

Hall thanked him, and each of the leaders returned to their men. The sun was beginning to show itself to the East, giving Hall a glimpse of massing men making their way toward them. They were still a few miles off, but he knew if they survived against this army currently assailing them, then the next would inevitably butcher them to the last man. "One thing at a time," he quietly whispered to himself.

"Lord?" Elias said.

Hall shook his head. "It was nothing. Just a thought I had."

They made their way to the lines to be greeted by Cyrus and Bors, then moved to the front rank of the shield wall. The torches had gone out sometime in the night, but Hall knew there could be no man brave enough to venture down to relight them. As the sun rose, he began to see the enemy forces assembling at the hill's base. By his count, they had enough men to occupy both of the other hills and still surround the bottom of the middle one with a sizeable force. After they had finished assembling, the horns began to blow their low, foreboding note.

Men were heard roaring in all directions as they readied

themselves for war. Gods were called, swords and axes were beaten onto shields, and the men from the North were now ready to exact their vengeance for Eidion's brutality.

"Shield wall!" Hall commanded loud enough for the whole hilltop to hear. "These Northmen have ransacked your villages, raped and enslaved your people, and now they want to butcher you for showing them the same kindness!" Hall strongly disapproved of Eidion's actions, but also knew some of the men considered it retaliation for their own loved ones being killed. He knew how important it was for them to think the commanders were united in the belief the brutality was necessary. "You are here to show them their actions will no longer go unpunished!"

The men around the hilltop roared behind him, briefly drowning out the greater numbers below. Once they ceased, the enemy finally came.

The cries of the men painted in blue were deafening as they approached the Britons. As they rushed forward, Hall knew they were there to kill every single man they found at the hilltop. "Keep steady," he said to the men around him. "Keep the shields tight and they won't get through. They aren't used to fighting against a wall of wood. Watch out for your neighbors and we may yet hold."

The men around him murmured among themselves as they braced for the impact of the first enemies, now two-thirds of the way up the hill. The Powysians were once again the first to be met by the Northmen, as a tremendous crash sounded from behind Hall. He knew it would not matter what he saw if he decided to look, so instead faced forward as the painted men with red hair were now about to crash into the men on either side of him.

The first enemy met Cyrus' shield and jolted him back to the man behind him before he managed to right himself and push back. Hall was second to take the weight of a man onto his shield, then after a short moment, the whole line was pushing against the enemy and stabbing their swords through the gaps between their shields. Hall's sword managed to find the throat of a man, slickening his hand with the blood that gushed from the wound. He always found it strange you could quite literally drain a man's life in such a way.

Is that what a man's soul is? Hall briefly wondered.

Bors and Cyrus were both faring well, as were others in the front rank of the wall. The line was holding firm as the painted men did what they could with their ancient swords and small axes.

Hall guessed the Picts must have thought his side the weakest, as most of the enemy force was lined up across from him. In truth, it probably was. The only men he truly trusted were the ones Bors had hand-picked to be in the first rank of the shield wall, while the others were mostly made up of the newer recruits he had only managed to train for a few days before they departed. The Powysians were faring well, having driven off the first wave of attackers without losing more than a handful of men.

Hall continued to push and stab through the cracks in the shield wall, keeping certain his shield did not drift too high and expose his lower half to the enemy. He had seen what a wound to that part of a body could do to a man. Men all around him were frantically stabbing over shields or through the gaps between them, all having the same ferocity that comes from a man who believes this will be his last day walking the earth. Bors and Cyrus were doing their best to prevent Hall from being overwhelmed, as it was apparent he was not as spry as he was in his younger years. Even so, he was performing well against the onslaught of strangely painted faces screaming into the wooden wall he held from his left hand. To Hall's relief, a uniquely pitched horn suddenly sounded from below the hill and the enemy began to draw back.

"What are they doing?" Hall asked Bors, who he watched brutally rip his sword from the neck of a man on the ground.

Bors looked around at the withdrawing enemy running down the lush grass of the hill. "I... Did we just win?" he whimpered in shock.

Hall was dumbstruck as he watched the overwhelming numbers below the hill run in the opposite direction. He glanced from side to side, then removed himself from the front rank of the shield wall, with Elias taking his place. The hilltop was crowded with wounded from the second attack, causing Hall some discomfort as he walked through the begging strangers around him. He walked further, toward the middle of the bodies until he noticed something odd near the wall they had erected shortly before the battle began. Hall slowly crept toward a group of men standing in a half circle, all staring into the ground. He approached to see the group mainly consisted of Powysians, then glanced toward what they were staring at. There was a bloody heap of rended flesh lying below Prince Aurelianus, who was sadly staring into it.

The Prince slowly looked toward Hall as he walked up. "Dead, Lord. Killed him before they left. You're going to need to watch yourself should we live this through."

"What was the purpose behind this?" Hall said angrily.

The Prince sadly looked toward the body on the ground before closing his eyes. "Eidion argued with him for a moment before killing him." He paused for a moment to rub his tired eyes. "He *smiled* as he killed him."

"How did you see it happen if you were fighting off Northmen?" Bors asked as he stepped in beside Hall.

Prince Aurelianus shook his head. "Poor luck. I glanced behind me when our attackers began to withdraw. I was too slow to prevent it."

The group stood in silence as they each stared into the vacant eyes of the body lying in front of them. The dead man was Aosten, and Eidion and his men were gone.

CHAPTER XVIII

Time aboard the captured Saxon vessel seemed to pass slower than usual. The rowers appeared to favor the lighter ship, explaining it was easier to propel it forward when compared to the Fortuna. After a day of sailing North, Drysten found he needed to add extra layers of clothing to brave the more frigid air, which was coupled with the icy spray of the wind driven sea. Under his new Roman armor, he wore a dark blue gambeson he always kept in his trunk, given to him by his father when he grew large enough to fit into it. At the moment, he had decided to remove the heavy metal plates from his chest, as they seemed to pull down on his shoulders and caused his back to ache.

The coastline of Britannia lay on the ship's left, while to its right was the open sea and the dreaded beasts lurking below its waters. Drysten had been told many tales of such creatures from fishermen and traders in his youth. Men working or passing through Burdigala never seemed to grow tired of the stories of the sea and tales of gods and monsters they defeated. Though now, Drysten feared the Saxons more so than any beast he had never laid eyes on. The Saxons now had a fleet based in Londinium, and Jorrit knew where Drysten and his men could be found should they ever venture to destroy them.

"We should be coming up on their tribal capital soon, Lord," Matthew put in from the stern of the ship. "We would do well to leave any Roman-looking men aboard the ship. Their presence could instigate... *resistance* to our being there."

Drysten nodded. "The only ones to join me will be Bors, Heraclius, and you. The others will stay aboard the Genii." That was the name Drysten chose for his new vessel. The Genii were popular deities in Britannia, being considered guardian angels by the island's inhabitants. Drysten knew the group would need the service of guardian angels if they were to see their task through. "We will manage with the four of us. What do you know of their lord?"

Matthew stepped beside Drysten at the bow of the ship as the smoke of cooking fires began to appear off in the distance. "I know he is the brother of King Ceneus. *Half*-brother actually."

Drysten turned. "I assumed you would know more than that when you talked your way aboard."

Matthew chuckled. "Lord, I assure you my presence in your company will not hinder you in any way."

Drysten skeptically looked on the priest before deciding it was time to don his exquisite armor once more. If he was to attempt business with a lord, he knew he would need to look like one himself. "How much longer until we arrive?" he asked Matthew.

"Not much longer, Lord," Matthew responded.

Drysten turned away from the bow and made his way to the area in the stern where the crew stacked their bags and armor. Once he was finished applying the metal to his body, he wrapped his shoulders in his father's cloak and silently hoped it would bring him some sort of good luck. He turned back to see a large wooden palisade encircling the smoke from the fires he spotted earlier. On the beach was a small wooden dock, just long enough for the Genii to safely tie lines to without the fear of being beached.

A group of a dozen men stood armed and waiting for them as they inched closer. All but one were bare-chested and carrying large wooden shields and small hatchets. Drysten saw Diocles give Heraclius a nervous glance before the ship finally slowed, then stopped for the lines to be tied off. Heraclius and Bors stood and waited for Drysten to make his way to the dock before beginning to follow, with Matthew trailing behind. Upon stepping off the vessel, the lone unarmed man of the group awaiting them stepped forward and spoke a language Drysten could not understand. He was rather tall compared to the others nearby, and had the glossiest bald head Drysten had ever laid eyes on. Drysten nodded to the man before gesturing for Matthew to interpret what was being said.

The priest stepped forward and appeared to ask the man to repeat himself, which earned the newcomers a scowl before he reluctantly did so. "He wants to know who we are, Lord."

"Tell him I have come with an offer for their king," Drysten commanded. Matthew translated, and once done, the man stepped closer to examine the newcomers to his lands. After a moment, he turned and spoke something to the guards, which Drysten assumed meant for them to stay put and gestured for Drysten and his men to follow.

The walk into the tribal village was a stark contrast to what Drysten was used to. The huts were mostly made from mud, with bits of wood mixed in for support. The one thing Drysten noticed as they wound their way through a dirt road leading into the center of the village was how the people all seemed to be inside their homes. "Keep your eyes open," he commanded his men as he put his hand onto his sword hilt.

"I wouldn't worry, Lord," Matthew explained. "People in these lands worship the old ways. They consider inviting a person into your home to kill them to be one of the *gravest* of sins."

"Then don't say anything to reverse that," Drysten commanded.

The man led them to a large building, mostly made of wood, then gestured for Drysten to go inside. Drysten began to step over the threshold but was stopped by their guide, who gestured for him to remove his weapons.

"I don't like this," Bors warned as he looked at Heraclius, who nodded in agreement.

Drysten looked at the guide for a moment, considering if he could change the man's mind until he gestured for the weapons once more. "Make sure nobody steals these," he said as he removed his sword belt and handed it to Bors, despite the guide wanting to hold onto it himself. He started to protest until Bors glared at him, then quickly turned and walked inside.

Drysten followed into the dimly lit chamber with a chair at the far side. The guide ushered him forward as Matthew entered behind.

"What business do you have for me, Roman?" a man said from the shadows. The voice seemed to echo somehow, though the building was a drabby wooden hall with a low roof. "Well? What does my good brother wish of me?"

Drysten took a small step forward. "Your brother does not know where I am, Lord King. What I have to say comes from me alone." Drysten was relieved he didn't stammer, as he was more nervous than he thought he'd be once he started to speak.

The king slowly rose from his drabby throne and stepped forward from the shadows. To Drysten's surprise, he shared a striking resemblance to King Ceneus, though the man before him seemed sculpted by hardship whereas Ceneus was obviously living a more pampered existence. The burly man also had scars running down the right side of his face resembling what you would find from an attack by a large animal. It ran from just above his eyebrow, then down the side of his face where it tapered off near the base of his cheek. "What's your name, Roman?"

"Drysten, and I am no Roman," he coolly replied.

The king stepped forward to examine his guest. "Well then, Drysten who is not Roman, I am Garbonian ap Coel, brother to King Ceneus and the once favored son thrown to the wild beasts in the North."

Drysten cocked an eyebrow. "*Once* favored?"

The king nodded. "I was chosen to inherit Ebrauc from my father. This place," he said, waving his hands around, "is the place of my father's birth and home to the Guayrdi tribe of the Brigantes. *This* is now where I reign." He slowly lowered his arms. It was clear there was a hint of sadness in his voice.

"How did King Ceneus inherit Ebrauc if your father once wished to grant it to you?" Drysten asked. Matthew was currently standing close to the doorway, seeming to Drysten as though he was attempting to conceal himself in the shadows for some reason. He figured the priest was nervous of the king, as the man was certainly intimidating.

"The plans of a dead man never play out the way he intended. Such is life. In any case, I do my best to preserve the lives of my people wherever I may reside," the king said with a sigh. "Rather than ask about my honorable father, why don't you tell me why you are here?"

Drysten stepped forward. "I have a proposition for you, Lord King."

King Garbonian chuckled. "I gathered as much. Now tell me, what is it?"

"My father is leading an army of undertrained and under-equipped men through the lands to your West. His job was to retake the fort of Segedunum from the men who claimed it not long ago, as I'm sure you knew." The king nodded. "He knew he did not have the strength to challenge the occupiers, so he was attempting to draw them out by raiding lands nearby."

"I know this. The village he sacked was once mine, though now the men from Strathclyde take their tribute," the king explained as he made his way to his throne.

Drysten turned in surprise. "The village was sacked? I knew he was planning to catch their attention, but killing the people of a village hardly sounds like something I would expect from him."

The king chuckled. "The men we know our whole lives typically surprise us the most. In any case, go on."

"What I have learned is that there was a Roman cache of iron and possibly silver located within the fort. If you help me drive off the men my father faces, and if you help me retake the fort, then the iron and silver are yours," Drysten explained.

The king leaned back in his throne, surprised by the generosity of the offer. "Your king approved this?"

Drysten smiled. "I fail to see the importance of his approval at the moment."

The king laughed, clearly amused by the prospect of stealing something out from beneath his brother's nose. "I like you, Drysten. Ha! Drysten who is *not* Roman!"

Drysten smiled. "Thank you, Lord King, but at the moment I am pressed for time and am in need of an answer soon."

The king continued to laugh. "Of course I will help you! The man usurped my throne and took my wife as his own before he whelped his children into her. I will grant your request, Drysten who is not Roman!"

Drysten was taken aback by the king's ferocity toward his brother. He expected him to be a reluctant man, only persuaded by the prospect of gaining a bit of wealth. "I thank you, Lord King. How many men could I expect?"

King Garbonian erupted from his seat. "All of them, boy! You will show my brother to the South what *real* men fight like! His precious fortress will be retaken by the very pagan filth he fears!" He turned to the man who guided Drysten and Matthew to the hall. "Dyfnwal! Assemble the men and ready them to march West."

"Yes, father," the man replied with a short bow of his startlingly bald head.

Drysten turned in surprise. "You speak the Roman language?"

Dyfnwal turned back and smiled. "All nobles are taught the language of the Romans."

Drysten stayed with the king for a short time, until a horn was blown and the cheers of men could be heard ringing out from all sides of the village. Drysten turned back to the king, who smiled and gestured for him to follow outside. Drysten walked through the doorway to see men running to and fro from building to building. Men were smiling and racing to grab weapons, and some were standing in a line while waiting for an old man and woman to paint their bodies and faces.

"These are the men whose ancestors struck fear through the ranks of the precious Roman legions sent to destroy them. They came to conquer, and instead their men were burned in the wicker, given to the gods, and never heard from again. There are still stories of great treasures to be found in the North, left behind by their Ninth Legion."

Drysten turned to ask who the Ninth Legion was, but was too distracted by the sight of the men racing around him to find their weapons. Drysten stood silently in front of his three companions and betrayed a subtle grin, knowing he would have these men at his back to face off against his father's enemies.

"How long before they will march?" Drysten asked.

The king peered around to examine the state of his men. More were coming through the gate, now adding to the numbers already inside the village. Drysten guessed there were a hundred already inside when he arrived. Now there seemed to be three times that amount readying themselves for war. "I would say you should go to your vessel and bring your men now. They will be ready shortly after your return."

Drysten nodded and returned to the Genii, followed by Bors, Heraclius, and Matthew. The three were just as impressed by the scene of the bloodthirsty men running around them. All of them painted with blue faces, and whooping and yelling to themselves in the ancient language of the Britons. Drysten's men outside of the palisade were now disembarking from the ship, all armed and confused by the men running around them. Amiram walked up to Drysten with an obviously confused expression.

"They will join us," Drysten said. Amiram looked around again in amusement. "I know. They seem to enjoy a fight. Better for us."

Amiram nodded and gestured for the rest of the men to follow Drysten into the palisade.

Upon entering, the king was shouting orders next to the man Drysten noticed to be his son, both watching their people as they were readying themselves for a battle they seemed to so desperately want. He then turned to Drysten. "My spies tell me your people can be found at an old hillfort to the West. It is a rather defensible position. Your father chose well."

Drysten nodded. "Then we march?"

"We march," replied the king.

CHAPTER XIX

Drysten and King Garbonian marched by night through the western fields and forests to his father's rescue. The king's scouts explained the defenses set up on the hilltop and how many men they could be expecting to fight through to secure the safety of Hall's army. He now knew they would face about seven hundred men in total, though the king was convinced much of the enemy force was made up of levies from the villages nearby. These men were lightly trained and fought with whatever they owned that could be used as a weapon. Their presence was not a concern to Drysten, as he knew that part of the force would be easy to break and rout. The summit first came within Drysten's view at dawn, finally seeing it a couple of miles to their West. The hill towered over the surrounding land and presumably the village he was told existed at its base.

"My people have been at war with the surrounding lands for a very long time. Those wars only intensified once the throne of Bryneich went to a man from the South," the king explained. "More to our advantage, these boys here have been born into wars for as long as there have been people here."

Drysten grinned. "I look forward to seeing them in action, Lord."

"I like you, Drysten who is not Roman," the king replied with a grin, "you do not strike me as a Roman. You have more mettle in you than they did."

Drysten graciously nodded. "Thank you, Lord."

"You know I have a daughter about your age," King Garbonian began.

Drysten laughed and shook his head. "I'm recently married, Lord. Though, thank you for the offer."

"Ha! What's one more wife!" the king laughed and slapped his hand on Drysten's shoulder.

It didn't take long before Drysten decided this man was much more likable than his brother. At first, King Ceneus had been kind to Drysten and his father, but soon after he showed his ineptitude. Drysten was easily convinced this man would have been a stronger and more capable ruler for Ebrauc.

The army finally made it to a small clearing, where they were met by one of the king's scouts. "We saw about a dozen horsemen riding down from the summit of the hill. They were venturing East."

The king looked at Drysten. "Your father?"

Drysten shook his head. "The last thing my father would do is abandon his men to die alone."

The king shrugged the news off as simple desertion and the men pressed on. The shouts ringing out from the hilltop spurred their pace on as they drew closer. Drysten began to see a massive line of men running up through a pathway, then being halted by what looked like a barrier of some sort.

Drysten quickly turned to the king. "Lord King, I believe you said it would be me who would lead the charge?" To which the king smiled and nodded, then gestured for him to step out in front of the army's column. Drysten did so, drew his sword, and turned around with his weapon raised. The army erupted in a roar to which the king sounded as though he contributed to half of it. To Drysten's surprise, Matthew of all people was standing in the front, face painted in blue.

"Figured why not, Lord!" the priest said.

Drysten began to oppose the idea of the priest being in

the front of the charge, then decided it was too late to give such orders. He turned to face the hilltop and screamed as he pointed his weapon toward his enemy. "Forward!"

The roar of the charging army from Bryneich seemed to send a wave of panic through the enemy soldiers piling up the hillside. As more and more of them figured out they were being attacked from the rear, heads began to turn, and blue-faced men began to turn and offer up a rearward defense. Drysten continued to scream as he led the mass of fury and barbarism forward. He took a quick glance to his right and saw Matthew and Amiram both charging beside him, with Bors and Heraclius on his left. the king was close behind with the man Drysten presumed to be his son while the army that followed was racing forward. There was no point in attempting a shield wall with these men. Aside from the fact not many even had shields, they all seemed content in the idea they would just rush into the enemy's backside and start hacking it to bits.

Men began to run down the hill to meet them. First a dozen, then about fifty, then half of what Drysten guessed was about five hundred men turned to face them. Spears and hatchets were being thrown at him, yet none came close enough to hit him. Bors shrugged one off as it clashed into his shield, and a few others embedded themselves inside some of the men around Drysten.

The first man to come close to him wildly swung an old Roman short sword toward Drysten's head, yet missed when Drysten sidestepped him. Drysten reacted by puncturing his own blade through the man's stomach. The man slumped forward and let out one last cry as Drysten wrenched the sword free.

More men came at Drysten, but were halted by Heraclius swinging his blade into one's cheek. King Garbonian cracked a huge axe over the head of another. The Fortuna's men finally reached the base of the hill, with Drysten now struggling to catch up with much of the force he was supposed to be leading. Matthew was nowhere in sight and Drysten hoped the man hadn't gotten himself killed in the first real battle he would find himself in.

"Drysten!" a man screamed.

Drysten wheeled around to see Diocles pinned to the ground with a man pressing a dagger into his chest. Diocles' jaw was clenched, and his eyes were narrowed as both of his hands were on the hilt of the crudely forged blade twitching over his chest. The Pict nearly succeeded in killing him until Drysten tackled the man away and shoved his blade so far into the man's neck it nearly severed his skull from his body.

He turned and helped his friend off the ground. "We're even," he said with a smile. Diocles plucked his blade back up and followed Amiram, who had also seen he was in danger and nearly beat Drysten to his side. The three men were now struggling to catch up to the main grouping of their army. The first wave of enemy forces to engage them had been routed quickly, with many of its men now disappearing into the surrounding forests.

Those men must have belonged to the levies, Drysten thought as they rushed forward.

A horn was blown, and suddenly the force still on the hillside abruptly turned to face them. To Drysten's horror, many of the enemy forces were also coming down from the summit of the hilltop.

"We're too late, they must have been overrun," Diocles whispered as Drysten looked to him in fright.

"Fuck!" Bors screamed with wide eyes. Drysten knew the pain his friend was experiencing. They each had gotten so close to seeing their fathers after so long apart. But now it appeared they would have to wait until finally meeting them in the afterlife.

"Kill every *fucking* one of them!" Drysten yelled as he watched Bors dash forward in a fury.

Heraclius ran forward to join him along with most of the remaining members of the Fortuna's crew. So much had happened since Drysten had last seen his father, but worst of all, the desire Drysten had of seeing Hall as a grandfather was no longer possible.

"Lord," Diocles said as he walked toward him, "there's more to do."

Drysten looked at Diocles through the tears beginning to well up, then ran up the hill toward his enemy. He never understood what it meant to truly hate a person, to hate them and wish for them to die in any way you could imagine. He felt this new hatred welling up from a small pit in his stomach to blazing heat in his temples. He felt it in his bones, his heart, and everywhere else. This feeling was different than first meeting Servius, as he somehow knew his woman was still alive.

You are no longer here to save them, the voice muttered, *now kill!*

And kill he did.

Hall and Prince Aurelianus quickly ushered the third ranks of each other's shield walls toward the now vacant defenses of the stone barrier. Both of their front lines would soon be overrun, but if they did not fill the gap left behind by Eidion, then the fight would be over even quicker. Luckily, a handful of men had seen the vacancy and rushed over once enemy forces had been seen sprinting up the path. To Hall's amazement the few men who positioned themselves there had held out well enough to prevent a mass of attackers from rushing into the top of the hill.

"Reform a line!" Hall commanded his men.

The line began to take shape just as new shouts could be heard from behind him. He quickly turned and saw the Powysian line break at the end closest to the wall.

"No!" Prince Aurelianus shouted as he rushed back to aid his men. Hall joined him with three others he had initially brought over from his own forces.

The Northmen were hacking away at a small group of

Powysians who had found themselves isolated when their line broke. Two men were simply tripped and rolled down the hill to be executed by men still attempting to make the climb. Hall was impressed with the prince as he watched him fight. The man had a strange grace to his movements, yet he also managed to have a rare anger behind each swing and stab. Northmen were now cowering as he drew closer rather than press their attack forward. Then, to Hall's amazement, they retreated.

"This is twice they've retreated for no reason," Hall said in complete confusion.

"Look!" the prince shouted. "They're fighting each other!"

Hall hurried to look at the sight. More men painted blue were savaging the others, driving them away in fear. As he was about to smile, men began to run from the Powysian breech, ignoring him and the Prince, and rushing down the hill. It would have been quite the sight if half of the men from Powys had not been dead or wounded.

"What the hell is going on?" Hall said to anyone who would listen.

"Christ...," the Prince said through a hushed tone.

Hall scoffed. "I doubt it."

The Prince looked at Hall and pointed. "Who is *that?*"

Hall scanned the hillside, finally noticing a Roman general slashing into the fleeing Pictish lines. Northmen were throwing themselves toward him, knowing he led the new forces which had attacked their rear and that killing him could disorganize their new enemy. Hall watched the general swiping his blade across throats and stabbing into naked stomachs as he neared. Picts began retreating from the fury which approached them, and as they did so, it finally gave Hall a clear view of the newfound ally. "That's... my son," he explained to the Prince.

The Prince looked on in astonishment as he watched the anger pour forth from Drysten. "*That* is your son?" he asked, prompting Hall to scarcely nod his head in shock.

Drysten was hacking and slashing through anyone who got close enough to him. Hall was completely taken aback by the anger that seemed to be emanating from him and driving him forward. He had a quick thought and wondered if that was the same anger he displayed toward the Saxons in the forests near Burdigala when he was younger, but tried not to consider the idea. He also noticed others from his crew. Amiram was seen chasing down men who were attempting to rush by him to safety, gutting them and then carelessly throwing them to the side before frantically looking around for more victims. The Greek who had befriended his son stormed through the gap between two men to slice the throat of a third who was standing behind them. The two he had run between were each gutted by others painted with blue faces, almost as brutally efficient as though a butcher was simply slaughtering an animal soon to be eaten.

Bors appeared by Hall's side to watch the carnage. "Boss, your son—," he stopped mid-sentence, "*My* son!" he said as he rushed forward.

Hall watched as Bors ran down the hill and disappeared behind a group of men attempting to rush up to the hill's summit. He turned back and watched as Drysten tackled a man to the ground, and held him up for his companion, the Greek, to stab with a knife.

"Drysten!" Hall called to no effect. There was too much noise coming from either fleeing or bloodthirsty men for him to be heard. He attempted to move down the hillside toward his people until Prince Aurelianus put a hand on his shoulder.

"It would be wiser to stay up top."

Hall turned and nodded. "It would be, but I don't intend to. Follow me if you want." Hall turned to his men. "With me!" he commanded, to which their shield wall dissolved, and the men followed him to the crest of the hill. Hall rushed down one of the only easily navigable paths of the wall, weaving in and out of men screaming in pain on the ground, and all the while attempting to keep an eye on his son.

A handful rushed toward Drysten on his way up, only to be butchered by him and his men as they worked their way forward at an impressive pace.

The Greek was stabbing into a man when he turned and noticed Hall and his men rushing from the enemy's rear. "Drysten!" he called.

Drysten pulled his sword out of a man's spine before turning to two terrified Picts and screaming a challenge toward them. The two men turned and ran when Drysten finally looked to where his friend was pointing. Hall assumed he saw nothing at first due to the chaos of men running in every direction, then his fury slowly began to subside as he noticed a familiar face erupting out of the haze. "Father!" he called with a smile.

Their gaze was momentarily interrupted by the sight of Amiram tackling a man to the ground, pinning him and allowing for a big-chested man wielding an axe to finish him off.

The enemy had been routed and was running in all directions, pursued by Drysten's men. Hall and his son walked toward each other and embraced for a moment before Hall withdrew and looked his son up and down. "Did you steal the armor?"

Drysten laughed. "It was a wedding present."

Hall smiled warmly as they each turned to watch the last of the fleeing enemy disappear through the trees.

A large man who resembled King Ceneus slowly walked up with brimming smile. "So about the contents of the fort," he began.

"For all I care, you can keep the fort too," Drysten quipped.

Hall shook his head. "I apologize, but I was instructed to retake it for the king Ceneus." He walked toward the man who seemed to have befriended his son. "I have not had the pleasure, lord. I am—"

"Hall!" the man roared with a laugh. He wrapped Hall in a bear hug for a moment before letting him go. "Your boy told me quite a bit about you on the march here. I am King Garbonian ap Coel, King over Bryneich."

"And the favored son thrown to the beasts in the North," Drysten added with a chuckle, prompting a confused glance from his father.

The king turned as laughter erupted from his belly. "Right, indeed!"

After a moment of conversation, Bors the younger limped up with the help of Heraclius, who was also bleeding from his side.

"Bors?" Hall said in surprise.

The man looked up with tears in his eyes. "My father is dead."

The group fell silent. Bors hung his head as Hall approached and put a hand on his shoulder. "Where is he?" Bors closed his eyes and half-heartedly pointed behind him. Drysten walked with his father while the king was instructing his men to see to the enemy wounded. They found Bors the elder hunched over with a sword through his chest, and blood pooling around him.

Hall walked over and knelt beside his oldest friend. "See to your men, son. I will ready him to be moved."

"Yes, father," Drysten replied through watery eyes. Bors was always extremely hard to like, but in a strange way, he was also widely known to be a good soul who watched over those he cared for. Drysten knew his presence would be missed.

Drysten walked around the hillside, hoping not to find any of his men in the piles of the dead. To his relief, there were no corpses of any real familiarity to him, only strangers whose names he had never learned. It seemed odd to him that a man who had no real association to him would have died for his cause.

"What purpose does all of this serve for these men?" he wondered aloud. "Why would they feel content with dying for a foreign man's cause?"

"Because that is how all warriors go. This was simply their time," a voice said from behind Drysten. He turned to see Amiram and Cyrus, one of Hall's closest friends walking to join him. "The men here did not fight for you specifically. They simply wished to die in a way that would appease their ancestors."

"Did they?" Drysten asked sadly.

Cyrus shrugged. "That is not for the two of us to decide. Hopefully so."

Drysten looked back down toward the bodies, noticing the lone familiar face he could find. There was a man who had been freed from Servius' island, yet he had never learned his name. "He was a slave not long ago."

Cyrus walked up and glanced over the dead man's face, also noticing the "FVG" brand on his arm. "One of Servius' prisoners," he said quietly.

Other than that lone individual, it seemed his people had yet again gone against the odds. He returned to his father further up the hill, who had withdrawn the sword from his friend's body and wrapped it in a cloak.

CHAPTER XX

King Garbonian and Hall both ordered their men to load the wounded onto their newly procured wagons. Burials were done for the deceased in a rushed fashion by piling stones from the hill's summit over the corpses of those who had loved ones back home. These men were to be exhumed and brought back to their respective homes when the danger in retrieving them passed. Those who did not have any known loved ones were burned over pyres hastily constructed atop the hill. Bors the Younger was the last to leave the sight of the temporary graveyard, with Drysten and Diocles walking at his side.

"We'll come back for him," Drysten assured his friend as he placed a hand on his shoulder. "I *promise* you we will come back."

Bors glanced over and nodded. "It's my fault he died, Drysten. I was surrounded by three men when he rushed to help me. Killed one before he got stuck from behind. It was my fault."

Drysten shook his head, but Bors moved off toward the column of men marching Southeast before he could speak. As Bors walked away, Drysten glanced at Diocles, who was shaking his head as if to silently tell him to give the man space. The men rejoined the army at the front, receiving cheers from the Guayrdians as they quickly moved to join Hall.

"That bastard prince of Ebrauc took all our horses and killed Aosten," Hall said as Drysten walked up beside him.

"Cyrus told me. We cannot fight for those people any longer," Drysten put in.

Hall looked over and sadly shook his head. "They are not honorable men. I held out hope King Ceneus just produced a terrible son, but it seems he is also not worth our trust. If I had known the main reason he wanted the fort back was for the metals it held, I would have turned down his offer immediately."

King Garbonian snorted in amusement. "I'll have you know I was the favored brother for a reason."

Hall smiled. "In the short time I've known you, I can surely guess your father would be much more proud of *you* than Ceneus."

The king smiled warmly, then nodded to Drysten. "Speaking of fathers who should be proud, this one fought almost as well as me! I was surprised to see such animosity from somebody cultured by Romans. Your lot should consider coming North."

"I'm sure King Ceneus would love seeing his men defect to his brother's lands," Hall returned with a smile. Drysten noticed his father was reluctant to address how Drysten was recognized as being a fearsome warrior by a Pict, and wondered whether he was truly proud of him for his fighting ability.

The king erupted in laughter. "By the sound of it, you would appreciate the sight as well!"

Hall and Drysten smirked at one another as they continued. Dagonet was scouting ahead of the marching column and occasionally came back to report the appearance of stripped men hanging upside down from the surrounding trees. They were presumably deserters who were caught by the fleeing Picts as they raced back to the safety of either Segedunum's walls or their own villages further away.

A few of the Britons were attempting to remove one of their friends from a tree when Drysten watched Diocles briskly walk up beside them.

"Let all of them hang!" he directed in a disgusted tone.

The men glanced at one another before ceasing their attempt to cut their comrade free, and slowly fell back into the marching column. The presence of deserters was not surprising and most of the survivors of the battle agreed the cowards didn't deserve a proper burial. What was surprising was the appearance of a group of Northmen who met the same fate as the deserters from Hall's army. These were not Northmen of King Garbonian's Guayrdians who were easy to recognize by the distinctive hue of their blue paint as well as the ancient runes drawn on their bodies. Most men did not give it a second thought, but Drysten wearily glanced toward Diocles and Amiram, who both simply shrugged it off.

The bulk of the army soon marched beneath the trees where the corpses were dangling, not bothering to stop and cut them down. King Garbonian was proud that none of the men in that area were painted blue, as most were noticeably from Ebrauc's forces marching under Hall. There was one body which was recognized as being part of Prince Eidion's entourage, but no sign of his lord was found. All Hall did upon seeing them was shake his head and look forward.

"Cowards," Cyrus murmured to Drysten.

The army continued on until dusk, where they found a clearing they judged fit for a campsite. Some of King Garbonian's men had raced ahead of the supply train, so scouts were sent to lead them back to their encampment. In the meantime, fires were lit throughout the clearing, with distinctive groups at each one. The open area was surrounded on all sides by the bodies of the deserters, all hanging upside down from trees. Most were too tired to try and cut any down, while those who attempted to were quickly stopped by others who felt their resting place fit their display of cowardice.

The remaining men from Powys camped with Hall's troops, while the Northmen camped together on the other side of the fires. the king was amused by the two distinctive groups that could be seen eyeing each other in suspicion, but no fights broke out between them. Drysten roamed through both groups, getting strange looks from the Britons and cheers from the Guayrdians before finally making his way to the Powysians.

"Lord," a voice called to Drysten.

Drysten turned around and saw a man of about the same age walking up to him. "Yes?" he said.

The man extended his hand. "I am Prince Ambrosius Aurelianus, of Powys. I understand you're the one to thank for the rescue."

Drysten shook his hand. "That would be me, Lord Prince, though it could be argued the good king of Bryneich is truly responsible."

"You fight well. There's a brutal sort of efficiency with you," the Prince complimented.

Drysten smiled and nodded in thanks. "You mustn't fight too bad yourself considering how many men you were up against. It's too bad that other prince I was told about doesn't fight like you. I doubt you would have had much of a need of me."

The prince smiled. "He is not cut from the same cloth as you and I, or your father for that matter." The Prince's eyes turned sad. "I apologize about Bors. I rather liked him, though I must admit he was... an acquired taste."

Drysten hung his head. "I wish I had arrived sooner. His presence will be missed by many."

The Prince was about to respond until angered jeering was heard from the Southern portion of the camp. He turned to look in the direction the commotion was coming from. "I suppose we should take a look."

Drysten nodded, and the two men slowly made their way toward the Southern end of the camp where they began to hear murmurs of prisoners. The two made their way to a group of men from both armies standing in a circle. As they arrived, Hall noticed his son and waved him over.

"Your scout found this one spying on our camp," Hall explained.

Drysten looked at the man with the blue paint covering his face and chest. He was nude, save for a scrap of leather wrapped around his waist. "Matthew!" he called.

After a moment, the priest walked over with a haunch of meat in one hand, most likely from an animal unlucky enough to wander too close to the camp. "Lord?"

"Ask this man what his name is," Drysten commanded.

Matthew spoke something in the man's native language, prompting a response. "He said his name is Muir."

"Where is he from?" Drysten asked once more.

Matthew again asked the man for an answer, then turned to translate. "He is from a village on the Western coast of the Pictish lands. He was paid to fight for a warlord named Drust to take Segedunum as part of something more."

Hall raised an eyebrow. "Something more?"

Matthew spoke to the man, who begrudgingly looked from side to side as if to consider the weight of his answer before he finally spoke. "He said he was to lead an army away from a large city to open it up for attack. That is all he knows."

"This was a diversion," Drysten whispered.

Hall turned. "What has happened?"

"Londinium was sacked and I presume it's now being occupied by Saxons. My man Titus lost all but a few men right before they were going to relocate to Petuaria."

Hall scratched his chin. "Londinium is much too far to the South for a northern army to defend. What force could he possibly be speaking of?"

Matthew asked the prisoner, but received only a shrug. "He says he doesn't know, Lord."

"I gathered as much," Hall said with a smirk. He turned to King Garbonian, who was nonchalantly strolling up with his son. "Lord King, if you will permit me, I would like to send some of your scouts further ahead."

"How far South?" the king asked.

Hall gestured toward Segedunum. "To the fort. This man here spoke of a plan to draw an army away, presumably as some kind of distraction."

The king turned and instructed his son to find some men fit enough to scout the areas just north of the fort, then turned back to Hall. "If this is true, then I would assume my brother might have his hands full at the moment."

Drysten shook his head. "A great Saxon army now occupies Londinium. I am thinking they were originally intended to move on Ebrauc, though something must have changed."

"Ebrauc," the prisoner said through a thick accent. "Ebrauc."

Hall turned to Drysten. "We need to take this fort and hurry home."

Most of the men wanted to execute the prisoner considering the bodies hanging upside down above them. They thought it would be a just punishment for the cruelty their own people were showed, never mind the fact those very men had abandoned them. Hall was ultimately the one who decided to let the prisoner go the next morning, citing the fact he cooperated, and that one man would cause no true threat since he was cut off from his people. Now the plan was to wake before dawn and march on the fort, which they should reach by noon the next day.

Drysten bid his farewell to the Powysian prince and made his way to the Fortuna's men as they were readying themselves to retire for the evening. King Garbonian walked with him and Hall, thinking it amusing the Fortuna's men were the only ones comfortable enough with the Guayrdians to camp near them.

"I'm thinking the force Segedunum sent to the hill may have comprised a sizeable portion of their men," the king noted.

Drysten nodded. "That's what I'm hoping for."

Hall scratched his chin, grimacing upon finding a painful bump within his beard. "They most likely saw an opportunity to try and gut the only force they needed to be concerned with."

The three men agreed before ultimately deciding to leave the matter for the morning. They bid each other a good night as they entered separate tents, now available upon the arrival of the wagon train from Din Guayrdi. Drysten's tent was small, and made from what he guessed was linen overlaid by wolf fur on the top. He threw himself down to the grassy ground as he began to unclasp his father's cloak, his sword belt, and then his armor, before he finally had a chance to rest.

"*Blood,*" the voice whispered.

Drysten slept poorly that night. He was drifting between being awake and asleep, all the while the memory of the day he came back from the forests near Burdigala was playing through his mind. Drysten tossed and turned on the ground of the tent, dreaming the painful memory under the bodies hanging in the trees above the encampment.

"What did you do?" a heavily armed and blood covered Hall had said quietly upon his son's return. "Where did you run off to with two dozen men I needed *here?*"

Drysten glanced to his side, seeing Amiram stand quietly in the corner of the room as he watched Hall question his son. They had taken a small group of men in pursuit of a retreating enemy and deprived his father of guards which were sorely needed at home. Drysten knew the shame on his face was more than visible, as he felt as though you could smell it in the air. The three men stood in the lower level of the Roman amphitheater they had claimed as a refuge for survivors of the attack. The civilians were there under the guard of Hall's men while the last of the raiders were being routed from the city.

"Lord..." Amiram started, attempting to take some

blame off his younger friend. "The first group to retreat went deep into the forest…"

"And you took men away from the amphitheater, from the people we are trying to protect, so you could find them? Was it not enough they were no longer a present threat?" Hall interrupted.

Drysten briefly glanced into his father's eyes before again staring into the stone beneath his feet. "I did what I thought to be right."

Amiram took a step forward to speak again, but was immediately hushed by Hall when he abruptly turned and angrily pointed toward him. The sight of his commander in a fit of rage was enough to keep him quiet no matter how much he wished to take some of the blame from his young friend. He slumped back toward the wall, failing to utter one of the last words he would ever be able to.

Drysten briefly lifted his gaze to his father's. "I thought it was the correct—"

"You did *nothing* correctly!" Hall responded angrily. "Do you even understand who we lost because you decided to leave half our fucking people unprotected?"

"I… What?" Drysten stammered.

Hall stepped closer to his son. "You look ashamed," he said as he took an uncomfortably long look into his son's eyes. "You should."

Drysten turned his head to try and hide the fact his eyes were welling up. "How many were lost?"

"About a dozen, though Isolde's family would most likely be the only three you care about," Hall responded harshly.

Drysten's eyes widened as he stared into his father's face. "Where is she?"

Hall scowled as he turned away in disgust. "Your plaything is fine. Her parents and brother were buried yesterday. The man who caused their deaths due to his feeling of inadequacy didn't even have the decency to be present for the funeral."

"That's enough, Hall!" Amiram blurted out.

Hall slowly turned toward his most trusted soldier, anger radiating from him. "You believe I am being too hard on my son?" he growled. It was obvious to Drysten his friend sorely wanted to leave the room, as he stutter-stepped back another pace before Hall spoke once more. "My closest friend is dead along with his wife and boy. My own son is the cause of this, and you think *I* am being too hard on *him?*"

Amiram's mouth slowly opened and closed a few times before he was able to create any semblance of speech. "Hall, I... he ordered us to chase them on the advice of another. He told us they had prisoners."

Hall glanced at his son, who still did not have the courage to meet his gaze before he looked back to Amiram. "Who told him this?" He inquired in a lighter tone. Drysten glanced toward his friend out of the corner of his eye.

"An old man on the outskirts of the town. He was badly beaten by the invaders and begged us to find his family," Amiram said quietly. "We failed."

Hall glanced back toward his teary-eyed son. "Is this true, son?"

Drysten looked on his father and finally spoke once he noticed his anger had faded. "Yes, father."

There was a long pause as Hall stared into his son's face. He was noticeably perplexed by the realization his son was following a stranger's instructions, but Drysten guessed it must have made more sense to him than the idea of gods ushering him forth.

"Then you did what you felt was needed to protect your people. There are certainly many still missing at the hands of the raiders," Hall responded softly. He closed his eyes for a moment to further release the tension from his body, noticeably becoming more relaxed to the other two men in the room. "You are all of fifteen. I suppose it is my own fault you did not understand how to weigh this situation correctly.

Use this as a lesson, son. Never doom a large group to save a small one, no matter... *who* wishes it." Hall then turned to walk toward the door while out of the sight of his father, Drysten gave his older friend a nod of thanks.

Amiram slowly walked toward his friend. "We should never speak of this after today. We did a terrible thing, Drysten."

Drysten nodded shamefully at the truth of the matter. He abandoned his people to pursue the idea of avenging those who could no longer be saved. What would disturb people more, was he did so based on the commands from a voice which nobody else could hear. "Isolde's family..."

"We can do nothing more for them now," Amiram said quietly. Drysten slowly turned to walk toward the door when he was halted by Amiram. "You have an obligation to watch out for that girl now. You *know* that don't you?"

Drysten nodded. "I do."

"Your life now belongs to her. This mistake we made cost her *everything*. You must be the very same thing she just lost by our error."

Drysten nodded. In truth, he loved Isolde more than anything, even if he only now realized it for himself.

Amiram patted him on the back, and the two followed after Hall.

When Drysten awoke from his night of sporadic sleep, the men were beginning to ready themselves for their march South. They had covered more ground than they intended the night before, and the scouts sent out the previous night returned to explain they would arrive at the gates of the fort well before noon of the following day. Drysten donned his gambeson and armor and before walking out of the tent, instructing two men to disassemble it for the journey South. He made his way to the head of the marching column where he found his father, Matthew, Dagonet, King Garbonian, and Prince Ambrosius.

"Have a pleasant night, Lord?" Matthew asked cheerfully. The priest dabbed a hand to the fading blue paint on his face.

Drysten rubbed the noticeable bags under his eyes. "Sleep does not come easy to some."

"Bad dream?" Dagonet inquired as he gnawed on the cooked leg of a small animal.

Drysten turned and nodded before glancing toward his father, who most likely understood his son's sleepless nights. Without going into too many specifics, Drysten had spoken to his father on multiple occasions concerning the contents of his dreams. What was more frustrating to Drysten was the fact that the only time he dreamed was when he had nightmares or flashbacks from Burdigala. In every single one, the massacre in the forests and the following discussion with his father was always a repeated theme.

The men silently waited until the supply train was ready to move off, eventually meeting up with the Roman road running through Segedunum. The Romans had only built one road running through the area north of the wall, but there were many paths built before they had ventured to the islands. The old roads were built by the ancestors of the Britons and Picts in the ancient days and were used ever since, well before the Romans had ever discovered the islands.

The army at their backs numbered about five hundred men after a handful were sent back to care for the wounded. They guessed the numbers would be enough when Dagonet found tracks that strayed in many different directions. This led them to believe that even if some of the enemy forces fled back to Segedunum then their numbers would have dwindled.

The following day was uneventful. Drysten led for most of the day before falling back to speak with Prince Ambrosius. Hall and King Garbonian led for the remainder of the day, as Drysten was detailing the last few months of his life to his new acquaintance.

"You truly stole everything?" the Prince asked, referencing his voyage to Frisia.

Drysten thought for a moment. "Likely not, but I would be surprised if we missed much."

The Prince glanced at the strange mix of men behind him. "Bad enough we worry about people already *on* the islands; I would hate to worry about a slaver as well. You did a good thing in killing that man."

Drysten quickly glanced at Amiram walking behind him. "I had an obligation to do so."

"We all do to the ones we care for," the prince agreed.

The two walked on, with the army soon stopping at dusk to once again make camp. Unsettling dreams would not be induced like they had in the previous night, as there were no lifeless bodies hanging above them. Drysten learned these nightmares had plagued many of the men in the army, with most not able to get any more sleep than Drysten.

Bors the Younger was still trying to take time to himself, but found it difficult due to the sympathetic eyes of his friends watching to make sure he was near. Nobody wanted to disturb the man. They just wanted to stay near him and provide what silent support they could. After some time, the king walked over and handed him a large skin which Bors assumed contained water or wine.

After taking the skin, the king patted Bors on the back and spoke softly. "Take it, my boy. I remember what it was like to lose my father. Still haunts me to this day."

Drysten watched from beside a campfire as Bors slowly removed the container's cork and sipped the contents. He instantly made a face indicating a pleasant surprise before looking up to the smiling king.

"Is that mead?" Bors asked happily.

"Keep it, my boy. We had a slave who knew how to make it. No shortage of it in Din Guayrdi." The King nodded and shuffled back to his tent beside Drysten's. "Seems a good man, that one. Shame to watch a good man brood by himself."

Drysten nodded. "Thank you. I think you may have slightly eased his pain."

The King shrugged. "Eased maybe, but that pain never leaves you. The loss of a father is hard, not as bad as a loving mother, but still hard."

"I lost my mother in my early years. I still think about her every day," Drysten said quietly. "I just wish I could remember her face."

The King looked over to Drysten and silently nodded upon seeing how intently Drysten was staring into the fire, focusing on trying to recall his mother's face. But for all his effort, all he could remember was her black hair and short stature. The two sat in silence for some time until they each decided to retire for the evening.

Hall and Dagonet had finished walking the perimeter of the camp, all the meanwhile Dagonet was detailing both the voyage to Frisia and the voyage to Din Guayrdi. "Your boy is still inexperienced, but I believe he will be a great commander. Certainly better than anyone Ebrauc had before your arrival."

Hall nodded. "I hoped as much. Always had a good head on his shoulders, but he inherited his mother's temper."

Dagonet snickered. "She must have been dangerous if he's anything like her."

"His strength, mixed with her temper will spell ruin for him if he is not cautious," Hall replied, "I only hope he never forgets to think before he acts."

"There are always mistakes at the start. Whatever mistakes your son has made led to the man you see before you. I would almost be thankful for them," Dagonet replied.

"He conducted himself well?" Hall inquired.

Dagonet nodded approvingly. "In every way. He showed mercy when it was needed and cruelty when it was required, but no more than the situations necessitated."

Hall nodded as though he wished to ask more of his son's scout, but decided against it. The two completed their examination of the outer areas of the camp before they went their separate ways to get some much-needed rest. King Garbonian was kind enough to let the Fortuna's crew get a full night's sleep, and put his own men around all sides of the camp, taking both first and second watch. The crew awoke the next morning and joined the men of Din Guayrdi in readying themselves for the battle to retake Segedunum. Bors the Younger returned the empty container of mead to the King, who laughed and patted the boy on the back before moving to organize his troops.

Hall and Amiram were speaking with Dagonet and Gawain about how best to approach the fortress, and Drysten and Diocles were speaking with Cyrus, Elias, and Heraclius about their options for employment upon the completion of their current task.

"Best to fight for Rome. They pay well," Heraclius began.

Elias shook his head. "No, they don't. They cannot pay their own people, let alone auxiliaries. Besides, Rome will be a corpse soon enough."

"Too many weak emperors," agreed Drysten.

Diocles nodded. "Honorius should have handed off the throne to Stilicho, but instead he decided to behead him. Did you ever hear how he had a favorite chicken? A favorite *fucking* chicken!"

Drysten raised an eyebrow. "The boy was a simpleton?"

"He's right," Cyrus stated, "he named the thing after a city that was sacked by barbarians."

Drysten chuckled. "Did he name it Rome then?"

Diocles snickered at the exchange. "Mars would be shitting himself if he could see what Rome has turned into," referring to the old Roman god of war. "The capital of the Roman Empire isn't even in fucking Rome anymore!"

"Nor do they welcome the old gods. Everyone in the empire is forced to worship the one from the East," Heraclius put in.

The men mostly agreed Rome would not be the best choice for employment, but were forced to table the discussion. The army was on the move and Segedunum was only a few short hours away. The march went through sparse woodlands before the men finally reached the road Hall was searching for. He did not know what the Romans had named it, but knew it ran directly through the lands toward Segedunum. It was not paved and had no markers, but the dirt was packed down hard enough to make it more than firm enough to hasten their movement.

The men from Din Guayrdi were setting an impressive pace, one which the Britons were occasionally struggling to meet. Jeers were coming from the blue faces, though not many men could understand them. The King eventually turned and quieted his people before he instructed them to slow for their less conditioned allies.

"Running is what they do. Few horses up in these parts, so even the women are used to having to run long distances," the king explained.

Drysten turned to respond but was interrupted by the sound of a man expelling his breakfast, then turned to see Amiram white in the face and hunched over. Upon finishing, the mute stood up and burped, then turned to keep pace.

"Your man there seems like he could use a break," King Garbonian observed.

Drysten nodded. "Soon, but he can go a bit longer."

The men continued until the edge of the woodland. Off in the distance, there could be seen columns of smoke towering up into the sky. The men knew they would soon reach the fortress and decided this would be the last break they would indulge themselves until the battle was completed.

No fires were erected through the camp, as men would only be resting for a short time. Hall ordered for the wagons to remain there and for a small guard to be placed over the area. After about a half hour of rest, the army rose and continued through the green fields and over the rolling hills. Drysten was struck by how beautiful this area was. During his early days growing up in front of Eboracum, he was always told of a harsh landscape with barbaric peoples reigning over the lands to the North. Now that Drysten was here, he saw how that description could not be further from the truth.

"Never been this far North?" King Garbonian asked Drysten, who shook his head as he stared out across the green hills. "It certainly has its own beauty, though it is most certainly just as dangerous. I suppose that may be even more true for the Romans considering they tried to claim it all."

"Nearly succeeded from what I was told," Drysten replied.

The King chuckled. "Not nearly as close as you would think. Further North there is a second wall built for the same purpose as the one we will see here. A wall of mainly dirt, from what I saw. The Romans could barely manage to keep it for more than a few decades due to constant war being brought against them. Now it only serves as a border-marker for kingdoms further North. The ones whose names *I* can't even pronounce."

"Not much different than this one then," Drysten said as he gestured in the direction of Hadrian's Wall.

"Quite right," the king said as he walked past Drysten to speak with Hall. "Your boy is a good fighter, but I would recommend you or I to lead the attack."

Hall turned and nodded in agreement. "He will lead men into his share of conflicts, of that I have no doubt."

"So which one of us will lead the army now? "I have the numbers, though your people are better armed and more suited for attacking a fortification," the king inquired.

Hall nodded once more. "You will be leading your men to the Northwestern gate, and I will lead mine to Northeastern entrance once the occupants believe you to be the extent of our numbers."

The king raised an eyebrow. "You wish to divide us?"

"I do. They sent out a sizeable force to fight us in the north. By my estimation, they would not have near enough the number of men required to man two sides of the ramparts," Hall explained. "We will attack one side to draw their forces there, then hammer the less defended side once they make their mistake."

The King thought for a moment, then nodded. "Makes sense to me. So long as I get the payment I was promised, I care not."

Hall smiled. "The iron and silver inside are yours," Hall assured him as he held out his hand for the king to shake. The deal was made, and he turned back to face the direction they would find the fort.

"Wonderful!" the king clapped his hands together and gestured for the army to march. "Ah, the things I will build for my people with this..."

It only took the men about two more hours of marching at a more leisurely pace before they were in sight of the fortifications. The stone walls were being lightly manned by groups of tribesmen from the area to the Northwest. The King was the only one who knew this for certain, as he had seen many different styles of the blue paint used in the different tribes of Caledonia. Hall explained the plan to the Fortuna's crew and the Powysians, then the force was split to make their way to their respective sides for the attack to begin. Thankfully, there were enough trees to conceal their movements as they were still about a half mile away.

Drysten led the force comprised of Britons through the trees as they drew closer to their target. The Northeastern gatehouse had a makeshift barricade built from the broken remains of the first gate the invaders had destroyed upon taking the fort. Dagonet led a small group of scouts closer to gain a better look. Upon their return, he detailed the strength and placement of the enemy.

"I saw about twelve men stacking bodies outside the gate, looked like men who had succumbed to fresh wounds or possible sickness," Dagonet began.

"Saw forty or so moving between the gate and the wall," Gawain put in.

Hall stood and turned to Drysten. "What would *you* do?"

Drysten turned, now noticing the attention from the Prince, the scouts, and his father. "Me?"

"You seem to have garnered quite a bit of faith in the men you lead. I'm simply curious how well that new faith has been placed." Hall nodded with a smile. "How would you approach this?"

Drysten scoffed and glanced to Ambrosius before looking back to his father. "Well, considering the state of the Northeast entrance, I would wait until nightfall and storm it. In the meantime, I would line the men up just behind the tree line to prevent any messengers from coming or going," Drysten suggested. "Your plan would have been the only way forward if both of the entrances were intact. *This* way, we may not lose as many men before we even get *inside* the fort."

Hall beamed as he looked to Prince Aurelianus and nodded. "My thoughts exactly. I'm glad my son has enough sense to use his eyes."

"Agreed," the prince responded. "I'll give the order."

Hall looked back to his son. "Did you hear the conversation I had with the prince before you walked up?"

Drysten shook his head.

"That was the same plan we devised upon news of the gate," Hall proudly added. "To the letter. Well done."

Drysten nodded happily. "Thank you, father."

Dagonet and Matthew informed the king of their plan to attack at night, then returned with his blessing. It was decided they would wait unless they were discovered, in which case they would attack as soon as needed. No fires were to be lit to keep their presence unnoticed.

Drysten was somewhat surprised the men from Din Guayrdi hadn't already tried to attack the fort before his arrival. They seemed bloodthirsty and ready for war at any moment, and there could be much to gain from taking old Roman fortifications. In a way, it made them even more intimidating considering the fact they were not only fearsome, but disciplined. The Britons were mostly quiet, occasionally betraying a whisper or sneeze, but the day drew on without much noise. Drysten was just about to doze off under the shade of a tree, when Diocles and Heraclius briskly walked over.

"Drysten!" Diocles whispered. "Men approaching from the East, walking along the riverbank."

Drysten rose. "Does my father know?"

"He does. He's sending Amiram with a small group to intercept them. You're to lead," Diocles informed him.

Drysten nodded and rose from behind the tree, then crept toward the Eastern tree line near the bank. Amiram was there waiting for him with a dozen Powysians and a dozen of the Fortuna's men. Drysten nodded as he approached and looked to the bank.

Drysten's eyes widened as he counted a hundred more men they would be facing. "We need to kill them now before they get too close to the fort," he declared as he spied the men marching toward Segedunum. "And tell my father our force will need to deal with this now. The king must attack if the men in the fort rush out to help them."

Diocles nodded, then gestured for Heraclius to send word to Hall before turning back. "We have no choice; we have to attack them before they reach the fort."

Drysten nodded. "Wait. They don't appear to be Picts," Drysten looked closer. The men he was surveying were very heavily armed, brandishing round shields with beasts not known to the men in this part of the world.

"That's because they're mostly Frisian," a familiar voice said from behind him.

Drysten quickly turned, clearly placing the voice which had crept up behind him. "You?" he said in disbelief.

Because there stood Jorrit.

CHAPTER XXI

Jorrit stood in the center of Londinium's bridge, quietly staring out over the waves. His hands were still sticky with blood from the dozen or so Britons who felt they could best him as they tried to defend their homes. The smoke from the fires choked at his lungs in a way he had never experienced, but such was the life of a raider. The whole of the city was burning, from the old Roman baths to the homes now vacant. He had seen many raids in his time with the Saxons, but never an invasion. It startled him to watch as defenseless Britons were savagely cut down all around him. He understood he had participated in the fighting, but also knew he did not harbor hate or resentment toward the Britons like other Frisians or the Saxons who led them.

After the raid, many prisoners were taken, with all the males being executed immediately. Men could revolt and cause discord in their homelands, but their wives and children could not, giving them value and more security in their investment. The port where he had docked with Drysten's crew was now being used as a slave market, with naked women and crying children being paraded up and down in front of watchful eyes.

Jorrit witnessed a child and her mother split after being purchased by separate chieftains. To his horror, the child was struck hard by her new master as a test of strength, quickly sending her down to the dirt. The girl laid still for long enough to make Jorrit question whether she was even alive, but to his relief, she finally rose, wailing at the realization the only people she knew in life were now gone forever.

I may be their enemy, but I will never be cruel to them in these ways, he thought to himself as he held Lanzo's hand tighter.

His son was mostly oblivious to the goings-on around him, and preferred to watch the seagulls fly overhead, occasionally pulling his father's hand and pointing up into the sky to show him.

"I know, son. I always enjoyed the birds as well," Jorrit stated with a smile. Lanzo smiled back as he watched a seagull float closer to Jorrit, and spread his arms out wide as if they were wings. Jorrit ruffled his son's hair as he turned back to the burning corpses and buildings of Londinium.

The invasion was a complete success, as the only sources of resistance were a group of Romanized Britons fighting in the forum and Titus' men near what Jorrit presumed was his villa. Titus himself was seen sailing toward the entrance to the sea earlier that morning, with a boat almost overflowing with women and children, but few men to speak of. Jorrit guessed the man assumed all his men were killed in the attack, but, in reality a lucky few were spared when they surrendered. Jorrit had not been there to see it, but heard from Colgrin that they fought too well to be executed. He planned to entice them into fighting for him instead of facing their deaths as prisoners, something Jorrit knew to be a fanciful thought.

Jorrit lightly tugged Lanzo's hand toward the Southern end of the bridge to spy the scene of the battle for himself. The boy followed obediently as they walked, weaving out of the way of men carrying their plunder back to their ships on the Northern bank of the river. Some walked by with baskets of food, some with precious metals, and some were parading around their newfound slaves. Jorrit cared little for such things. All he wanted was to take his payment and find a home in which he could raise his son.

"Ah! There he his!" a familiar voice said as he reached the end of the bridge. "You certainly were not wrong about this place. Good fields, good walls, and most of all, good women!"

"I am happy to have helped, Colgrin," Jorrit replied as he gripped his son's hand a little tighter.

Colgrin pushed a naked and terrified woman off his lap before he walked over to Jorrit. "Oh, help you did, brother. This will prove to be a wonderful choice for our new kingdom."

"So long as I am paid, I care not what is done to this place," Jorrit replied.

Colgrin laughed. "Ha! Of course you will be paid! You are the architect of the Briton's destruction after all. The one who made this possible."

Jorrit felt a pang of guilt ring through his body. He had grown to dislike Colgrin more and more the longer he was around him. The only reason he guessed he was still there was because he would have been killed had Colgrin's attack failed. "What will you do now?"

Colgrin gestured around him. "Rule!"

"You wish to be a king?" Jorrit inquired.

Colgrin nodded. "Is it not obvious? I crossed the water to be a king, not to serve chieftains such as yours any longer."

Jorrit nodded. "Well, I suppose that is certainly understandable."

"So you do not like your chief?" Colgrin asked in an amused tone.

Jorrit shook his head. "I believe him to be incompetent. I have my own aspirations for my home that do not entail serving him."

"Well, you will not be serving him any longer!" Colgrin responded with a laugh. Before Jorrit could ask him his meaning behind that statement, he abruptly turned and walked back toward the table at which he left his woman and grabbed up two cups of ale. "Your chief, if he was ever worthy of the title, is dead."

Jorrit stood there dumbstruck. "By whose hand?"

"Once we left the old bastard by himself, that Marhaus fellow went and killed him for me! Burned the village and everything in it!" Colgrin laughed as he spoke.

Jorrit's heart sank down to his stomach. He hadn't meant to, but he gripped Lanzo's hand too tightly once he heard the news, causing him to squirm. He noticed and instantly apologized to his son before looking back to Colgrin. "Why was that done?"

"Because he fulfilled his use to us," he replied matter of factly. "He was a useless old fool on an island with no more worth to *you* than *me*. You cannot tell me you will miss the man, though I admit the slaver's *total* destruction of your village was more than I had originally ordered."

"I won't miss him, but I did not believe it necessary to kill him. I could have simply taken the role of chief without bloodshed. I had more than enough supporters for it," Jorrit replied coldly.

Colgrin's smile faded as he put his mug down. "You believe yourself important enough to question me?" he asked harshly.

"I do not question you; I simply fail to understand the need for him to die," Jorrit responded. "They were my people, Colgrin..."

Colgrin scoffed and threw his hands in the air. "Gah! Such small-minded people I am surrounded by." He then turned and began to utter something under his breath, making Jorrit uncomfortable before the Saxon turned back to face him. "He *had* to die!" he screamed as he waved his arms through the air. "People fight harder if they don't have a home to go back to!"

Jorrit slowly nudged Lanzo to move him behind his leg. "You think these men will follow you if they have no choice?"

Colgrin's eyes lit up. "See! You *do* understand!" He quickly stepped toward Jorrit, who moved back a pace until he was abruptly met face to face with Colgrin. "I am ushering in a new future for our people! There will have to be sacrifices along the way, many sacrifices. But what I aim to bring this land will last centuries, Jorrit. Centuries!"

"And how many of your own have to die before your dream becomes a reality?" Jorrit responded softly.

Colgrin's maddened eyes were beaming as he stared up toward the sky. The dusk began to settle in over a newly conquered Londinium, eerily illuminating the pillars of smoke rising throughout the city. "Their lives will be given to a higher purpose. The numbers do not matter. How many soldiers died for Rome to conquer most of this world? How many men did they lose and butcher on their way to greatness? Nobody ever remembers them, Jorrit. But they will always remember the one who leads them." Colgrin slowly gazed around at the faint stars poking through the Eastern sky, seeing something in them that Jorrit couldn't. The silence from Colgrin was almost more unsettling than when the man spoke, as Jorrit had no way of knowing what the crazed brute would do next.

Jorrit stepped back, nudging Lanzo as he moved. "Your dreams are certainly grand. Though I wonder what my purpose for being here is now that my job is finished."

"You are a skilled boat builder. Your services will always be needed in my lands," Colgrin assured him.

Jorrit raised an eyebrow at the strange comment. "Then, I require labor to make certain my skills are put to use. I think it would be fitting if you granted me the prisoners taken from the battle on this side of the river."

Colgrin paused, scratching his chin as he considered the idea. "I suppose that would be fitting, though I did have my own plans for them. They are familiar with you from what I am told. If there was a man here to convince them to fight for me, then that someone may indeed be you."

Jorrit deceptively nodded. "My thoughts exactly. How many do they number?"

"Fifteen from what I am told," Colgrin responded.

"Then I will be expecting them tomorrow morning. We have much work to do if I am to be building another fleet," Jorrit quickly stated as he turned to walk back over the bridge. Colgrin did not speak to him as he left, only laughing to himself as Jorrit moved slowly away toward the Northern bank of Londinium.

Fantastic, he thought to himself, *I serve a deranged madman.*

He and Lanzo moved through more men rushing around to claim their plunder, undisturbed by busy men and the crying women being dragged behind them at the end of long ropes.

I need out of this fucking city.

His ship was now docked in the same spot the Fortuna had once sat upon Jorrit's first visit to the city. He approached the vessel through the temporary slave market, subtly calling to him the members of his crew who were sparsely located around the dock. With nowhere to go, he would not be attempting to leave, he just needed to speak with his crew to sort out a plan of action.

The men were mostly trying to take in as much ale as they possibly could on the night after a fight. Jorrit remembered those days well, but at this point in life, the only joy for him came from the idea of raising his son, the last gift his wife was ever able to give him. He looked down to his side at the boy, tired from a long day of walking and taking in the sights of the city brought to heel by Colgrin.

"We will not need to rest on the ship anymore, son," he said with a smile. Lanzo looked up at him and extended his arms, requesting for his father to carry him. Jorrit complied with a beaming smile.

"Such a kind man wrapped in such a *dangerous* skin," a woman said from behind him. Jorrit turned to see Colgrin's wife, Inka standing behind him with a smile. "I take it you spoke to my husband."

Jorrit nodded. "He explained how he murdered my people for his ambitions; how he intended to conquer this land and remake it in his image, and how any losses he incurs along the way will not hinder him."

Inka frowned. "Father *did* warn me about him, of that I am sure you remember."

Jorrit did remember. The marriage between Inka and Colgrin was to strengthen both of their tribes, but in the end, all it did was strengthen one and lead to the other's destruction.

"He wanted my people to build ships, man them, and then die for him," Jorrit said as the anger welled up inside him. "Your husband will be a plague on anyone he comes across. Once I lose my usefulness, he will surely kill me too."

"Of that I have no doubt. We are in the same position, you and I," Inka said as she stepped toward Jorrit. "Now that he has no need of our marriage, what do you think will happen to me once he finds another bride to grant him land and power?"

Jorrit paused. "He wouldn't dare harm you. You are too beloved to his people, as well as mine."

"You have no people, Jorrit. The only survivors from your village sailed under Colgrin's banner to Londinium. Your only people are here now," Inka said quietly. Jorrit turned toward his men, most of which were now eavesdropping on their conversation. Murmurs could be heard aboard the ship as men began to realize their homes were gone and families killed.

Jorrit turned back to Inka. "What would you do in my position? He is too powerful to stand against. He has too many men to try and kill him."

Inka stepped closer to Jorrit, glancing around to try and prevent anyone from overhearing her. "We leave. We leave and find others to come with us."

"There are none. He has members of the strongest tribes of Frisia, Northern Germania—"

"We fight with the Britons," Inka said, causing a stir among the men around them. "You already know some we could appeal to for sanctuary."

Jorrit turned to view the men who were listening. All but a few belonged to him, so their silence was assured. The few who did not belong to him were scarcely paying any attention to their conversation now that Inka was whispering. "We just raided one of their most populated cities. How do you think they would respond to my presence now?"

Inka shuffled her feet as she considered her next words. "You... would you take me with you?"

Jorrit shook his head. "All I can imagine happening is our people being killed and turned into slaves once we arrive. I am sorry, Inka."

Inka turned away in frustration. "You will see what he is truly capable of. You will build his ships and fight in his name, and then you will see." Inka turned and stormed off toward the forum of Londinium, the space where most of Colgrin's household guards had taken up residence.

Jorrit stood with his son in his arms, wondering if Inka's advice should be heeded. He now understood the kind of man Colgrin was. He showed himself to be ambitious, cruel, and insane. What he did not yet know was how far the man's reach extended. His first aspiration had been Eboracum, yet now he was further South and not yet a danger to those parts.

What if I did try to appeal to Hall? he thought, *Surely he would at least keep my son safe.* He stood there considering his next move and its consequences.

"Lord?" a voice said from behind him. Jorrit turned to face the man who walked down from his ship.

"What is it, Braxus?" Jorrit said as the burly, black-haired man with symbols all over his arms walked over.

"What happened to our homes?" Braxus asked in a worried tone.

Jorrit frowned as he looked on the nervous man in front

of him. "I don't know. Colgrin said they had been raided," he responded, not sure if he should tell the truth quite yet. "I will get more information when it becomes available."

Braxus' face turned white. "Our people are dead? There were no survivors?"

Jorrit shrugged. "I don't know, but I will soon find out. I promise you. Tell the others to always keep the ship ready to depart at a moment's notice," Jorrit commanded. Braxus nodded and hurried back to the ship to relay what he had been told. Both the news of the raid, and the order.

He probably thinks I will send them home, Jorrit thought with a guilty conscience. *I hope someday I will.*

He looked at Lanzo, still sleeping on his shoulder, then walked to the building directly across from the ship. It had been a Roman customs office in its heyday, but the building's old purpose did not interest him. The fact it had an upstairs dwelling with a lock on the door was the only thing he cared about. He slowly ascended the stairs, careful to prevent Lanzo from waking, then slowly opened the door. The inside was dark as the sun was almost completely down in the West, so he had to carefully maneuver through the scattered bits of broken table toward the crib he brought from Frisia. He carefully laid Lanzo down, then piled a small bundle of skins below for himself to rest on for the night.

I don't know what will happen, but I promise you I will always protect you, son, he thought as he looked to his son's crib from the floor below. *We will find our place in this new world of Colgrin's making, even if it is apart from it.*

At that, he slowly closed his eyes, and tried to sleep.

Lanzo stirred in the early hours of the morning, waking Jorrit to the smell of his filled trousers. This had been the routine they were living for the better part of two weeks, as Jorrit was still waiting for Colgrin to grant him the prisoners taken from Titus' people.

Wonderful, he thought to himself.

He rose from the floor beside his son's crib and carefully picked Lanzo up to be brought outside for cleaning. The smell was overwhelming for Jorrit, as he dry-heaved before walking outside into the fresh air.

"What the hell did I feed you to cause this?" he quietly whispered.

Two women who journeyed with the army knowingly laughed amongst themselves as he passed. One kindly stepped over, betraying a smile; as she offered to take care of the child, which Jorrit greatly appreciated.

He handed his son over along with one old Roman coin as thanks, then began shuffling toward his ship. The woman followed a short way, also surprised at the rankness of the young boy's filth. Jorrit chuckled to himself.

Definitely mine, he thought.

He walked across the narrow street toward his ship to find his crew speaking to a gangly man accompanied by his two guards.

"The bastard, Marhaus," Jorrit declared as he approached.

The man turned and scornfully looked over the Frisian. "I brought you the labor you were granted by Colgrin. The men from the other bank of the river."

Jorrit nodded as Marhaus gestured to the group of fifteen men on their knees aboard his vessel. "Then why are you still here?" he said in a cold voice.

"Watch that tone of yours, Frisian. I have no qualms making you into a slave. You seemed to enjoy it with the Britons, but I wonder how your boy would fare." Marhaus gestured toward the woman cleaning Lanzo by the bank of the river. He had gotten away from her and was running around, trailing excrement in a wide circle and laughing the whole while.

Jorrit calmly walked toward Marhaus. "If you threaten my boy, you will spend the rest of your days in the dark, wearing your eyes on a chain around your neck."

Marhaus cracked a half smile as he began to move away from the vessel. "Have a good day, *Lord*," he sarcastically replied.

Jorrit watched the man until he was safely away from both Lanzo and himself before turning to his crew. "Get everyone up and ready to leave. We go north within the hour," Jorrit called to Braxus. His second in command walked over with a leg of meat in his hand, offering a taste to Jorrit, who refused. "I need you to run an errand for me."

"That is?" Braxus asked.

Jorrit looked around to make sure the only men who could hear him were his own. "Find Inka, find her and tell her to bring her things to the ship."

Braxus adopted a confused expression. "We're taking her?"

Jorrit nodded. "We're taking her and the slaves we were given. If anyone asks, tell them we found more suitable wood for boat-building upriver, but say nothing of Inka's presence to anyone."

Braxus nodded and handed off the meat to the closest man. "I will be back shortly, Lord." He left with one other man from the crew, named Veqreq, then disappeared behind a crowd.

As Jorrit turned back to his ship, he caught a glimpse of Marhaus walking across the bridge, this time with more than the two guards he had a moment before. He was walking to the Southern side, so Jorrit did not feel threatened, but did take notice of the more significant numbers at his back and the fact he gestured in Jorrit's direction.

Time to leave, he thought to himself.

The woman who had taken care of his son walked over, gently tugging him along as she walked. Jorrit nodded in thanks and picked the boy up. "Certainly *smells* better!" he thankfully chirped to the woman.

"That he does, Lord," she replied before returning to her daily chores.

Jorrit carried Lanzo to the ship, setting him down on the stern and instructing one of his men to look after him for a short time. "I will be back soon," he said. The man nodded and placed Lanzo on his lap, then started playing with the young boy.

Jorrit turned to walk off the ship when, for a reason he could not understand, he glanced toward the bridge. At first, he saw the normal mix of slaves and women roaming across, but then he noticed small groups being pushed aside in favor of a bigger one. Marhaus and a large group of men were briskly walking back to the Northern bank and pointing at him once again.

"Get the oars ready!" Jorrit yelled. He turned back to the surprised men on the ship and made his way toward the prisoners. "Which one of you is in charge?"

The men all stared at each other, unsure if they should answer.

"I aim to *free* you! Now, which one of you is in charge?" he insisted.

"I am," announced a man with long brown hair tied up on the back of his head. He had a short beard of the same color and blue tribal markings over his left arm. "I am the highest ranking of our people."

Jorrit drew the knife at his side, causing the leader of the prisoners to nervously glance at the men to his left and right. Jorrit hurried over and cut the man's bonds. "What is your name?"

"Citrio Bardas," the man answered as he stood, rubbing his wrist where the binding had made the skin raw. "Exactly what do you aim to do with us?" he asked in confusion.

Jorrit glanced to his right, noticing most of the men under Marhaus' command were now all the way across the bridge. "I need to know where your people were going. If it is where I think, you will need to vouch for me in saying we freed you of our own will."

Citrio nodded, then looked at the rest of his men before

turning back to Jorrit. "No trouble from us, Lord."

Jorrit smiled and gave the man a pat on his shoulder when one of his crewmen walked over. "Lord, what exactly—?"

"It is not safe for our people here," Jorrit answered as he watched Braxus emerge from the crowd with Inka running behind him. "We must leave."

"I thought we had no home to go back to," the man said.

Jorrit turned back to face him. "We go North. I know of a people who may take us in, provided we serve them as we would Colgrin." The men aboard the ship began to protest until Braxus, Inka and Veqreq made it onto the vessel. Jorrit raised his hand to silence the crew and explain the situation. "Colgrin instructed the man coming to kill us to murder our people. It was his belief we would fight harder for him if we had no homes to return to. In his mind, we would be fighting to carve out our new place in the world he envisions for himself to rule over. I will not be a party to such lunacy. If any of you wish to leave, then do so. But my place is in the North, and I would caution you not to march for Colgrin, as he sees no value in any of our lives. We are simply tools or instruments to him. We will serve a purpose for the man, and when we outlive our purpose, he will cast us aside like animals. I will not allow that for my son, I will not allow that for any of you."

The men stood for a moment, silently coming to the understanding of what their current state was. Jorrit was relieved when the first few men began to move to their seats by the oars. One by one, every other man joined them, all mostly staying silent as they did so. Jorrit cautiously turned and handed his knife to Citrio. "Undo the binds on your people. Once we are free of this place, I will take us all North to Ebrauc."

"You're going to take us to Drysten's people?" Citrio asked in surprise.

Jorrit tuned to face the man. "I am. He may consider

taking my people in if I bring you with me. At least that is my hope. I do not know for certain. Either way, your people will be safe."

"That was where we were supposed to be moving to when you attacked us. Drysten had given our leader enough gold to convince the men and their families it was the best option," Citrio explained. "All of these men will have family in a place called Petuaria by now, that is if they were not stopped during their escape."

Jorrit nodded. "They made it through the ships we left at the mouth of the river. They were pursued upon leaving, but the two that chased them did not return. I would expect your people made it North."

Citrio smiled widely. "Then why are we still here?"

Jorrit turned to Inka, still breathing heavy from the long run from the forum, then turned to the men assembling about a hundred yards away from the boat.

"We go!" Jorrit commanded.

The ship's lines were cut, and men began to push oars into the dock to slowly heave the vessel into the river. As the ship began to move, Jorrit held onto the hammer amulet around his neck, then glanced behind him to see Marhaus giving a shifty and disconcerting smile.

"I will see you soon!" Marhaus shouted. "I hope you have a safe journey; I wouldn't want anything to happen to little Lanzo!" Jorrit gritted his teeth as the boat began to move further into the center of the river.

"Let him squawk," Inka said as she moved in beside him, grabbing his hand as she did so. "They have a powerful army, but even Colgrin does not yet have the strength to hold Londinium and attack Ebrauc simultaneously. If we make it, we will be safe for a time."

"I pray you are right," Jorrit responded. The ship began to gain speed as the oarsmen on both sides were now able to freely row their vessel down the river. After some time, the only indication the crew had of the presence of Londinium were the cooking fires set inside the city since the raid. The sun was high in the air and Jorrit, for the first time since leaving his village, felt like he was about to go home.

CHAPTER XXII

The two days of sailing North proved tiresome for Jorrit and his crew. There had been multiple scuffles between the men who were branded as slaves by Colgrin and Marhaus, and his own crew who had recently played a small role in sacking their home city of Londinium. Jorrit was pleased there were no deaths, though one man in the company of the Britons was struck hard enough by Braxus to knock him out for a few minutes. Thankfully, that was the worst of any argument and no blades had been drawn. He kept both groups of men isolated to different ends of the ship for most of the trip and that seemed to be enough to prevent further altercations.

"How long until we reach Petuaria?" Inka asked Jorrit.

Jorrit glanced around before answering. "We should be there by the end of the day."

Inka nodded. "Funny how we weren't chased upon leaving. I almost feel like Colgrin won't miss his dear wife."

"The Saxon ships are not as fast as ours. The Frisians made theirs of equal quality to mine, but they are all raiding into a kingdom called Cantia to Londinium's South. Even if they were to chase us, they would be dealing with a head start they could not overcome. As for Colgrin missing you, most men don't know what they've had until it's gone," Jorrit said with a smile, causing Inka to blush and look away.

The Frisian-made ship was certainly faster than any Saxon vessel, solely on account of the sleek design coupled with a sail. Many Saxon ships were not fixed with a sail and solely relied upon rowers to propel it forward. This was not uncommon, and the obvious reasoning behind Colgrin's desire to have Jorrit on his side to make him more vessels of Frisian style. If he had a fast-enough fleet, he could assail all sides of Britannia, then leave before real resistance showed up. Without a fast navy, that option would be taken away from him. Jorrit oversaw about twenty ships built for the fleet before he was instructed to leave on his errand, but a handful were lost to a storm, meaning most of Colgrin's fleet consisted of slower ships.

Jorrit sat next to Inka, occasionally glancing at her when she was not looking. She reminded him so much of his wife, it almost made him uncomfortable. The way she held his son was that of a mother, and the love she had for the child was strange to him until he figured out Colgrin had not let her raise their own children to prevent them from becoming soft. Jorrit could not imagine the feeling for a mother if she was not allowed to see her children. The very notion of it infuriated him. He wanted nothing more than to see how his wife would have loved their son. Now it seemed he was getting a similar picture of it with her sister. The feeling was slightly confusing, yet made him happy all the same.

"Lord," Citrio said as he shuffled toward Jorrit, "we should be there shortly. The mouth of the river is just around the coastline. I think it would be wise to discuss what you want me to tell the people we find there."

Jorrit nodded. "Well, to start, I wish for my people to be given asylum in Ebrauc."

"You realize it will not be easy to achieve that considering your people already waged war on the Britons there. Raiders from Frisia have been known to sail these shores for generations," Citrio cautioned. "There is a chance you will all be executed by the lord who rules here, regardless of your intentions."

Jorrit nodded. "I feel I can be persuasive enough to prevent that for my people. Myself on the other hand…"

Citrio awkwardly scanned from Jorrit to Lanzo. "I... I will do what I can, Lord. You have all our thanks for letting us go free. At the least, I promise you I will make sure your son is in good hands."

Jorrit politely nodded. "I thank you."

Citrio nodded. "The fact you set us free might go a long way with my commander. The king here is who I am more concerned with, considering he does reign supreme over these lands. If I were you, I would try and find another way to convince him other than the fact you freed my people."

"Do you have any ideas?" Jorrit asked, prompting a shrug from the former prisoner. "I hope I will be able to speak to Titus before I have to see the king. I rather like him, the king not so much."

"You have met the king already, Lord?" Citrio asked.

Jorrit sighed and nodded. "We have met once. When I was a prisoner."

"Do you always give people such a wonderful first impression?" Citrio said, prompting a mischievous smile from Jorrit. "Regardless of what happens, I swear I will do what I can. The fact you were our enemy does not change the fact we owe you."

Jorrit nodded. "You have my thanks."

Citrio nodded, then gave a "Lord," as he walked back to the bow of the ship with the rest of his men.

Jorrit sat with Inka and Lanzo a while longer before getting up to stand at the bow of the ship in preparation for his arrival to Petuaria.

I really hope Hall or Drysten is still here, he thought to himself.

He knew Titus was a good man, yet was not sure if he could trust a Roman. His experience with Romans always ended up with him getting tricked into either paying more money than intended, or receiving less than he was supposed to. Titus did seem different to him, but he still believed he would have to be cautious around a man of his descent.

The ship made its way into the mouth of the river where he had fought against Drysten and his crew not long before. As the ship sailed, he moved a hand to his still raw wound at his side where Drysten had stabbed him in a blind rage. The wound was nothing close to serious, but was still sore to the touch.

"It might be best if I did the talking at first, Lord," Citrio suggested. Jorrit turned and nodded as the smoke from the pottery kilns was seen rising above a tree line to the West.

Inka laid down Lanzo in a pile of furs for a nap before she made her way over. "Will they take us in?" she asked in an anxious tone.

Jorrit shrugged. "I would guess they'd like to have more men who can fight, and having one who can build effective boats would be beneficial as well, but I could not say for certain."

Inka turned and muttered a prayer to herself, but Jorrit could not hear who it was that she could be praying to. If he had to guess, it would most likely be Woden, but recently the Christian God had made its way to their homelands, so he was not sure.

The ship slowly drew on before rounding a bend in the river to see a dock off in the distance. Once their ship was visible to the people fishing and going about their daily routine, a horn sounded, and people began to run to their homes. Jorrit spied another Frisian made vessel at its dock and wondered if they too had been attacked by Colgrin's people, but decided it must be a trader just going about his business. This belief was further reinforced once he saw a shield wall beginning to form at the edge of the docks numbering about forty men in total.

"Hardly much of an army," Jorrit said to himself.

As they drew closer, he began to see the shield wall was almost totally made up of villagers wielding pitchforks or other farming tools, with the front row being the only line with shields and swords. Jorrit glanced to Citrio as he gestured toward the line of shields. "Recognize anyone yet?"

Citrio narrowed his eyes and scanned over the men lined up to oppose them. "I recognize the man in the center; the one walking in front of them giving orders. His name is Gaius. He's Titus' boy."

Jorrit turned to Citrio. "You do not see Titus anywhere?"

Citrio again strained his eyes, yet shook his head before turning back to Jorrit. "All I see are strangers aside from him. I thought Titus would be alive, his wound did not look fatal."

Jorrit cursed under his breath before turning to the rest of the crew. "Not a single man is to brandish a weapon or equip a shield! You will leave those on the floor of the ship and do nothing to cause an alarm. We are not here as conquerors." Jorrit turned back to Citrio and gave him a pat on the shoulder. "You will be the first ones off the ship."

Citrio nodded and informed the rest of his men what the plan was. They would step off the vessel, then Jorrit would accompany them to speak with their leader. Jorrit's own crew would either stay with the ship or follow any instructions given to them by the commander of the Britons. After a few short moments, the ship finally docked, and the men began to depart. At first, there were shouts and taunts from the shield wall, as they naturally assumed the foreigners were coming to raid, but the shouts soon died away upon the realization the first fifteen men to disembark were Titus' own who had been left behind in Londinium.

A shout to keep the line of the shield wall came from its commander in the center. Gaius then stepped forward and handed his shield off to one of the men behind him in case there would end up being a fight after all. He cautiously stepped forward to Citrio. "We thought you were all dead," he said in amazement.

Citrio hesitated as he watched the rest of his men leave the ship. "We... the man in command of that vessel brought us back. They seek asylum from the people who sacked Londinium."

Gaius glanced over to Jorrit, who calmly nodded upon meeting his gaze. "You're telling me *that* man set you free?"

Citrio nodded. "He did, Sir."

Gaius glanced back toward the shield wall before returning his gaze to Citrio. "Take the men inside. My father will speak to you there." Then glanced back to Jorrit. "I know you, do I not?"

Jorrit slowly stepped forward with his hands gently raised to prevent anyone seeing him as a threat. "I briefly sailed with your father a short time ago."

Gaius stepped toward him. "Who are you? Tell me your name," he commanded as he drew his blade.

Jorrit glanced behind him to make sure his men were following his instructions of being unarmed, then glanced back to Gaius. "I am Jorrit. You might have seen me waving to your father as you made your escape from Londinium. I... am sorry for the role I played in the city's attack."

Gaius' eyes narrowed in anger. "I knew I recognized you. You murdered my people, and now show yourself here?" he screamed, causing Jorrit to step back and slowly put his hands up higher to show he meant no harm. "You want me to let you live even though your people are all *murderers?*" Gaius began stepping toward the Frisian, causing Jorrit's men to slowly reach for their weapons.

Jorrit abruptly turned and pointed to his men. "No!" he commanded, causing them to look around anxiously. Jorrit turned back to Gaius. "We were enemies once. I do not wish for that anymore."

Gaius drew his blade back to swing it at Jorrit's neck before a voice rang out from the road leading to the market. "Stop!" it screamed. "Stop this now!"

Gaius turned to look behind him, then slowly lowered his weapon upon seeing his father limping forward with a crutch under his arm.

"Stop it, boy. We will hear him out."

Gaius slowly turned back to Jorrit and sneered as he put his sword back in its scabbard, then slowly walked back to the shield wall.

Jorrit felt a wave of relief wash over him as the familiar face hobbled his way toward him. He was unsure if he would be forced to defend himself from Titus' son, and thankfully he now knew he could deal with his father instead. "It's good to see you, old man," he said with an awkward smile, as Titus finally reached him.

Titus half-heartedly chuckled. "Old man? I'm sure I could take you in a fight if I could only shave off a half-dozen years."

Jorrit smiled and nodded. "I'm sure you could. I don't see Hall or Drysten anywhere," Jorrit said as he glanced around, "nor do I see any Frisians to be manning this vessel. What has happened?"

Titus sighed. "We fled here once your people attacked us—"

"Not my people," Jorrit interrupted. "I wish to have nothing to do with that murderer who attacked Londinium."

Titus' face adopted a perplexed look as he glanced around toward Jorrit's crew. "Fine, we fled here and were pursued by two ships all the way from Londinium. They attacked us once we arrived, and Drysten led a defense against them."

Jorrit nodded. "And the men aboard these vessels?"

"Dead mostly. The rest are under guard outside the village, while the leaders are in the same place I was told they kept you," Titus responded, "though I do not know what Drysten will do with them once he and his father return."

Jorrit nodded. "I suppose myself and my people will be joining them under that damn storage shed then."

Titus hesitated, then nodded. "Depending on what it is you have to say, then yes. Though I knew there were rumblings of Drysten wishing to retain you in his crew."

Jorrit had suspected Drysten and his men had taken a liking to him, but did not know it was enough to ask him to stay. "That is certainly welcome news. We came here to get away from Colgrin."

"Colgrin?" Titus asked.

Jorrit let out a sigh accompanied by a heavy nod. "He is the man who led the attack on Londinium. He murdered my people in Frisia to prevent us from returning home. Now, it would seem we have no home to go back to, and I was hoping Drysten or Hall would allow my people to settle here with them."

"Why would he do that?"

"It's what I was told he allowed for some of the more hostile tribes near his homeland. He kept some of them busy earning a wage instead of stealing from his people," Jorrit added with a shrug.

Titus chuckled. "Britons, Romans, men from Gaul, what's a few Frisians while we're at it. If it were up to me, I would be more than willing to replenish our ranks with you and your men, but alas it is not up to me. Drysten left for the North and Hall has been gone since you were last here. I suppose I am in charge to some capacity, though only until the king decides to leave the bathhouse in Eboracum. The man has shown himself to be... less than an ideal leader thus far."

"In what ways?" Jorrit asked.

"Not only did he send ill-equipped and undertrained men with Hall, he arrived here shortly after Drysten left to try and stop him. He spilled that he wanted a small amount of wealth that may still lay inside Segedunum, and was worried what Drysten would do with the knowledge."

Jorrit nodded. "So he wants it all for himself. How much is it?"

"I doubt it is little more than a few bars of iron and possibly a small amount of silver. I was briefly in charge of the men stationed in various forts along the wall and never heard of any sizeable caches to be looted. Certainly not enough to fund any kind of army the king may desire. He was also less than enthused when he heard I had pledged my service to Drysten instead of him. But what was I supposed to do? The boy took me in when I believed I had nothing left to offer."

"He's a good man," Jorrit said of Drysten. "His father raised him well. I found it hard to dislike him despite him stabbing me."

Titus smiled. "So you aren't here to kill him then?"

Jorrit quietly laughed. "Only if he tries to stab me again." He held up a finger. "*Once*, I can forgive."

Titus turned to his son. "Take this man's crew to the tavern across from the villa. I see no reason to treat them the same way as the Saxons who chased us." After turning back to Jorrit, he said "Keep your men in line until I can work out the best way to settle them here. I would prefer it if they did not leave the tavern, but if they feel the need to, I will have my son place them under guard as they roam the town. No weapons either until we sort everything out."

Jorrit was overcome with relief. "I truly appreciate this, Titus. My people had nowhere to go and I was not sure how much of a risk I was taking by bringing them here."

Titus smiled. "What's a few more mouths to feed?"

The two shook hands and the instructions were relayed to Jorrit's crew, who quietly complied and left their possessions aboard the ship before walking to the tavern under the guard of Gaius. Jorrit waited until the ship was fully disembarked before waving over Inka, carrying Lanzo in her arms.

Titus looked on Jorrit with a surprised look. "Your wife and boy?"

Jorrit shook his head. "The boy is my son Lanzo, but the woman is Colgrin's wife."

Titus was shocked at the news. "You kidnapped the man's wife?" he said in surprise. "And brought her *here?*"

"She believed she was in danger from him. I agreed and

told her she could come with me. She's my sister-in-law as a matter of fact," Jorrit responded.

"And you do not believe this Colgrin will come looking for her?" Titus asked.

Jorrit shook his head. "There was not much love in that marriage. He married her to secure ships and good craftsmen."

Titus sighed and gestured to the woman carrying the boy over. Inka walked over, but could not understand Titus, as she had no knowledge of Latin or the old Brythonic language. She just looked at Jorrit for help when Titus greeted her. "What's he trying to tell me?" she asked.

Jorrit chuckled. "Waving is normally the same in every language." To which Inka awkwardly smiled and nodded her head to Titus. "You can trust him," Jorrit assured her before looking to Titus, "I would appreciate it if she and my son could stay in the villa. I can stay with my men, but I would only trust my son in her care, and her in yours."

Titus nodded and waited for Jorrit to relay the request to Inka, who cautiously looked toward Titus and nodded.

"She will be cared for," Titus assured him. The four of them made their way to the villa, where Jorrit was greeted by the two Cretans he had sailed with under Drysten, each with a deer slung over their shoulders. They both looked at him in surprise before nodding as they passed Jorrit by.

"Told them to go South of the river and find some game. Not enough meat here at the moment," Titus said as they walked on.

The streets were filled with local tribesmen, cautiously eyeing Jorrit and Inka as they finally made it to the gates of the villa. "Never thought this would be a welcome sight after my first visit," Jorrit noted.

"What did you say?" Inka awkwardly asked.

Jorrit chuckled. "Nothing of importance," Jorrit responded.

"What did you say?" Titus then asked.

Jorrit sighed. "Nothing of importance. I really need to find a way to teach her the language the Britons speak," Jorrit replied as he gestured to Inka.

"Are you speaking of me?" Inka said in annoyance.

Jorrit chuckled. "I was saying I need to find someone who can teach you their language."

Titus noticed Inka's nod and was able to gather what was said, and smiled. "One crisis at a time, Jorrit."

Jorrit himself was granted a room inside the villa, right alongside where Drysten and his wife lived. As a precaution, Isolde slept with two guards outside her door due to the newcomer's presence. She somewhat trusted Jorrit considering the role he played in freeing her, yet still was uneasy about him given the mixed reports she received about his character. Inka also slept in the room with Jorrit, and Lanzo was laid to rest in a crib. The boy slept the whole night, even during the time Jorrit crept into the bed with Inka. He awoke with her resting on his chest, and carefully crept out from under the furs and into the cold morning air.

Jorrit was unsure why he awoke so early until he heard a loud heave and liquid splatter on the ground outside.

"What the fuck was that?" he whispered to himself.

He briefly checked Lanzo to make sure he was sound asleep, then covered Inka up before donning some clothes and walking outside. He was thankful he spent extra moments putting on his fur boots, as he immediately stepped in what he came to find was vomit.

"My apologies," a hunched over woman said from a bucket nearby. "I slipped on the way over and... missed."

Jorrit sighed as he carefully stepped around the remainder of the vomit. "I take it you are Isolde then?"

The woman heaved more contents into the bowl before turning. "What gave me away?"

Jorrit laughed as he walked closer. Isolde had attempted to draw away from him, but felt more vomit coming and again leaned over the bucket instead. "My wife told me the Romans once drank breast milk to cure the sickness accompanying pregnancy, though I don't think she ever tried it herself." Jorrit walked over and placed a hand on Isolde's shoulder as she wretched for the last time. "There is also some sort of fruit the Romans ate."

Isolde took a deep breath and sat on the ground. "Thank you for the advice," she said politely. It was clear she was still trying to draw away from him.

Jorrit stepped back and sat on a bench in between their two bedrooms. "How many months are you?"

"I think five," Isolde responded as she wiped her lips on the linen dress she had worn to bed.

"That was about the time the sickness got my wife the worst. She would wake up before the sun and vomit all over," Jorrit said with a laugh. "I do miss her."

Isolde glanced toward Jorrit's room. "That's not your wife?"

Jorrit shook his head. "Her sister."

Isolde's jaw dropped. "You left your—"

Jorrit interrupted her with a smile. "No, no, no. My wife died in childbirth with my boy, Lanzo. Her sister is the wife of the man we are attempting to run from."

Isolde chuckled. "I assumed that was your wife from all the noise I heard last night."

Jorrit's face began to turn red. "I... well... my apologies," he said awkwardly. The two of them laughed and spoke for a short while, until Isolde finally decided it was time for her to get cleaned up. As she stood, Inka walked out of the bedroom and politely smiled at her while walking around a small dog which scurried by her.

Isolde walked over to her. "I am sorry for what you are going through," she said softly.

Inka glanced at Jorrit. "What?"

Jorrit chuckled. "Just take her hand and say, 'thank you'." Inka did so, and Isolde made her way to the villa's baths, leaving Jorrit with Inka.

"She seems nice," Inka said as she watched Isolde walk away, "though she certainly smells funny." Jorrit chuckled and gestured toward the bucket on the ground next to Inka, who made a disgusted face and walked closer to Jorrit.

The two sat silently as the morning drew on. Jorrit was pleased to find his men had kept to their orders, and had not engaged in any altercations with the locals. This was of considerable worry for him, as many were still grieving the loss of their homes and families. Because of this, Jorrit could not gather whether that would make it more or less likely they would be susceptible to taunts and jeers.

"Frisian," a man said through an obviously distrustful tone, "my commander wishes to speak with you before the king arrives."

Jorrit kissed Inka once more, and followed the man outside to where Titus was speaking to a local farmer complaining about the quality of some horses. "They're malnourished and some don't even seem to have been broken properly. I have quite a job on my hands with this lot."

Titus sighed, but brightened once he saw Jorrit walk up. "Jorrit! Good morning," he said as he nodded to the man who brought him, signaling the farmer's job was done. "King Ceneus is on his way. Scouts reported him riding from the North about an hour ago. He should be here soon."

"I suppose I should play nice for the moment," Jorrit woefully answered. "I would rather just tell him I already pledged myself to Hall or Drysten."

Titus chuckled. "Believe it or not, I have a feeling we are about to have a similar conversation with him," prompting Jorrit to turn in surprise. "The king will undoubtedly hate the idea of a force so strong serving Drysten after he sailed away on bad terms with him."

"The king really dislikes the boy that much?" Jorrit inquired.

Titus nodded. "He believes him to be a threat."

Jorrit sighed. "Why are these things never simple?"

"Life is *never* simple anymore, Jorrit. Just do not get on the man's bad side like the one you are hoping to serve," Titus suggested.

Jorrit was not given much time to think of a way to address the king, as right when the two stopped talking, Ceneus came riding in from the North. He had a Christian priest as well as a dozen men around him, most likely his entourage, and held his head up high with an air of authority.

Titus limped over toward the king with Jorrit by his side. "Lord King Ceneus," he said with a half bow of the head, "a good day indeed when a king graces our presence."

King Ceneus politely nodded to Titus and turned his gaze to Jorrit. "I thought you would be back in Frisia, or dead," he said in surprise.

Jorrit politely bowed. "I was home for a brief time before coming back to Britannia."

"And what purpose did you have for returning?" King Ceneus asked.

Jorrit nervously glanced at Titus before looking back to the king. "I came back as an invader to the South, though I was forced to." Jorrit figured he could tell a half-truth without much consequence and decided to commit to his gamble. "The man who took Londinium threatened to kill my people if we did not join him. I later found out he killed them anyway, and now I am here to appeal to you, Lord King, for mercy."

King Ceneus raised an eyebrow in surprise. "You wish for me to let you stay here?"

Jorrit nodded. "I do, Lord King. Before Titus so generously let me journey home, he offered me an invitation to join the crew belonging to Drysten. At the time, I did not accept due to other obligations, yet now I seem to be without choice."

The king scoffed. "That damn *boy* is more trouble than he is worth. He comes into my home conducting himself as though he is a fucking Roman emperor and makes demands of me."

"He also saved your people here not two weeks ago," Titus shot back, drawing a glare from Ceneus. "Lord King," Titus finally added.

The king turned away in frustration to pace toward his guards, and listened to the priest whisper something toward him before he eventually turned back. "So what is it you ask of me then? Come out and say it."

Jorrit stammered at first before being saved by Titus. "He wishes to fight for me. He is a good warrior and a good man, regardless of how we first met. He is no enemy of yours or mine, Lord King."

King Ceneus paused for a moment. "No!" he finally stated. "You will not fight in my name unless you pledge yourself to me, and *only* me."

Jorrit gave Titus a worried look before turning his eyes back to King Ceneus. "I... I do not think I have a choice in this matter. Do I?"

The king shook his head. "No. You do not. Pledge yourself to me here, or leave under penalty of death. I do not look upon idlers fondly, so make your choice."

Jorrit peered around him. His men were brought there because they believed they would fight for a good man of honorable quality, if they were even to be asked to fight at all. However, now they all wondered about this new king and his questionable morals. Jorrit finally sighed deeply, then walked to the king and knelt. "I swear an oath to fight for you," he whispered.

"You what now?" the king said mockingly. "I could hardly hear you. Speak up."

Jorrit grimaced before looking the king in the eye. "I swear an oath to fight for you, Lord King," he repeated in a loud, clear voice.

The king smiled and gestured for him to stand. "Your first order of business will be to go North and help take

Segedunum and reclaim its contents. You will take what men you have, as well as the Saxon prisoners we have kept here under guard."

Jorrit gave the king a surprised look. "They will not fight for me, Lord King. They have no reason to."

The king smiled. "Threaten them, bribe them, lay with them, I do not care. But you *will* make them fight for you, Jorrit. I will give no men of my own, so make do with what you have here, Saxon."

"I am Frisian," Jorrit whispered.

The king leaned forward. "What was that. I do not believe I heard you?"

It will be done, my lord," Jorrit replied.

"As I thought," the king nodded and walked back toward his men as Jorrit turned toward Titus. He could not see it, but knew all the color had left his face. He walked beside Titus, who stepped with him to the villa before he would go and speak to the prisoners.

Neither of them said a word until Braxus jogged up beside him. "Is it safe to say it could have gone better?" the man said.

Jorrit shook his head. "I will not fight for that man."

Titus shook his head. "Neither will I, but thankfully he did not ask me to swear him any oaths. He will expect you to fight against Drysten if he commands it, and I suspect it will come to that at some point."

Jorrit nodded. "The boy sure knows how to make powerful enemies."

The three men walked toward the storage shed before instructing one of Titus' men to bring the leader of the group up to speak. The man nodded and obediently disappeared into the small building. After a moment, the guard reemerged with two men instead of one.

"I said to bring their leader," Titus said in a frustrated tone, "that entails just one person."

The guard looked at each man. "Sir, they each led one of

the ships. Neither is above the other."

Jorrit nodded and looked at Titus. "Many of the ships were crewed by families. A different family owned each vessel, meaning a different leader in each as well. Some were chiefs, and some were simply wealthy landowners." Titus nodded and gestured for Jorrit to speak to the two men standing in front of them.

The Frisian glanced to Braxus before he finally took a step forward. "I am called Jorrit, and I was commanded by my king to urge you to fight for me." The man on the left scoffed while the one on the right openly laughed, causing Jorrit to glance awkwardly at Titus. "My orders are to either convince you to serve, or to kill you. I would rather not be known as an executioner."

Each of the two men slowly looked at one another before the man on the right stepped forward, looking Jorrit in the eye as he spoke. "I am Octha. I was convinced by Colgrin this land would be easy to conquer and settle. While it seems he may have been mistaken, I still see no reason to fight under the banner of a *Briton*."

Jorrit smirked. "I am Frisian, and the man promised me much of the same before he burned my village."

Both Saxons looked at each other in surprise before Octha turned back to Jorrit. "What purpose did that serve?"

"He said men fight harder if they believe they are fighting to carve out their place in the world. Their old home would be gone, so they would be trying to carve out a new one," Jorrit responded in a disgusted tone.

The other Saxon stepped forward. "What proof do we have that you're telling us the truth, and what proof do you have that the same fate has befallen *our* people?"

Jorrit shook his head. "I could not tell you whether or not the man killed your people as he did mine. All I know, is this king is not fit to lead or rule over anyone. What is your name?"

"Ebissa," the man responded.

Jorrit looked between the two men. "Well, Octha and Ebissa, it would seem you have a choice to make. I cannot guarantee you much wealth if you go down this road with me, but I can guarantee you a place where you can raise your families. That would seem to be the reason all of us made our journey West."

The two Saxons looked at each other, each silently considering the deal before Octha turned back to Jorrit. "I will speak to my men. If they choose to join you, then I will send for the rest across the sea." Jorrit nodded, then turned to Ebissa. "I will do the same," the Saxon responded.

Titus nodded to the guard to take them back into the building, then turned to Jorrit as they vanished through the doorway. "You know they *cannot* be considered trustworthy."

Jorrit nodded. "I will speak to them more frankly once I am out of earshot of the locals," he whispered. "I will offer them more than just land, but not yet."

Titus smirked and nodded. "You and Drysten are just as crafty."

"So long as I don't fail," Jorrit said mildly.

CHAPTER XXIII

Jorrit awoke the next morning to the sound of rain hitting the villa's tile roof. All things considered, it was a mild storm and would not impede his efforts when he set out North. He knew he would first need to see what the Saxon prisoners decided, and thus kissed a sleeping Inka on the cheek before finally making his way through the villa toward the storage shed. Once in sight of the building, he noticed there was a small hole developing in the roof and couldn't help but wonder why such an easy fix was being left undone.

He slowly stepped inside, followed by the guard stationed there at all hours of the day and night, and proceeded down to the familiar basement level. The space was dimly lit with two small torches on either side of the room, both illuminating the bowls of food set out near the sleeping bodies of both Saxons nearby.

"Wake," Jorrit loudly commanded, causing the bodies to slowly stir.

"Would you like me to get Titus, Sir?" the guard inquired.

Jorrit shook his head. "That will not be necessary. Remain outside unless I call for you."

The guard nodded and began to walk toward the exit as Jorrit turned back to the Saxons, both now standing in front of him.

Octha stepped forward first. "We decided to fight for you," he said as he stepped forward, "we just have one request."

Jorrit nodded. "You wish to be set free upon this fight's completion."

Octha nodded as Ebissa stepped beside him, both silently waiting for Jorrit's decision.

Jorrit rubbed his chin before he finally gave a nonchalant shrug. "Your request makes no difference to me. I will allow it with no conditions."

The two men smiled and happily looked at each other before Jorrit finally beckoned for them to follow. The two looked capable enough, as most Saxons did. Jorrit perceived he would have good fighters at his back when the fight finally came, but still understood he must be careful around these new members of his crew. Jorrit gestured for the men to come forward, and one by one, were cut from their bindings.

"Colgrin really killed your people?" a skeptical Octha asked.

Jorrit nodded. "He sent someone else to do it, but the decision was his all the same. I doubt he had enough men under his command to murder your people as well, though I don't doubt he eventually intends to do so in the hopes of preventing fighters from abandoning him."

Octha worriedly looked to Ebissa. "We should send for our families. We could find somewhere North to settle instead of living under Colgrin's thumb."

Ebissa nodded. "I agree, but we must not worry about that until the time comes."

The remaining Saxons were brought back into Petuaria from whatever enclosure was housing them outside the village. Their bonds were cut once Octha and Ebissa each spoke to their own men, explaining to them that they were temporarily fighting under Jorrit for their freedom. None seemed to find issues with the idea, as Jorrit was the kind of man they were accustomed to in their homeland. He was big, hairy, and smelled of the sea. Most importantly, he personally assured their freedom should they fight.

Titus and his men piled the weapons and armor of the dead Saxons inside the walls of the villa, and groups of five were let inside to handpick their gear before the voyage. Most of the men were quick to find their own trusted equipment. However, some decided their dead comrades would no longer be needing theirs and left their own in favor of better-made weapons. Most of the shields were oval shaped with depictions of an assortment of beasts feared by the people in their homelands. Octha and his men picked up shields with black bears painted on red backgrounds, while Ebissa's people had a more varied assortment with depictions of fish or trees. Jorrit did not care what the men used to fight. He only cared that they would.

"Lord," Octha said as he walked toward Jorrit, "what was done with our dead? Nobody has told us what became of their bodies."

"They were burned atop pyres with their ashes scattered in the river," Jorrit answered. Octha nodded upon hearing the response, but Jorrit wondered whether their funeral rites were similar to those of his. Both the Frisians and the Saxons worshipped similar deities but Jorrit did not know where the similarities ended.

The Saxons were mostly ready to depart when Titus gimped his way toward them from the main building of the villa. He walked with the aid of his son and stopped once he saw Jorrit with the new additions to his crew.

"Seems you're almost ready, Frisian," Titus observed.

Jorrit nodded. "I will need a heading before I can go anywhere. North is not quite specific enough to follow."

Titus chuckled. "No, I suppose it isn't. Drysten went North of the wall, to a place called Din Guayrdi. The king's brother rules there."

Jorrit sighed. "Another fucking Roman to deal with."

Titus shook his head. "He is anything but. From what I remember of the brief power struggle for Ebrauc's throne, King Garbonian was the original heir. He was somehow pushed out and sent to rule over Bryneich. More than likely, Ceneus thought his brother would offer a buffer between the Picts and his own lands. Probably did not expect his brother to survive too long."

"How *did* he survive so long?" Jorrit asked, moderately impressed.

"The Guayrdi tribe has some impressive warriors. If I had to guess, I would say that had something to do with it," Titus answered with a shrug.

Jorrit looked over his new additions one final time before gesturing for them to walk through the gates of the villa. "So North to Din Guayrdi then," he said aloud.

"Actually, I don't know if that would be a good idea," Titus said skeptically.

Jorrit sighed as he turned to Titus. "What is it now?"

"If Drysten already made it to Din Guayrdi, he won't be there anymore. I would suggest patrolling the coast near the fort until you see any sign of them," Titus explained, "once you find him, you'll be able to help, but dealing with the locals may not be a good idea for you if you have nothing to offer them."

Jorrit ran his hand over his head in frustration. "I couldn't just take a few Britons along to show I am not opposing them?"

Titus shook his head. "They are not friendly to most outsiders. I actually wonder whether or not Drysten could convince them to help him."

"I hate this place," Jorrit said in a frustrated tone. "You and your people make things too complicated."

Titus laughed and nodded his head. "Well, we were all Roman once. That could have something to do with it."

Jorrit began to pace from side to side. "What I will do, if there is not some glaring issue I have not been told about, is sail my men around the fort until I finally find signs of the boy and his father. Then, supposing there aren't locals who would burn my people and I alive in a giant wickerman, is help them take the fort and reclaim the contents inside."

"Drysten planned to give the contents of the fort to King Garbonian," Titus said with a chuckle, causing Jorrit to throw his hands up in the air in frustration.

"Then I will figure it out when we arrive!" Jorrit yelled, attracting the attention of a few curious villagers nearby.

"Best thing to do," Titus replied in amusement. "You better be off soon, otherwise the king may return and force someone to swear another oath."

Jorrit ordered his men to begin boarding the vessel before going back inside the villa to say his farewells to Inka and his son. It would not take long before the men would be ready, as most had already assumed they would need more supplies and were preparing the ship. Jorrit walked through the main building of the villa, where he nodded to Isolde and Titus' daughter as they walked by, then sauntered into the room shared with Inka and Lanzo.

"Ah! There you are," Inka said happily as he entered. "Are you going to be off soon?"

Jorrit nodded. "I am."

Inka smiled as she walked toward Jorrit, kissing him briefly before Lanzo ran up from the other side of the room. "I will take care of him while you're away."

"Thank you." Jorrit smiled. "I am happy you are with me."

Inka smiled and kissed him once more before turning and picking up Lanzo. "He really isn't much trouble, aside from how often he shits. Must get that from you because my sister never had a weak stomach."

Jorrit chuckled. "Just make sure he doesn't run around trailing it everywhere. Did that in Londinium. Quite the sight."

The two laughed for a moment before Jorrit finally kissed Inka and ruffled his son's sparse hair. He then departed, and walked through the villa to the gate where he was met by both of the Cretans he sailed with under Drysten.

"Nice to see you still live. Did not get the chance to speak with you when I first arrived."

Paulus stepped forward and shook Jorrit's hand briefly. "We wish to come with you."

"Why is that? Did Drysten not tell you to stay behind to defend your families?" Jorrit asked.

Both men nodded. "We don't believe we are needed now that Titus has some of his own men back, we feel as though our people would be safe for the time being," Paulus explained.

Jorrit shrugged. "Grab your things, but if you sail on my ship, you follow my orders."

Both men smiled and nodded. "We already put our supplies aboard a few moments ago."

Jorrit chuckled. "Then what are we waiting for?"

The three men walked through the market, with Jorrit still drawing skeptical looks from the local tribesmen as he moved. He returned their stares with a smile to further confuse them of his intentions, as well as for a bit of his own enjoyment.

Most of the men were on board and ready to move when Titus joined him at the edge of the dock. "Make sure you warn Drysten of the king's opinion of him. I'm sure the boy already has some idea, but you can never tell with the younger ones."

Jorrit chuckled. "If I were you, I would worry more of what the king does when we come back."

"What's your meaning?" Titus asked. A wave of fatigue ran over him, causing him to stumble slightly before being caught by Jorrit.

"You need rest, old man. That wound won't heal as quickly as it would have thirty years ago," Jorrit said. He then gestured for Citrio, who was sitting near the docks, to come and help his commander.

Titus began to stammer. "I... I will be fine. Just make sure you hurry back with our people so I won't need to look after Petuaria. I will certainly heal faster if I can remain in the villa."

Citrio took Titus' weight from Jorrit. "Come now, Sir, time to get you back to your wife. She'll be rather unhappy if you keel over after her putting all that trouble into wrapping your leg."

Titus sadly nodded to Jorrit in farewell, then turned and slowly began to hobble his way back to the villa. Jorrit was watching him limp, as a feeling of guilt began to well up inside him. He knew it was ultimately his fault the man was attacked, though if he had not suggested Colgrin change his plans, then Drysten and Hall would quite possibly be homeless and many of their people dead. If that had happened, there is no telling where Jorrit would have run with his people. He finally boarded his ship and made his way to the stern, where it would be his job to steer.

"Is everyone aboard?" Jorrit called to his men, causing murmurs before Braxus and Octha both nodded. "Then, we go!"

The men found their seats at the oars and the ship began moving. The men knew it would be about two days of sailing before they reached the area around Din Guayrdi, but nobody knew whether they would make it without some sort of altercation between the Frisians and the Saxons. Jorrit was hopeful there would be nothing to worry about, but to make sure, he instructed both groups stow their weapons at the stern. He ordered them not returned until they reached their destination, or if they had to defend themselves against another ship.

The vessel reached open water after a short time and turned North. "We will keep near the coast for the time being," Jorrit said as he handed steering duties off to Braxus. He walked down to Octha at the bow, who was speaking with Ebissa. "How many men will you have at your backs should we decide to bring the rest of your people over from the East?" he inquired.

Octha and Ebissa both glanced to each other. "Assuming Colgrin hasn't sent for them, we both have about one hundred men each," Ebissa replied.

"I doubt he would have. He did not look favorably upon my father before we departed," Octha put in.

Jorrit was interested by the news. "Why was that?"

"Colgrin wished for more of our men to accompany him from the start. My father knew he already had enough to take one large city, and did not think it necessary to leave the rest of our people undefended until they had a guarantee of land to settle them in. What worries me now is that they are all living in tents," Octha explained. "They would be easy pickings for rival clans who may have followed them."

"Your people were most likely intended to meet the same fate as mine," Jorrit concluded. "If they were to be left undefended, then Colgrin would have likely massacred them as well."

Both Saxons glanced to each other uncomfortably, finally beginning to be swayed by what Jorrit was trying to explain to them. Ebissa sighed. "My people sent most of our strength along with me. It is... possible... they may have been attacked once we left."

"We will find out soon enough," Jorrit said as he placed a hand on the worried Saxon's shoulder. It was evident to him now that he was the only one to have the luxury of knowing what kind of man Colgrin truly was. It seemed the man was good at hiding his cruel ways from most of the people under his command. They probably had no idea they had just placed their people in danger by siding with him.

"Your people were camped close enough to mine to have a place to run if anything was attempted," Octha assured Ebissa.

Jorrit nodded in the hope the assurance from Octha would be enough to relieve some of the stress for Ebissa. He did not want to have to deal with any people trying to desert to find their families, though it would certainly be forgivable. On some level, Jorrit hoped the people belonging to these two men had been attacked, as it would be much easier to secure their support once this voyage was over. For now, there wasn't any way to tell one way or another.

Jorrit moved back to the stern to sit besides Braxus, who was currently steering the vessel. He was half asleep and sitting on the bench at the back when Jorrit walked up. "How do you think we will fair with the Saxons aboard?" Jorrit inquired.

Braxus looked around him, making sure none of the newcomers could hear him. "I don't trust them, Lord. If they tried to take the ship, we would have quite a fight on our hands."

Jorrit nodded. "I know. I just hope I was able to put enough doubt in their original cause to persuade them it would be in their best interest not to attempt anything."

Braxus looked at his captain curiously. "What did you tell them?"

"I told them the truth. I told them what Colgrin ordered Marhaus to do to our people and what he intended to do for more of his followers," Jorrit explained.

"You know, we may be the only ones who understand what he did. Even if he did attack other tribes, he could have blamed the Britons and Romans," Braxus began, "meaning the only ones who may be swayed by what you're saying would be these two right here," Braxus said as he gestured to the two leaders of the Saxons.

Jorrit nodded. "It is better to convince a few rather than none at all."

The two men sat in silence for a time before the estuary leading to the River Abos began to fade from view. The coastline was all the men aboard the ship could see not long after, with brief glimpses of the seagulls flying above a dense fog that began to settle in around them.

Braxus turned to Jorrit and finally broke the long silence. "Do you intend to keep that oath to the Christian king?"

Jorrit chuckled. "I only repay my loyalty to those who show me kindness. Not those who demand it. Drysten and Hall have my allegiance, not some weak man who connived his way into power."

Braxus nodded in approval. "That is good to hear. I was told by a local that he forces his oathmen to convert to his religion. I would never go to my ancestors should that ever happen to me."

"How does he manage that?" Jorrit said in surprise.

Braxus shrugged. "I haven't the faintest idea. I was only told the Britons in Petuaria had to strike down the depictions of their idols in favor of Christian images. Strange religion if you ask me. Their God demands his followers to only acknowledge him, even though there are gods all around us."

Jorrit nodded. "I am sure that is not true. I have never known a religion that does not at least acknowledge the existence of other powers. If anyone is demanding the allegiance, it is the king, not his god. They may openly worship him, but I would not be surprised if they still retain their heritage when they are behind their own walls."

Braxus shrugged once again. "Either way, so long as I am not forced to renounce my own heritage, I do not care."

The ship rowed against the current for most of the first day until, finally, the sail could be unfurled at dawn of the second. Jorrit was relieved the men would not need to work quite as hard, considering he did not know if there would be a fight facing him in Din Guayrdi. He decided that was his best option for finding information on Drysten's whereabouts, and ordered his men to keep sailing North despite reaching the entrance to the river where Segedunum was located. Before long, he started seeing signs of people along the coast and knew he was drawing closer and closer to their main settlement.

Over the hills, the first fires of the day being lit inside

huts and shacks could be seen, signaling that Jorrit and his men were nearing their destination. The coastline of Britannia was dotted with various tribes, all taking advantage of the sea for their livelihood. This area was no different in that fact, though the Guayrdi tribe was not like the others located in the island's North. These people were undoubtedly Picts, much like the men and women further North, but they were ruled by a Briton. Jorrit hoped this simple fact would mean his people were not going to be killed on sight.

"Lord!" Octha said from the bow. "Lord, there's a group of men matching our pace on the shoreline."

Jorrit looked to the coast and indeed saw the people Octha was warning him about. "We press on."

The ship finally spied a dock filled primarily with small fishing vessels not suited for sailing in open water, but there was one other that caught Jorrit's eye. "Octha, Ebissa, do either of you recognize that ship?"

The two Saxons both nodded before Ebissa stepped forward. "She's mine, Lord."

So the boy made it North. Hopefully, there won't be a mound of corpses waiting for us when we arrive, he thought to himself as he turned back to the Saxons.

"You two will accompany me ashore along with Braxus. Veqreq, you're in charge of things until we make it back."

The ship finally made it to the dock, where they were met by a small group of men wielding spears and small axes. Jorrit spied the men as he waited for his ship to finally bump the wooden dock connecting the land to the sea. They stopped parallel to the Saxon vessel, yet across from it on the dock and he slowly stepped forward. Jorrit gave a sideways glance into the ship to see its contents, being satisfied that Drysten must have at least been alive since there was no blood to be seen.

He led his three companions toward the group who had been stationed on the dock to greet them. "My name is Jorrit. I am here to speak with Drysten or Hall," he said.

The small group of men spoke a language Jorrit could only make small sense of, then gestured for him to follow. He looked to Braxus and the two Saxons, who each looked back at him and offered a shrug, then began to follow the Guayrdians into the village surrounded by a palisade.

The four men followed the guides through small groups of people and up into a poorly built hall which looked as though someone must have raised it from driftwood found on the nearby beaches decades ago. Jorrit signaled for Braxus and the two Saxons to wait outside and followed one of the guides inside.

"What is this then?" a blonde man with fair skin said as he entered. "Come to sell my uncle some more of that disgusting fucking *fish* have you?" The jeer was followed by a series of laughs from a small group of people situated around the man sitting in the throne.

"Your uncle?" Jorrit asked. He looked around and noticed most of the people inside the building were not like the people he passed by on the way from the dock. They were cleaner, well-armed, and Briton by their language.

"My uncle, the good King Garbonian ap Coel!" the man said sarcastically. "King of what, precisely? I cannot tell. All I've seen thus far has been fishermen and filth." He drew more smirks from his following.

"Then I suppose I am here to speak with your uncle," Jorrit said as he eyed the young man. "I am to find Drysten and his father."

The boy rose from his seat and walked a couple paces toward Jorrit. "Do not speak of Hall to me! The man's only use is on the battlefield with the other *dullards* who dwell here."

"Has your mother's breast run dry?" Jorrit said with a smile.

The small insult was met with all the men around him rising to their feet, and placing their hands on their weapons. Jorrit looked around and laughed at what he saw.

"Do you think I am frightened of you?" he said as the local tribesmen in the room slowly made their way to the door. "You think I care what some little twat surrounded by his gaggle of friends has to say?"

The man's mouth fell open as the realization that he held no authority over his new guest began to seed itself inside his mind. "I... You *dare* insult me? You dare insult a *prince?*" The prince waved a hand at two of his companions to attack Jorrit. They unsheathed their blades and slowly walked forward.

Jorrit saw both of them, and drew his own weapon in response. "You really want to die, do you?" he said with a smile. The two men were much younger than Jorrit, and obviously unseasoned compared to him. He knew he could overpower them both if the need arose.

"Lord?" Jorrit heard from behind him. Jorrit turned to see his three companions enter the building with their weapons drawn.

"You lot are more fun than I thought," Octha said with a chuckle.

Jorrit turned back to the prince. "It would be wise for your people to sit their skinny asses back in those seats."

The men complied as they saw the three others enter the room, causing their prince to contort his face in anger as they did so.

"Good dogs," Jorrit said with a laugh. "Now, where are Hall and Drysten?"

The prince looked at the half dozen men, all red in the face from either embarrassment or fear, then looked back to Jorrit. "Dead on some hill, most likely. Not my problem anymore. Not the *king's* problem."

Jorrit's eyes narrowed as he stepped toward the prince, sword still in hand. "Where exactly is this hill?"

Eidion smirked. "What will you do if I don't tell you? Kill me?"

"Yes," Jorrit responded as a broad smile began across his

face.

The prince awkwardly stepped back in response. He gave a quick look to his men before finally turning back to Jorrit. "It's... not far to the East. Go and die with them if you wish." The prince waved Jorrit off as he turned to go back to his uncle's throne. His group of companions slowly sat down in response, signaling to Jorrit that their little exchange was now over. He sarcastically bowed and tossed out a "Lord Prince", before walking back to Braxus and the Saxons. All weapons were sheathed at their sides as the three men followed their captain out of the hall and back toward the dock.

"That boy really *is* a twat," Braxus said, amusing the Saxons and Jorrit.

"That he is," Jorrit agreed with a smile and nod.

Braxus turned to Jorrit. "So what is our plan?"

Jorrit paused for a moment, thinking their options over. They could venture West to try and find Hall and Drysten, but Jorrit knew any battle that took place would long be over by the time they arrived. Even if they won, they would surely move back toward Segedunum. If they lost, then the trip West would surely be a waste, as all they would find would be corpses they would have to bury. "We go South. We go South and we wait."

Octha glanced at Ebissa before turning to Jorrit. "Wait for what?"

"If we arrive near the fort early enough, we can prevent any of the men who would have left to go fight our people from returning. Whether they won or lost, there will surely be men returning from the battle. We need to prevent them from reinforcing the ranks of the people left behind to man the walls of Segedunum. If there is no sign of our people in a couple of days, we will try and take the fort ourselves," Jorrit explained.

The four men made the short walk back to their vessel, gazing over the strange people who dwelled in the area as they proceeded. They resembled those who lived in Petuaria if those men and women had been allowed to live as their ancestors had.

Before long, they arrived at their ship and set of South.

"So you've been harassing them all this time?" Drysten asked of Jorrit, who responded with a smiling nod. "Very useful of you, though I worry about what sort of reception we will face when we return South."

"I do not believe that princeling will be much of an issue. He's the type who hides behind his rank and tries to make others do his bidding for him," Jorrit responded.

Hall crept up from behind Drysten to see Jorrit and his Saxon companions. He noticed the conversation, so was not startled by a Saxon presence outright, but still looked on the people wearily. "Son," He said, catching Drysten's attention, "I see you've made more friends."

Drysten smiled. "Apparently he's with us now."

"That I am," Jorrit said with a nod. "When our task here is over, I suspect we could take Ebrauc from the Christian king should we desire it."

Hall smiled. "That will not be necessary, Frisian."

"No?" Jorrit replied.

Hall crept closer to the group, speaking as he did so. "If we moved on the king, he would undoubtedly win with the support of Powys. Besides, at the moment we are fighting in his name, and I overheard something about an oath being sworn."

Jorrit grimaced as he was reminded of the embarrassment he endured in Petuaria. "Unfortunately yes, I did swear the man an oath."

"Then that cannot be broken. A man is only as good as his word," Hall said as he patted Jorrit on the shoulder, seemingly trying to reassure him the deed may not turn out unfavorably. "I heard he treats those loyal to him well." The Frisian again grimaced and turned to think quietly to himself.

Hall turned to Drysten after witnessing the Frisian's discomfort. "We should attack soon. Some of the men have begun to desert."

Drysten chuckled. "Let me guess. The men the king sent with you."

"Who else would it be?" Hall said in a frustrated tone.

"One thing before we begin," Jorrit began. "I'm sure you have noticed our handiwork with the Northmen we hung from the trees alongside your deserters." This prompted Drysten to glance toward his father before nodding. "Right before some were finally sent to their otherworld, there were mentions of a General Plautius. Do we have Romans with us? I don't understand why they would fear a man who has been dead for generations."

Hall glanced around before seeing his son and smiling. "They must have believed Drysten to be his ghost. The man was one of the first Roman governors of Britannia. Brought much of the lands to heel when they first arrived."

Jorrit laughed as he looked on the finely dressed son of Hall. "I suppose they would still fear the man's ghost, since he was the reason for much of their ancestor's suffering."

"An infamous man indeed," mentioned Paulus, who walked up alongside Drysten with a grin.

Drysten smiled back to both Cretans. "I thought I told you to stay in Petuaria."

"Greeks do not follow orders well," mentioned Diocles, a recent deserter from the Roman army.

Heraclius scoffed. "Speak for yourself."

The group laid low in the cover of the trees as they crept back toward the fort. The Saxons joined with Drysten's men, who had been moved in the attempt to intercept what they first thought to be an enemy. There were many nervous glances between the men, as many did not trust their new comrades. That could hardly be helped, as much of the army was currently made up of people who had fought against each other at one point or another in generations past. The army was doing a diligent job of forming a line of men around the Northern side of the fort being concealed by what tree or hill cover they could find. Drysten knew if somebody tried to enter or leave the immediate area around Segedunum, they would easily be spotted by their men.

"Fort looks bigger up close," Jorrit whispered to Drysten as they crawled closer to get a better view.

The fortress was one of the last to be abandoned by the empire fifteen years prior. It had been manned by an auxiliary unit comprised of both infantry and cavalry up until that point, and had been kept up in good condition by the men of Ebrauc ever since. The fort was surrounded by a long ditch, which had large overgrown bushes of thorns at the ditch's top near the base of the wall. The land on the other side of the ditch was once used for farming, though now most of the local Brigantes tribe had moved South because the Picts began to raid the areas once protected by the Romans. Since then, the land had shifted to overgrown grass, mixed with weeds and small patches of crops once harvested many years ago. The Western side of the fort was joined to Hadrian's Wall and small groups of Picts could be seen leaning up against the still-standing fortifications at the wall's top. There were multiple bastions on each side of the wall, along with one on each of the four corners of the fortress. These structures would prove to be the most troublesome for the army, as any approach taking place during the day could be easily spotted from the higher vantage point.

"Can't go around," Hall whispered to his son.

Drysten nodded. "They repaired the Eastern wall going down to the river."

Hall nodded. "Them or King Ceneus. Either way, the Southern side of the wall is not accessible."

The Western side of the fortress had a small village at its base. Drysten noticed it the moment they were near enough to see the burned-out walls of the homes. It was not of impressive size by any means, but from what Cynwrig had told Drysten, his home was surely welcoming.

Reminded of his childhood friend, Drysten turned to Jorrit. "Did you happen to see Cynwrig while you were in Petuaria?"

Jorrit thought for a moment, then shook his head. "Saw no sign of him. Why was he not with you?"

"Wounded in Rodanum and needed time to heal," Drysten replied as he turned back to continue surveying the fort.

A handful of men were walking in front of the destroyed gate on the Northern section of the wall. This would be the easiest way in once night fell, and Drysten instructed Diocles to inform the newly arrived Cretans their task was to thin out the men stationed there. A smaller barrier jutted from the Eastern side of the wall, extending out toward the beaches. Drysten could easily tell there would be no marching over that patch of soggy earth and turned to Jorrit. "Ideas?" he asked.

"The gate is our way in," Jorrit acknowledged. "If we try anything else, we will lose just as many to water as we would to their ranged weapons."

"Should they have any," Diocles put in.

Hall tilted his head to the side as he thought up a strategy. "We... may have *one* more option." The group of men turned to face Drysten's father as he spoke. "Jorrit, your people were originally intended to reinforce this garrison?"

The Frisian thought for a moment. "I was not told of any such plan, but it would seem like the sound thing to do at some point."

Hall nodded. "If we send in Jorrit with the Saxons, they can pose as those reinforcements. Jorrit can tell them of a plan by our enemies to assault Ebrauc from both the North and the South. Your people can pose as the vanguard sent to inform the Picts to prepare for a march."

Drysten smiled. "And when they do, they can take the

gate and hold it for our entry," prompting a nod from his father.

"Do you really trust these men not to betray us?" an unfamiliar voice said from behind them.

Hall did not bother to turn. "I do," prompting a smile from Jorrit. "When nightfall begins, you will take your men down from the road. You will march them in a column as if you've just journeyed from the North. Say whatever you have to for them to believe you."

"Sounds like a good enough idea," Jorrit began. "My only worry is we have no clue as to the strength of their forces. We could well be overmatched and not even know it."

"Not likely," Hall answered back. "They sent some warriors North to fight us on the hill. There's a good chance many of them were killed."

The men debated for a short while until everyone was satisfied with the plan of attack. Only Jorrit was somewhat apprehensive, leading Drysten to believe he did not fully trust the Saxons, a fact which worried him. In any case, the Hall ordered everyone to stay out of sight until dusk.

CHAPTER XXIV

The twilight hours approached alongside a thick fog that covered the fortress' overgrown farmland. This proved useful to the army, as Hall could now position his men closer to Segedunum's walls. This would cut down the amount of time it would take before the main group finally made it to the gate on the Northernmost side of the fort. It was decided the Britons under Hall's command, including the remnants of the Powysian forces, would ready themselves on the Western side of the road, while King Garbonian's men would now set up on its Eastern side. The Northmen under the king would also be reinforced by Drysten's Britons who sailed with him from Petuaria, as they were the only men comfortable enough with the Guayrdians to fight alongside them. Jorrit's newcomers would march up to the gate and announce their presence in an attempt to trick the Pictish forces into thinking they are reinforcements. Once they took the gate, Jorrit would send a runner out to inform the awaiting army of its capture.

"Fight with a shield this time, boy," Hall ordered his son.

Drysten scoffed. "I'm quick enough to fight without one."

Hall turned. "This fighting will be different. You won't be out in the open with space to move around in. Take mine. It's Roman-made. Should serve you well enough for the kind of fighting you will face inside. I will use one of the heavier ones from Ebrauc."

Drysten smirked. "What do you know about fighting?" he replied as he took his father's shield.

Hall smiled and turned back to the road as the Saxons marched toward the fort. They were moving at a leisurely pace to try and persuade the men inside they were fatigued from a nonstop march. Hall instructed Jorrit to mention they arrived at the battle on the hill too late to be of any aid, but followed the directions of locals back to Segedunum without any altercations between them and the Britons.

"All things considered, I believe this is going to work," Drysten said to his father.

Hall smiled at his son. "You're a pup. What do you know about fighting?"

The two laughed briefly before they noticed Jorrit and his men had reached the gate of the fortress. Prince Aurelianus moved up beside Hall and offered a nod to Drysten before he turned to watch the events unfold in front of them.

From what Drysten could see, Jorrit was speaking to a lanky man with raunchy and unkempt hair. Jorrit could be heard raising his voice, but nobody could understand what was being said until the blonde man finally gestured for him to enter.

Drysten saw his father was about to order his men to ready themselves until he saw one of Jorrit's men carefully slip away from the gate and nonchalantly walk back to their lines. The man only peered behind him once, and upon being satisfied he was under enough cover, he subtly began to rush toward the main army.

"What's all this then?" King Garbonian asked as he watched the man running toward them.

The few short moments it took for him to reach Hall felt like years to everyone wanting to know why he was sent back so soon. As the man came closer, Drysten recognized him as Braxus, who was introduced to him as Jorrit's unofficial second-in-command. He finally made it to the tree line. After frantically glancing around, he made his way toward

Hall. "They're ready for us, Lord," he announced through heavy breathing.

Hall shot a glance toward the fort. "How do you mean?"

Braxus took a small sip of liquid from a skin handed to him by Bors before coughing violently and shooting a glance at the Briton. Bors smiled as the man's surprised look faded into one of satisfaction. "Mead?" He asked Bors, who responded with a nod. "They blocked off all of the alleyways. If we charge in from either of the two gates, they will trap us in the Northern portion of the fort."

Hall cursed under his breath. "What did Jorrit say you were doing before he sent you away?"

Braxus smiled. "He said he would need to send for the rest of his force. He wanted them to hurry up and get behind their walls before they were caught by the Britons on their trail."

"Good man!" Hall said louder than he intended, before turning to his men. "Take off your armor!"

The men looked at him wide-eyed before a lone voice could be heard from behind them. "Why the *fuck* would we do that?"

Hall slowly raised his voice loud enough for the men nearby to hear. "Take off anything that makes you look like a Briton! Cover yourself in skins and put away any images of your gods under your clothes." Men donned confused expressions as they slowly complied with the order. Hall then looked at King Garbonian. "Your men will attack once my people are inside. When they are focused on you, we will attack them from behind."

The King bellowed out a jovial laugh. "About time!"

The restless men from Bryneich hurried their way toward the bank of the river, quietly running through the cover of the trees. King Garbonian decided it would look the most convincing if they were coming from the coast, meaning they would not have been able to see the Saxon reinforcements on the road. It also had the added benefit of a slightly heavier layer of fog they could stay concealed in until they got reasonably close to the Eastern gate.

The men finally marched their way toward the fort, following the road coming from the North. Every man toward the front of the marching column now looked as much like a Saxon as they could manage. Drysten thought it was somewhat strange as he walked through the rear portion of the Britons to meet with King Garbonian on their Eastern flank. Each man shed their Roman-like tunics and armor, then put furs from their blankets in their place. Drysten, Diocles, Bors, Amiram and a small number of other Southerners slowly made their way to the king's men, spying the weary faces of the other Britons.

"Strange they never sent out any scouts," Diocles remarked.

Drysten nodded. "Could mean they did not have any men to spare."

Bors scoffed. "Better hope for an advantage seeing the state of men from Ebrauc."

Even Amiram, who seldom used his voice on account of not having a tongue, let out a nervous "Mhm" before the men finally made it to their positions. The king was grinding a whetstone on his axe while he sat on a fallen tree near the tree line.

"Boys," the king greeted.

Drysten and his men nodded in return as they formed up with the men from Guayrdians. From what Drysten could tell, Jorrit had stirred no trouble upon his entrance. No shouting or fighting to be heard inside.

"Your father might be relying too heavily on trickery, boy," the king said as Drysten settled in.

Drysten shrugged as he tried to readjust the leather on his right shoulder. "From what I can tell, he doesn't have much of a choice. The king hardly gave him any fighting men worth speaking of."

"None at all besides the Powysians," Diocles put in.

The king nodded. "I have done more impressive feats when given less than this. Though I knew the size of the force I was facing well beforehand."

"When was that?" Drysten said intrigued.

"In Ebrauc," King Garbonian said sullenly. "The long battle for the crown."

Bors crept up besides Drysten to listen. "You fought against Ceneus?"

"Just the once, though he did not participate until he knew he was sure of victory. Even so, the reason he needs that damn bath is because my firstborn cut him deep in his leg. The waters soothe his limp," the king said proudly. "If it were not for the Powysians coming to save him, Ebrauc would have a king fit to rule."

"I take it Ceneus did not inherit much of your father," Diocles guessed sullenly.

"No," King Garbonian said grimly, "no, he did not."

Drysten's group looked on in silence for a short while longer as the last few men belonging to Hall were making their way into the fort. Before long, two familiar silhouettes appeared at the top of the bastion closest to where the attack would start from. Both Cretans had strung their bows in wait of the moment they would turn and fire on the Picts inside the fortress.

"Care to give the order, boy?" the king said as he patted Drysten on the shoulder. "Seemed to work out well the last time you led the way."

Unable to contain his excitement, Drysten nodded happily and rose to his feet, followed by most of the Britons under his command. Drysten stepped toward the men lying in wait and raised his sword in the air. "Stand!" he roared. A handful of the men who understood the Brythonic word followed the command, then were soon followed by the rest who took the hint. Drysten then turned and pointed to the fortress. "Make them scream for mercy!" he bellowed at the top of his lungs.

The men behind him did not need to wait for a translation, as every single one of them broke out in an impressive sprint toward the Easternmost gate. Drysten led for a few moments before a score of men ran by him, one noticeably laughing as he did so. It did not take long for the first Northmen in the fort to sound a horn as a warning to the others. There were two horns blown before both were noticeably cut short. Drysten guessed it was most likely the Cretans who had silenced them as the charge finally began.

As they ran closer, intense fighting could be heard ringing out inside. A handful of Picts ran out through the gate as the first of the king's men reached it and were quickly cut down, with their bodies thrown into the ditch at the base of the fortress. The men ran on, nearing the sounds of combat inside. The king's men began to enter the gate as a hail of short spears and axes came down from the ramparts above, skewering some and sending them down to the ground screaming and bleeding onto the earth.

The disturbing sight almost gave Drysten pause, until Diocles ran up beside him and gestured for them to enter the gate. Diocles raised his shield as cover for Drysten's sword arm as they started stepping over the squealing men at their feet. Drysten watched as two men ran forward to intercept them, until a pair of arrows danced through the air and embedded themselves deep into their chests, sending them to the ground with shocked expressions and hollow breaths. He glanced up at the wall to see Petras pointing to the right of the gate mouthing and yelling something unintelligible to the group of Britons.

"Follow!" Drysten commanded as they raced to the right after reaching the fort's interior. King Garbonian finally made it through the gate with a roar as his men reached the line of enemies who came from the Southern portion of the fort. The last thing Drysten saw before the wall of men formed in behind him was King Garbonian bringing his axe down into the face painted blue.

"Shield wall!" Drysten cried out. After a brief moment, his men formed a defensive line on either side of him. Drysten glanced to his left, then his right and finally took a deep breath. "Advance!" he ordered. The shield wall crept toward a hastily prepared barricade at the Northeast part of the fortress. As they inched closer, hands could be seen prying the wooden scraps of the barricade apart. Drysten pointed and ordered a handful of the of his men to aid whoever was on the other side as a group of Picts began racing through an alleyway on his left. Drysten's men were seasoned enough to not need an order to reform a new shield wall between the barricade and the screaming Picts charging them.

"Hold here!" Drysten shouted from the wall's center. He glanced over and saw Bors and Matthew defending the leftmost portion of their line from the screaming Northmen. "Swing left!" he shouted. The right side of Drysten's shield wall began to swing around to close off the alleyway from the larger street. Two large buildings on either side would provide them with barriers, as the rearmost line of Drysten's men would quickly try and tear down the barricade in the way of Hall's forces. The left portion of the shield wall slowly began to pivot, keeping an orderly line with the men on their right as they moved around toward the buildings across from them. After a brief moment, the shield wall stretched from one side of the alley to the other, with Northmen attacking both ends in an attempt to make it fold.

Drysten turned to Diocles after he pushed back an attacker and drove his sword into his stomach. "Get more men working on that barricade," he ordered as he gestured to the corner. Diocles glanced in the direction of the obstacle before turning back and nodding. He ran through the back ranks of the shield wall, shouting for men to follow. Drysten turned back to face the Picts now gathering on the other end of the shields. All but a few were painted with the customary blue war paint seen by the Northmen from above the wall. Drysten did not fear the way they looked but was smart enough to understand how his enemy's ancestors had driven back centuries of Roman invasions. These men seemed as though they had never been taught fear and were instead taught ferocity in its place.

The dying men at the shield wall's base prevented the Northmen from gaining a steady footing as they threw themselves into its wood and metal. Drysten's men were stabbing their short swords forward and withdrawing them coated with blood at their tips. The enemy's number had been thinned out to about sixty, while Drysten's men had lost only a handful.

Pays to be organized, Drysten thought to himself as he glanced above him.

Every few seconds, an arrow could be seen flying from the ramparts above and embedding itself through a neck or abdomen. The screams from the wounded were now slowly beginning to drown out the battle-cries of the blue faced men still trying to break the shield wall.

After a few moments of pushing from both sides, a horn was sounded from somewhere in the middle of the fort. Every Northman who was still able to run turned and made his way in the direction of the sound.

We cannot let them regroup, Drysten thought silently. His men looked to him for an order as he took a pace forward from the wall of shields forward from the wall. "Chase them down!" he shouted.

The Britons under his command broke from the shield wall in pursuit of the men running down the wide alleyway. Any who were caught were quickly cut down by a sword in their spine or a spear thrust to the leg. Men were frantically trying to reach the safety of their barricade at the end of the alley, with a small opening big enough for a man to walk through. As Drysten's men ran forward, a group of about twenty Northmen rose from behind the barricade with spears and throwing axes in hand. "Shields!" Drysten yelled. His men obediently stopped and raised their shields high, placing them between them and the projectiles as they were thrown.

A shout could be heard from behind Drysten, who turned to see Amiram holding a wound from an axe on the side of his face, while more men around them began falling prey to the deadly metal or wood flying through the air.

"Shield wall!" Drysten screamed once more. "Form up in front of the wounded!"

The Britons placed themselves between the men sprawled out on the ground and the Picts hurling weapons into the air. The wall formed quickly enough to protect the fallen men and allow time for them to be brought behind the rearmost rank of the shield wall.

Shields in the front were being dragged down by the weight of weapons being embedded into their planks, freeing men up to be targeted by more projectiles thrown by the Northmen.

"Advance!" Drysten yelled, causing the line to slowly move forward.

As he took his first couple of steps, an axe thrust itself into the center of his father's shield, jarring him for a brief moment before he was able to keep pace with the rest of the men.

Drysten risked a peek through the gaps of his shield and that of his neighbors to see there were now about forty men hurling weapons over the barricade into his ranks. They had only twenty feet or so before they would reach the barricade, where Drysten knew they would need to dismantle it quickly. If they got themselves stuck at its base for too long, then the spears originally intended to be thrown at them would be used to stab down into their necks and heads. To make matters worse, the barricade had small gaps, which Drysten could see men peeking through.

"They're going to jab at us through those fucking things," Bors said from behind Drysten.

Drysten knew his friend was right. They were about to

meet the barricade the moment more men appeared at its top. They hurled more spears and axes into his ranks, narrowly missing him with a spear which stuck itself into the shield behind him.

"Fucking hell. Pull back!" Drysten yelled. "Drag the wounded and move back!"

The shield wall halted no more than ten feet from its intended destination before gradually moving backward. The Guayrdians, who were taking advantage of the last row of the shield wall by throwing projectiles overhead, were reluctant to withdraw until more spears flew over Drysten's shields and into their ranks, sending yet more men to the ground screaming and bleeding. The wall itself was holding firm against the barrage from the Northmen, inching away slowly and carefully to avoid gaps being created between shields which could be exploited.

After a few moments, the Britons and their allies from the North were safely out of range. It was the same moment when Diocles came up from the Northeastern corner of the fort. "Drysten! Your father needs you at the gate. We made a space in the barricade! Jorrit's people held out long enough for him to be relieved, but there are more men here than we anticipated. They hid in the old Principia until we were too committed to withdraw and slammed into our center."

Drysten looked around at the wounded men under his command. "King Garbonian!" he called. After a few moments, the king limped up, blood flowing from his hip.

"What's the plan?" the king asked.

Drysten pointed to the barricade he just lost a handful of men assaulting. "Stay out of range of their spears. Just set up a defensive line here and prevent anyone from coming up behind us. We're going after their center."

The king offered a tired nod as he turned and spoke in the Guayrdian language. Men began creating a barricade of their own out of the remnants of the one torn away by Diocles, using the bodies of the fallen enemies as mortar.

"We may have bit off more than we can chew with this one," Diocles said wearily.

Drysten slowly glanced around at the bodies of the dead and wounded. There were noticeably more Northmen than Britons, leading Drysten to believe this fight could still be won. He shook his head, took a deep breath, and turned to his men.

"Back!"

Drysten's men raised their shields as they methodically paced backwards. After a few moments, the projectiles ceased pounding their shields and the men turned to race toward the barricade. Britons ran through the space created by Diocles and made their way toward the northern gate. Drysten could see bodies along the ground, some Briton, some Pictish, and many from Bryneich. He glanced behind him toward his men to get a rough estimate of his numbers. He estimated he had about fifty men remaining, and wearily prayed to whatever god might be listening to help him take the center of the fortress. Smoke was beginning to fill the air, as a fire could be seen on the fort's Western side. Most likely it was burning through one of the fort's old granaries placed near the Western gate.

As Drysten reached the gate, he could see the shield wall commanded by his father, with Heraclius' big body towering over many of the other men in the front rank. Next to him was someone looking vaguely like Dagonet, and one more who may have been Jorrit. Drysten ordered his men to reinforce the line as he made his way through the back ranks of the shield wall to find his father.

"Father!" he shouted. "Where is Hall?" he asked the men in the back. He was not able to get anything more than a shrug or a vacant look until a hand grabbed Drysten's shoulder. He turned to see Prince Aurelianus and his handful of Powysians running toward him.

"Your father was wounded when we first arrived. This way!" the prince said urgently.

Drysten followed the prince back through the rear ranks of the shield wall and into the Northwesternmost building by the gate. The fire was now in the neighboring building and began to burn brighter with each passing second.

"Boy!" a voice called to Drysten as he entered.

Drysten turned to see his father being bandaged by his scout, Gawain, to the right of the doorway. "How bad is it?" Drysten said as he knelt beside Hall.

Hall grunted as Gawain applied the last bandage around his chest. "It doesn't tickle," he said in a tired voice.

Gawain turned to Drysten. "I've seen people survive much worse, though the blade cut deep. I have managed to stop most of the bleeding, but he needs better help than what I can give him."

Drysten glanced around to his men, who were all looking for him to give them some sort of direction. At first, he was reluctant to do anything without his father's guidance, as he had never led an attack on a fortress. He knew the best two minds in the army were his father's and the king's, but both were not in any situation to make battle plans. He looked to Diocles, who simply gave him a reassuring nod before he looked back to Gawain. "Take him out of the fortress," he ordered before turning to Diocles. "We need torches."

Diocles nodded and ran outside of the building to find scraps of wood.

"What's the plan?" a weary voice said from behind Drysten. He turned to see Matthew; blood caked in his hair but seemingly unhurt.

"We burn *everything* they're hiding behind. I doubt they will be able to douse the fires and fight us all at the same time," Drysten said.

The fort was mostly made of stone, but the forces from Ebrauc who inhabited the buildings before its capture had no knowledge of how to upkeep the tile roofs, so all but the Principia was covered in thatch. Drysten knew he could cause enough chaos with well-aimed torches thrown behind the enemy lines to at least redirect some of the Northmen's attention. Diocles returned with two lit timbers in hand, each wrapped in cloth.

Hall chuckled slightly before grimacing. "The king wanted his fort back. Though, I suppose he said nothing about the state of it."

Drysten nodded then turned to Gawain. "Like I said, get him outside the walls." The scout lifted Hall under his arm, then slowly walked out of the building toward the gate.

"Burn everything," Drysten said to Diocles. "Throw those torches into the barricades and onto any roof behind them."

Diocles began to speak, presumably to question him when Drysten simply repeated his order.

"Burn *everything*, Diocles."

The Greek nodded and left the building with two other men Drysten did not know, all carrying fire in each hand.

"Reinforce the line and find me the Cretans," he ordered Bors.

Drysten rose and gestured for Prince Aurelianus to follow him to the back of the shield wall. The two stood and watched as the Northmen and Briton weapons were brought down on skulls and necks, spewing blood on those around them.

"Drysten," a voice said from behind him. Drysten turned and saw both Cretans were walking up with Bors.

"I need you two looking for whatever man leads them. Save your arrows for him and him alone," Drysten commanded.

Petras and Paulus nodded, each counting the arrows they held in the bags at their waists before moving to get themselves back on top of the ramparts above the Northern gate.

Drysten turned to Prince Aurelianus. "Send your men with them. I need them alive until they can pick out the leader. You stay with me."

"I would prefer to stay—" the prince began.

Drysten shook his head. "The men need to see their leaders in the front of the fight. Your men will be fine on the ramparts. I have no interest in losing the small number of Powysians we have left."

The prince nodded and gestured for his men to go with the Cretans before turning back to Drysten.

Fires were now starting up on the rooftops behind the Picts, sending a small number back to find water to halt them. The one silver lining for the current situation was the fact the Britons had held the ramparts from the start of the battle, meaning nobody had yet attempted to rain spears down from above them. A mix of Britons and Saxons held firm at the stairways on either side of the fort, meaning the Caledonians were confined mostly to the center of the enclosure.

Drysten picked up his blade once again and hefted his father's shield before he began to move through the rear ranks of the shield wall and into the front. He settled into the second rank behind Heraclius, who was covered in blood and screaming profanities at the men attempting to assail him. Nobody was too keen on getting close to the man, as he quickly stood out as the fiercest fighter of all the men in the shield wall. Drysten thought it was somewhat funny how the Picts were throwing themselves into the shields of his men, while in this one small area there seemed to be a gap in which nobody would enter. Heraclius had a small mound of corpses at his feet and reluctant looking men standing across from him.

"Forward! Drive them toward the fires!" Drysten shouted. After a moment, his men began attempting to push the fort's occupants back little by little. A man could be heard yelling in a language Drysten could not understand before it seemed he was cut off mid-sentence. Drysten glanced overhead to see two blurs rush through the air in the direction of the voice, and wondered whether Petras and Paulus had found their target.

"Let's hope Cretans still don't miss," Diocles yelled from behind him. Drysten could not turn to respond, as a spear came at him from a tall man on the other side of his shield. He ducked at the last second and was relieved when the man in front of him was able to skewer his attacker's belly right after he had thrust the spear toward Drysten. The spear was let go and rattled down from Drysten's shoulder before clattering to the ground. The line pushed forward until the Northmen began to give, with some turning and running toward the main building of the Principia.

"Keep pushing!" Drysten choked out through the thick smoke. He glanced behind him to see Diocles had disappeared and was replaced by the prince, who nodded to Drysten before he turned back to face front.

The Northmen's defense was beginning to waver. It seemed they were faced with the decision to either move backward into the heat of the flames, go forward into the shields and swords of the Britons, or run toward the Principia for some semblance of safety.

Drysten estimated their army had lost over two hundred souls in total, leaving about two hundred more without counting the Saxons. Jorrit and his men were to Drysten's left side of the shield wall, and doing well in the face of the Northmen. Their defense in that area had yet to weaken like much of the rest. After a moment of pushing and stabbing, a familiar horn sounded, and the Picts broke their defense and ran toward the Principia.

"Hold!" Drysten yelled, causing pause among the men who were about to break ranks to pursue the fleeing defenders. "Hold your positions!" he yelled once again.

After a quick moment of reassembling the shield wall, the men were standing from end to end of the wider middle road running South down the center of the fort. Drysten remembered what happened when he pursued the Northmen the first time, and was sure they would try to use similar tactics with ranged weapons should he advance.

"What are our orders?" Jorrit said as he pushed his way toward Drysten, who had just moved himself into the front rank. "We should pursue them to the entrance of the stone building there," Jorrit said as he gestured to the Principia. "Surely they are close to beaten if they fell back."

Drysten glanced at the burning buildings on either side of the street. "We wait until those fires are about to burn out. Order your men to burn any barricades they see."

Jorrit sighed and nodded before moving back to his men, who removed themselves from the shield wall to be replaced by the Britons who had fallen in behind them. Jorrit was about to protest what he thought to be hesitation on Drysten's part until a building's roof gave in from the flames causing blue-faced men to limp out before the whole thing came down on top of them. Drysten waited for the screams of those still stuck inside to die out, then turned and ordered his men to burn everything that could be flammable.

"Lord," Dagonet said as he approached. "The king and his men are weakened. We do not have the strength to both reinforce them and take the Principia."

Drysten looked down as he thought of his next move. "Have them fall back to the Western gate. Place the Powysians with them," he ordered as he turned to Prince Aurelianus, who overheard the conversation and left after nodding to Drysten. "Matthew!" he called.

The man walked up from his right, a shallow cut on his sword arm, but mostly unharmed. "Lord?" he asked through a tired voice.

"Come with me. We're to have a conversation," Drysten said as he lowered his shield and handed it off to Bors. "They look beaten. They may just need further convincing."

Matthew gave a reluctant nod and followed Drysten as he began walking toward the Principia with his hands outstretched to show he meant no harm. A spear struck the ground ten or so feet in front of the two, causing them to wearily glance at each other before a voice shouted from the second story of the stone building.

"They wish to know if we want to surrender."

Drysten scoffed. "Tell them I will only speak to their leader, and I will only do it here."

Matthew obediently shouted something in the language of the Northmen. After a moment, the tall blonde man with the unkempt hair limped from the doorway of the building, limping from two arrow wounds he had taken from the Cretans. One arrow was broken off in his shoulder, while the other was recently removed from his right thigh. The man took a few steps toward the two men and shouted something in his native language.

"He says his name is Drust. He wants to know why we are trespassing in... I think he said Gododdin, though I have never heard of the place."

Drysten turned to the man and briefly sized him up before he looked back to Matthew. "Tell him we will allow them to surrender and leave with their lives. Tell him we want no further bloodshed."

Matthew translated what needed to be said, all the while Drysten slowly glanced across the faces of his enemy. They undoubtedly looked beaten, but Drysten guessed the men were still ready to meet their ancestors, something he would grant them should this leader choose to continue fighting.

Drysten counted the number of men his Britons would have to cut through to secure the fortress. To his dismay, he found the numbers seemed to be a bit more even than he'd anticipated. Snapping him from his thoughts, the man limped closer with the aid of another blue faced soldier and shouted something to Matthew.

"What did he say?" Drysten asked.

Matthew turned with a nervous look. "He said there will be no surrender without the assurance of their lives.

They want to exchange prisoners. People of equal importance."

"Did they have anyone specific in mind?" Drysten asked.

Matthew nervously glanced toward the man seemingly called Drust. "You for him. The leaders." Matthew then turned and shouted something else without Drysten's permission, causing Drust to let out a frustrated sigh, before yelling something in response.

"What did you tell him?" Drysten inquire.

"I... informed him you are not in charge," Matthew replied.

Drysten took a step toward the former priest. "Matthew, what *specifically* did you tell him?" he asked in a raised voice.

Before Matthew could answer, Drysten's father slowly walked through the front line of the shield wall. "He correctly informed them who was in charge. Tell him I accept."

Drysten turned and grabbed Matthew by the collar. "You tell that fucker I am the one in charge. My father needs medicine and won't survive more than a few hours without it."

Matthew's eyes went wide as he tried to find the words to calm his commander. All he could do was open and close his mouth as Drysten stepped closer and closer. "Lord... I—"

"Tell him now!" Drysten screamed into the priest's face.

"No!" Hall said as he limped toward his son, who was noticeably red in the face. "It is time you led these men yourself, son."

"Father..." Drysten muttered, wide-eyed. "You'll die..."

"Most men do." Hall nodded and calmly smiled. "I have gone too long without seeing your mother. The only thing of hers I have had in all these long years of her absence, is you. I wish to meet my daughter. I know now I can leave you in the knowledge you will be a great man and will lead my people well. Everything I have is now yours, Drysten. That means my small amount of wealth along with all my responsibilities," Hall said as he smiled at his son, proud and satisfied with the man he had become, "I know you will do great things. Things I was not capable of. Things the gods above have chosen you for."

Drysten's eyes began to well as he realized this would be the last time he ever spoke to his father. The two silently embraced for a moment before Hall gave Drysten his ring of the Legio Victrix, with "VI" carved into its golden band, and his golden chain around his neck. Amiram slowly walked from the front of the shield wall, holding a hand to his bloody cheek as he slowly made his way toward his captain.

Hall turned and placed a hand on his shoulder. "You take care of my son. He will need good men working the ship." Hall removed his hand from Amiram's shoulder and looked on the faces of the men he led into battle. Most were noticeably spent from the fighting and some were still trying to fight through wounds that may eventually take them. Hall nodded to the prince before turning to Bors. "Anything you wish me to tell your father, boy?"

Bors looked at Hall with tears in his eyes. "Tell him... tell him I am sorry," he answered before lowering his head. "Tell him I am sorry," he whispered to himself as he lowered his head.

Hall chuckled. "Bors, look at me," causing the man to slowly lift his head, "your father would never want any kind of apology from you." Hall nodded his head and briefly placed a hand on his son's shoulder before looking to the enemy lined up ahead of him. He took a deep breath and finally began to step toward the enemy line. Drust began to walk forward as well, keeping pace with Hall.

"Father," Drysten called, waiting for Hall to turn. "Thank you. Thank you for everything."

Hall smiled warmly at the son he was so proud to say was his, then once again turned and marched his way toward his enemy. Drust again kept pace with Hall until they were about to pass one another. They offered each other an uncomfortable nod as they did so, and each man continued forward until they reached the other side of their respective lines.

"Order your people to withdraw immediately," Drysten ordered the enemy commander before turning away and looking to Jorrit. "Make a path for them," he commanded.

Matthew translated for the enemy leader, who turned and gave a nod of his head. The Picts slowly moved their lines toward the Northern gate as Amiram slowly walked up to Drust and placed a knife at his throat, insinuating the man's fate if his army did not withdraw peacefully. Jorrit mouthed something to the men to create an opening. As it began to widen, the beaten men from the North walked through and out the gate.

The whole process took little more than a few moments, but for the men involved, it felt like years. Everyone was expecting the other side to pick up a weapon in resistance to the retreat, but to Drysten's relief, nothing happened. Before long, the Britons were left with nothing more than smoke-filled air grabbing at their lungs and the bodies of their brothers laying on the ground around them.

No men were heard cheering for the victory. Each man simply thanked the various gods the diverse army worshipped that their lives had been spared.

"Two day," Drust said to Drysten through a thick accent, "the man... return... two day."

"Both of you will be dead well before then. I am no fool. You chose this because you understand your wounds will be fatal, much like my father does." Drysten gestured for Amiram to help him into the Principia, taking a handful of others with him.

He disobeyed you! Kill him!

"Matthew," Drysten said coldly as he turned toward the priest.

Matthew took a step back, unsure of what Drysten would do next when he reached him. Drysten eventually did, then paused for a short moment before closing a fist and abruptly striking him, sending him down to the ground in a heap.

"I expect my men to follow my orders. I expect them to do what I *tell* them," Drysten said as he pointed to himself, still towering over the surprised man looking at him wide-eyed in terror. "If you ever do anything like this again, I will kill you slowly and painfully." Drysten then turned and faced his men, ordering them to reinforce the gate to prevent any kind of attack from the Northmen should they change their mind about retreating.

A handful of men stayed behind with Drysten, mostly his closest friends and the leaders of the army. Nobody said a word, each man understanding the best thing to do for Drysten was offer their silence. He stood gazing into the fires of the buildings around him, but he knew his life was different now. Where he once had to find his place in the world, his father had now given him one. He was to lead the men who served his father, and do what he could to provide for them.

"Lord," Matthew said as he finally got up from the ground, slightly dazed, "I meant no harm by my actions, Lord. His wound was fatal, and I feared to lose both you and him in one day. The men need leadership. The men need a man to *follow*."

Drysten obviously heard him speak, but refused to turn and face the man who sentenced his father to die.

"Lord?" Matthew said again. He took two small steps closer before whispering. "Drysten?"

Drysten finally turned to face him.

"I am sorry," Matthew whispered before leaving to help the men at the gate. "I truly am."

Bors walked up to Drysten with the king once Matthew had gone. Garbonian looked at Drysten with sad eyes. "Like the great Coel Hen, your father was also a noble man. Certainly better than most I have ever met. It's a shame Britannia demands the blood of such men for her altar."

"Thank you, Lord King," Drysten said weakly before looking down at the ring and chain in his hands. "I fear I will not live up to what he expects of me. I have half a mind to go after him, but I know that would cost more lives. Should we even succeed, he would never forgive me for those sacrifices. Especially considering he likely won't survive his wounds."

The king walked up and placed his hand on Drysten's shoulder. "You're quite right about that, boy. And as far as living up to him, I'm not sure how to help you with that. All the advice I can give is for you to live the way you were taught. I am certain he would be quite satisfied with that."

Drysten returned a weak smile before placing his father's "VI" ring onto his finger and golden chain around his neck. The weight of the chain was strange to Drysten, almost as though it had more to it than its *physical* weight. It had belonged to the chiefs of Hall's tribe for generations. And now it belonged to Drysten, the newest among those names.

Drysten turned and looked over the men still standing behind him. "Where is Diocles?" he asked.

Dagonet gestured toward a man laying with his back to the wall of the Eastern granary, a hand to his face and covered with blood.

Drysten jogged over with Bors to meet his friend. "How bad is it?" he asked Diocles as he knelt beside him.

"Dagonet did what he could for the eye." The Greek let out a frustrated and strained sigh. "Not fatal. Not pleasant either though."

Drysten called for Bors to find Magnus and some bandages before turning back to Diocles. "I am sorry this happened to you. I promised you a stable occupation and a small amount of wealth, and I gave you war in the name of a petty *fucking* king."

Diocles returned a half-hearted grin. "I suppose you did. You owe me, but I would not feel too guilty. I have a decent reason to live."

"Yes, you do, I need my second-in-command," Drysten

replied.

Diocles shook his head with a smile. "Have you met Oana?"

A perplexed look crossed Drysten's face. "Titus' daughter? Did you—"

"I did!" Diocles said with a satisfied smile. "Hopefully she doesn't mind my missing an eye, but we will have to see.

CHAPTER XXV

Three days passed with not so much as a sighting of any Northmen while the Britons, Saxons, and Guayrdians fixed up the fort. Surprisingly, the old Roman water tank and baths were still in service, which meant the job of dousing the fires was much easier than anticipated. The silver and iron were found under a loose floorboard in the Principia, in an old office on the second story of the building. King Garbonian took almost all the metals to Din Guayrdi with half of his forces. For Jorrit, he granted one silver ingot and four of iron before inviting him to bring his people to Din Guayrdi. A proposition Jorrit declined.

Drysten ordered the wounded men to be sailed back to Petuaria under the command of Amiram and the now one-eyed Diocles. Diocles was convinced he needed to remain in Petuaria upon their arrival, but both he and Drysten knew how well the Greeks on the Fortuna's crew followed orders. Drysten then sent Jorrit, the Saxons, and Matthew back to inform the king of their success, and to return with word of King Ceneus' response.

Bors journeyed out the morning after the battle to reclaim his father's body from the hillfort he had died on. He took Heraclius and Dagonet along with him, partly for company, and partly for protection. After the second day, there was still no sight of Hall, though Drysten knew there was no chance of him being alive with the wound he endured.

In the afternoon of the fourth day, Bors arrived back to Segedunum with not one, but two bodies on the back of his horse. One was Bors the elder, and the other belonged to Hall. Drysten slowly walked up to the horse to examine the body for signs of torture or maltreatment and found his father naked with deep marks across his neck and wrists.

"What happened to him?" Drysten said in a disgusted tone.

Dagonet stepped forward. "He looked like he must have died shortly after the battle. I don't think he was tortured, but—"

"The fuckers hung him naked and upside down from a tree about a mile North," Bors interrupted, visibly angered.

"The rope marks?" Drysten wondered aloud.

Dagonet shuffled his feet. "They torment their prisoners before they execute them, Lord. There's a chance he was still..."

Treat them in kind, the voice commanded.

Drysten clenched a fist around the blade at his hip. "Bring me Drust and prepare twenty men to join me," he said coldly.

The men did not hesitate and after a few short moments the group departed to the tree where Hall had been hanging from. Drysten's guess, Hall died shortly after the battle ended but that did not change the fact the barbarism of the Picts was unnecessary and demanded punishment. Drust was brought from the Principia, white in the face from an infection in one of his wounds. He struggled to keep up with the group following behind Drysten, but was forced to nonetheless.

Drysten was content in the knowledge the enemy chieftain had nothing more to hide from him, as he endured a rather aggressive round of questioning from Gawain and a handful of Powysians. He told of the various Pictish tribes who swore oaths not to attack one another until the Britons were driven back, and that there were even a handful of Gaelic tribesmen in attendance serving a man named Abhartach.

Abhartach was apparently some feared warrior from the West, but Drysten doubted he'd ever run across him. Those men were now corpses under a bonfire outside of Segedunum, but Drysten did indeed notice their cold look as they were piled with the Picts. All were bald, and appeared to have each had their tongues cut out in some sort of ritual of initiation some time ago. In any case, Drysten believed he had all the information he needed from the man, and watched the ravens float overhead as they began nearing the final resting place for Drust.

After a moment, a tree with a rope beside it was found, and Drysten looked to Bors, who nodded his head in confirmation. "Hang him the same way they did my father. Make certain his people can see," Drysten said coldly. "Hang him high."

Drust was stripped naked and the rope was tied around his ankles. The other end was thrown over the strongest looking branch to be caught by Bors. He handed a section to Heraclius at the base of the tree and the two men looked to Drysten for permission. Upon receiving a nod, they quickly hoisted Drust up. His head hit the ground with a loud thud, as his feet were pulled out from underneath him. After a moment of pulling by the two men, the rope was tied off.

"Tie it off around a trunk," Drysten ordered. Bors and Heraclius complied, and the man was soon hanging from the branch. A few stones were thrown by people standing around and after one hit him on the side of the head, he became motionless.

"He would have died soon anyway," Dagonet nonchalantly put in.

Drysten nodded and gestured for the men to proceed back to the fort. They were silent as they returned, but did not seem to be in poor spirits, and arrived to find a tired-looking King Garbonian readying his force to leave.

"Going home?" Drysten asked.

The king nodded. "I fear reprisals will begin in my lands

for my participation here. You're certainly more than welcome to join me in defending them. You could serve a proper king for once," he added cheerfully.

Drysten smiled. "I would, but there is a matter of payment I must discuss with your brother. Besides, our families are waiting for us."

The king smiled, patted Drysten on the shoulder, and yelled to his men in his people's tongue to move North. He glanced back to Drysten once more to nod farewell, then departed.

Jorrit returned with Matthew later in the day, both visibly worn from sailing with an undermanned ship. Many of Jorrit's Saxon and Frisian sailors had been wounded in the battle and were taken with Amiram, unlikely to return. The ship was beached on the sand closest to the fort, where Drysten and Dagonet walked out to meet the men as they disembarked. Joining them was Titus's son, Gaius, as well as a small number of others needed to reinforce their numbers.

"Well?" Drysten asked as he approached the Frisian.

Jorrit shook his head. "The prince returned shortly before we did. He said your father killed the man they called Aosten and said something about you both trying to usurp the king."

Drysten chuckled. "What the fuck would I want to rule Ebrauc for. Being surrounded and unable to protect my borders does not seem like an enjoyable way to live."

"I know it, but the king doesn't. He wants to speak to you, though I would not trust him," Jorrit responded wearily. "Should you decide to return to Petuaria, you will most likely be arrested."

Drysten was dumbstruck by the accusations brought against him and his father. He had barely known Aosten but knew he was a good man. From all he heard about the prince, he was quite sure the opposite was true. And it did not seem fair to him that the good man should be the one killed at the hands of the cruel one.

"The *real* murderer is the heir to the bastard's throne. Prince Aurelianus told me as much."

"I'd wager we saw him riding off before the battle on the hilltop," Dagonet confirmed. "Always has been a gutless little twat."

Drysten turned to Dagonet. "Tell Gawain he is in charge of the fort. All our forces not belonging to Ebrauc are to be marched back to Eboracum at once." Dagonet quickly turned and walked inside the fort's Southwestern gate to relay the orders to the men as Drysten turned back to Jorrit. "Did he look like he was readying forces as you left?"

Jorrit shook his head. "Hard to do when you know nothing about war and only have one general remaining. Especially when that one general is the man you are attempting to arrest." Jorrit ran his hand over his head as he thought of a possible solution, but came up empty. "How many men do we have?"

Drysten thought for a moment. "Out of the ones who will be coming South, I would say we have two hundred left. I believe forty or so are Powysian, so I cannot say whether or not they will fight for us should the need arise."

"They will," a voice said from behind them. Drysten turned to see the prince walking up to greet them. "Powys values traits of honor and loyalty over those of treachery and cruelty. We only helped Ceneus retain the throne because the man trying to take control of Rheged was much worse. At least at the time, it was believed he was worse. Now, I believe we were simply tricked into believing so. I also wonder what he had to do to attain his kingship now that I have been acquainted with King Garbonian."

"He never told me specifically, but made it known that his brother was untrustworthy and vile," Drysten said with a shrug. "Either way, we must journey home. If for no other reason than to go to our families and take them someplace else."

"Again," Bors quipped.

"How did Eidion's men even get back so quickly?" the prince asked as he walked toward Jorrit.

Jorrit chuckled. "They showed themselves in Din Guayrdi soon before I found you. Apparently, he stole fishing boats shortly after that from some villagers and made it to Arbeia. They have a light garrison there and he was able to take some horses before running back South."

Drysten wheeled around. "Are you telling me the king has more men at the fort on the other side of the fucking *river?*" To which Jorrit nodded his acknowledgment.

"I hate him," Bors said in a frustrated tone. "I don't even *know* him and yet I hate him."

Jorrit chuckled. "Most kings have that effect on *some*. This is the first one I have met one who has that effect on *all* people."

Drysten sighed before returning Jorrit's gaze once again. "How are the wounded we sent back?"

"The Greek fared well enough, but my man Braxus may succumb to a stomach wound. A few others perished as well, but Magnus did quite the job in keeping everyone alive," Jorrit responded.

Drysten nodded. "I am sorry about Braxus. He seems like a good man."

"Aye," Jorrit said as he nodded, "a good man indeed. He may yet live, he is unnaturally strong for such a skinny man."

Drysten's men were ordered to gather their belongings at once to prepare for the march South. They would be crossing over the River Tinea by way of the Pons Aelius bridge about four Roman miles to the West. The area was uninhabited, but there were recent stories of Roman ghosts wandering old buildings in search of their families. There were many such stories in the Roman territories after the empire's exit, although the people who were alive to remember the Romans mainly viewed them as superstition. It also seemed to Drysten it was the newer generations who were the ones dreaming up the stories of roaming spirits in the first place.

The army departed from the Western gate, walking through the burnt-out buildings that once belonged to the village situated just outside the entrance on the Southern side of Hadrian's Wall. It was apparent from the fires that very few people survived the initial attack by the Picts, and Drysten found himself wondering which home had belonged to Cynwrig before he was forced South.

The marching column made its way through the village and came upon the stone bridge built by the Romans so long ago. It stood in the shadow of an unoccupied fort, making Drysten wonder whether any of these places would ever be occupied in the future.

"Continue on, we will not be stopping until we reach Concangis," Drysten said, speaking of a small settlement built around a timber fort. Drysten did not know if there were any villagers still living in the area, but remembered there was once a street stretching from the village all the way South to Eboracum. "We should reach the village in about five hours, give or take."

"About right," Dagonet confirmed.

Drysten turned to his lead scout. "You spent significant time this far North?"

Dagonet nodded. "When I was first tasked to become a scout, I was based in the North. I roamed around these parts, trying to warn others of raids from Northmen and often found very good hunting along the way."

"You mean game or Northmen?" Drysten inquired.

"Both," Dagonet returned with a smile.

The army trudged on through mud caused by heavy mist coming down from overhead. It was not causing much of a hindrance to the march, but was still viewed by many as a slight inconvenience. Much of the area South of the bridge was comprised of open fields, filled with verdant green foliage in all directions. It was a pleasant change from the blood-soaked earth of Segedunum his men had grown accustomed to. As he walked, Drysten found himself fiddling with his father's ring, twirling it around his finger as he gazed off into the distance.

Bors chuckled as he pat Drysten on the back. "We'll give them both a proper funeral."

"I hope we will have the opportunity," Drysten said as he looked behind him. "The king may have other ideas."

The sun was now setting over the Roman stonework of Eboracum's fort. Ceneus paced its courtyard from side to side with the uncomfortable news he received from his eldest boy. "I do *not* believe it!" King Ceneus roared as his son stood quietly in front of him. It had been little more than a few minutes since Prince Eidion returned with news the king's newest general planned to usurp his throne. "The man has no aspirations to speak of."

Prince Eidion smirked. "The man killed Aosten. What more do you need to hear, father?"

The king dismissively waved his hand toward his son and turned away in frustration. *How can he believe that I would accept this nonsense?* he wondered.

His son was sent with his most trusted commander alongside a man who he all but promised the world to for his service. Now, it would seem Eidion returned with an obviously fabricated tale of that man being a murderer.

"The lords of your court will demand the head of Aosten's killer," Bishop Germanus added as he strolled closer to the king. "For all your faults, Ceneus, I *know* you to be a man of justice."

"You simply wish him dead because his presence is inconvenient," King Ceneus angrily returned.

"What of Prince Aurelianus?" a worried voice trembled from behind the king.

King Ceneus felt a wave of calm wash over him as he turned to see the beautiful face of his daughter approaching alongside his wife, Heledd. These were the only two people

Ceneus had which he knew he could trust without question.

"That dullard of a prince is fine, sister," the prince responded. "Last I saw of him, he was bedding a farmgirl he met North of Hadrian's Wall."

Something the king knew of Prince Ambrosius was his faithfulness to his daughter came without question, even if Ambrosius believed nobody knew of their relationship. It was unsettling to know Ystradwel would marry the man and leave this place, but he knew she would be taken care of by possibly the best man Ceneus had ever met.

Yet another lie, the king thought.

Ystradwel calmly walked toward her brother, pausing a moment while she glared at him. Ceneus' heart skipped a beat as she quickly raised her hand and angrily slapped it across her brother's face. "You lie. That is all you ever do."

Bishop Germanus seemed to nearly choke on his tongue as he waddled forward. "Discipline this whore, Ceneus!"

"No, no I will not," the king replied with a shake of the head. "What she says is true. My son *is* a liar. A liar who is about to cost a good man his life."

Prince Eidion scoffed. "A good man who does not share the values of our kingdom."

"Quite right, boy," stated the approving bishop.

King Ceneus slowly walked toward Bishop Germanus. "I have little choice but to punish the man for his actions. I know this, but what I also know, is if you ever call my daughter a whore within earshot of myself or any of my guards—"

"My king!" a rider said from behind the group.

Ceneus wheeled around to see an exhausted-looking messenger approaching through the main gateway from the city. "What news? Has my son returned?"

The rider shook his head. "I encountered Prince Gwrast as I rode through the gates, Lord King. He should be here momentarily should you choose to wait for him here. But I was sent from Segedunum."

"Out with it," the king said as he narrowed his eyes at

the grinning Eidion.

The messenger nodded. "Segedunum is yours, Lord King. Lord Hall is presumed dead, as he sacrificed himself as a hostage to end the fighting and secure the capture of the fort."

"Hardly what a usurper would do, don't you think, boy," Ceneus said to his son with a sideways glance. He could easily see the contorted expression Eidion wore in response to being outed as a liar.

The messenger was clearly confused by the statement. "Usurper, Lord King? Lord Hall served you well, of that I can personally assure you."

King Ceneus nodded. "I expected as much," he warmly replied. "Forget what you heard here. What of the losses?"

"King Garbonian's—" the messenger began.

"My *brother* aided them?" a surprised Ceneus said with a gasp. He turned to his son, who appeared to the king to be as confused as he was. "I suppose that was why he was not present when you journeyed to his lands for aid."

Prince Eidion shrugged. "I suppose, father. The only man of any rank I encountered was your new Frisian pet."

"Yet another thing we have yet to discuss," the king responded before training his attention back to the messenger. "You may leave."

The messenger nodded and turned his horse back toward the town, disappearing into the darkness shortly after. The group awkwardly stood in silence as Ceneus turned around, seeing a striking rift between the two sides. On one, stood his beautiful wife and daughter and on the other stood the bishop and his hateful firstborn. A strange sight, as he knew these two groups would somehow find a way to war with one another shortly. Of that Ceneus had no doubts.

"Father..." another voice said from behind.

The king turned to see his favored son dismounting from his horse, trailed by twenty of the fifty royal guards he sent with him.

"My son…" Ceneus whispered, "where are the rest—"

"Dead, father." Gwrast's voice cracked as he slowly shuffled toward the king. "I do not… I did not mean to disappoint you."

King Ceneus attempted to show a warm smile to his son, but wasn't certain he could. The sight of his strongest boy in a distraught state seemed to create an uneasy feeling in everyone around. Even Bishop Germanus was confused by the display. Everyone stood silent as a hooded man was brought up from behind Prince Gwrast, with the two men leading him sporting uncomfortable expressions as they halted in front of the king."

King Ceneus glanced toward his wife before gesturing toward the nearest building. He waited for her and his daughter to walk through the door before turning back to the prisoner. He could somehow feel the evil emanating off the man in front of him, almost as though the Christian devil himself was standing there. As he slowly extended a hand toward the burlap bag covering the stranger's face, Ceneus thought he could hear him sniffing like an animal catching the scent of its prey.

"Father," Gwrast whispered.

Ceneus glimpsed to his boy and noted he was shaking his head. The prisoner's hands were bound in front of him, covered in furs which looked aged and stained a dark brown on the cusps over his wrists. The stained hands slowly lifted toward the sack, gripping the bag and slowly peeling it away.

"Christ almighty…" Bishop Germanus whispered, barely audible to the king as he gazed on the gangly looking creature standing defiant in front of him.

The man was pale, paler than a corpse even. His pupils were tiny, yet his eyes were rather large. The strange man slowly gazed over the men standing in front of him, and a smile began to curl his lips, which were an odd hue Ceneus could not place.

"Abhartach…" the beast whispered.

The man's movements were slow and deliberate, and his gaze seemed to draw the life from Ceneus as the man's hairless head turned to face him.

Ceneus straightened his back. "I am—"

"*Meat*," the prisoner interrupted. The man's smile widened, causing Ceneus to betray a hint of revulsion as he felt the corner of his mouth curl up.

Gwrast tore the sack from the prisoner's hands and stuffed it over the man's head. "Take him to the darkest cell you can find," he stammered to the guards, both of whom wrenched the prisoner away from the king and toward the fort.

The king waited until the man was out of earshot before walking toward Gwrast. "He called us... meat. And what way of life turns a man's features to that of a *corpse*?"

Gwrast stepped toward his father. "We attacked their camp after we tracked them through the night. I didn't realize it at the time, but they knew we were coming. They killed thirty of your men before we found him," he explained through a stutter.

Ceneus let out an uncomfortable sigh. "These men are more dangerous than we realized."

Gwrast nodded. "We did not know any of our men were gone until we found him. All of mine were alive, but they went after yours exclusively. I don't even know how many attackers there were, as they barely left any tracks."

"You did not fight them?" Eidion questioned. Normally, the boy's tone would be antagonistic, but Ceneus could only hear his confusion and fear.

Gwrast turned to his brother. "There was no fight. We found one man at their camp. We saw no others. We heard no screams, only the sound of one man nibbling on..." Gwrast's gaze dropped to the ground.

Ceneus placed a hand on his son's shoulder. "I have heard enough. Rest, my boy."

Gwrast lifted his head and nodded before shuffling toward the building his mother and sister disappeared into. Ceneus was left staring into the ground as he imagined the sights his boy couldn't put to words.

"Lord King," the bishop beckoned. "It would be wise to send patrols to the west."

Ceneus glanced to the bishop and his eldest boy, both failing to hide their uneasiness. "I will send Hall's boy out upon his return."

The king received no response from either man, and thought that was the end of it.

Just before nightfall, the army finally reached the village of Concangis. The villagers were mostly inclined to stay indoors, considering they had no way of knowing the intentions of their new guests. Drysten gave a reassuring wave toward a few children, who had stopped whatever game they were playing to gaze upon the man wearing the extravagant, yet bloodstained armor. They scurried away at the call of their mother, a gorgeous woman who had hair as bright as gold and unmarred skin.

"Morrigan's tits," Dagonet whispered to himself. "Now that right there is the most beautiful thing I have *ever* seen."

To Dagonet's great disappointment, her smiling husband chose to neglect his orders and march home with the Fortuna's men. The beaming man jogged over to his excited wife and four thrilled children.

"Damnit! Every time!" Dagonet said in frustration, amusing the men around him.

The woman's husband turned to Drysten and began to walk over, most likely to ask for forgiveness at being caught, or for permission to remain with his family. Drysten simply smiled and waved at him to stay put, finding a bit of amusement from the man's boldness. "You're home already, brother, stay with your people." The man smiled and nodded his head in thanks, returned to his beautiful wife, and disappeared inside their home. Drysten turned to the men at his back. "We make camp here for the night, so do not stir up any trouble. I want no more grievances the king may choose to throw against me," he commanded.

"Did we not leave the men from Ebrauc in Segedunum?" Dagonet asked.

Drysten shrugged. "Some chose to follow us South. If they should choose to be with their families instead of fight under Ceneus, I do not care."

Dagonet chuckled. "I'm certain Gawain would not be very pleased to see some of his men had left their posts."

"That makes two of us. I was not pleased to see how many men were hanging from trees when we arrived. Those are the *real* cowards. I will not punish a man who loves his family. Besides, he was called to fight and now the fight is over," Drysten shot back.

"The fight is never over, Lord," Dagonet sullenly returned.

The army halted and men began to disperse throughout the town, with most going toward the small market for more provisions. Drysten briefly looked around before Titus' son, Gaius, caught his attention. "Lord," he began, "the armor suits you well."

Drysten smiled. "I do hope you're okay with the gift from your father. If not, I will gladly return it to you."

Gaius shook his head. "I feel as though there is only one man here who should wear it. Though I would not say no to a proper set of lorica segmentata if one were available."

"I will have my father's given to you once we make camp. It is only right considering the kindness your father has showed me," Drysten responded. The armor was found tossed aside a few yards away from the tree Hall was hung from. A scout had brought it back to Drysten the evening Drust was hung in Hall's place.

Gaius raised an eyebrow. "You would not wish for your *own* boy to wear it?"

Drysten smiled and shook his head. "I cannot worry

about my son until I see him born. Besides, Isolde may be growing a girl."

"I thank you, Lord. I'll wear it proudly," Gaius said with a smile.

The two continued to speak for a few moments until Gaius finally bid Drysten farewell and went to join a group of his men who had accompanied him with Jorrit. Drysten watched the group as they made their way to the market, wondering if he was truly ready to lead his people. Right when he was questioning his leadership, he found himself again twirling his father's ring around his finger, instantly reminding him of all the things his father had taught him. He felt reassured at once and held his head up a little higher as he finally moved toward the tents being erected on the Southern edge of the town.

Men were laying down their bedrolls and preparing for what they hoped to be a moderately restful night's sleep. Some had the good fortune to obtain ale from the local taverns before it was all bought up, while others were content with drinking water from a well located in the village interior. Drysten spied a few men playing a game involving dice and small pieces placed along a pathway. He stopped and watched for a few moments before one man noticed his presence.

"Would you like to play, Lord?"

Drysten shook his head, reminded of the game Maurianus would play as he cheated the Fortuna's crewmembers. "I am content to watch for a moment, but thank you."

"It's a fun time, Lord. The game is *centuries* old and played by many men from the East. My father taught me to play when I was young," the man said.

"Your father was from the East?" Drysten inquired.

The man shook his head. "He was born in Italia, but served in Judea where he learned it."

Drysten nodded. "Well, don't let me ruin your enjoyment, but get some rest soon, as we have a long march ahead of us tomorrow."

The man nodded happily and returned to his dice while Drysten continued to walk through his camp. He found himself in the area where most of the Powysians had camped, and watched Prince Aurelianus doing much the same thing, before the two looked at each other and nodded in greetings. Drysten slowly stepped toward the prince, weaving through groups of tired soldiers relaxing beneath him.

"How are your men doing?" he asked.

The prince sighed. "We lost many to this little errand Ceneus sent us on. I fear my uncle will withdraw many of our forces from Ebrauc when he learns of all the details."

"Hard to argue with that decision. From what I was told, they were supposed to provide security, not fight in wars," Drysten responded.

The prince nodded. "We were sent as an envoy at first, then were turned to safeguarding roads and old Roman forts. King Ceneus practically begged us to help him regain Segedunum, convincing us of its strategic importance to the kingdom's protection. Now that I know he just wanted to regain lost wealth..." The prince hesitated mid-sentence, unsure of his next words. "Ah, no matter now. We will learn from our mistakes and choose our allies better in the future." He shuffled a little closer to Drysten. "Also, I regret I have not expressed my sorrow for the loss of your father. He was a good man. He taught me much in the short time I knew him."

Drysten glanced down before returning Ambrosius' gaze. "I thank you, Lord Prince. He will be missed by many."

"I am sure he will be, but please, my friends call me Arthur." The prince placed a hand on Drysten's shoulder. "If you are half the man your father was, I would feel safe placing my men under your command in the future. Should you need a new lord to follow, I hope you understand where to look for him."

"Well, I have never been to Powys, but I will surely consider your offer. Especially since the man who I am currently fighting for has shown himself to be a greedy fool with no real morals to speak of."

Arthur smiled and withdrew his hand from Drysten's shoulder. "He fooled us both, brother. I don't know how he managed it, but he has fooled many since he took the throne. We should just be glad to have found him out, rather than die in his service."

Drysten nodded as he gazed over the Powysians observing the two speak. "And your men? How are they faring?"

Again, the prince sighed as he turned to his people. "Well, we have scarcely a quarter of our original numbers remaining. These men will return home, and a new army will be raised to replace those lost, but I could not ask any more of the ones you see here."

"I heard Prince Eidion abandoned your flank on the hill," Drysten began. "Treachery such as that cannot go unpunished. Especially, when it caused your people so much loss."

Arthur nodded. "We can agree on that."

The two stood in silence for a moment, gazing over the campfires being lit throughout the camp. Both men did not know it, but their futures would be intertwined for decades to come. For now, they were simply thinking about warm beds and smiling loved ones to return to.

Drysten turned and nodded to the prince before making his way back into the village.

The rest of the march took a few days at the leisurely pace Drysten chose. He originally hadn't planned on traveling this slow, but many of the men in his army lived in villages along the way, so he thought it best to allow them to return as the journey continued. It was about seventy Roman miles from Concangis to the gates of Eboracum and he let about twenty of his men go to their families and homes along the way. He was surprised by how many were not professional soldiers. Instead, they were levies raised by Ceneus comprised of common villagers. He was later told by Dagonet that in return for their service, the men were granted small pieces of land. What he neglected to inform them of was where this land was located.

They expected to find lush farmland to till and raise families on. Instead, they received plots located in woodland areas or swamps, hardly conducive to living on. Many of these men were then forced to move to nearby villages and work under tribal chieftains to feed their families. The whole arrangement was designed to keep the peasants reliant on chieftains loyal to the king and prevent unrest in his kingdom. Drysten was sickened by the unfairness of the whole ordeal and was hopeful for their futures should Eidion and Ceneus be overthrown.

"His two other sons do not see eye to eye either, though they are much better men than the king and his firstborn," Dagonet informed Drysten as they entered the city. "I saw men with their insignias walking by as we arrived, so it may not be a bad idea for us to try and speak with them if they are indeed present."

Drysten looked at his scout and nodded, even though he understood agreeing to speak with the two men could be seen as inciting rebellion. "We will speak with the king first, and see what he has to say."

Drysten and Prince Aurelianus led a small group of men into Eboracum, leaving behind most of their forces. Upon reaching the interior of the city, they were greeted by a group consisting of Titus, Diocles, Oana, and to Drysten's delight, Isolde.

Drysten greeted them all warmly and introduced the prince, but fixed his eyes on his wife. "I told you I would return," he said quietly, before pulling her in for a quick kiss. Isolde gave a half smile before turning to Titus, causing Drysten to wonder as to what could possibly have ruined a seemingly happy moment. "What has happened?" Drysten asked his wife.

Isolde turned back to her husband and met his gaze. "The king is calling your father a murderer."

"Eidion..." the prince said angrily.

Drysten scoffed, "And what would the king base this on?"

Titus awkwardly stepped forward. "Your father is said to have murdered Aosten, supposedly the king's most trusted advisor. It is also said your Frisian attempted to kill the prince under your orders."

Drysten stood awestruck by the allegations. "I... I have never met the fucking prince, and when would Jorrit have been able to try to kill him?"

Titus shrugged and gestured for Drysten to follow. The group walked through the markets and toward the bridge leading to the former legionary fortress on the other side of the River Abos. Diocles and Oana were trailing behind Drysten and Isolde, seemingly oblivious to the current crisis at hand.

"Been like that ever since the cyclops got back," Titus said in amusement. "Not that I'm complaining. It was always hard to find her a suitable man. At least this one seems to have a good head on his shoulders."

Arthur smiled. "Well, he has most of his head left if you're not counting the missing eye."

Drysten and Titus turned to Arthur, showing their amusement just loud enough to prompt Diocles to crane his neck to overhear what was being said. The group continued until they finally reached the river's crossing where they were abruptly stopped by a guard, this one clad in black.

"You will go no further," he ordered with a hand raised, "and will remove your weapons at once."

Drysten glanced to Titus before looking back to the guard. "There were no such restrictions during my last visit."

The guard gave a toothless smile from underneath his

old Roman leather helmet, crackled and dried from the sun during countless marches of its original wearer. "You did not try to kill the prince the last time you were here. Surrender your weapons now, as I will not repeat this order again, *usurper.*"

"Usurper?" Prince Arthur snarled. "You believe your kingdom important enough for people to steal it from you?"

The guard smiled. "Important enough for your people to die in its name, Powysian."

"Enough!" Drysten yelled as Arthur brought a hand onto the hilt of his sword. "There will be no more blood drawn in Ceneus' name. Not from us." Drysten gave Arthur a reassuring nod as he began undoing his sword belt.

"I will take them to the gate," Diocles whispered from behind Drysten. "I will make sure they are not stolen."

"The prince as well," the guard said with a chuckle. "Not that we worry too much about Powysians; they seem to only be good for dying."

Arthur ripped his sword from its sheath and began to surge forward until Drysten gripped his arm to halt him. The prince wheeled around and met Drysten's gaze with his own. It startled Drysten to see the sheer anger in his new friend's eyes. As the prince slowly began to relax his arm, Drysten watched Diocles saunter over and gesture for Arthur's sword. The prince glanced to the guard before handing it over, with Diocles making him the same assurance he made Drysten.

Drysten turned and stared the guard in the eye, wondering what was about to happen when he crossed the river. He slowly handed his sword and dagger to his good friend and glanced to Isolde. Drysten then gestured for her to follow Diocles away in the hopes of keeping her safe. But when nobody was looking, he slipped his father's ring off and crept it into one of her hands.

"Wait, why—?"

Drysten calmly shushed Isolde quiet. "Everything will

be okay." He gave his wife a reassuring nod before turning back to the guard. "If I wished to kill anyone, I would've done so already. There is a whole hill's worth of dead men to the North as a testament to that fact. Now move," Drysten commanded as he took a step forward.

The guard drew back a pace at Drysten's slight advance, and upon looking to his comrades, turned back to Drysten and Arthur. "Go, but do not take your time about it. The king was expecting you days before you finally arrived."

Drysten began to walk over the bridge before he finally glanced behind him to make sure Isolde was indeed following Diocles away. She was, but there was now a larger group of men making their way toward the bridge. Drysten vaguely recognized one of them, but could not place where he had seen him. Dagonet, Jorrit, and Gaius had also met up with Diocles and Titus, all of them looking apprehensive at the realization Drysten was venturing forth without his weapons.

Drysten turned back and began to make his way forward once more. Arthur and himself had finally made it inside of the old legionary fort's stone walls, slowly walking beneath the gates manned by a larger group of black-clad guards.

Drysten guessed there were about two dozen men tasked with watching over himself and the Powysian, all doing their best to not look conspicuous. Most were standing around near the two workshops once used by the Romans next to the entrance of the fort. They were walking through both buildings on either side of the street, but none of them strayed far from the building's entrance, most simply standing in front of them. Drysten and Arthur worriedly looked at one another as they turned right onto the first path leading to the baths.

A nervous guard quickly stepped toward them with his hand on his sword hilt. "He will greet you in the old Principia," he stammered, accompanied by a nod toward the middle of the fort. Drysten nodded before turning around and making his way to the building standing tallest in the very middle of the fortress.

"This feels rather ominous," Arthur said as he viewed the men still eyeing them as they walked.

Drysten glanced behind them, and just as he expected, the guards had begun to follow them deeper into the fort.

"You would think we would get a better reception considering our people *died* for this man," Arthur muttered under his breath.

"No doubt he believes the shit spewing from his boy's mouth."

"Sadly, it seems he is blind to the true quality of him," the Powysian replied as he ran his hand over his head. "I assure you. I will not let him harm you or your people. He relies too heavily on Powys to anger our lords."

"I hope you are correct," Drysten wearily responded.

The two men finally reached the Principia and made their way inside. For the most part, its stonework looked much the way Drysten guessed the Romans had left it. They stepped through the entryway and made their way forward into the forum, an open aired space used by the commanders of the fort for centuries. Many different classes of men once stood behind the podium to address the troops stationed in the city. Some were simple chieftains or petty lords of the locals, while others were prominent military commanders. An emperor even graced the city with his presence on two occasions, with Lucius Septimius Severus even passing away there three centuries prior.

Shortly after arriving, the two made their way through the open space and reached the main building. Right as they entered, both men heard a door shut loudly behind them. Neither man turned to look, but they were each positive the guards had most likely barred the door. They entered the building once used as offices and resting areas by Roman soldiers before Arthur let out a frustrated scoff.

"Bastard took down the statue to Mars!" he angrily proclaimed. "Absolutely ridiculous." He gestured to an empty pedestal which had once held the marble statue atop it.

"There would be many men rolling in their graves if they were to see this," Drysten noted. "My father spoke of times when soldiers would come here to worship various gods before being sent on scouting missions or raids."

Arthur sounded worn out from the realization the gods of his ancestors were slowly being abandoned. "Those times seem to have passed us by. The world is changing..."

"That it is," a voice said from behind the two men. Neither Arthur nor Drysten could recognize the voice. "You know what it is we must speak of, I presume."

Drysten finally turned to face the man, seeing an older man with a powerful brow adorned in a priest's robe. "My business is with the king."

The priest took a step toward Drysten. "Why should a king be bothered with the fate of a murderer?"

"There are no murderers here, priest," Drysten responded.

Arthur placed a hand on Drysten's arm as he stepped forward. "I do not wish to cast accusations, but Aosten's death was surely not caused by a man who was fighting in the king's name. It would make no sense, as I am sure you could agree."

"It truly does make no sense, Prince Aurelianus," the priest responded. He looked away from the men for a moment before returning his gaze toward the Powysian. "How would you approach this issue? I am being told this man here wishes to claim my lord's crown," the man said as he motioned toward Drysten. "How would you respond to these allegations if it was your own title at stake?"

"I would seek the truth, however inconvenient it may be," Arthur abruptly responded.

The priest rubbed a hand to his brow. "It was not *only* the prince who made these allegations. All his men vouched for him as well. Good *Christian* men."

Drysten scoffed. "You really think they would go against their commander?" The question prompted the man to smirk as he stared into Drysten's eyes. Drysten could sense enjoyment in what was about to happen. "This conversation does not matter, does it?" he asked weakly.

"No, boy. No, it does not." The priest drew in a breath before continuing, his smile becoming wider as he readied himself to speak. "By order of King Ceneus ap Coel of Ebrauc, I, Bishop Germanus of Rome, sentence you to imprisonment until your execution at the hands of the king's men. Your lands and possessions are now property of the kingdom, as well as the Church."

Kill him! the voice demanded.

Drysten did not hesitate. He lurched forward and got within a breath from the bishop when men began storming in from doorways on either side of him.

Bishop Germanus smiled as he took a pace backwards. "Guards!" he shouted, prompting Vonig, the guard Drysten had assaulted when he first arrived in Petuaria, to step through a doorway. "Take him below. Leave the other one alone, I do not wish a war with Powys for his return."

"Tell Ceneus he has lost his most powerful ally for this!" Arthur roared as two black-clad men grabbed each of his arms.

Two more men reached forward to grab Drysten, who slunk back out of the way of the closest and connected with a forceful blow to the side of the man's head. The force of his fist sent him down to the ground in a spiral. He looked to Arthur, struggling to free himself from the two men holding him back.

"Do nothing!" Drysten commanded as the second man grabbed his father's mantle, ripping the brooch at its center and uncovering the impressive armor hidden beneath. Drysten grabbed the bottom of the cloak as it was being pulled away and tossed it over the man's head before connecting with a second man's chin, forcing him back a few paces.

He was about to move forward until out of his peripherals a black blur came toward him and the left side of his head felt the blow of a blunt object. He did not feel himself hit the ground, but knew he was still conscious to some degree. He could hear the faint shouting of his new friend, the prince, as well as the orders being barked at by the bishop. He could not make out what was being said, just that the tone of the prince's voice seemed to startle Germanus in some way.

Bide your time, son, a familiar voice whispered in his ear.

Drysten felt calm for a moment, like a benevolent spirit was watching out for him. But then his world started to shift between his ears. Colors began running darker in his vision as shadows danced just out of view, with new voices ringing through his ears.

Another voice slowly began to rustle through Drysten's mind. In a strange way, this one, which had been nothing but malevolent in the past, was strangely comforting.

You will kill him and his brood. You will steal his crown and pillage his lands; you need only wait.

As Drysten tried to turn his head and see the one who spoke, the whole world began to fade out, and he heard no more.

CHAPTER XXVI

Bishop Germanus was sitting in the corner of the remodeled Roman bathhouse, directly across from one of his personal guards, as well as King Ceneus. "The Prisoner should be hung from the gatehouse of Petuaria, you useless *fool*."

The king shook his head. "I will determine the course of action to be taken in this matter."

"Agh! You and your soft spot for the apostates. It was *their* presence which caused the loss of Rome to the barbarians," the bishop replied.

King Ceneus sighed heavily. "I have no soft spot for anyone, Your Excellency. It is merely the idea of executing a man who I did not arrest. Not to mention he was arrested on the word of a liar. Surely Christ—"

"Do not pretend to have a more knowledgeable outlook of our faith than *I*, Ceneus." Bishop Germanus glared at the king with a stare so intense it caused a tingling sensation to be felt over Ceneus' brow. "Agh, no matter. Just lock him away then. He will succumb to either insanity or malnourishment soon enough."

The king leaned back, guilt forcing his mind into places it rarely journeyed. *How have I let myself become a puppet?*

The bishop stormed into his kingdom, made violent demands and now was attempting to murder someone which King Ceneus had actually grown to admire somehow. He knew he would be harboring a dangerous enemy below. The longer he remained there, the more dangerous he would become.

"So long as he does not go free, he should be no concern to us," a voice said from behind Ceneus. He instantly recognized it as his firstborn son, Eidion, and was too ashamed to look back. "Though, I agree with His Excellency. We should skewer his head atop the city gates as a warning to his followers. So long as he lives—"

"Do you never tire of *killing*, boy?" the king screamed. "You have one solution to all life's problems! You are a simpleton with no regard for the sanctity of life."

Prince Eidion cast a wide grin as King Ceneus turned to face him. "Well, father, I have you to thank for all that I have learned in life."

"Away with you!" Ceneus responded as he angrily gestured toward the door.

Bishop Germanus chuckled at the sight of the bickering father and son. "You should listen to the boy. He has a more auspicious outlook on life than you think, Keneu," he said as the prince happily glanced to his feet.

"My name...," King Ceneus began, furious at the bishop forgoing the Christian name given to him upon his conversion, and addressing him by the name of his heathen birth, "is King *Ceneus* ap Coel. That is the only way you will address me. The boy will stay where he is, and your words will cause no more death in my lands."

The bishop stood, clearly amused by the anger he stoked in the king. He nodded to his guard as he stepped out of the water and began making his way toward the door. "We will speak further of this in the morning. I grow tired of your insolence, as does the Vicar."

"The Holy Father is not here, Your Excellency," the king replied with a scoff. "I only see you."

Germanus scowled as he pointed at the king. "You forget who sent me on my errand. Pope Celestine's vision of a world blanketed in God's grace will begin on these vile shores, whether you are willing to face it or not."

Eidion, silent until that moment, sauntered forward. "Are my instructions still the same, Your Excellency?"

Germanus reclined back as he relaxed his shoulders. "Yes, Lord Prince."

Eidion nodded before gesturing for his guards to follow him out. Ceneus watched his son give him a sly grin before he finally walking out of the bathhouse.

Ceneus glared into the bishop's eyes. "Have I not made myself—"

"I have not ordered for the boy's execution, you halfwit," Germanus interrupted. He dismissively waved a hand at the king before exiting the bathhouse after the prince.

After a heavy sigh, the king sat quietly for time, pondering the options he had for Drysten and his people. He contemplated sending a secret envoy to Powys to appeal for asylum on his behalf, staging a mock rescue, or even giving in to the bishop's demands and executing him. The only solution he could muster, one which did not entail war with the bishop, Drysten's people, or anyone else for that matter, was imprisonment. Imprisonment for a time at least. Drysten could prove to have another use which had not yet become apparent. His people will understand he would be executed should they try to rescue him, the bishop would not send word to Rome to summon a holy army to oppose him, and Ceneus' conscience would be clear, as an innocent man would not be put to death in his name.

Eidion was finding it hard to contain his excitement. He journeyed alongside Vonig and a handful of his guard to Petuaria, going over his speech in his mind the whole way. He loved the idea of causing the usurper's people the pain they deserved, and hoped he would remember the face of the man's wife once his speech was over.

Hall and his boy will fade into memory, Eidion mused, causing a smile to cross his face.

"The people of Petuaria have placed guards at the gate,

Lord Prince," Vonig stated.

Eidion could see his second was also relishing the opportunity, as his face was lit with joy and his eyes were wide with happiness. It had been so long since they were able to reassert their authority in the area.

"It does not matter, Vonig. Just make sure you throw the bag with the man's belongings at their feet before I make the grand announcement," Eidion returned with a smile.

Eidion was accompanied by thirty of his personal guards, all of which shared his hatred for the newcomers to the kingdom of Ebrauc. The Frisian's presence in particular seemed to aggravate his men more than anyone. Eidion knew they would relish the opportunity to make an example of him should the opportunity arise.

Eidion glanced back toward the line of men following him, seeing the banner of Ebrauc waving over the head of its bearer. "Not too long now, boys!" he triumphantly declared.

The men responded with a cheer of approval as they approached the muddy path leading to the gate. A handful of men wearing old Roman mail were standing on either side of the entrance, none of which were recognizable to the prince.

"You!" Eidion called out, catching the attention of the nearest guard, "bring the people of this shit-smelling town together!"

The guard glanced to the others stationed near him, clearly ambivalent at the idea of following Eidion's command.

No matter. Not even the insolence of a lowly peasant could dampen my mood now. Eidion thought. Soon, he led his people through the gate to see a pathetic gathering of wounded men and haggard women. *Disgusting wretches.*

The men the prince gazed over looked tired and beaten, likely a side effect of their leader being taken by the bishop. Or as far as they knew, the king. They truly had no idea who held the true power of Ebrauc, and while the prince was aligned with the bishop, he knew it would stay that way. They would see a member of the royal family acting as though he was following the orders of his father, giving the bishop the cover he needed to root out the internal enemies of the kingdom.

"Lord Prince," a man cheerfully yelled, though Eidion could sense the deception in his voice, "to what do we owe this pleasure?"

Eidion glanced to his side and waved Vonig and his guards forward, signaling for them to dismount and create a wall of shields between him and the people of the town, with him mounted behind them. "I have been tasked by our king to deliver you with news!"

"News, Lord Prince?" The lone man who spoke to Eidion slowly limped forward from the group of people on the other side of his shield wall. Many men were backing away from Eidion's spears, while this man curiously seemed unfazed by them.

Eidion was mildly impressed by the old man's resolve. *Should it come to force, perhaps this one would need to die first,* he wondered. "What's your name?"

"I am Titus Octavius Britannicus, of the Sixth Victorious Legion, Lord Prince." It was obvious this man was proud of his past service to Rome, as he held his head higher when he divulged the legion of his service.

"Well then, *Titus,* could you be so kind as to show me this legion?" Eidion replied with a smirk. He now recognized the man as the mercenary once tasked with training his father's men, the bastards in the royal blue cloaks who watched Eidion and the bishop all hours of the day. Their constant presence was beginning to prove a nuisance to the prince.

"I... Lord Prince, I no longer serve—" Titus began.

Eidion raised a hand. "I no longer care." He cleared his throat and looked over the faces of those who remembered his last visit. The visit where he took the head of their lord. Drumond was an old fool, and Drysten was no different. Eidion knew he would enjoy this, as he waved to Vonig to throw down the sack containing Drysten's finely crafted armor and sword. It clattered to the ground in front of Titus, who went white in the face as he saw the armor spill out.

"By order of Lord King Ceneus ap Coel, the *just* king of this *great* kingdom, your lord, Drysten ap Hall, has been executed for the crimes of murder and treason!"

The deafening roar created by the news startled Eidion, who jumped in his saddle at the response. He found himself wondering how Drysten managed to foster such love in the hearts of his people. As he looked to the frantic villagers assembled on the other side of his shields, he noticed many were people who were present during his fight with Drumond.

How? How did such a fool inspire loyalty from those who barely knew him?

"Lord Prince!" Titus yelled, though had Eidion not been able to see him, he likely wouldn't have been able to tell. The noise from the screaming villagers was so deafening it caused his temples to throb. "Lord Drysten—"

"He is a lord no longer!" Eidion screeched. He heard his voice crack from the nerves. His head began to spin as the people seemed to inch closer to his spears, almost as though they didn't care they would easily be killed should they venture too close.

"We'll fucking *gut* you!" a voice yelled from the back.

Eidion spun his head around to find the voice, but failed, seeing only a man with no tongue madly screaming at him.

"Fucking *twat!*" another man yelled.

Eidion raised a hand to cease the madness, but not a single person heeded the gesture. He glanced to Titus and saw him slowly back through the lines and whisper something to a man with a bloody bandage covering one eye. The man looked to the prince, a tear falling down one side of his face, and turned to race toward the villa. That was when Eidion saw him.

Ambrosius Aurelianus erupted from the gates of the villa, leading a column of his Powysians toward the Prince's lines.

That fucking pest. Eidion quickly looked to Vonig. "If anyone gets close enough to kill, do so."

Vonig smiled as he relayed the order, and two men were immediately stuck in the belly before the prince from Powys was able to move the villagers aside.

"You will harm no more of these people!" Aurelianus screamed. The man halted in front of the villagers as he waited for the rest of his Powysians to form a barrier between Eidion and the men and women of Petuaria. The two people skewered by Eidion's spears were squirming around on the ground before being dragged away by a pregnant woman and the man with one eye.

Ambrosius stepped closer to the spears, with the man across from him glancing back for his instruction. Eidion was no fool, and understood killing this Powysian would ignite a war which Ebrauc would never win. Eidion simply looked to his man and shook his head, signaling the Powysian prince would not be harmed.

Ambrosius inched closer, his eyes locked on Eidion. "If I see you harm *one* more villager... *one* more man who I bled with while *you* ran off... you'll be fucking your own face with that sword on your hip before the day is over." Fury spilled out of his glazed over, wide-eyed stare.

Eidion began to calm as the screaming villagers began to run deeper into the town. He gazed over the line of Powysians, seeing the formidable warriors lined up and more than ready to attack. But what Eidion was disappointed to see was the additional men who must have belonged to Drysten piling into the rear lines of the shield wall.

That would certainly tip the scales rather unfavorably.

"Lord Prince," Vonig whispered. "Lord Prince, it would be wise to leave now." The fear in his voice was obvious.

Eidion looked over his men, seeing their wide eyes as they gazed back to him.

You fucking cowards.

Ambrosius kept his gaze locked onto Eidion. "You will leave," he said in a stern tone.

Eidion cleared his throat. "I have also been tasked with the apprehension of two more criminals which served the traitor. My spies told me of their crimes this very morning. Our king's justice works rather quickly, does it not?"

"You will get no more blood from these people," the prince replied.

Eidion glanced at his rival counterpart. "How would your uncle like to hear his nephew, the one man in his royal family not in line for the throne, ignited a war with Ebrauc by assaulting Ebrauc's heir?"

"I don't think you know my uncle," Ambrosius replied with a smile.

"Nevertheless, it would likely cause many problems in his court. You Powysians have already bled much in these lands. I doubt they would want to shed more blood on *your* account." Eidion was relieved to see the fury in Ambrosius' eyes turn to frustration. "Now," Eidion said with a raised voice, "bring me the one known as Matthew, and the man known as Diocles."

The Powysians refused to move, with their commander still glaring at Eidion. Ambrosius knew he couldn't start a war with Ebrauc, but Eidion was also aware he was in a similar position.

Eidion dismounted from his horse and quickly stepped through his shield wall, stopping right in front of Aurelianus. "I will find those two men, as they have crimes to answer for. The king wishes—"

"I will come voluntarily," a timid voice rang out, causing Aurelianus to wheel around. A nervous man with a cross dangling from his neck slowly walked toward the two princes. "I am Matthew, and I am confident I have done nothing wrong. I will come without struggle," he announced. "I look forward to meeting your king."

Eidion smirked. "Not many have said that in recent times." He glanced to the prince and winked, causing a grimace to cross Aurelianus' face. The sight of it gave Eidion a sense of joy he struggled to contain. "Now, where is Diocles."

Behind the Powysian line, the man with the bloody bandage across his eye tried to subtly back away. Eidion saw it immediately and pointed before looking to Aurelianus. "That one belongs to me. He will face the king's justice."

The Powysians began to uneasily glance to their commander, clearly wondering whether they were about to ignite a war.

Try it, you fool.

Eidion watched as Aurelianus slowly glanced behind him, then turned back to Eidion with a smile.

"Diocles!" the Powysian yelled.

The man with one eye began to lose the color in his face. "Lord Prince..." His remaining eye was wide with fear as he reached for the blade at his hip. He fumbled with it as he glanced to the men near him. Eidion saw the Frisian was now with him, with the other huge Saxons from Din Guayrdi lining up next to him.

Aurelianus' smile became wider. "Did you not tell me you wished to serve me?"

Diocles glanced from Aurelianus to the Frisian, the latter of which was giving him a knowing stare. "I... yes, Lord Prince. I did..."

Eidion knew in that moment he had been beaten. "Fine, *whelp*. Take the man and fuck off back to Powys. I grow tired of your kind staining Ebrauc's ground with blood." At that, he turned and mounted his horse, violently yanking it toward the exit to Petuaria.

Vonig followed, screaming the command for the black-clad men to break the formation and follow.

Titus watched as Matthew's hands were tied, and wondered what madness drove the priest to volunteer himself up in such a way. All the old veteran could do for the fool was watch him leave. He looked down to his feet as the sack of extravagant armor lay below.

"Father," Gaius whispered as he placed a hand on Titus' shoulder, "Drysten and his people helped us when we needed sanctuary. We must find a way to return the favor."

How do I tell these people I don't know what to do. I haven't known since Londinium.

Titus ran a hand over his brow as he caught the faint sobbing of a woman coming from behind him. "Oh no..." He turned and saw Isolde sobbing in Marivonna's arms.

Diocles approached from the Powysian line, still white in the face at the idea of being executed. "We need to find a way to get all these people away from here."

Titus slowly bent down and picked up Drysten's sword, gradually bringing the blade out from the brown sack it had been carelessly placed in. He turned the blade over in his hand, wondering how much he had paid for it. The weight was almost perfect, but the length was greater than the blades Titus had used in the Roman legion.

"Sir?" Diocles continued.

But Titus didn't hear him. He was so transfixed on the Drysten's sword he couldn't hear much of anything. He no longer heard the wailing of Drysten's woman, nor the frantic questioning by Diocles, nor the orders being given for the Powysians to usher everyone to the Fortuna and prepare to set out.

"Titus!" the Powysian prince yelled, gently grabbing Titus' arm and snapping him from his thoughts. "The people here need a leader, and they need one *now*."

Titus glanced around. "I..." The words stuck in his throat. All Titus could think of was the similarity between these grieving people and the ones who made the voyage from Londinium with him a few weeks prior. He thought he'd found a man those people could follow, but all he found was another good man who had been turned to a corpse.

"Everyone!" the prince shouted, causing every man, woman, and child to halt what they were doing and turn to face him. "I am Prince Ambrosius Aurelianus of Powys. I know I arrived shortly before that bastard who executed your lord, but I assure you, I am not like *him*." He jabbed a finger toward the Eidion's departing band of men. "This kingdom has showed its true colors to you today, and I wish to extend an invitation for every single one of you to join me in my lands."

A large murmur started through the gathering crowds as the prince slowly looked over each face. Titus gazed over those same faces, seeing something he hadn't known for weeks.

He saw hope.

"In my lands, I am known as Prince Arthur, and I now extend a hand of friendship to every one of you here. I applaud you for all that you have endured in this cruel land, but you will not have a need to endure it any longer."

"How can we leave the place of our birth, Lord Prince?" a voice screamed. Titus recognized it to be that of Conway, the farmer who was tending to Drysten's horses while he was away.

Arthur looked through the crowd as he carefully chose his words. "By putting one foot in front of the other, my friend." The smile the prince produced warmed Titus' heart in a way he didn't understand. He knew everything would be alright should he decide to follow him, but he also knew he couldn't.

Titus met with Ceneus a few days before Drysten's return, and was given a villa across the river from Petuaria. It was shabby compared to Petuaria's, with numerous repairs needed before it could be called a home.

But it was the rest of the deal which Titus knew he couldn't ignore. He was given roughly same deal as Drysten's father, only the lands were to the south. He would have total control of that area on the condition he would keep it safe for the king's people. When Titus began to express his concerns regarding Eidion, Ceneus explained how Germanus and Prince Eidion rarely ventured south, and would surely never go further than Petuaria. Ceneus personally assured him his people would be out of the reach of Eidion and the bishop. Every person Titus still had in his life would be safely across the river, and he knew they would never wish to leave their homes again.

"Lord Prince…" Titus whispered.

Arthur looked behind him. "Speak, man. What would you say to a home you can grow old in?"

"I would say I am already old, Lord Prince," Titus said with heavy eyes.

Arthur grinned. "What of your people then? Will you join me?"

"I cannot, Lord Prince," Titus responded with a heavy sigh. "I swore an oath to Ceneus to keep watch over the Southern bank of the river. As of a few days ago, the king has placed the Frisians in my care as well, as are his Saxons. The king is very good at forcing oaths," Titus explained. He briefly lowered his head before continuing. "He assured me I would find no trouble from…"

Arthur's grin turned to a disappointed frown. He nodded before turning back to the people of Petuaria when Titus began again.

"Lord Prince, take as many of these people as you can aboard the Fortuna and my own vessel. The Victrix is yours."

Arthur looked back and smiled. "You are a kind man, Titus. Thank you."

Titus nodded as he walked back to his wife, still clutching a sobbing Isolde in her arms. Oana was also present, placing a hand on Isolde's shoulder. "You are now under my care, Isolde. You and the child will want for nothing. I swear this to you on my life."

Isolde could only manage a nod as she sobbed into the arms of Titus' wife. Marivonna looked to Titus and gave him a proud nod, much as Oana tried to before a strange looking puppy jumped into Isolde's arms.

"Maebh," Isolde whispered.

Titus pursed his lips in anger as he turned back to the crowds now racing from home to home to grab their items. It was obvious the Powysian prince managed to move the people into believing his promise, but whether he was telling the truth, Titus did not know.

Suppose it doesn't matter so much. Any place is better than Ebrauc.

"Gaius! Citrio!" Titus called, gaining the attention of his two most trusted men. "Bring every person under our command back to the Southern bank of the river. We are not to venture to this accursed town under any circumstances. Anyone who chooses not to join the Powysian, but wishes to be rid of the *filth* that rules this kingdom can accompany us."

Both men nodded as Titus began walking toward Arthur, who was helping a young girl carry a satchel much too heavy for her. They were moving to the Fortuna when Titus caught his attention.

Titus cleared his throat. "I want you to know, if there is ever a war between Ebrauc and Powys, you would be a fool to forget that we are here."

Arthur smiled as he picked the young girl up and slung her satchel over his own shoulder. "I assure you, Titus, we won't. This will not be the last time we speak."

Titus nodded and gestured for the prince to keep moving to the Fortuna, whose crew was ransacking the villa for the provisions needed to make a journey to Glevum, the Powysian capital near their Southern border. He saw Diocles pleading with a handful of men for some odd reason, and overheard each wished to stay behind with Titus to try and form some sort of resistance against Ceneus' rule.

Not yet, boy. Titus thought, producing a smirk. He hadn't

realized it until that moment, but Prince Eidion had accidentally given Titus one last purpose in life.

He would see Ebrauc burn.

Drysten finally awoke to see he was stripped bare, with a sizable portion of blood caked to his left temple. He had no idea how long he was unconscious, nor where he was taken. He slowly stood, instinctually covering his manhood until he realized there was nobody around to see it. The walls and floor were crafted by interlaced stones, with iron crossbars facing a hallway. The enclosure looked old, very old. There was the trickling sound of water nearby, but Drysten could not tell where it was coming from. As Drysten stepped forward, he could see light from a torch coming from around the corner, as well as hear two men speaking.

"Where are the rest of your people?" a man asked.

Drysten quietly walked to the edge of the stone wall, directly next to the source of the torchlight. As he peered around the corner, he saw a man who vaguely reminded him of King Ceneus, only with more unkempt hair and twenty fewer years to him.

Must be another son of his, Drysten thought.

"Your *people* are all that concerns me," another man said, this time from the cell next to Drysten's. This voice was strange, as it seemed hollow, yet hoarse in a way Drysten could not explain. *Off* would be all he could use to describe it.

The man with the torch seemed flustered at the prisoner's response, though Drysten wondered why. The comment seemed rather ambiguous in its nature.

The free man pursed his lips and glanced toward Drysten's cell. He finally grumbled something to himself and began walking in front of Drysten, who could only stand there, naked, as the man finally stopped to gaze inside.

"There isn't supposed to be anyone else down here," the stranger whispered.

Drysten stepped forward. "Perhaps that would be because *I'm* not supposed to be here."

The man chuckled. "Another innocent criminal? I suppose that response is to be expected." The man glanced back to Drysten's neighbor. "That one has done worse than any crime you could have committed. I would stay away from that side of your cell."

"You could also sue for my release considering I truly *am* an innocent man," Drysten quipped as he dabbed his forehead to check for blood, finding none.

The man with the torch smirked and shook his head before turning toward a stairway Drysten had not been able to see in the darkness.

As the man left, Drysten heard his neighbor snicker to himself and shuffle closer. "What was your crime?" The man's voice had an air of authority to it which Drysten instantly found familiar. His father spoke in much of the same way. Or rather, had spoken.

"I committed no crime," Drysten responded.

The man chuckled. "Then what crimes are you *accused* of?"

"Murder." Drysten felt a pang run down the back of his neck as he spoke. "The fuckers are saying I murdered someone. A good man."

"Ah. Good men tend to meet that end," Drysten's neighbor responded. "As for myself, I am accused of stealing *cattle*."

Drysten scoffed. "Hardly worth warning me about."

"These fools are so easily panicked," the man observed. "What do they call you?"

"Drysten. As for yourself?"

"They call me... Argyle."

Drysten noted the pause, but decided the man could simply be reluctant to share his real name. "A pleasure."

"Likewise," Argyle responded.

"Perhaps my people will free us *both* when they hear of my imprisonment," Drysten thought out loud. Truthfully, he wasn't sure how a handful of men could assail a city in the hopes of locating him when he didn't even know where he was.

Argyle laughed. "That would *indeed* be fortunate, but I believe I am right where I am supposed to be."

Drysten glanced toward the stairway as the last light from his captor's torch faded away. "What kind of criminal desires to be in a place like this?"

"Simple," Argyle said through thick laughter. "The sort who desired to be captured."

"You really are a strange one," Drysten stated.

"Maybe you would have preferred the company of the other man they held here. They took him while you slumbered so nicely," Argyle replied.

Drysten instantly thought of Diocles or Titus, men who were the most important to his warband. "Tell me of him."

Argyle sighed. "He was simply a priest, though I did not know his name. He knew you, shouting *Lord, Lord* as they yanked him up the stairs shortly before you awoke. The black ones took him."

Surely, he couldn't mean Matthew, Drysten thought. As unlikely as he thought it could be, he also knew it to be true.

"Like most men I come across in these lands, he truly detested the idea of speaking to one such as myself," Argyle continued. "One thing he *did* manage to divulge, was your people all seem to have been told of your death."

Drysten's heart felt as though it exploded out from his chest. His knees were weak, his neck felt cold, and he felt the crystals of sweat developing on his palms. *No,* he thought, fighting his tears. *They have no idea I still live.*

"Briton?" Argyle yelled, somehow unsure if Drysten hadn't heard him. "Briton!" he yelled louder.

"I..." Drysten managed.

"Ah, you did hear me then." Argyle chuckled to himself as Drysten heard him shuffle away.

Even the voices had left Drysten. They normally

hounded him in times like these. Time where hope seemed lost, but even they dared not venture into the places Drysten's mind was going. Drysten didn't know where they went, only that for the first time in his life, he was truly alone.

EPILOGUE

A smirk began to creep its way across Bishop Germanus' face as he glared into Mathew's eyes. "You stand accused of heresy," the bishop explained. "What do you think a fitting punishment for such a crime should be?"

Matthew glanced down to his hands, tied by old rope found near the cell he was thrown into earlier in the day. He recalled how he was told of his lord's fate by Ebrauc's prince, and thought he could beg for his release. "One Christian to another," he had said to Ambrosius as he walked through the Powysian shield wall.

"Well?" Germanus insisted. "Perhaps we should have you share in the fate of your lord, or maybe death like the other Pelagians from Londinium…"

"Other Pelagians, Your Excellency?" Matthew questioned as he lifted his gaze.

The bishop's face contorted into a wicked smile. "I have known of your kind for quite some time, priest. I have had the pleasure of rooting others out who shared your misguided beliefs. You…" he slowly rose from his seat, flanked on either side by Prince Eidion and a bald-headed guard, both smiling. "are also suspected to be a man who was taken from my people not long ago. Taken by the one who killed the king's man."

"My Lord Drysten did no such thing, Your Excellency!" Matthew stammered.

Bishop Germanus cackled as he gestured for Matthew to

be pushed to his knees. "Is *he* your lord now? What of *our* Lord, priest?"

Matthew was about to answer until a man kicked him in the back of his leg, violently sending him down to his knees. "I... my Lord and Savior has all the love of my heart, Your Excellency."

Germanus glanced toward the prince, whispering something inaudible before turning back to Matthew. "And how could we prove this?"

"I... am at your disposal, Your Excellency." Matthew struggled to make that statement. He heard of the bishop's cruelty from others in Londinium, not to mention his own more recent observations.

"Ha!" Germanus let out a sinister laugh and slapped his hip. "Why should I believe the word of a man who has forsaken our Lord?"

"I have done no such thing!" Matthew glanced down at his feet, trying to will his mind into thinking up a way to convince the bishop to let him live. He had come to Eboracum with the intention of meeting with the king, and now understood where the true power was held. He only found one option which may convince Ebrauc's true ruler to let him live. He lied.

"Your, Excellency, I was taken against my will to fight for the traitor. I am a man of God and would not raise my hand against another man of my own free will."

Bishop Germanus glanced to the prince, who snickered in disbelief until he noticed the bishop's expression. To say Germanus was interested would be an understatement. Luckily, Matthew was able to hide the small feeling of relief which washed over him.

"Explain," Germanus ordered.

Matthew felt an immense sensation of shame flow through him. He found himself wondering whether this lie of his would save his own life at the cost of his lord's. "I was kidnapped from Londinium because I speak the language of the men in the North. Lord Drysten treated me well, but I would have very much liked to have stayed in Londinium."

Germanus gestured for the prince and his guards to leave, and waited until they did so before finally speaking. "You mean this man *kidnapped* you?"

Matthew nodded.

"If this is the case, then it would seem you have cause to feel a sense of strife toward your lord?" The Bishop turned away and gazed over the crucifix mounted on the wall. "What would your punishment be for a man who had no wish to commit his latest crimes...?" he whispered.

Matthew glanced around, wondering what teaching the bishop received which led him to believe the Lord would physically answer him. That was when he noticed the knife on the table next to him. It was crude, with its only intention to be the carving of bread or fruit, but Matthew picked it up just the same. Silently, he crept closer to the bishop, who was still staring at the crucifix as he pondered the decision he was about to make. Matthew had killed before; he was even taught to before he became a priest. The bastard grandson of the Emperor Constantine, The Usurper, needed such knowledge to survive should anyone reveal his true heritage.

"You will live," the bishop announced.

Matthew was frozen for a split second, until the instinct to place the knife back onto the table took over. He slowly paced back and carefully placed it in its original position before watching Germanus slowly turn around.

"You will be rebaptized to cleanse you of the Pelagian heresy which has infected your soul and you will serve our Lord anew."

Matthew fought the urge to smile and lowered his head. "I thank you, Your Excellency. You are most merciful."

Germanus smirked. "Mercy has nothing to do with this. You have a purpose, otherwise the Lord would not have brought you where you are now." Germanus shuffled toward the doorway, calling in a handful of his guards. "Take him to the river, I will follow shortly."

The guards nodded and ushered Mathew out of the Roman baths, eventually making their way to the bridge adjoining the two sides of Eboracum. Matthew peered behind him, seeing the king and one of the sons Matthew hadn't met standing in the stone gateway of the fort. Both men were whispering to themselves as a handful of guards adorned in royal blue cloaks stepped beside them. It was strange to see the king with a confused expression, almost as if he had no idea what was occurring. Germanus finally walked by them, with the king and the prince glaring at him as he passed.

They hate him? Matthew silently observed. *Are they not working hand in hand?*

The bishop sauntered over and gestured for Matthew's hands to be untied and for him to be led to the riverbank. The small group of men marched down the slope, with Matthew's hands being unbound once they arrived near the water.

Germanus walked toward Matthew. "Your sins are about to be washed away, and you will rise a *true* member of the faith." He gestured toward the water.

Matthew nodded before entering the frigid water. The sting of the cold slowly died away as his legs became accustomed to it, but the shame remained. He wondered if the Lord would turn a blind eye to his lies, as well as find it in his heart to spare Drysten.

"Kneel," the bishop commanded.

Matthew complied, and the bishop placed a hand on his forehead before forcing him below the river's current. Words were spoken, but Matthew could scarcely hear any from underwater. For what felt like years, Matthew waited for the moment the bishop would let him breath. Germanus finally allowed him to rise, pulling him up from the water.

"Galahad," Germanus said through a wicked grin. "You now serve the church in a greater way than you could have ever imagined. You will be my shield protecting Christendom from the darkness of the apostates. Most of all, you will make certain the people of Petuaria never raise a finger to their king."

Matthew looked away in disgust. *If being a pawn keeps my lord alive, then a pawn I will be.*

The story continues in book two, Usurper, out now!

Find it on Amazon today!

Printed in Great Britain
by Amazon